Meant to Be

JUDE DEVERAUX

Meant to Be

mira

ISBN-13: 978-0-7783-3373-9

Meant to Be

First published in 2021. This edition published in 2023.

Mira
22 Adelaide St. West, 41st Floor
Toronto, Ontario M5H 4E3, Canada
BookClubbish.com

Printed in U.S.A.

Meant to Be

CHAPTER ONE

Mason, Kansas
May 1972

ADAM IS BACK.

Vera Exton couldn't get that thought out of her head. The man she had always loved, the man who held the keys to her future, was finally home.

She was on the front porch of her family home. As always, she was surrounded by newspapers and magazines. She paid to have the *New York Times* sent to her. That it arrived three days late didn't matter. At least she got to see what was going on in the world. The *world*. Not just Kansas, not just the US, but everywhere.

In college, she'd majored in political science, with a minor in geography. She knew where the Republic of Vanuatu was, where Rajasthan, India, was. She could tell Bhutan from Nepal by a single photo. She'd studied languages on her own and knew a smattering of several. *Rhodesia*, she thought. *Madagascar.* She'd send her sister photos of herself with a lemur when she got there. Kelly would like that.

Vera closed her eyes, leaning back in the old chair that her mother had bought at a craft fair. It had been made by someone local, using local materials. That was the difference between them. Her mother and her sister prided themselves on "local," while Vera could only see the world.

"And now it's all going to begin," she whispered, and opened her eyes.

Bending, she began stacking the newspapers and magazines. Her mother complained about the mess that always surrounded Vera. "We can hardly walk through a room," her mother often said, frowning. Since her husband died two years ago, Nella Exton did little but frown.

If Kelly was around, she helped Vera clean up. Or helped Vera do anything, for Kelly was deeply glad her big sister was there and doing what everyone expected her to do.

When Kelly mentioned her gratitude, their mother just sniffed. "She's the eldest child, so of course she takes care of things." Even though the sisters were only ten months apart, to their mother Vera was to take on the family's responsibilities, so she was doing what she was supposed to do. There was no other choice.

But Kelly didn't feel that way. In what people tended to call "the drug culture," many kids ran away, never to be seen again. The idea of "family obligations" was becoming obsolete. But not to Vera.

She had postponed the future she'd dreamed of, had studied for, to give her sister what she wanted and Kelly was ever thankful, grateful and appreciative.

For all her sister's appreciation, right now all Vera could think of was that Adam's return meant the ordeal of staying at home was over.

He'd arrived just in time for his father's funeral, as there'd been delays on the long flight from Africa. Vera had searched the newspapers to find out what was going on in Kenya. During the years he'd been away, Adam's letters were full of stories of floods and bridges collapsing, infestations and diseases with exotic names. His letters had made her heart pound with excitement. She'd read them to her mother and sister, then was shocked by the horror on their faces. "But doesn't it sound *wonderful*?" Vera would ask.

Nella said a flat no, and Kelly would say, "If you like that sort of thing." Then she'd pick up a few of her animals and feed them or groom them or whatever she did with them.

Vera had seen Adam after the service, but she'd not spoken to him. He was surrounded by people offering condolences. His father, Burke Hatten, had been a big shot in the county. "Ask Burke" was a common catchphrase.

In Vera's opinion, the man thought he knew much more than he did, which is why he and his eldest son had always butted heads. Burke's temper and his son's matching one was why Adam had run off to join the Peace Corps.

Well, that and Vera's endless talk of how she was joining the second she finished college. She'd begged Adam to go with her, but he'd always said no. He said he'd be waiting for her in Kansas when she grew tired of moving about the world and came home.

Funny how things work out, she thought as she stacked the papers. Adam had the big fight with his dad and had run off to the Peace Corps. Vera had planned to join him, but her father had died suddenly, leaving no one to care for the farm. To Vera, the solution was to sell the farm, but Nella had refused to leave the place. In just a few weeks, everything changed. Vera had agreed to stay behind until Kelly finished veterinary school. The new plan was that as soon as Kelly graduated, Vera would join Adam wherever the Peace Corps had sent him. .

Now everything was going to change again. Burke Hatten's horse threw him and he'd died instantly, so Adam had returned. But this time when he left the country to go back to his job in Africa, Vera wouldn't be kissing him goodbye.

They'd leave together. The goodbyes would be to her mother and sister, to the farm, to her job at the travel agency. Goodbye to the town of Mason. The world she'd been reading about was out there and calling to her.

At last, she was going to answer its call.

She heard Kelly before she saw her. But that had always been the case. Schoolkids tended to call her Pig-Pen after the *Peanuts* character. But while he was surrounded by dust, Kelly was followed by and covered with animals. Today there was a parrot on her shoulder and some kind of lizard had its tail wrapped around her neck. Three dogs, tails down, were following her. In her hand was a fat textbook that had bird droppings on the cover.

Kelly was almost finished with veterinary school and the "almost" was the key to Vera's life.

When Kelly was out of the school, Vera could *go!*

"So where is he?" Kelly asked as she sat down. She removed the lizard from her neck and put it on the porch railing. The bird flew to land on the lizard's tail. One of the dogs looked longingly at the bird, but Kelly gave the dog a stare that made it lie down, head on paws. Kelly didn't believe in discourteous animals.

"He'll be here," Vera said.

"Sure? I saw Miranda Miller at the funeral. She was eyeing him and she looked good in her miniskirt. I bet she was afraid to sit down or she'd show all."

Vera didn't take the bait. For one thing, Kelly didn't like Adam. She thought he was too full of himself, too bossy. Too much like his father. "I didn't talk to him, and we didn't reaffirm our love for each other, if that's what you're hinting at. And Miranda Miller is an idiot."

"Men like dumb girls," Kelly said.

"Until they marry them," Vera shot back.

"And that's when she gets to stop pretending to be stupid."
Vera laughed.

The bird had flown back to Kelly and she was feeding it
something she took from her shirt pocket.

All their lives, they'd heard, "You two are sisters?" said in an
incredulous tone. They looked very different. When they were
younger, they'd answered truthfully. Vera explained that she
took after her father's family while Kelly was like their mother's side. As they grew up, they began to play jokes. Kelly was
a good actress and she would pretend to be shocked. Sometimes she'd even pull up tears, saying that maybe her father
wasn't really her father. Mac Exton had played along with the
joke but his wife had never liked it.

Vera was tall and thin, flat chested, and had an explosion
of corkscrew ringlets of light brown hair.

As best she could, she kept her hair pulled back and tightly
tied down. Her face was pleasant but not cutesy pretty. Even
as a child she'd looked like an adult. Her truly spectacular fea-
ture was her legs: long, lean, shapely. Vera in a swimsuit was
a sight to behold.

Kelly was the prettiest girl in the county. Big blue eyes,
naturally blond hair, a perfect figure eight of a body, and she
was inches shorter than her sister. She was so pretty that she
surprised everyone by being smart.

Their personalities differed as much as their bodies. Vera
was acerbic; Kelly was sweet. When someone annoyed Vera,
she told them so. Kelly was the diplomat. Vera wanted to save
the world; Kelly wanted to save all the animals in Mason. For
her, Kansas City was too big and as far away as she wanted
to go.

They were so opposite that they never collided. They were
a perfect match.

For minutes they were silent, looking out from the front of

the old house. There was a gravel drive shaded by fifty-year-old oak trees. Every sunny spot was filled with flowers, lovingly tended by Nella.

There had been a running joke in their family. Nella took care of the plants, Kelly looked after the animals, Mac took care of the farm. "What about me?" an eight-year-old Vera had asked.

"Honey," her dad said, "you take care of the world." Vera had smiled at that. Even then she'd been fascinated by the whole planet.

"You're going to miss us," Kelly said softly.

"Of course I will, but I'll write constantly. Adam and I will send photos and tell you everything. We'll—"

"You're *sure* nothing has changed between you two? Sometimes when high school sweethearts lose touch, they grow apart. He's been in Africa for years and you've been here, and..." Kelly trailed off.

Vera could hear that Kelly was near tears. "I'm sorry," she said. "I wish I could change what's inside me. I wish I could find a career or a man, something, that made me...satisfied. Fulfilled me. I've always envied you. Since you were born, you've known what you wanted to do." She looked at her sister. "I'm a volcano about to explode. I have to go or I'll erupt."

"I know," Kelly whispered. "We all see it. Mom has done all she can to keep you from spewing up fire but nothing has worked."

The way Kelly said it was serious, but the image made Vera laugh. "Hasn't she just! What was that boy's name? The one she sent to pick me up?"

"Kevin. He was a nice guy. She was just trying to tempt you into staying."

"To get me away from Adam since he'd left the country. By the way, where was Pauly today?" Vera wanted to get the conversation and the weight of guilt off her. "I haven't seen him in days."

"He's around."

"Uh-oh. Is there trouble in paradise?"

"Of course not. I see him at the clinic every day."

Kelly and Paul had been together since elementary school. His stepfather, Dr. Carl, was the local vet and to Kelly that meant Pauly was the crown prince. She'd spent much of her life in the veterinary clinic with the doc. She'd helped deliver her first calf when she was eleven.

As for Pauly, he adored her. He was willing to follow wherever Kelly led. They were inseparable. "So where's your engagement ring?" Vera asked. "You're twenty-four. Time to get married and have babies."

Kelly smiled. Vera was mimicking their mother. "School costs too much for such frivolous things. Maybe later."

Vera nodded. It had never been said aloud, but the plan was that after she left, Kelly and Paul would marry and live on the Exton farm with Nella. Kelly would work with Dr. Carl and eventually take over his clinic.

"Maybe you should—" Vera began, but halted at the sound of a horse. Thundering down the road, barely visible through the trees, was a black stallion. Vera knew who was riding it.

At the far end of the long drive, Adam drew the big horse to a halt and sat there for a moment, his eyes on Vera.

Adam was tall, lean, broad shouldered and muscled from a life of sports and digging wells and hauling rocks in Africa. Wearing jeans and a denim shirt, broad-brimmed hat down low over his eyes, he was something from the cover of a novel.

As Vera stood up, she felt her whole body vibrating.

Behind her, Kelly snorted. "Really! Does he have to make everything into a drama? He'd better not run Xander or I'll—"

Adam did just what Kelly said he shouldn't. The horse, retired from a racetrack, needed only a nudge to take off fast. Gravel and dirt spewed.

Vera's heart leaped to her throat, pounding in anticipation.

Kelly ran down the porch steps and stood to the side of the path Adam was taking. He and the horse stopped less than a foot from the porch railing.

Kelly ran forward. "If you hurt his mouth I'll murder you!" she shouted.

Adam's eyes never left Vera's as he tossed the reins to Kelly. "He's fine, kiddo. Give him a bath. My truck is here." He held out his hand to Vera. She took it and the two of them walked down the drive to where his pickup was parked.

Adam held the door to his truck open as Vera got in, then went to the other side and got behind the wheel. In the distance, Kelly was still yelling that he was a pompous ass and if Xander was harmed she would report Adam to the ASPCA.

"Your baby sister hasn't changed," Adam said as he started the truck. "Was that a lizard on the porch?"

"Yes. And a bird and three dogs."

He glanced at her so hotly that even her ears turned red.

"Miss me?" he asked.

"Madly," she said.

Smiling, they rode in silence. She knew exactly where they were going. Burke Hatten's widowed mother had refused to leave the ranch that she and her husband had built. No amount of enticements of travel or city life interested her. But she'd been a quiet woman and she'd needed to get away from her bigger-than-life son and her two energetic grandsons. Burke had built her a cabin about a mile from their main house.

One room and a bath was all she wanted. The windows looked out over the fields with their grazing cattle. After her death, Burke had locked the door and no one used the cabin. Until, as teenagers, Adam and Vera had claimed the place as their own. They'd cleared it of mice and spiders, repaired the leaky roof and used it whenever they could escape their families. If Burke Hatten knew where the teenagers were spending their afternoons, he never let on.

Adam parked to the side of the house. It was a plain little place, with a porch along the front.

They got out, stepped onto the porch, and Adam swept Vera up into his arms. Like a groom carrying his bride over the threshold.

She snuggled her head into his shoulder. So familiar, yet it had been so long that it was almost new.

When he tossed her onto the bed, she gasped, expecting dust to encase her. But it was clean. She raised herself on her arms. The familiar place practically sparkled. The bedsheets felt new. "Is this—?" That was all she said before he fell on top of her.

As they tore at each other's clothes, Adam said, "Forey," and she nodded. Fortunata was Vera's mom's best friend and she had cleaned the cabin for them.

They made love quickly, waited just minutes, then did so again more slowly. They didn't say a word until after the second time and Adam fell back on the pillow beside her.

"I should have—" he began.

"Shh," she said. She knew he meant that he should have used protection. She didn't want to tell him that she'd started on the Pill weeks ago. She planned to fly to Kenya the minute Kelly graduated and she wanted to be prepared. Since it was barely legal for women to use birth control and the Pill was considered dangerous, she hadn't told anyone.

Birth control was the last thing she wanted to talk about. What she *really* wanted to do was jump up and down on the bed and shout, "When do we leave? When do we leave?"

She needed to control herself. She snuggled in his arms, bare bodies pressed together. "How's Robbie?"

She knew the answer to her question but she wanted to hear Adam's reply. Actually, she wanted to know what he planned to do about his eighteen-year-old hellion of a brother.

Adam groaned. "I don't know what Dad was thinking. He created a monster."

Vera and Adam had a code of honesty between them. They didn't lie and didn't hold back. "Your dad blamed himself for your leaving. He told my dad he was too hard on you."

"So he went soft on Rob?" Adam sounded angry.

"I think so."

"Dad bought him cars. How many has he wrecked?"

"Two," Vera said softly. Her hair had come loose. Brushing it aside, she looked at him. "He's going to college in the fall. Until then he can stay with my mother." She'd thought a lot about this problem.

"And you think your mother is strong enough to control him? Ha! The way he is now, I wouldn't want him near your little sister."

"Kelly will sic a dog on him." She meant it as a joke but Adam didn't laugh.

"That won't work."

She knew him well enough to know that he had a plan. "What are you going to do?"

He moved her hair aside and kissed her forehead. "I've not had time to think about anything much, but I don't believe Robbie wants to run the farm. He wants to do something in a city. I don't know what it is, but…" He took a breath. "I need to stay here until he's in college." Adam ran his hand through his hair, dark brown but with sun streaks through it. "I need to get back to Kenya. We're putting in wells and I've been teaching classes on crops and—"

She turned to him. "I can help."

He kissed her. "I want to plan for you, too. I've told everyone about you. Showed them your photo."

Vera began to relax again. Everything was still on. Everything was going to be all right.

"Let me figure this out," he said. "I'll get Robbie settled, then..." He took a deep breath. "I think the best thing would be for me to sell the farm."

"Yes," Vera said. "Cut your ties."

"I'll give Robbie half the money. Then you and I can start a life somewhere else."

"We can help people in the world."

"Yes, exactly."

They were silent for a moment. He rolled over to face her. "I bet I know something you don't."

"Not from around here, you don't. *I* have been here, remember?"

"Yeah, well, this just happened."

She waited. "Go on. Tell me."

"Miguel is back. Remember how the three of us ran around during the summer?"

"I remember that summer when we were eleven years old and you decided to jump out of the top of the barn. You broke your leg and were in a cast."

"Oh, right. I forgot that bit. But I remember us as a threesome."

"That's because Miguel and I entertained you."

"I don't remember any dancing or singing."

"You don't remember us pushing you in the wheelchair?" she asked. "Helping you master crutches?"

"Only vaguely."

"Kelly helped, too," Vera said. "She brought you a parrot. Noisy critter."

"And a rabbit and a fox cub. I thought it was a puppy. Dad was the one who knew what it was." There was sadness in his voice. She knew that later they would talk about his father. But not yet.

"I was always glad when she didn't show up with a bear cub," Vera said. "With the mother ten feet behind her."

"Kelly would have charmed the mother."

"Probably so."

Adam lay back down. "I'm glad you remember Miguel."

"I would never forget him." Her mind wandered to that summer. It was before sex came into their minds and spoiled everything. With Adam down with a broken leg, there was no one to preach sense to her and Miguel. No one to declare that rotten logs across a stream were too dangerous to cross. Or that a tree was too tall to climb. Miguel was as fearless as Vera. They ran and climbed. They sneaked through the grasses to see the fields full of illegally growing marijuana. They—

"Hey! Come back to me."

"I'm here. I was just remembering the carefree days of summer as a kid. So Miguel is back at his uncle Rafe's house."

"Yeah. I talked to him for a few minutes. Miguel said that right after he graduated from college, Rafe sent a letter to his family asking if one of their boys could help out this summer. Miguel said that an hour later he was packed and driving east. Goodbye New Mexico."

"No overlong partings, then?"

"I think he had good memories of his time here and wanted to return," Adam said.

"Did he ask about me?"

"He did."

"Well?"

"I told him that your hair had taken over your body so that you now shave like a man and—"

"You jerk." She rolled toward him, ready to make love again, but the loud grumble of Adam's stomach made them both laugh.

"Think Forey left us any food?" he asked.

"I'll put money on it that she did." There was a kitchenette along the wall, with a little table under a window.

Adam got out of bed and pulled on his jeans. He reached for his shirt but Vera grabbed it. "I'll wear this. We mustn't hide our best features."

He got her meaning. His bare chest, her legs. Laughing, he bent and kissed her. "I missed you a lot." He went to the fridge and opened it. "Ah, yes. The finest of Mexico-Kansas. And a pie. Bet that's from your mom."

Vera got out of bed and put on Adam's shirt. It was very short on her. She twirled around. "How do I look? As good as Miranda Miller?"

Adam nearly choked on a bite of cold pinto beans. "Heard about that, did you?" He put the food on the table and his arms around Vera's waist. "She said she's been waiting for me."

"Did she?"

He kissed Vera's neck. "She asked if I thought she was as pretty as the girls in Africa."

Vera leaned back to look at him. "And what did you say?"

"I told her to take off her top so I could make a comparison."

"You didn't!" Her eyes were wide.

"No, but I wanted to." He released her and went to the table. For a moment he stood still, his back to her. "I wasn't faithful to you." He spoke so softly she could hardly hear him.

Vera took a few breaths. This was a turning point. Did she storm out in anger? Or cry? She didn't feel either of those emotions. "Did you learn anything?"

She saw his shoulders drop down in relief and he turned

to her. "I'm sorry. It was more time and place and need than anything else."

She was starting to feel something and she didn't like it. In the time he'd been away, there'd been opportunities for her with other men, but she hadn't taken them. All she knew now was that she didn't want to think about this. "Want me to heat this up?"

"That would be great." He was still waiting for her judgment about what he'd confessed.

"Let's not mention it again." Her head came up. "Later, if we're, you know, together, uh, forever, you wouldn't—"

The look he gave her made her stop talking. No, he wouldn't.

She put the foil-wrapped food in the oven. "I wish there was a way we could talk to people all over the world, and see them. Like on a TV."

"Sounds like something off *Star Trek*. They didn't put that show back on, did they?"

"Sadly, not."

He sat down at the table. "We don't get much news where I've been, so tell me what I've missed in the world."

Vera smiled. Her favorite topic. "East Pakistan renamed itself Bangladesh. Shirley Chisholm says she's running for president."

"Couldn't be worse than Nixon. Does everyone still hate him?"

"Yeah. Especially *Maude*."

"Who?"

"It's a TV show you haven't seen. And there's a new movie you have to see. *The Godfather*."

"Sounds boring. Too romantic for me."

Vera chuckled. "Not really. Anyway, Libya and the Soviet

Union signed a cooperation treaty. And Congress is sending the Equal Rights Amendment to the states to ratify."

"Any hope they'll sign it?"

"None whatever. The US and the Soviet Union and seventy other nations have agreed to ban biological warfare."

"But they haven't agreed to ban war," Adam said.

"No," Vera said softly. Three young men they'd gone to high school with had been killed in Vietnam. Vera had participated in sit-ins and walkouts. Adam and her father had supported her, but her mother had been angry and scared. But still, the useless war continued.

"Hey!" Adam said. "How did we get morbid?"

"You started it by telling me that you'd bed hopped with half of Africa and—"

"I didn't! It was once and—" He halted.

"One girl or one time?" she asked.

Adam turned away. "You and I aren't officially engaged."

"Right. We're not." For the first time, there was anger in Vera's voice. "Free love and all that."

Adam cleared his throat. "Did you know that Paul is spending the summer in Europe? Are he and your little sister still an item?"

Vera got the food out of the oven. "They are, and no, Kelly didn't mention it."

"That's because Paul only has two legs. Not important to her."

Vera smiled as she got plates out of the cabinet. "Pauly's so mad about Kelly he's probably only going away for a week. Just seems like the whole summer to him."

"Nope. He'll be away all summer. And Forey told me that Miguel will probably marry Gabby. I got the idea he was asked to come more for matchmaking than to help on the farm."

Vera put out plates and glasses and the food. "This was all told to you since your father's funeral? All this *gossip*?"

He finished chewing before he spoke. "It's all because of Dad. He wanted to be told everyone's business. Today I got the idea that people expect *me* to take over everyone's problems and to solve them. Why are you looking at me like that?"

"You've *got* to see *The Godfather*."

"A woman's movie about christenings?"

"No, not quite. I'm sure my mother made the pie."

"So she was in on this? She knew we'd come here and... and...?"

"Hoped is more like it. She hopes you and I will elope and I'll be pregnant by Christmas. With triplets."

"She wants them to hold you in place?"

"Exactly!" Vera got up to get the apple pie. Pretending it wasn't of monumental importance, she said, "So what *are* you going to do? And when?"

"O ye of little faith," he said. "Tomorrow I'll show you my photos." He hesitated. "I know Africa is far away, but I feel like I belong there. The people *need* me and that's a powerful connection."

"Very powerful," she murmured, her eyes never leaving his.

Adam sighed. "If it were up to me, I'd go tomorrow. Tonight even, but I've got to get Robbie settled. We have to take care of the youngsters in our life. You and Kelly, me and my hardheaded, disaster-loving brother. Are we agreed on this?"

Vera could only nod.

He leaned forward. "You really want to go, don't you?"

"More than you can imagine. At work I envy my clients with all my heart. They fly to places I've read about but I can't go. I—"

He kissed her. "I know. You've sacrificed yourself for your family. We should put a plaque up for you. Or maybe a statue."

"It's what had to be done."

"My house in Africa, if you can call it that, has a dirt floor. I saw hyenas. They—"

"Save the animals for Kelly. What's the hierarchy of the tribe? Or do they let you know that? Tell me the politics. How are the women treated? Did you—?"

He smiled. "Slow down and come here, and I'll try to answer all your questions."

CHAPTER TWO

KELLY YELLED AT ADAM UNTIL SHE SAW his truck drive away. But maybe she was shouting in anger at both of them. With Adam's reappearance, everything was going to change. She had an idea that Adam would want to stay until the end of summer and of course Vera would agree. But then, her sister would do/say/agree to anything if it got her out of Kansas.

Kelly nuzzled against the big horse. She knew him well, as he was ill last summer and she'd been the one to sleep in the stall with him.

Kelly adjusted the length of the stirrups, then hoisted herself up to Xander's back. He pranced a bit, but she leaned forward and stroked his neck. "Calm down. I'm not Adam showing off. Let's go for a walk."

There was woodland between the crop fields and she knew it well. There was an old wagon trail, but it had too many potholes to risk running on. A quiet stroll would do them good.

Thirty minutes later, they halted at a stream. She dismounted, tied Xander loosely since rabbits tended to make him run off, checked the area for poisonous plants, found none and let him graze.

She wanted time to think. The last couple of years had been relatively peaceful. Well, sort of. Vera had been like Xander and wanting to run, but she'd done her duty. She took care of her mother, her sister, the farm, and held down a part-time job in Kansas City. It would have been too much for most people, but not Vera. She could do *anything*!

Kelly ran her hands over Xander's neck, then leaned against him.

"Can I do her job?" she whispered. The minute Vera left, everything would be handed over to Kelly. Nella Exton was a "taken care of" woman. She did her canning, freezing and baking, and she expected others to do the rest. First it had been her father, then her husband, then Vera. It would soon be her youngest daughter's turn to do the things that Nella didn't.

Kelly sat down on a patch of grass by the stream.

"Adam will stay for Robbie," Kelly said to Xander. "Everyone knows that it wouldn't be safe to leave Robbie alone for a whole summer. He'd do nothing but party. A deputy sheriff would have to move in with him."

She sighed. "And of course Vera will wait for *me*." Xander nudged her with his head and she leaned into him. "She just might stay here to wait for, you know, my wedding." She stroked the horse's head; he gave a snuffle, then went back to eating.

Kelly lay back on the grass, her hands behind her head, and looked up at the sky. This plan was all about the future of her with Paul.

He had entered her elementary school when they were in the third grade—a small, quiet boy, with blond hair and blue eyes. He was the son of the woman Dr. Carl had recently married and they were all curious. But Paul didn't reply to their questions, just stared at them in silence.

In the evenings, Kelly often heard her mother complaining about Dr. Carl's new wife. "She thinks she's better than us," Nella said to her husband. "We invited her to a potluck and she said she couldn't imagine eating food made in a private kitchen. She said, 'What if it wasn't *clean*?' We told her—" She cut off when she saw Kelly in the doorway, a puppy in her arms.

"What's the new boy like?" Mac asked his daughter.

"He's very quiet," Kelly said. "He won't talk to anybody, so we leave him alone."

"Good idea!" Nella snapped.

Mac, who was kind to everyone, said to his daughter, "Be nice to him. Everything's new and strange to him."

With a nod, Kelly went to the barn to give the puppy to its mother.

The next day at school, she tried to be nice to Paul, but he just looked at her in silence. He was a pretty boy, with dark lashes and a small mouth, and he was never dirty like the other boys. Kelly tried for a week to draw Paul out but she could get nothing from him, so she, too, left him alone. Besides, Kelly was a very popular child. She had lots of friends and invitations to join everything.

When Paul had been there three months, everything changed. Their teacher had to leave the room and she threatened them with death if they so much as moved while she was out. Then she'd run out, slamming the door behind her. The kids looked at each other. All their mothers had told them that Mrs. Wilson was expecting a baby.

The room was quiet for about three minutes. Then Susie Brown let out a scream. She jumped up so fast her desk fell over. She was staring at the back of Paul's neck. Sticking out of his jacket was the head of a large brown snake.

In seconds, the room was in chaos. Children leaped up; desks fell. There were whispers of fear and a few screams.

All of the children were slammed against the walls, scared, or trying to pretend they weren't.

Except Kelly. She hadn't moved out of her desk, and her eyes were as wide as theirs, but in wonder.

As for Paul, he was just sitting there, not moving, and his eyes were beginning to fill with tears. Kelly got up, went to Paul and gently pulled the long snake out of the boy's jacket.

"He was cold," Paul whispered. "He didn't move. I thought he might die."

Kelly had never held a snake before and she was fascinated with how smooth it was. Its eyes were bright, its tongue flicked in and out, and it had a beautiful white underside. "He's beautiful," she whispered.

"Dr. Carl—I mean, Dad—says he's good for a garden," Paul said.

The children against the walls were beginning to loosen up, but none of them stepped forward.

They were all watching Kelly as she let the snake wrap around her arms. She rubbed her cheek against its head.

Charlie Barts was keeping watch out the window. "Mrs. Wilson is coming," he yelled.

The children reacted instantly. Kelly opened her metal lunch box, took out her sandwich and cupcake, put the snake inside, closed the lid and latched it. With the speed of light, the kids righted the desks, picked up books and papers, and sat down.

When Mrs. Wilson entered, everyone was exactly as she'd left them. She didn't notice the fast breathing or the red faces. At lunch, she saw that Kelly Exton, who usually had a dozen kids sitting by her, was isolated at the end of a table with the new boy. Kelly's blue lunch box was in front of them on the table. *Good*, Mrs. Wilson thought. *Kelly's bringing that odd little boy into the fold.*

On the Day of the Snake, as they came to call it, Kelly got off the bus with Paul and walked to Dr. Carl's house, with his clinic next door. She'd always loved animals, but that day, when she saw the doctor's surgery, with animals being kept under his watchful eye as they recovered, Kelly knew what she wanted to do with her life. She was going to be a veterinarian. When she told Dr. Carl, he smiled. "Not many girls become vets," he said.

"I will." She was so solemn that he stopped smiling.

"In that case, why don't you come over Saturday morning and help me clean cages?"

She agreed readily. As for Mrs. Carl, which, to her annoyance, was what everyone in town called her, she was thrilled that her son had brought home a friend. And that Kelly was pretty and "normal" made her nearly frantic with happiness. She fed the children, asked Kelly a barrage of questions and called her son "Pauly."

As Kelly was leaving, she heard Mrs. Carl say, "She's not a Hatten, but she's better than nothing in this hick town."

That night, as Kelly's father was tucking her in bed, she told him what Mrs. Carl had said and asked him what she meant. Her father frowned. "The Hattens are rich but we're not. And Mason doesn't have subways and tall buildings."

"But we have cows," Kelly said.

Her dad smiled. "I'd rather have cows than skyscrapers."

"Me, too." Kelly yawned.

He stood up. "Let's not tell your mother what you overheard, okay?"

Kelly turned over. "I want to go to Dr. Carl's again, so I won't tell her."

Mac chuckled. "What a smart child I have."

"I'll be Dr. Kelly," she said as she closed her eyes.

"I'm sure you will be." He shut the door behind him.

It was in the fifth grade that she realized Pauly didn't want the same things she did. Kelly and Pauly spent so much time with animals that she had assumed he wanted to be a veterinarian, too.

They'd only been in the fifth grade for a week when Paul contradicted Mrs. Acton. The class gasped. They knew Paul was strange, always quiet, never joining in their games, but correcting a teacher was too much! If the teacher told a parent, there'd be a belt applied to a backside.

Mrs. Acton had told them of Johnny Appleseed, who went all over the country planting seeds to grow apple trees.

Paul spoke up. That was odd enough, but when he said, "That wasn't a good idea," the room became silent.

"What did you say?" Mrs. Acton asked.

Any of the other kids would have backed off at that tone, but Paul kept on. "That's not good, as apple seeds aren't true to the parent. A seed from a green apple doesn't necessarily grow into a tree with green apples. They could be red or yellow, or any color or size. The only way to be sure to get a specific apple is to graft a branch onto a sturdy rootstock."

No one had ever heard Paul say that many words before and he'd sounded so adult!

They all turned to look at Mrs. Acton. She was a new teacher. She could congratulate or punish, all based on her whim.

"On Monday, I want you to give us a report about that.

And I want pictures and drawings and…and an apple tree on a graft."

The kids didn't move. They weren't sure if that was a punishment or a reward.

They looked at Paul and, for the first time, they saw him smile. In fact, he was so pleased all he could do was nod.

After class Kelly asked Pauly if he knew how to draw. "No."

"Do you have any apple trees?"

"No."

Kelly rolled her eyes. "My dad would say we're up the river without a paddle."

"What does that mean?"

"That we need help."

"My dad can—" Pauly began.

"Dr. Carl doesn't know an apple tree from a cactus. Let's get your mother to bully people into helping us."

Kelly was usually so nice that he blinked at her statement. Then he smiled. "She bullies me all the time."

"And Dr. Carl, too. Come on. Let's run."

By the next day, everyone in Mason knew of Dr. Carl's stepson's project, and they loved the idea of helping. Dr. Carl was well liked in town. Kelly got all the kids in their class to use their talents.

On Saturday, Mrs. Carl was ecstatic when eight children showed up to help with posters and handouts and dirt-filled pots for demonstrations. One of the kids was the principal's daughter and she coaxed her dad into having an assembly so Pauly could tell everyone about fruit trees.

The big nursery in Ottawa lent four apple trees, and a parent offered a truckload of horse manure.

Kelly said no to the manure, but her mother took it for her roses.

Pauly's presentation was intelligent and interesting, well

thought out and made every kid in school tell their parents they wanted an apple tree for Christmas. "One that's been grafted," they stipulated.

The local nursery took out a full-page ad in the *Ottawa Herald* offering 40 percent off on apple trees. "Buy now, give a gold-rimmed certificate for Christmas and the trees will be delivered in the spring."

After that day, Paul was still a bit different but he was accepted, and he and Kelly were forever considered a twosome. In high school, when the girls played "Who will you marry?" for Kelly it was "When will you and Pauly get married?"

Smiling at the memories, Kelly turned to Xander. "I don't know what's wrong with me. I should be happy. And excited. I'll soon be a full-fledged veterinarian. Dr. Carl is going to expand so I'll have my own space to work in and I'll see clients. Pauly and I will marry and move in with Mom and..." She couldn't go on. The truth was that she'd miss her sister very much. Vera was interesting. There was never a second when she wasn't creating something, coming up with ideas, and she was *always* passionate. Every moment, Vera was in a frenzy about some injustice. Every nightly newscast sent her into anger.

Kelly walked around Xander and hoisted herself into the saddle. She wanted to get to Dr. Carl's and check on the animals, see if he needed her.

As she rode, she thought that sometimes it was as though she could see her entire life in front of her. It was a perfectly straight road, with no side roads, no paths, no surprises anywhere.

She patted Xander's neck. "Wonder where Vera is now? And what she and Adam are doing?" She grimaced. As if everyone in town didn't know about their trysts in Adam's grandmother's hideaway. People in town said, "Bet Burke Hatten never foresaw that that place would become the Sex Shack."

Kelly told herself Vera and Adam's shenanigans were shameful. Embarrassing. She turned red when she heard the gossip, but sometimes… Sometimes she envied her sister. She and Pauly had had sex but it wasn't anything that would cause giggles and blushes.

She shook her head. "I'm in a weird mood today." They were at a straight path and she nudged Xander a little faster. It didn't take much to make him gallop.

By the time she got to Dr. Carl's office, she felt better. She went in the back way so no visitors would see her.

"Didn't expect to see you here today," Dr. Carl said. He was tall and thin and had gray hair. The people of Mason unkindly said his wife had given it to him.

"Adam Hatten kidnapped my sister and…" Kelly shrugged. There was a German shepherd on the table. "What's wrong with Sergeant?"

"The kids fed him chocolate, so he has a tummy ache. How's Adam taking his father's death?"

"No idea, but it doesn't seem to be bothering him."

"What's he going to do about Robbie?"

"I don't know!" Kelly snapped, then said, "Sorry. He rode up on Xander and took Vera away. I don't know anything. Maybe they'll leave for Nepal or wherever tomorrow. Robbie be damned."

Dr. Carl looked at Kelly. "You're going to miss her a lot, aren't you?"

Kelly sat down hard on a chair against the wall. "Do you ever feel like you have no control over your life? That everything has been planned for you and you have no choice about any of it?"

"Every day," he said softly.

Kelly saw the sadness in his eyes. His first wife had died of cancer. Two years later, he'd gone to a convention in Dallas and had returned with a wife who had a son. He'd been ecstatic, floating on air, as he told people how happy he was. It was a year before all the air had gradually left his balloon. His new wife didn't like small-town living, his stepson was in his own world and, worse, his wife had told him that birth complications had made her have a hysterectomy. There would be no more children. One night, after Dr. Carl had had too many beers, he told Kelly she was the child he was never going to have. If he remembered it the next morning, he didn't mention it.

Kelly was about to say something when the door burst open. It was Mrs. Carl. She was plump but squashed into a girdle that prevented any part of her from moving. She was like a statue by Rubens that could turn its neck but the rest was immobile.

"Kelly, darling," she said. "I'm so glad you're here. Have you eaten? There's a big horse outside. It looks dangerous, so don't get near it. You look sad, so I guess Pauly told you. I told him what I thought of his plans, but it's done no good. *You* need to talk to him. He's postponing everything! I was so hoping for a spring wedding for you two. Apple blossoms. Lord knows there are enough apple trees around this town. Messy old things. Why aren't you wearing the ring? I told Pauly to give it to you before he left. I guess he hasn't done it yet. The wedding will have to be in the fall. Your attendants will of course wear green and—"

"Lillian!" Dr. Carl said loudly. "The children must make their own decisions."

She gave her husband a look Kelly had seen many times. It was usually accompanied by, "If things were left up to *them*, they'd never *happen*."

Frowning, Mrs. Carl glanced at her watch. "I'm going to

be late for the beauty shop." She looked at Kelly. "As soon as you have a date for your wedding, I'll make appointments for you. Who will be your bridesmaids?"

"Uh…" Kelly said.

Dr. Carl stepped forward. "Are you going to cover that gray hair at your temples? I hope not. It gives you a nice look of maturity," he said. With a gasp of horror, Mrs. Carl ran out the door.

"Sorry about that," he said.

"That's okay. I'm from Kansas, so I'm used to tornadoes."

He laughed. "I take it by your expression that you have no idea what Pauly is up to."

"None whatever."

"I think I better let him tell you."

"What's this about a ring?"

"Lillian got the idea that Pauly hasn't officially proposed to you because he's been saving up for an engagement ring."

"Was he?"

Mr. Carl shrugged. "I have no idea. But Lillian bought a ring for him to give to you. It's rather nice."

Kelly frowned. "And expensive?"

"Yes."

Kelly didn't ask but she knew that he had paid for the ring. "Where is he?" His expression said, *You know where he is.*

"Do you need me here?"

"No. Go see Pauly and sort out your life."

"In that case, I'll be back in about ten minutes."

He gave a snort of laughter, and Kelly left, mounted Xander and rode back the way she came. Four years ago, Pauly had bought the ten acres that lay between the Hatten and Exton farms. It was farmland, with rich soil, and no artificial fertilizers had been put on it in over thirty years. Both Burke Hatten and Mac Exton had tried to buy the piece, but old man

Anders had sold it to Pauly, saying, "I like what he plans to do with it." As the town of Mason had seen, when Pauly wanted to, he could be very persuasive.

Kelly rode across the edge of the property her family had owned for three generations. Ahead, she could see Pauly's land. There were hundreds of fruit trees, all in long rows, perfectly pruned, all weedless. There were about fifty chickens pecking away at the bugs that tried to eat the trees.

Over the last couple of years, Pauly had spent most weekends traveling around the Midwest, gathering branches of trees that people said had been planted by their great-great-grandfathers. "Only one in existence, that I know of," the people said. "Best eatin' apple you ever put in your mouth."

Sometimes Kelly went with him on his trips. Pauly dealt with the plants while Kelly tended to any animals the farmers had. She never charged and it gave her experience.

In the middle of the property was a pretty little shed with a greenhouse attached to the front of it.

It's where Pauly did the work needed to graft all the branches that he so carefully cut and labeled.

His dream was to eventually open a mail-order company. "Only I want to sell the old varieties, not the new, lifeless ones," he said.

They never discussed it, but she knew that, someday, he planned to use the hundred and thirty acres of Kelly's family's farm as part of his tree business. If it all worked out, that is. After he and Kelly were married, and if people ordered the trees.

She saw him beside the greenhouse, a pot in his hands. He was a very good-looking young man, with his blond hair and blue eyes. Mrs. Carl said Kelly and her son were so alike they looked like a pair of salt and pepper shakers.

Kelly had shot back, "Who's the pepper?"

"You are," Pauly answered. "And I'm the salt of the earth." They'd all burst into laughter.

Pauly nodded when he saw her and gave a bit of a smile. For a second, Kelly frowned. No fireworks in greeting. No expressions of undying love. No feeling of *I'll follow you to the ends of the earth* ran through her.

She dismounted and tied Xander up tightly. She didn't want him wandering about and munching on Pauly's young trees. "What's going on?"

"Just some cross-pollination and staking," he said. "The wind's been bad this week, so I—"

"I was told you're leaving."

"Oh. That. Vera will be here so you won't be alone, and Adam said he's staying until Robbie enters college. I'll be back in the fall."

"And you didn't think to tell me about your plans?"

"I was going to talk to you about it first, but then Adam told me about Robbie and..." He shrugged. "It just came out. I didn't think the gossip would spread this fast."

Kelly sat down on the edge of one of the raised beds Pauly had paid someone to build. For all that he was great with a grafting blade, he knew nothing about carpentry. "Tell me everything."

"Remember Brian Tayman?"

"The guy you met at...?" She couldn't remember where.

"In San Francisco. Agriculture show."

"Right."

"You know we exchange letters. He and two of his friends are spending the summer in the British Isles—Scotland, Ireland, Wales, all of it. They're collecting seeds and studying farming methods and I—"

"Let me guess. You're going to cut branches off fruit trees."

Pauly gave her a look that said he didn't like her tone.

"What about your job?" He was manager of the Ottawa Safeway. Young for the position but he was good at it.

"Mr. Dunham. Remember him? Used to manage the store? His wife said that since he was retired, they could spend the summer in Mississippi with her relatives. Mr. Dunham offered to pay me to say he had to take over for the summer."

Kelly knew she was supposed to laugh but she was deeply annoyed. Vera would be with Adam, so with Pauly away, Kelly would be left with her mother and an increasingly unhappy Dr. Carl. There were wonderful summer activities in Mason. Pond swimming. Picnics. Barbecues. Just plain laughter. For the first summer since she was eight years old, Kelly would be *alone*. Or worse, the object of pity.

She looked at Pauly in speculation. And after the summer, then what? When he returned, would they have an autumn wedding? "Your mother said something about a ring. I think it cost your dad a lot."

Pauly turned away from her and she could see that he was frowning. "Mother can be extravagant. I returned the ring to the store."

Kelly sat still, staring at him, knowing the reason he wasn't meeting her eyes. *No* mention of an engagement.

"That's good to hear." She slapped her hands on her thighs. "I think all this sounds great. Really fabulous! I'm sure you'll enjoy yourself very much." She stood up. "I need to take Xander back. I wonder if my sister and Adam have finished their afternoon of lust? Their sexual fulfillment will give the town something to talk about. How many hours can Adam Hatten last? We should make bets."

Pauly had turned and was staring at her. Never, ever was Kelly crude. He was shocked.

She smiled, mounted Xander, then looked down at him.

"I hope you found someone to take care of your little trees. I have too much to do to tend to them."

She didn't wait for his answer, but turned Xander around, then pulled on the reins so he went two steps back. As she knew he would, Pauly leaped to the side. He didn't like big animals. She gave him one last smile, then urged the horse forward, knowing that Xander's iron-clad hooves were digging into the carefully tended soil. She didn't lead the big horse down a row of trees and flatten them, but she *wanted* to!

CHAPTER THREE

ADAM FELT LIKE HE WAS DROWNING IN paperwork. His father believed that paperwork would get itself done, so he rarely bothered with it. As the mayor of Mason and the "fixer of problems," Burke had been forgiven for his foibles. When he was late with a payment to a local merchant, a pretty girl would be sent to get a payment from him. Burke and the young woman would spend the day laughing, eating and drinking, and eventually someone would drive her home with a check in her hand.

But Adam wasn't his father. He believed bills should be paid and things kept in order.

When he heard a car engine, he glanced out the big window. Robbie had finally come home. It was 7:00 a.m., his clothes were rumpled and a cigarette was hanging out of his mouth. He looked like he'd been up all night, with *up* being the key word.

Wonder who it was? Adam thought. He hoped it wasn't some local girl who would be planning to move in with the Hattens.

Robbie came into the house and went to the kitchen without so much as a glance at his older brother. "Who'd you get to cook?" he asked.

Adam didn't answer.

Robbie rounded the corner, a plate piled high with chicken and tortillas. "This is from Forey. Did you know that she's got a nephew staying with them? I hear he's old. Like you."

Adam glared at his brother.

There wasn't as much difference in their looks as between Vera and Kelly, but Robbie was the pretty one, with a face of such sweetness that he made people smile. Adam was handsome, but he tended to scowl. No one bothered Adam when he didn't want them to.

The brothers were the same height but Adam was wider, built more strongly. In high school, he was a coach's dream, good at all sports, played well with his teammates. A quintessential man's man. For years, it was thought that Adam might go pro in several sports. But when he was a senior, he hurt his knee badly enough that the sports life was out of the picture.

As for Robbie, he was lean, flexible. In school he'd joined the swim team but he missed many practice sessions. Eventually, he quit. Burke said his youngest son's problem was that he was too easygoing, too likable, too much loved by women.

Unlike the Exton sisters, the differences between Adam and Robbie Hatten made them incompatible. They didn't understand each other at all.

Robbie plopped down in a big chair, facing his brother. "I thought that after yesterday with Vera, you'd be in a better mood today. Or are you mad because you think you have to stay here to keep me out of trouble?"

Adam continued to glare at his brother. "Where were you all night?"

"I don't kiss and tell." His eyes were sparkling.

Adam thought how he wished his brother was ugly. But

Robbie looked like something off a poster of a rodeo star: dark brown hair, dark blue eyes, dressed in denim and leather. He'd been a cute kid and now he seemed to be endlessly surrounded by women, young and old. "Do you have everything ready for college?"

Robbie laughed. "That's months away." He put his empty plate on a side table. "We can't all be like you, big brother. We're not perfect in everything we do. You were great at sports and had top grades. And now you love a girl who is sane and sensible. She's not even overly pretty. Nothing flashy for you. Now, that little Kelly...she's enough to make a man sweat."

Adam bared his teeth. "Man? You're just a kid."

Robbie stopped smiling. "I grew up fast after you ran off to save the world. Dad was depressed. His favorite son was in far-off Africa, and all his dreams were gone. I tried to put his attention on me but it didn't work."

"By 'attention' do you mean getting yourself arrested for drunk driving?"

"That was cleared."

"Of course it was. Dad got you off."

Robbie frowned. "Kids today aren't like you and Vera. You've been more or less married since you were, what? Two years old? Dad and Mr. Exton were like medieval lords plotting to join the farms. After you ran off and left Vera behind, nobody was sure what was going on. Dad said it was too bad Kelly was older than me or I could marry her. One day she was here at the pool wearing a bikini. I said I was more than willing to help him join the farms."

"And what did Dad say to that?"

"That he'd thought of asking for Kelly's hand himself. He said, 'Think she'd have me?' I told him he should ask."

Adam could only stare at his brother. He'd never had that

kind of camaraderie with their father. Their conversations had been about school grades and how well or poorly Adam was doing on the sports fields. Trying to get himself back under control, he lowered his voice. "You wouldn't really go after Kelly, would you? She's years older than you and she's about to become a veterinarian."

Robbie stood up. "Five years, four months, one week and two days. That's the age difference." He turned away, lit a cigarette, then looked back at his brother. "You go to far-off Africa to take care of kids, but you ought to look at people around here. Kelly Exton will probably marry that half-wit stepson of Dr. Carl. She's afraid that if she doesn't, she'll piss off the doc. If that happened, she wouldn't have a vet job around here. Then she'd have to go somewhere else, which means she'd have to leave her mom. Mrs. Exton won't leave the farm but she can't run it by herself. Vera is running away with you, so Kelly would have to stay here in Mason. And do what? Take on Vera's job at the travel agency? Give up her animals? Might as well rip out her *soul*."

Adam was surprised that Robbie knew so much about Vera's kid sister. "I get it. It's a stack of building blocks. If Kelly doesn't marry Paul, everyone's expectations of life will be destroyed. But she *is* going to marry Paul. Vera told me so yesterday. *You* need to stay *out* of it!"

Robbie gave his brother a cold look. "You never see past whatever *you* want, do you? You and Dad had a fight, so you ran away. And now you come back and give us orders of what to do with our lives. Then you plan to leave again. Tell me, who died and made *you* king?"

"Dad," Adam said before he thought. It was too flippant.

Robbie's anger increased. "You think *you* are fit to take his place? That it's your birthright? You haven't *earned* any rights around here. And as for Kelly Exton, I like her. A lot! And I have the money to open a clinic for her. Screw Dr. Carl and his loser son. That guy would sell Kelly for a bag of apple tree branches."

Robbie smashed his cigarette in an ashtray. "Oh, hell. It's no use talking to you. Go back to Africa, where they make you feel good. Don't get involved with *us*." He stormed up the stairs and slammed his bedroom door.

Adam fell back against the big desk chair made of leather and carved oak. He and Vera used to call it "Burke's throne."

"He rules the world from there," Vera had said.

"The world of Mason, Kansas," Adam had said, and they'd laughed together.

He looked around the big house. His parents had built it when he was just a kid and he remembered marveling at it. Lots of wood, lots of stone. The fireplace went to the ceiling and covered most of a wall. Burke's huge desk and chair were situated so he could see everything: kitchen, living room, dining room, outside to the garage.

As Adam looked around, he thought about what Robbie had said and what he'd said in return.

Vera's little sister was not someone Adam had thought about much. She'd always been a cute kid with big blue eyes and animals all around her. She'd never been afraid of worms or bugs, or the big animals, either. Last night when she'd brought Xander back, he waved at her through the window. She'd barely moved her chin in recognition.

He didn't know when their bickering started. She'd always seemed so quiet and complacent that maybe he just wanted to get a reaction out of her. Of course she knew his barbs were all in good fun.

Didn't she?

For a moment, he thought about his younger brother and Kelly. Robbie was good-looking, rich, adored by women. Was

Kelly the one he couldn't get? The unattainable one? Would Rob think of it as a notch on his bedpost if he could break up Kelly from the man she loved?

For a moment, Adam closed his eyes. Robbie going after Kelly and probably getting her would cause masses of problems between the two families. If Robbie broke Kelly's heart—which he would, of course—Vera might hold it against Adam. Robbie's lechery, his insatiable need to conquer, could hurt a lot of people.

He had a vision of Vera flying home from Africa to try to settle the mess her sister was in because of Robbie. On the other hand, maybe Robbie was right about Pauly being a wimp. Sometimes it felt like the marriages in this town were arranged in childhood. He and Vera; Kelly and Paul. They may as well have been betrothed when they were in elementary school.

Adam felt he'd had to admit to Vera that he'd not been faithful, but that wasn't the whole story.

The young woman had been a social worker from Boston, a bit older than Adam and way more experienced. She was the one who'd said, "Don't fall in love with me." He had, at least for a while. He'd been the one whose heart seemed to break when she left. "Go home to your girlfriend," she'd said. "Go home to Kansas and stay there."

He hadn't liked her implication. It was almost as though she was saying he wasn't cut out to be a world traveler. And maybe it was true that he'd made his little hut into a home. He had a garden with plants he'd found growing on the savanna. And he'd bought some nice, locally made furniture. He'd told himself that he was doing it to welcome Vera, but sometimes he thought he was making a home for himself.

He got up from the desk. He wasn't sure what he was going to do, but he needed to do something about Robbie.

CHAPTER FOUR

KELLY HADN'T SLEPT MUCH. SHE'D FLOPPED around in bed, her mind awhirl, thinking about her life. If she were like Vera, she'd march over to Pauly and demand to be told what was going on. He'd been given an engagement ring and told to put it to its proper use. But he'd returned the ring to the store. So maybe that was good. It showed that he was money conscious. Maybe he wanted to buy a ring on his own and was saving for one.

That idea calmed her down for about five minutes. Then she turned over and stared at the ceiling.

She knew that any money Pauly got he invested in his future business. This trip to Britain must be costing him a lot.

"So he doesn't want to get married *now*," she said aloud. "But what if he never wants to get married?" The future that possibility showed her was too horrible to contemplate. If she and Pauly broke up, Dr. Carl would keep her as his assistant. He needed her. But Mrs. Carl was a woman of strong emotions. She hated as hard as she loved. Kelly had a vision of Dr. Carl in tears as he told Kelly how his wife was making his life hell. He would be sorry, but Kelly *had* to leave the practice.

She got up before dawn, as she often did, got into her four-wheel-drive Jeep and headed toward Dr. Carl's clinic. The animals needed to be fed and watered and given some exercise. Dr. Carl would do it, but Kelly usually helped.

When she reached his driveway, she couldn't bring herself to turn in. She had no doubt that Mrs. Carl would find her and quiz her about what Pauly was doing, as if Kelly knew anything. She felt that her mood was bad enough without being questioned.

She headed back home. She needed to study for her finals, but when she approached the long Hatten drive, she turned into it. It was early enough that Robbie and Adam would be asleep, so she could go to the barn without being seen. Right now she'd like to be with Xander. "Best listener in town," she mumbled as she parked and got out.

The Hattens had six horses. The men who worked the big farm rode them through the pastures, to the places their trucks couldn't go.

Beautiful Xander had been Burke's pride. Hands taller than the other horses and with a strong personality. Xander liked and disliked people, and he didn't hide his preferences.

As she entered the stall, Xander nuzzled her in greeting. She led him out to the paddock to let him prance around.

"You're here early."

Kelly frowned at Adam's voice, but when she turned to him, she had cleared her expression. "And you're awake early."

"Couldn't sleep."

"Missing your friends in Africa?"

"At least no one there hates me."

Kelly blinked in surprise. Adam Hatten didn't usually reveal anything to her. "I guess you mean Robbie."

"He yells at me."

The way he said it, with such deep self-pity, made her smile. "Robbie's angry at the world."

"You know him well, do you?"

She narrowed her eyes at him. "Are you implying something?"

Adam stuck his hands in his pockets and let out a sigh. "I think he wants to marry you. Unite the farms, that sort of thing."

At that, Kelly let out a full-blown laugh. "Your dad asked me, too. Robbie would be a pale second." Adam's eyes widened.

"It was a joke. He was drunk." She stroked Xander's cheek. "If you go out today on Xander, take it slow. He's not as young as he used to be."

"Go with me."

"What?"

"The house is full of paperwork that I don't want to do, and I haven't had a chance to look around. I've never seen Paul's tree farm. We can visit it and—"

"No!" she said with too much emphasis. "I mean, he's busy. He's going away for...for the summer and..." She turned away. The last thing she wanted to do was show weakness to Adam. He'd tell Vera. Then she'd run to Pauly, who'd tell his mother. By nightfall, Mrs. Carl would have Kelly in a chair, interrogating her.

"Okay." Adam had moved to stand near her. "No visiting Paul. But I do need to look around this place. We're going to be relatives soon, so maybe we should spend some time together."

She'd lived next door to the Hattens all her life, and Adam had been joined at the hip to her sister since they were kids, but she'd spent little time alone with him. And if it was just the two of them, it was usually silent. To him, she was a kid.

To her, he was the person who took Vera away so much of the time.

But Kelly needed time away from all of them: her mother, Mrs. Carl, Dr. Carl, Pauly. Everyone!

Adam kindly let her ride Xander, and from the way the horse twitched its tail, he was pleased. "He certainly does like you."

"Most people do," she said.

Adam mounted Jagger. He wasn't magnificent like Xander, but dependable and unimpressed by anything. "Are you defending yourself or aiming at me?"

She ignored his question as they rode side by side on an old trail between crop fields of soybeans and sunflowers. "So tell me about Africa."

He got a faraway look in his eyes. "You'd love the country. The animals are majestic. They roam wild. Giraffes and zebras run together. There are herds of water buffalo. And the lions! They're lazy most of the time, but they'll take off in a leap. They're ruthless killers."

Kelly was nodding. Since she was a child, she'd watched documentaries about animals.

"What about human hunters?"

Adam took a while to answer. "People pay so they can kill the animals. I saw a rhino dying because his horn had been cut off."

"I can see why you'd want to be there and not here."

"There are a lot of problems here, too."

"I take it you mean Robbie."

"Can you keep a secret? One I haven't even told Vera?"

"Of course."

"Robbie doesn't know this, but Dad left me two-thirds of the farm. He didn't divide it equally."

"He was probably trying to give you a reason to stay here."

"That's what I think, too, but Robbie won't believe that," Adam said. "He'll think Dad liked me better."

"That's ridiculous! Robbie is much easier to love than you. Don't look at me like that. I'm just telling the truth. Robbie will stay because he wants to, but *you* have to be coaxed."

"Or bought." Adam grimaced. "You sure know how to crush a man's ego."

"Sorry. Robbie is *friendlier* than you. Is that better?"

"Not much. He's certainly friendly to women. And he acts like he can't stand me."

"He's trying to make you angry."

"Why?"

"He's trying to make you stay, of course. Robbie loves you. You should have seen him and your dad after you ran away."

"I didn't 'run away.' You make me sound like a kid running off to the circus."

"You went off to lions, elephants and rhinos. Seems to fit."

Adam shook his head. "I guess so." He took a deep breath of clean air. "I needed to go. The pressure on me to be 'Burke Hatten's son' was too much for me."

"Being Adam Hatten's baby brother is almost too much for Robbie."

He looked at her. "You're smart, aren't you?"

"Top of my class in vet school. Of course, I'm no match for Vera."

He looked puzzled. "She's ahead of you in Elephant Class?"

Kelly laughed. "If she took my classes I'm sure she would be. She'd know the history of every animal back to the Ice Age."

"But you just know when an animal is feeling bad. Remember the baby foxes you sneaked into your house? I thought your mother was going to take an ax to them."

"She was scared."

"Uh-oh." The sky had opened up to rain. Kelly started to

turn back. "Fredericks," he called over his shoulder and she knew where he meant.

She had on a little sun hat but it wasn't much protection. She put her head down and went east toward the old homestead. Xander, not liking getting drenched, took off at a racer's pace. Despite her warning to Adam about running him, it was exhilarating as they sped down the trail.

The old Fredericks house was in bad shape but it still had a fairly good roof, and there was a big shed in the back.

With his head down against the rain, Adam slid off in front of the shed. When the double doors stuck, he kicked them in and his horse hurried inside. He put his arms up for Kelly and lifted her down. Big Xander barely fit through the doors.

It took them a while to get the horses settled. Then Adam said, "Let's go."

They ran through the rain and into the house, then through the old kitchen and into the living room. There was a fireplace but it looked to be full of nests. With a clogged chimney, they both knew that a fire would fill the house with smoke.

Against the far wall was a stained mattress and there was spray-painted graffiti on the wall. *Henry loves Diane.*

"Another Sex Shack," Kelly said.

"Another one? Where's the—?" Adam stopped and his face turned red. He realized she meant the place he and Vera used.

Kelly sat down on the mattress.

"You're soaked," he said. "I'd offer you dry clothes and a warm drink but..." He shrugged. "It's Kansas. Any rain that isn't from a tornado makes me happy." He was looking around for a place to sit. She nodded toward the other side of the mattress and he sat down a couple of feet from her.

The rain was loud on the roof and Kelly was beginning to feel cold in her wet clothes. The room was dark, with the only light coming from a window that showed the grayness outside. Something about the place made for a kind of intimacy and Kelly desperately wanted to talk to someone, a person who wouldn't go into a panic, about the disrupted future of everyone in her life.

She looked out the window at the rain and blinked hard at the tears that were coming.

"Tell me what's wrong," Adam said.

"I think Pauly is breaking up with me," she said softly.

"What makes you think that?" He sounded surprised.

She told him about the ring Mrs. Carl had bought and given to Pauly to use for their engagement. "I went to him expecting a marriage proposal. It wasn't as though I didn't know it was coming. It wasn't 'if' but 'when.' But he said nothing about the ring, so I asked." She paused. "Pauly said he'd returned it to the store."

"You're kidding!" Adam almost shouted.

Kelly started to get up, but he clasped her forearm and she sat back down. "Sorry. It's just that you're so much...so much *more* than he is! I'm not denigrating him but everyone thinks that."

"Pauly has been safe, and I—"

"You what?" When she hesitated, he said, "You can talk to me."

"Only if you swear on your life that you won't tell Vera. I have to protect her."

"*Protect* Vera? What does that mean?"

"She has to be free to leave. No obligations. No chains holding her here. She stayed here for *me*. She gave up going to Africa for *me*."

"And for your mother," he said.

"Yes. For us. I can't allow things to fall apart now. Vera will only leave if I'm settled."

"I understand," he said. "Robbie told me about this. Actually, he shouted it at me. I gather that Mrs. Carl is a problem."

"She's an absolute witch to most people, but she often tells me she loves me."

"But if you don't marry Paul she'll take you away from Dr. Carl. Then where will you work?"

"Exactly!"

He leaned back against the wall. "Have you ever been on a date with anyone other than Paul?"

Kelly shook her head. "How about you and Vera?"

"In Africa—" He waved his hand. "I've never asked a girl out to dinner or a movie. Except Vera and that was more—"

"I know," Kelly said. "You don't ask. You just say, 'Which movie do you want to see on Saturday?'"

"Or 'Wanna eat at the diner or the burger place?'"

They were quiet for a moment.

"If Pauly and I are broken up, how do I...?"

"Get into dating?" he asked.

"Yes. I admit that I've wondered what other boys are like. All through high school my girlfriends would fall in love one week, then break up the next. I was always glad that I didn't have to go through that."

"You couldn't have done that *and* worked with Dr. Carl *and* studied so that now you're the top of your class."

Kelly smiled. "That's true. Pauly never complained when I canceled something because I was helping his dad."

"And besides, he had his tree obsession to occupy him."

"And I never had to worry about him and other girls. Although I did have a few moments of jealousy when the trees were in bloom and he wouldn't leave them. One time I wore a very short dress that was the exact pink of the flowers."

"Did he notice?"

"I think so, but he didn't say anything."

He was looking at her. "Are you a…?" He didn't finish.

"A virgin? No, I'm not, and if this gets that personal, I'm leaving."

"Sorry," he mumbled. "How are we going to solve your problem? Other than marrying Robbie, that is. I can't see him as husband material."

She looked at him. "I don't know. I bet Robbie could teach me a few tricks about boys and girls. Or maybe you could explain things to me. I'm quite curious. Which animals do mating humans most imitate?"

"Well… I, uh…" He saw the light in her eyes. "You brat! I'm not about to explain the facts of life to you. Ask Vera."

"Oh, so you taught her and now she's to tell me?"

Adam laughed. "We were talking about *you*, not me. And I agree that if you tell Vera that Paul isn't going to be part of your future, she'll panic."

"I know. She and Mom think my graduation is the moment all problems will be solved. I'll marry Pauly, we'll move in with Mom and I'll become a partner with Dr. Carl."

"And Vera will leave with me for Africa."

"Everybody gets a happily-ever-after."

He looked at her. "Think Vera will agree to leave if you and your mom are alone? Can just the two of you take care of the farm?"

"I don't know. It was all planned so perfectly. Pauly is good with numbers. He was going to keep the books."

"In exchange for how many acres given to him to plant his old trees?" Adam's disgust was evident.

"Heritage," she corrected. "His business is called Heritage Harvests. And we agreed on twelve acres."

Adam whistled. "That's a lot." His head came up. "Wait a minute! You worked all this out but he never officially proposed?"

"We did."

"This is a problem," he said.

"Not for you. You'll leave and—"

"Stop saying that! It's thrown in my face every three minutes. That I left! That I'm going to leave! When I first went away, it didn't matter. My father was the ruler. He treated me like a kid and always would. I needed..." He couldn't go on.

"I know you loved him. A lot of people said bad things after you went away, but I never believed any of it. Burke Hatten had to have his own way. That's hard to deal with. Who else worries you?"

He laughed. "How'd a kid like you get so smart?"

"May I remind you that I am only eleven and a half months younger than you?"

She had on wet clothes that clung to her body. She certainly didn't look like a kid! He looked away. "I always think of you as Vera's pest of a little sister."

"We'll hire someone to help Mom and me."

"Some hippie who'll grow Mary Jane in the far fields?"

"I've got all summer to find someone."

"You'll search while you study and work? You're not going to have a minute to yourself. And as soon as this town hears that Pauly is going away and the perky little Kelly Exton is unchaperoned, every man for fifty miles will come running."

Kelly could feel blood creeping up her face. "I don't think so!"

"Dances, hayrides, barbecues by the dozen. They'll take you to make-out places. They'll send you flowers and burnt ends. The smart ones will show up with birds with broken wings."

"I could stand that," Kelly said. "First one who brings me a sloth and I'm his."

Adam didn't laugh. "Robbie will sleep on your doorstep."

"He already does."

"What?"

"You haven't been back long enough to hear all the gossip. Vera should have told you. Unless you two were too busy to talk."

Adam gave her a look to cut it out.

"Mom and Forey cooked for him, listened to him and generally adored him. He was quite happy."

Adam was frowning. "So maybe he thinks he's in love with you because he doesn't want to give up your home life. Your mom and Forey are great cooks."

"Take that back. Now!"

"What did I say that was wrong?" He looked perplexed, then smiled. "Oh. Right. Sorry. I'm sure Robbie fell for you because you're the prettiest girl in the county." His eyes were twinkling.

"Pretty doesn't last."

"You're also talented and a hard worker. Of course he's crazy about you." He shook his head. "Does Vera know what you're really like?"

"She has no idea. She thinks I'm a helpless child."

"Hmm. If she *thought* you were settled, she would leave with me. She just has to *believe*."

"So Robbie and I should pretend that we're a couple and madly in love?"

"No! My little brother is off-limits!" He narrowed his eyes at her. "Robbie is to go to college first. Then he'll meet someone. We just need to figure out what to do with *you*."

"Put an ad in the paper? 'Husband with a horse wanted'? 'Send photo of horse.'"

He snorted. "It's stopped raining. Let's go." He stood up.

"Maybe Robbie would show up with Xander."

Adam was going out the door and shaking his head. Behind him, Kelly was smiling.

By the time they got home to the Hatten barn, the rain had stopped but they were still wet. They removed the saddles and began rubbing down the horses.

"Thanks," Kelly said. "You made me feel better."

"I enjoyed it. It was nice to be around someone who isn't angry at me. And it's good for you and me to get to know each other better."

"I agree. Wherever we live, we'll be family." When Xander dropped a pile of manure, Kelly got the fork hanging on the wall and scooped it up.

Robbie's voice came from outside. "Kelly? I saw your Jeep. Are you in here?"

Adam was about to call out to his brother, but to his shock, Kelly flicked the fresh, hot, steaming pile of horse manure onto him. It hit him smack in the middle of his chest, then began to slide down. "What the hell?" He wiped a piece off the side of his face. "Why did you do that?"

"We just spent two hours at the second-best make-out spot in the county. If we were seen sopping wet and smiling, by noon gossip will have me pregnant. With *your* kid."

He grabbed straw and started wiping himself down. "I never thought of that."

"Really? And you're the brother with the brain?"

"It's not my brain that would cause the gossip."

She laughed.

"Kelly!" Robbie shouted. "Where are you?" He was close to them.

She raised her voice to an angry shout. "I told you, Adam Hatten! What I do or don't do is none of your business. Stay *out* of my life!" As she ran past him, she mouthed, "Thanks," then stomped toward Robbie.

Adam went to the door, but stayed in the shadows. Robbie was next to Kelly's green Jeep, his back to the barn.

"If my brother is bothering you, let me know. I'll deal with him." Robbie sounded like he was about to strap on a six-shooter.

Adam rolled his eyes.

Kelly saw him and had to suppress a giggle. She got into her car and started it. "I can handle myself."

Robbie put his hand on the door. "I hear Paul is leaving town for the summer. I don't want you to think you have to be alone. You won't have to miss out on any fun just because he's not here. How about going to the dance on Saturday with me?"

Behind him, a smelly, dirty Adam was shaking his head in a vigorous no!

"It's just a temporary separation," she said. "I'm still engaged." Immediately, Kelly regretted her choice of words. She meant engaged as in that she had other things to do. "I mean—"

But Robbie stepped back, his eyes wide. "You and Paul are engaged? That's really big news."

Adam was shaking his head at her lie. He held up his left hand, wiggling his fingers. She had no ring.

Robbie was still talking. "People are going to be disappointed to hear that you're off the market. Where's your ring?"

"Being resized. I have to go." She put the Jeep in Reverse, turned it around and left the Hatten farm. The slip about the engagement was bad, but maybe she'd said it on purpose. She didn't want to admit that Pauly had maybe dumped her. After he left town, she could tell everyone *she* had broken up with *him*. She was smiling. She'd started the day feeling very bad. She still had the same problems, but Adam had made her feel better. He'd made her believe there was a way to solve everything.

CHAPTER FIVE

ADAM WENT BACK INTO THE BARN. HE thought about sneaking out and getting cleaned up, but that would mean leaving Xander wet. As he started rubbing, he braced himself for the ridicule of his little brother.

Robbie didn't disappoint. He looked at his brother, his chest coated in horse manure, and said, "What the hell happened to you?"

"I fell."

"And kept your hands clean? No, it looks like you had a pile thrown on you. It was Kelly, wasn't it? I heard her yelling at you. What did you do to her?"

Adam held out his towel. "Here, you finish this."

Robbie didn't take the towel. "I don't want to go to town smelling like horse."

"Then rub carefully. I need to go take a shower."

Robbie still didn't take the towel. "When Xander comes down with pneumonia, I'll tell Kelly it was your fault."

With a groan, Adam kept wiping.

"What *did* you do to her to make her do that to you? I know she dislikes you, but this is the worst yet."

"Dislikes me? Kelly is going to be my sister-in-law. I've known her all her life. We're friends."

"Kelly can't stand you. Everyone knows that."

"Because Vera is going to leave with me?"

"No. Because you're a know-it-all who thinks he owns the town. You're a clone of Dad, but without his love of the place."

Adam stopped rubbing and stared at his brother. "That's not true. Dad lived in his own world. He was oblivious to anything outside it."

"Just like you." Rob was grinning, seeming to be glad that he'd upset his brother. "I gotta go. There's no food in the house but I guess you're too good to go to a grocery. The Great Hatten Heir. King on the football field, ruler of the basketball court, saving Africa, engaged to a girl who plans to change the world. It's a wonder you don't wear a cape and fly over us."

The hostility behind his brother's words left Adam speechless. He felt like he'd been hit with a baseball bat.

"See you at dinner. Maybe." With a smile, Rob turned and left.

Adam thought he should demand to know where his brother was going, but he didn't have the courage to ask. "I can't wait to leave this place," he muttered as he headed to the house and the shower.

Robbie wanted his brother to think he was heading off to some wild rendezvous but, as he often did, he was going to the Exton house. Vera was at work today, so there'd be no one to say, "Are you here again?" For the life of him, he couldn't understand what Adam saw in her.

If he was lucky, Kelly would be there. Since Mac Exton died, their house had almost become an animal hospital. Dr. Carl didn't care about what he called "the exotics" but Kelly loved them. Turtles with broken shells, injured possums, wounded birds. One summer Kelly took care of a young deer in the backyard. That ended when it escaped and ate all of Nella's lettuces. After that incident, Kelly gave Robbie a copy of *The Yearling* by Marjorie Kinnan Rawlings. He loved it.

As he pulled into the drive, he sighed. Alas, Kelly's Jeep wasn't there. He gave a single knock, then entered the house.

As he hoped, Nella was in the kitchen and the old stove was covered with big pots. The smell was delicious.

He rounded the corner, then halted. Not only was Nella there but so was Fortunata. To him, they were a beautiful sight. Two women, older but certainly not old, comfortably plump and smiling at him.

He took turns hugging and lifting them while they giggled like girls. "What smells so good? Besides you two, that is?"

They giggled some more.

"Beef and chicken broth," Nella said. "We're getting it ready to make soup."

"And we made bread," Forey added. "Think you could manage a slice or two?"

Robbie took a seat at the old kitchen table. It was stainless steel with a red Formica top. It had been scrubbed so many times that white showed through in places. "I'm starving. There's no food in my house and Adam is being a jerk and…" He gave a sad sigh.

The women weren't fooled; they knew him too well. They put before him a platter heaped with food. It was part traditional American and part Mexican. No matter what could be said about Kansas residents, they ate well!

As Robbie dug in, he wondered if he should say that he knew about Kelly's engagement. She'd said it quickly, so maybe she was waiting for the ring before she announced it outside the family. "So what's your news?" Did anything in the world taste better than bread fresh out of the oven? Nella bought cream from a local dairy and put it into her blender to churn it into butter. There was a pot of it on the table and he slathered the bread.

"Miguel is here!" Forey said. She and her husband were second generation from Mexico, living in Kansas. They didn't have a lot of land and her husband did many outside jobs. They had two grown daughters, both of whom had moved to far-away California.

"Tell him the rest of it," Nella said.

"I think he and Gabby are in love." Two years ago, Forey and Rafe had sponsored the daughter of a friend to move to the US to live with them. Gabrielle had recently turned twenty.

"Sure about that?" Robbie kept his head down so they wouldn't see his eyes.

"Oh, yes," Forey said. "We'll build them a house beside ours and we'll have grandbabies we can see every day."

Robbie didn't look up. "So how's Miguel doing?"

"You won't remember him, but—"

"Are you kidding?" Robbie said. "I remember him very well. The summers when he was here were the best of my life."

There was a stool by the end of the counter and Forey put a dish of cold flan there. They knew how much he loved the dessert. Robbie left his empty plate and went to sit closer to them. "That was the summer Adam broke his leg. I used to…" He didn't finish the sentence.

"You used to what?" they asked.

He felt a warmth creep up inside him as his memories came back. He'd adored his big brother. Seemingly from birth, Adam had been a star athlete. Not clumsy like other kids. First time he picked up a bat, he hit the ball. Hard. Burke had nearly popped the buttons on his shirt in pride.

Robbie, diaper clad, had always followed his brother when-ever possible. Adam would ruffle his little brother's hair now and then but there was too much to do to give him any real attention.

But that summer, Adam had been confined to bed, his leg in a harness suspended from the ceiling. Burke had hired nurses to look after him. The women were bored and glad to let young Robbie hang about to let them know when they were needed.

That summer, Robbie was by his brother's side often. Adam read to him, told him stories, coached him as he tried to learn to throw a ball in a way that was natural to his big brother.

"I liked all the things Miguel and Vera did."

"What does that mean?" Nella asked.

"Just their talks and telling of where they went and what they saw. They used to ride a lot. And Vera brought books." Robbie smiled. "Her books were for teaching, but Adam read Louis L'Amour to me. And Kelly came, too. She was the best. She always brought animals. Mom was afraid one of them would bite Adam, so they weren't allowed inside, but Kelly didn't obey. She used to climb up the side of the house and through the window with the animals. One time a bird got loose and Adam fell out of bed trying to catch it. Kelly barely got out the window before the nurse arrived. Adam had to go back to the hospital for three days." Robbie was smiling in memory.

"I don't know anything about this." Nella's voice was low, that mother-voice of warning.

"I'd like to hear more about it all," Forey said sternly.

Robbie didn't know what he'd said to set the women off, but their intensity made him know he had to change the subject. He gave a little cough. "I thought you two would be planning Kelly's wedding cake."

Nella's eyes went so wide he was afraid her skin would break. "He asked her?" she whispered. "She said yes?"

Forey put her arm around her friend. "When did this happen? And why did Kelly tell *you* before her own mother?" Her frown was fierce.

Robbie swallowed. "Maybe I have it wrong. Maybe—" He got off the stool. "I have to, uh… I need to go." He hurried out of the house, lit a cigarette, got into his pickup and drove onto the road. It appeared that he'd broken some kind of girl-law by knowing this important thing first. So why *had* Kelly told him before she told her family? *Maybe*, he thought, *Kelly does feel a bond between us.* He smiled as he drove home.

Adam had taken what had to be the longest, hottest shower of his life when he heard the front door open. Then Robbie ran up the stairs. He got to the bedroom door before his brother could close it.

"Hey!" Adam said. "I don't want us to get off on the wrong foot. We're brothers. We—"

"Save the preaching for church." Rob removed his shirt and took a clean one out of his closet.

Adam, with an athlete's eye, looked at his shirtless brother. He had certainly grown up in the last years! He no longer looked like a kid but an adult male who was finely toned. Adam stretched out on the bed, hands clasped behind his head. "Still swimming?"

"Some."

"Why don't you and I go to the grocery together?"

"As fun as that sounds, I'm going to go—" He cut himself off with a quick glance at his brother.

"Where are you going?"

"To see Miguel. Remember him?"

"Of course. He used to run after Vera."

"If that's the way you remember it." Robbie went to the adjoining bathroom but left the door open.

"So where are you *really* going?" Adam asked.

Robbie couldn't help smiling at his brother's perception. He went back into the bedroom. "It's not your business, but I'm going to apologize to Kelly. I put my foot in my mouth and I need to warn her."

Adam sat up. "What did you do?"

"It wasn't my fault. I was boxed in and I had to get out any way I could." Adam was glaring at him. "I told Nella and Forey that Paul asked Kelly to marry him. They hadn't been told yet, so they weren't happy. You'd think I had—"

Adam recovered his shock. "You had no right to tell them that!"

"Don't give me that look. Paul thinks he can put a cage around Kelly by giving her a ring. But he's going to be gone all summer, and *I* will be here."

"The dance," Adam said. "Paul will be away, so you're going to ask Kelly to go with *you*."

Robbie didn't answer but his smile said yes. "See you later." He left the room.

Adam stayed where he was until he heard the front door close. Then he picked up the bedroom phone and called information. The operator gave him the number for Dr. Carl's clinic. "Would you like for me to dial that number for you?" the operator asked.

"Sure," Adam said, then waited.

"Betty Lewis," a woman said. She was chewing gum in that way that made constant bubbles that popped.

Adam asked if it was the vet clinic.

"Isn't that who you called?" she snapped.

Adam looked at the receiver in disbelief. "I need to speak to Kelly," he said.

"She's busy. Call back later."

"Wait!" Adam said. "This is an emergency. Tell her I have a sloth."

"A what?" Click, pop, click, her gum went.

He gritted his teeth. "This is Adam Hatten. Get Kelly Exton on the phone *now*!"

"If that's what you want," she said tiredly, and he heard the receiver hit the desktop.

It was several minutes before Kelly came to the phone. "Adam! Is it Mom? I'll be right there. Or is it Vera? I'll—"

"No!" he said loudly. "No one is hurt. Robbie told your mom and Forey that you and Paul are engaged."

The sound Kelly made was half a cry, half a whimper of fear.

"My little brother is on his way to you now and I think he's going to make a serious play for you."

"I might take him up on it," Kelly muttered. "Pauly will tell one person that he dumped me. Then everyone will know. I'll be the laughingstock of the town. Poor dumb Kelly and all those wasted years." She was heading toward tears. "Mrs. Carl will fire me. She'll—"

"Kelly!" Adam was loud, firm. "I will take care of this. Tell Rob you *are* engaged. Yell at him for blabbing your secret, then say you will *not* go to the dance with him. Say you already have a date."

"A date? Oh. Seth Murray just broke up with his girlfriend. Maybe he—"

"He failed geography class and he can't hold on to a ball."

"But he's nice to look at," Kelly said.

Adam grunted. "If you like that sort. Look, I'll fix this. Go back to whatever you were doing, but send my little brother away. Meet me…" He thought. "Meet me by the frog pond at five thirty and I'll explain everything. Okay?"

"Yes," she said. "Adam? Did you tell Betty you had a sloth?"

"Yeah, I did. You bring a wombat and I'll bring sandwiches."

She laughed. "I look forward to it."

Adam was smiling when he hung up.

Adam was frowning as he drove to Paul's little "hippie farm," as Vera had told him the town called it.

The little trees that produced small and gnarly and often bug-infested apples were a great source of laughter to the town. "At least he's not trying to make a living off of them," they said, meaning that Paul had sense enough to work at a grocery store.

As Adam drove up, he saw that the place was quite pretty, as though waiting for a photographer.

He parked and got out of his truck.

Paul was holding a hose, individually watering his precious trees. "Hi," he said, but he didn't seem glad to see Adam. They'd never really been friends, just people who lived near one another.

"There's a problem," Adam said. "I'm afraid my little brother told people that you're engaged to marry Kelly."

Paul moved the hose. "We're not engaged. Someone misunderstood."

Misunderstood the years you kept her locked down, Adam thought. "Kelly was caught off guard. She said the ring you gave her was being resized."

Paul didn't reply, just kept his attention on his trees.

He could see that Paul was upset by this. Adam turned off the water. "Tell me what's going on."

Paul's eyes were burning in anger. "Why? So you can tell the whole town what a monster I am? That I'm evil because I'm not ready to settle down? That I don't want to work forever in some grocery store and play with my little trees on the weekend?"

Adam took a step back. "Whoa, man. I was just asking."

Paul took a few breaths to calm down. "I was offered an opportunity to travel with some guys who have the same interests as me and I took it. I admit that I turned coward and didn't tell Kelly right away, but now I'm paying for it. My mother..." He took a breath. "I don't want to think of the hysterical, grandiose fit she's going to throw when I tell her there will be no autumn wedding."

"That's your side, but what about Kelly?"

Paul closed his eyes for a moment. "I love her. Always have. She was kind to me when others weren't. I've enjoyed every minute I've spent with her." His voice began to rise. "I'm just not ready to move in with her mom and take on a farm and an animal clinic and..." He looked at Adam. "And all those women!"

Adam couldn't help a smile of understanding.

"I'd be living with Kelly's mom and Forey, who practically lives there, and my mother will be there constantly. And all Kelly's damned animals. I live with them now with my step-dad, but—" He took a breath and stopped talking.

"Did you tell Kelly all this?"

Paul groaned. "No. My mother doesn't believe in not getting what *she* wants. Especially when it concerns *me*. She bought that ring for me to give to Kelly. Then she told Kelly what she'd done. When Kelly came here, I think she was expecting a marriage proposal."

"But she didn't get one."

"No, she didn't, but when she got on that big horse and it looked like she was going to trample my trees, I almost gave her one."

Adam grinned. "*How* can this be solved?"

"In a way where she doesn't hate me? Where the whole town doesn't want to murder me?"

"Do you plan to ask her when you get back?"

"I don't know," Paul said. "I just know that right now it's not what I want. Marriage, kids, snakes slithering across the floor and a mother-in-law who expects me to be a reincarnation of her husband and take care of cows, and my mother criticizing everything I do. I just…plain don't *want* it!"

Adam sat on the back bumper of his truck. "I'm not an expert about women, but I know they should do the breaking up. If it gets around that *you* dumped Kelly, she'll—"

"I know." Paul sat on the other end of the bumper. "Everyone will feel sorry for her."

"You need to talk to Kelly and tell her all of this."

Paul gave a false laugh. "Any way I say 'I don't want to marry you' will make me into a villain. But the truth is that if Kelly and I did marry, she'd be as unhappy as me. She dislikes my trees as much as I dislike her crap-producing animals."

"I don't see how you two ever got together in the first place."

"I had one day of lunacy. Trying to please my stepfather by warming up a snake."

Adam put his hand up. "It all seems to revolve around your dad."

"My *step*father." Paul grimaced. "If Kelly and I were ever in a situation where he could save only one of us, guess which one he'd choose?"

Adam nodded. He hadn't been in Mason for the last few years, but even he knew Paul was telling the truth. "You still have that ring?" he asked.

"I lied and told Kelly I'd returned it but I didn't." His car was nearby and he got it out of the glove box and handed it to Adam.

He opened the little box. "Wow! That's some ring. Mind if I borrow it?"

"The longer you have it, the more time before Mom finds out the truth."

"So when are you leaving?"

"Tomorrow morning."

"You planning to say goodbye to Kelly?"

Paul's face drained of color. "Not many people know this but Kelly has a temper like a volcano. If you ever want to see it, let her think you're mistreating one of those flea-ridden creatures she hauls around."

Adam was looking at the ring. "How much do you care about your reputation in this town?"

"Is that a joke? I'm already a laughingstock. People like the fruit they buy at Safeway. It's all perfectly shaped and colored and sprayed with every pesticide known to mankind. Ever hear the word *organic*?"

"Just that it's from the earth."

"Close enough. I want to put nonpoisoned food in the grocery stores. I want the whole world to know what 'organic' means. I want—"

Adam stood up. "I get it. You should do what drives you, and what other people think be damned. I think Kelly should flash this ring for a while. Then later this summer she can break up with you. How does that sound?"

"I'll do most anything to keep Kelly from hating me. She's my best friend. She's..."

When Adam saw tears gathering in Paul's eyes, he looked away. "I'll take care of this."

"That's great. I want the best for her. I heard that Seth Murray broke up with his girlfriend. He's very good-looking and he plays sports and—"

"She can do better than him!" Adam was frowning. "I need to go. I'm meeting Vera for lunch."

What looked to be fear flashed across Paul's face. "Can you clear it with *her*? If she thinks I've hurt Kelly, she might…" He swallowed.

"Break your bones into little pieces and use them for plant stakes?" Paul didn't smile but he nodded.

Adam took his keys out of his pocket. "Leave tomorrow early. Before daylight if possible. The sooner you're gone, the faster I can do whatever needs to be done." He held out his hand, they shook and Adam drove away.

He frowned on the drive into Kansas City. It was a fairly long way but the highway made it clear driving, and he admired the surroundings. A lot of people said Kansas was too flat, but to Adam, the fields, the open spaces, were beautiful. It reminded him of Africa. Add a few giraffes and a zebra or two, change the color of the soil, and it could be Africa.

The travel agency where Vera worked was on the beautiful Plaza, built in 1923 to look like Seville, Spain. It was the first shopping center in the world made to accommodate motorcars, so there were covered parking garages everywhere. He pulled into one, got out and walked to Vera's office on Wyandotte.

Like all the other buildings on the Plaza, it had a romantic look about it, old Spain in Kansas.

She was on the phone and motioned for him to take a seat and wait for her. The walls were covered with posters of places in the world to visit.

"I'll call you as soon as I know," Vera said, then hung up. She smiled at him. "Hungry?"

"Starving." He held the door open for her. There was no need to talk about what they would eat for lunch. It was Kansas City, so they'd have barbecue. Beef and how to cook it was practically a religion in the state. Burnt ends, brisket and ribs said it all.

"Enjoying your time off?" Vera asked as soon as they were seated.

"Actually, I've had a busy day. This morning I—"

He stopped as the waitress took their orders.

"Joe Harding called me," Vera said as soon as she left.

"He owns that big farm in Garland?"

"No, silly. *The* Joe Harding." Adam drew a blank.

"I wrote you about him. He did that series on modern-day Pakistan for the *New York Times*. There's talk of a Pulitzer for it. Anyway, I wrote him a long letter about how I would soon be traveling and I told him I work in a travel agency. Today he called me and asked if I'd plan his next trip for him." She fell back against her chair and waited for Adam's exclamation.

"That's great! Really, it is."

"I think so. In fact…"

The waitress put their platters in front of them. It was a huge amount of food. "In fact what?" Adam asked.

Vera moved her food around. "I think I'd like to do some journalist work. Tell me about where we'll live in Kenya. What access do you have to political leaders?"

Adam's face showed his puzzlement. "I wrote you about all of it."

"I know. Clean water. That's important, but what about the big picture? A lot of countries send money to Africa. Where does it go?"

"Not to us," he said, smiling.

But Vera didn't smile back. "I'd like to look into that. You should read what Joe wrote about Pakistan. He thinks the separation of the countries was a failure. It was over twenty years ago but people *still* don't have homes."

People at nearby tables looked at them as Vera was getting loud.

He leaned forward, his voice low. "We workers live very quietly. We're teachers and well diggers. I play a lot of football—that's soccer in the US. We..." He broke off as he could see Vera's attention was wavering. He put his hand over hers. "I probably don't know anything because I haven't asked. When you get there, you can question everyone." He went back to his food. "So you're going to arrange the travel for this guy Harmon?"

"Harding. Joe Harding. Very famous. He's going to be in Saint Louis next month and I am going to go see him. You okay with that?"

"Depends on his age and what he looks like."

Vera smiled. "He's fifty-two and seems to live on beer and cigarettes. He's spent a lot of time in India. I'd really, really like to go to that country." Her eyes seemed to glaze over.

"I need to talk to you about something. Kelly—"

Immediately, Vera came back to the present. "What's wrong? That little twerp Paul hasn't done something to her, has he? So help me, I'll rip him apart."

Adam looked at the couples at the next table. "It's nothing. Paul leaves tomorrow morning. He won't be around all summer."

"That's good. Hope he stays away."

"Kelly's afraid of losing her job with Dr. Carl."

Vera frowned. "I know, and his wife would make sure Kelly was kicked out. The woman dotes on that son of hers. Him and his little trees."

Adam couldn't help frowning. "Paul has some good ideas about organic food."

"What's that?" Before Adam could answer, Vera looked at

her watch. "I have to go." She stood up. "Kelly needs to open her own clinic. I've told her that a thousand times. She could put Dr. Carl out of business. Then she could dump Paul and she could meet other people."

"Like Seth Murray?" Adam asked.

"Great idea. Very nice guy. Works for the volunteer fire department. I'm late." She started toward the door.

Adam caught her hand. "You planning on going to the dance on Saturday?"

A look of horror flashed across Vera's face. "I usually work on Saturday nights, but if you want to go, I will."

"No," Adam said. "I mean, I may go, but only to catch up with people. I haven't seen them in a long time."

"Good idea." She gave him a quick kiss on the cheek, then left the restaurant.

Adam sat where he was, feeling a bit like he'd just weathered a storm. Had Vera always been like that or had his absence made her that way?

The waitress came to clear the table. "We have pie."

"Apple?"

"Of course."

"I'll have a slice, and could you wrap up a couple of pulled pork sandwiches? I'll take them with me."

As he ate, he realized that it was better that he hadn't told Vera what was going on with Kelly. And certainly not with Paul. Poor guy. He was right—the whole town was going to hate him. But the worst problem was keeping Kelly employed by Dr. Carl. Adam thought of Vera saying Kelly should open her own clinic and Dr. Carl be damned. Vera could do that. She could snub her nose at everyone, but Kelly couldn't. She would hate it if there was animosity between her and a man who'd been a second father to her. As Paul had said, if Dr.

Carl had to choose between his stepson and Kelly, everyone, including Mrs. Carl, knew who he'd choose.

There *had* to be a way to solve this!

When Adam got home, he made another stab at sorting the paperwork, but his heart wasn't in it. He kept thinking about Kelly and Paul. He wanted to be on one person's side, but he understood both of them. He admired Paul for wanting to create a business, even though it seemed ridiculous. It had taken centuries for farmers to learn how to protect food from insects and now Paul was going backward. It made no sense.

Adam admired Kelly for her love of animals and giving her life to them. Although marrying someone just to keep a job was way too much.

An idea began to form in his mind. It couldn't work, could it? It was too far-fetched. On the other hand, if his idea did work, it would be nice for everyone: Kelly, Vera, Adam. And for all the adults who seemed to believe that marriage was the one and only goal of every human being.

At four, he rummaged in the kitchen looking for his mother's big picnic basket. How he missed her! She was the peacemaker, and after she died, Adam and his father never stopped arguing.

He found the basket in the top cabinet. The two sandwiches took up little room inside and Robbie was right that there wasn't much food in the fridge.

He showered again—a coating of wet horse manure could make a man paranoid—then headed toward the frog pond, making a quick stop at the tiny local grocery. He had no idea what food Kelly liked, so he added potato chips and candy bars and cans of Coke.

"You and Vera goin' on a picnic?" Hal, the store owner, asked. "Nice day for it."

Adam just smiled. The village in Africa was as bad as Mason. Everyone knew everything about everybody. A lifetime of gossip had taught him to keep his mouth shut. "It *is* a nice day," he said as he left.

The pond was a half mile off the road, surrounded by trees, and as far as Adam knew, it wasn't a "make-out site." He drove across the flat, hard ground and parked his truck. When he was a child, he'd ride his bike to the pond to get away from his father.

Kelly was already there and she was feeding the ducks. It didn't surprise him that they were at her feet. Even as a kid, she'd had a magical touch with animals.

"Hi," she said. "Hope you brought something good to eat."

"All vegetables. And some of Paul's apples."

Kelly looked at him in shock.

"Beef. Fresh off the hoof. And fried potatoes."

"That's better."

In the shade of a big tree, he opened the basket and pulled out a red-and-white-checked tablecloth.

"That's your mother's. She said it made her feel French. We had some good meals on that cloth."

Adam realized that he didn't remember Kelly at any of his family's picnics. But then, if she'd been there, she would have been playing with animals and staying apart from the humans. What he remembered most was his father and Vera arguing. Every political side there was, the two of them were on opposite ends. Only Adam's mother could get them to stop going at each other, but the truth was that Burke and Vera adored each other. "My third son," he called her.

Kelly and Adam sat down on opposite ends of the cloth and he handed out sandwiches and drinks. She was no longer feeding the ducks but they still stayed near her.

"Paul's leaving in the morning." Adam was watching her closely. "He thinks it's better that he doesn't say goodbye."

She didn't look at him, just nodded, but he saw the muscle in her jaw working. "Mind if I ask you some personal questions?"

"Like what?"

"About you and Paul," he said. "You were planning to *marry* him? Are you that much in love with him?"

She took a while to answer. "It's not easy living with a perfect sister and a perfect mother. Vera plans to save the world, and she's made great sacrifices *for me*. Mom is always cooking and cleaning. She never rests. Pauly was someone I could complain to. He has an air of peace around him."

"That sounds great, but there's more to marriage than talk. What about sex?"

"Sex?" she asked.

"Yeah, you know. Passion. Can't keep your hands off each other. Slammed up against a wall. That kind of thing."

Kelly gave a little laugh. "It's not like that between us." She looked at him. "I heard you visited his tree farm. What did he say about me?"

"That he cares about you and doesn't want to hurt you."

"So maybe in the fall, he'll come back and we can…" Her eyes showed what she was asking.

"Maybe." He knew he didn't sound hopeful, but he didn't want to tell her the truth of what Paul had said. She didn't need to hear that he hated the idea of moving in with her family and running the farm with snakes slithering around and—

"What aren't you telling me?"

He didn't answer her question.

"Dumped," Kelly muttered as she put her empty sandwich paper into the basket. "I was discarded. Like garbage."

He winced at her phrasing. "I have an idea about how to

solve everything. It's dishonest and kind of silly, but at least it'll keep people from feeling sorry for you."

"I'm all for anything that will stop the pity. Celeste Wigman is going to cut me to pieces. One time she tried to kiss Pauly, but he backed away from her. Ever since then, she's been out to get us. She—" She looked at him. "Is that too high school?"

"Definitely!"

"So what's your plan?"

"It's simple, really. You will wear the ring Mrs. Carl bought and say you're engaged to Paul. This summer you'll go places with Vera and me, and spend time with a whole new crowd of people. Eventually, you'll say *you* decided to break up with Paul."

"Vera won't do that," Kelly said. "It's too dishonest. She'd tell everyone what a jerk Pauly is for dumping me."

"She doesn't have to know the whole truth," Adam said.

"You'd *lie* to the woman you love?" She was looking at him in speculation.

"Okay," he said, "let me introduce you to Selfish Adam. *What's in it for me?* is my life's motto."

"All right, Mr. Selfish, what *is* in it for you?"

"I want Vera to leave with me. You could even wait until *after* we're gone to say you broke up with Paul."

Kelly was smiling. "Actually, this whole idiot plan, this stupendous lie, rather appeals to me."

"You won't be the object of pity. Mrs. Carl won't start a vendetta against you for not doing what she wants and—"

Quickly, Kelly stood up. "Wait a minute! Mrs. Carl! My mother! Forey! I don't know what I was thinking. I can't do this. If they think I'm engaged, they'll start preparing the wedding. Thanks to Robbie's big mouth, the cake is probably already in the oven. They'll nag me to choose a dress. Then what? In September, I call off the wedding? Waste all that time and money?" She sat back down. "I think I better wait until Pauly returns and we can talk about the future."

Adam gave a big sigh. "Okay. Time for some truth. Your dream isn't going to happen. Paul won't live with your family and what he calls your 'crap-producing critters' and—" He cut himself off. "Sorry."

"I'm not surprised," she said. "Pauly forbid me to even have a dog around his trees. But this is bad. Mrs. Carl will throw me out of the practice. And Vera won't leave, so I'll take away *more* of her life." She looked at him. "The wedding to be planned should be yours and Vera's. She'll wear a long white dress and you'll be married in a church with lots of flowers. Then you two will jet off to Bali or wherever."

"Do you even know your sister? If she marries me, she'll wear whatever she's traveling in and tell the minister to hurry up because we're going to miss the plane. There won't be any cake cutting or champagne drinking. There'll be no sharing with people we've known all our lives. None of that."

She was looking at him. "But what about you?"

"There are photos of my parents' wedding, and I've always assumed I'd have a ceremony like theirs."

"Me, too. I know what my dress will look like and the cake and the flowers. All of it."

"How many legs does your ring bearer have?"

"At least four."

Adam gave her a hard, serious look. "I'm an old-fashioned guy. I want a *legal* marriage. If I did get Vera to agree to a wedding, she'd turn it over to you and your mother to plan. Am I right?"

"Yes."

"So you work it all out for you and Paul. Then you break up, and…" He raised his eyebrows at her.

"You and Vera take over the wedding."

Adam nodded. "With a few lies, we might both get what we want."

"I don't know if I can pull this off," she said. "But if Mom gets one of her daughters married, she'll be happy."

He could tell that she was leaning toward the idea. "You'd get to pick out cake and flowers and—"

"I'd have to buy a dress, but maybe I'll be able to use it later. And I can get Vera into something nice. My dad left me some money and I've saved it."

"Don't worry about money. I can—"

"No! You are *not* going to pay for *my* wedding dress."

"But if this whole thing is eventually for me, I *should* pay for things."

"The bride's family does all that. I think the theory is that you pay for everything after the wedding."

They were quiet for a moment, thinking about their plan. Kelly spoke first. "If you leave in September, will Robbie be running the farm? While he's still in college?"

Adam hesitated. "He can't do that and I don't think he *wants* to." He took a breath. "This is between you and me and Vera, but I may sell the farm. In that mass of paper Dad left behind, there's an offer from someone who wants to buy it. It's a good price."

"I never thought of that." She turned to him. "These are big changes. If you and Vera run off, and your farm is sold, Mom will be devastated."

"Add that if you don't marry Paul Mrs. Carl won't let you work with her husband, and it's a catastrophe. You'll spend the next twenty years saving enough money to open your own place."

"This doesn't sound so good after all."

"Kelly, please let me lend you the money to open a clinic. It can be in Ottawa. That's far enough away that there won't be too much competition and you can easily drive there every day."

"You can't—"

He cut her off. "We're going to be *family*. That means something. You can pay me back every cent. And when you think about this, it's all for me."

"And Vera," she said. "To free her. And to release me from being a burden to her." Her head came up. "And besides, maybe I'll find somebody else. This sex against a wall interests me."

Adam laughed. "Tell you what. While you plan a wedding for Vera and me, you and I will look for a clinic for you."

"My own clinic," she whispered. "I love Dr. Carl, but his filing system is very bad. And he doesn't like what he calls 'weird pets.' That means turtles and birds. And goldfish."

"You work on goldfish?"

"When needed."

"I hope you get a secretary better than the gum chewer who answered the phone."

"Betty was Mrs. Carl's choice. Utterly incompetent. And rude. But no chance her husband would be attracted to her."

Adam was watching her. "Are we set on this?"

"We have a Dagwood sandwich of lies." She was smiling. "I'm engaged to Pauly but I'm really not."

Adam grinned. "And you will plan a wedding for you two that will actually be for Vera and me."

"You have to help."

"I'm sure you can do it all by yourself. Have confidence."

"Okay. Then it'll be pink. Pink flowers. Pink cake, pink ribbons in the church. Maybe the pastor can wear pink. I bet we can find a pink jacket for you in KC. And—"

Adam threw his hands up in horror. "I'll help! I promise.

And I'll help you find a clinic. I'll enjoy doing that. And I will introduce you to some men."

"That's not necessary."

"Yes, it is. I'll weed out the scum that'll come running when they hear Paul is out of the picture."

"I was kidding about other men. I don't have time for that now. I'll have a wedding to plan, a clinic to find, my studies and working for Dr. Carl. It's all I can handle."

"No. You're going to meet some people."

She gave him a hard look. "Mr. Selfish, is this about your little brother?"

"I'm caught. Robbie will be at your doorstep. He's too young for you. Too much of a...of a kid. You need a man who won't get upset when you're called out in the middle of the night to deliver a calf. Or somebody who won't pout because you like four legs better than two."

"I didn't realize I was such a problem person," she said.

"Women might have jobs but they don't have careers. That's reserved for men."

"Maybe that will change."

"Someday, but right now it's the way things are. So are we set? Do we have a plan worked out?"

"I think we do."

He held out his hand and they shook.

"I nearly forgot," Adam said. He rummaged in the bottom of the picnic basket, withdrew the ring box Paul had given him and handed it to her.

She started to take it but then pulled her hand back. "I want at least some of the magic of this great lie." She held out her left hand to him.

With a chuckle, he took her hand and slipped on the ring. "Me, too. Can you imagine if I gave Vera an expensive engagement ring?"

"She'd sell it to help famine victims."

"Yes, she would. Your sister is a better person than we are."

"That she is." Kelly was looking at the way the ring sparkled in the fading daylight.

Adam moved the picnic basket. Then he and Kelly took opposite ends of the tablecloth to fold it.

Suddenly, the sound of a truck motor made them drop to the ground like combat soldiers. Flat on their bellies.

They waited, breaths held, until the truck kept going.

Adam was the first to sit up and he shoved the cloth into the basket. "I guess we should address this secrecy thing."

As she sat up, one of the ducks nudged her leg. "We can't be seen together. Not out here, anyway." The area around the pond was secluded, too private. "The gossip would be rampant."

"In public, I guess we should keep arguing, like we always have."

"I can tell you you're an arrogant ass and that if I want to spend time with your sexy little brother I will?"

Adam gave a one-sided grin. "And I will tell you to get your filthy animals off me."

"You wish they liked you that much."

Adam scooped up a squawking, flailing duck that had been pecking his ankle, then released it. "When you're around, even the cockroaches like me."

"Lucky you." She said it with such sarcasm that he laughed. "Where do we meet when we must? Your grandmother's retreat belongs to you and Vera. The town kids use the Fredericks place."

Adam took a moment, then said softly, "Dad has an apartment in KC."

"Had it for long?" She was trying to sound as though it was an ordinary question.

"He bought it twenty-one years and seven months ago."

Kelly knew what he was saying. It looked like Burke Hatten had the apartment even when he was married to Adam's mother. Kelly thought about saying some platitudes but she didn't. "Sorry," she whispered.

"I found the deed and keys in the safe. I haven't seen the place. I asked Robbie about it, but he knows nothing."

Kelly stood up. "We'll meet there when we need to. I have to go. Mom will be…" She looked at the ring. "This is going to cause a lot of commotion."

"Call me if it gets too bad. It's just Robbie and me in that big house, so I can talk in private."

"I bet Mom and Forey will want the reception in your house. Do you have enough champagne glasses?"

Adam groaned. "I'm already regretting this."

"Come on, Mr. Selfish. There's a dance on Saturday. You and Vera can—"

"She's not going. Did you forget that she works on Saturday nights?"

Kelly tried to keep her face straight, to give away nothing. Vera did *not* work on Saturday nights. "Then I'll go alone. Or maybe I can get Seth Murray to escort me. Platonic, of course. No wall slamming allowed."

"I'll be there."

From the way he was frowning, Kelly guessed that he'd seen her look of surprise when he'd said Vera had to work on Saturday. If Vera wasn't working that night, where was she going? Was she with someone or alone?

They shook hands again when they left. A deal had been made.

CHAPTER SIX

KELLY HAD KEPT THE RING HIDDEN while she was at home, but the next morning, she put it on. She thought she should get used to it before showing it. Mrs. Carl spotted it immediately. But then, she was the one who'd chosen it, purchased it and told her son what to do with it.

Her squeal was so high-pitched that three dogs started howling. "What's going on?" Dr. Carl asked, alarmed. "They sound like werewolves."

Kelly had just finished stitching up a four-inch-long cut in a dog's hind leg. She didn't reply as she tossed away her gloves.

"It is!" Mrs. Carl screeched. "It's the one."

Dr. Carl was staring at the ring and he didn't look happy. "Go on," he said to Kelly. "I'll finish here."

Mrs. Carl was in a trance of happiness and she grabbed Kelly's hand so hard it hurt. "When? Where? Why didn't you tell us? Pauly already left and he never said a word, but then, I was crying so hard I couldn't hear anything. I'm sure he wanted to surprise me. My darling son." She dropped Kelly's hand. "I have to tell people."

She ran out of the clinic and back to the house. Within an

hour there wouldn't be anyone in Mason who didn't know. In three hours all of Kansas would know.

Dr. Carl was staring at Kelly. "Are you positive you want to do this?"

Lying wasn't easy. "Sure" was all she could manage to say.

"I can't see Pauly living in your house with your mother and…" He nodded toward the cages of animals. "Pauly is a very quiet person. The silence of trees suits him better than a squawking parrot."

Kelly kept her head down. "We'll work things out."

"With the deep love you have for each other?"

His tone was so cynical that Kelly looked at him in surprise. She saw that he was waiting for her to tell him the truth. But if she told him, she'd lose a boyfriend and her job in one great swipe of a diamond blade.

Kelly took off her smock. "Mind if I go home? My mother will want to, uh…talk to me."

"Sure," he said, but he didn't look up as she left.

As soon as Kelly entered her house, she knew she was in trouble. She hadn't told her mother *first*. Even though Forey's car was parked in front, the house was eerily silent. *Maybe they're outside*, she thought in hope.

But no. They were in the kitchen and suffering. Kelly's mother's eyes were red and Forey looked hurt.

"Could we see it?" Forey asked solemnly.

With a sigh, Kelly held out her left hand to show the big diamond ring. "Lovely," Forey said.

Her mother gave it a glance but said nothing.

"I'm sorry I didn't tell you right away," Kelly said. "I should have, but I didn't. I'm *very* sorry." Forey gave her a look of sadness, but Kelly's mother stirred a pot and didn't look up.

"I have to study," Kelly said, and went to her room. She flopped down on the bed, textbook open, but she couldn't concentrate. *This is not going to work!* she thought. *Lies on top of lies.* She'd never be able to keep it up.

There was a quick knock on the door and Vera came in. "So what's going on? Rafe called me and said there was an emergency with you at home. He swore it didn't deal with blood, but from the look of Mom and Forey, I'm not sure that's right. What gives?"

Kelly held out her hand.

Vera plopped down on the bed beside her sister and took her hand. "That's some rock. It would probably feed a whole village."

"That's what—" She stopped. She couldn't say that Adam had said the same thing.

"It's what?"

"Nothing."

Vera leaned back against the headboard. "I take it the ring is from Paul."

"Of course."

"Kelly, you don't have to do this."

"Do what? Get married?"

"Get married, fine, but not to some reclusive, withdrawn guy like Paul. You deserve an actual *man.*"

"You mean a man like bossy, know-it-all, rules-everyone Adam Hatten?"

Vera chuckled. "I know you've never liked him, but he's better than the vet's stepson. And is it him or working for Dr. Carl that you want?"

That her sister was so very right was making Kelly angry. "There's nothing wrong with Pauly. He's ambitious and wants to make something of himself, and he—"

"With those trees that produce ugly little fruit? I'm all for growing our own food, but at least make it produce enough to actually feed people. But those little things—"

Kelly stood up. "Pauly has a vision. He wants to save what we once had. Why is what you want to do so much better than his goals? Why is your boyfriend fabulous and mine isn't worth anything? Vera the Great and Kelly the Worthless. Is that how you see us?"

Vera was looking at her with wide eyes. "I didn't mean anything bad," she said softly. "I'm just worried that you feel you need to marry Paul so you can stay with Dr. Carl. And so I can leave."

Kelly nearly choked. But she couldn't tell Vera what she and Adam planned to do. She sat back down on the bed. "Pauly *is* quiet and he's good for me. I didn't tell anyone about the engagement because…" She couldn't think of a reason.

"Because people like me would give you hell?"

Kelly had her head down to hide the tears that were starting. Her life had been so planned out. Then Pauly said he didn't want to play his part and it had all crashed. "Mom isn't speaking to me," she whispered. "And Forey…"

"Ah," Vera said. "Now here's where I come in handy. Want me to jerk a knot in their tails? Bawl them out and make them happy again?"

Kelly started to say no, but she looked at her sister. "Would you? Please?"

"Love to! Give me ten minutes with them and I'll have them baking your wedding cake." Vera went to the door.

"Wait!" Kelly said. "When you and Adam get married, what kind of cake do *you* want?"

"Married? What an outdated concept. I think we'll just fly away together."

"But what about Adam? What does *he* want?"

Vera shrugged. "We've never talked about it, but I'm sure he agrees with me. You just rest and I'll take care of Mom."

"Thank you," Kelly said.

★ ★ ★

Three days later, Kelly was hiding in her room. *Too much and too little*, she thought.

At work, Dr. Carl's silence was too little. Oh! But she missed going to school. This summer was all hands-on casework. Her adviser visited every other week and got a report of what was being done. Kelly wondered what Dr. Carl would tell the man. *"She's going to marry my stepson, so she deserves to fail."*

Kelly knew that if she were Vera she'd confront Dr. Carl and ask what he was thinking. Instead, she had cowardly mumbled, "Are you okay?"

He had snapped, "Of course!" then walked away. If it hadn't been for the arrival of an alpaca, Kelly would have been miserable. She nuzzled the soft fur of the sweet animal's neck and told herself it would all be okay.

At home, it was worse. Vera had laid into her mother and Forey so hard that they'd gone the other way. Vera had told them they were selfish, thinking only of themselves. She said poor Kelly was facing a whole summer without the man she loved and having to plan a spectacularly beautiful fall wedding all by herself because *they* were angry that snoopy, gossiping Mrs. Carl had been told *by her son* first. Vera had made the women dissolve in apologies.

Kelly heard them through her bedroom door, and if she didn't know it was all a lie, she would have laughed.

Since then, her mother and Forey had launched into jet power. The moon landing had less planning than what was being done for Kelly's wedding.

Now, Saturday morning, she was in her bedroom, textbook open and unread, when Vera knocked and opened the door. She tossed a magazine on the bed. *Brides*. "Are they including you in any of what they're planning to do?"

Kelly picked up the magazine and her eyes widened at the sight of the gorgeous dress on the cover. "No. Last I heard, they're making a strawberry cake. But it might change." She put the magazine down.

"Go on," Vera said as she sat down. "You can look at it."

"I think Mom wants me to wear *her* dress."

Vera groaned. "That thing is from right after the war. It's probably made of parachutes. I'll take care of that."

"You can't keep rescuing me!" Kelly grabbed the magazine. "What do you want *your* wedding dress to look like?"

"Whatever I'm going to wear on the plane. Speaking of clothes, what are you wearing to the dance tonight?"

"The same as you. If I go, that is."

"I'm not going. But you need to. Call one of those horrid girls you used to hang around with in high school and go with her."

"Ellen is married and has two kids. Sue has a husband and a child. Janice is nine and a half months pregnant. Why aren't you going?"

"Have to work." Vera stood up.

"You never work on Saturday."

"Special client."

Kelly tightened her lips. "You're not telling the truth."

"Oh?" Vera raised an eyebrow. "And *you* are? I don't know what's going on with this engagement but something is."

"You didn't see Adam for years and now that he's here you run off to work. Does he want to go to the dance?"

Vera's eyes were sparkling in amusement. "Good pivot away from whatever you don't want to tell me. I imagine that Adam will be at the dance. He's taking his role of trying to control his little brother very seriously." Vera's hand was on the door. "I'm taking Dad's old truck."

"That ugly thing on the beautiful Plaza? Are you sure it's still running?"

"I tried it yesterday and it was fine."

"What's going on with you?" Kelly's voice showed her genuine concern.

"Nothing interesting." Vera nodded to the magazine. "Why don't you make an appointment at that fancy bridal store in Lenexa? You and I will go together to look at dresses."

"Mom and Forey have already said they want to help with the dress. I have to—" Kelly stopped as a vision came to her. Trying on wedding dresses would bring tears and complaints and disagreements and they would be from Kelly. But Vera would be honest and maybe even fun. "Okay," she said. Maybe she could get an idea of what kind of dress Vera would like. If she did have a wedding, that is. If Adam could persuade her. If Pauly returned and wanted nothing to do with marriage and kids and...alpacas.

"Kelly?" Vera asked. "You still here?"

"Yes, of course I am. I'll make an appointment and we can meet there."

"Tell no one," Vera said. "Our secret." She left the room.

"Secrets," Kelly mumbled. *Maybe I should make a list of them so I can keep them straight.* With a grimace, she picked up the magazine and began to turn the pages. If she did marry Pauly, what dress would he like the most?

She took a breath. This wasn't going to be *her* wedding. *She* had been dumped. She tossed the magazine aside and picked up her textbook.

CHAPTER SEVEN

"IS THERE ANYTHING ELSE I CAN GET for you?" Gabby asked. She was short, round and very curvy.

"No," Miguel mumbled. Gabby was a good cook, a good housekeeper, good at everything a wife needed to do. He pushed away from the table.

"You should take Gabby to the dance," Forey said. "You'd like that, wouldn't you?"

"Very much," Gabby answered. When she looked at Miguel, her eyes seemed to turn liquid.

"Can't," Miguel said. "I have to…work."

"You can take the night off," Rafe said. He was reading the newspaper. "Gabby would like to go. She never gets out of the house."

Miguel looked at the three of them, with their identical expressions of pleading, and headed for the door. "Sorry. I have to go. I need… I need money for something." He knew he'd regret it but he glanced at Gabby's left hand. Let them think what they would.

He ran out the door, got into his pickup and raced out. He had no idea where he was going. Maybe he'd keep going until he reached his home in Taos. At the moment, his loud, overbearing brothers seemed easier than the soft, pleading eyes of Gabrielle.

Miguel was driving as though demons were chasing him, which, in his mind, they were. He took a farm road, where no one would think to look for him, but he kept glancing in his rearview mirror. He wouldn't be surprised to see Rafe following him.

Because he was distracted, he didn't see the old truck was sticking out in the road.

He went around the sharp curve too fast, saw the rusty bed with the stakes sticking out of the back, then cut hard right. Just before he went into a ditch, he cut left and stopped about twenty feet from the old truck. As he looked in his side-view mirror, he could feel his temper rising. Who the hell had left a truck there? Someone could have been killed. They could— He leaned forward toward the mirror. Stepping around the truck was a woman. She was tall and thin and had hair that he'd recognize anywhere. "Vera," he whispered.

She was hurrying toward him, a worried look on her face. She'd grown up to be pretty, but then, he'd always known she would. He opened the door.

"Are you all right?" she asked. "My truck died on me as I went around the curve. I tried to push it out of the way but I couldn't."

Miguel got out and stood in front of her. He was glad to see that he was now taller than she was. When they were kids, she'd been half a head taller than he was. Frowning, he advanced on her. "Well, why couldn't you move the truck?" he said angrily. "Just pick the damned thing up and twirl it around. How hard could that be?" She didn't back away from him. He halted when his face was close to hers. She was alone on a country road with an angry male stranger. Most women would be fearful. But not Vera.

"My truck is made of kryptonite," she said.

It took him a moment to understand what she was saying. It was from the Superman comics they used to read.

Realizing that she *did* recognize him made him laugh. He put his arms around her and swung her in a circle. "When'd you get so short? At least your hair is the same."

He set her down and they looked at each other.

"I see you lost your fat cheeks. Still have a belly?" Smiling, she put her hand on his stomach. It was hard, flat, strong. "Oh my goodness. You must have a lot of girlfriends."

Laughing, he took a step back. "Haven't you heard the town gossip? I'm a mail-order bride."

She gave him a look he remembered well. She was trying to figure out something. That summer they'd shared, it had been a constant job to keep Vera interested. She was curious about everything in the world. He would ride his bike to the library and search for books on subjects Vera knew nothing about. He'd stay up late reading them so he could impress her the next day.

"So I heard," Vera said. "Gabrielle. Rafe and Forey brought you to Kansas not to work but to marry her."

He grinned. "You may be short but your brain still works."

"You do know that everyone in town thinks you and Gabby are in love, don't you? I think Forey wants a double wedding with Kelly and Paul."

"Paul? Is he new in town?"

"Nope. Been here for ages. Dr. Carl's stepson."

Miguel shook his head. "Still don't remember him."

"Me neither and I see him all the time. Kelly says he's scared of me."

"Scared of a little thing like you?"

She laughed. "Will you stop it? You grew taller than me. You made your point."

"Remember when we were in the cellar and you said I should stand on your shoulders because I was the shorter one?"

She was laughing. "I can tell you're still deeply hurt."

For a moment they stood looking at each other, smiling in memory.

Miguel was the first to look away. "Isn't this your dad's old truck? The one we drove that day?"

"Yes. I'd forgotten that. It's a wonder we didn't kill ourselves. I'm glad Dad never found out that we stole his pickup for an afternoon."

"Or maybe he didn't say he knew. Your dad was the nicest man. He..." Miguel paused. "I was sorry to hear of his passing."

Vera stopped smiling. "It was hard on all of us and changed everything. I couldn't leave Kelly. She would have dropped out of school to take care of Mom and—" She waved her hand. "I need to go. Is it possible that you know how to start this truck?"

"Is there something on this planet that Vera Exton doesn't know how to do? What's that in the back?"

"No!" she yelled, but she was too late.

Miguel grabbed a stake and pulled it out of the truck bed. It was a placard. End the War Before It Ends You. He reached for another one.

"Don't," she said.

But he didn't obey. He leaned the sign up against the truck and pulled out another one, then another. Hell, No, Don't Go. Stop the War. Bring the Troops Home. Get the Hell Out of Vietnam. Heil Nixon.

The last one was Not Our Sons. Not Your Sons. Not Their Sons.

"For the mothers who show up," Vera said softly.

Miguel looked at her. "Who in your family knows you do this?"

"No one. Not even Adam."

"Adam? You mean Hatten? You and he are...?"

"Together, yes. In the fall I'm leaving with him to go work in Africa. The Peace Corps."

Miguel stepped back, looking at the signs. "So you're going off to be a part of a protest and no one in your family knows where you are or what you're doing?"

"Correct." She was looking at him in a hard way, with no humor. Was he going to tell on her?

"After Kent I can understand why they wouldn't want you to be part of a protest." Two years earlier, the Ohio Army National Guard had been called in on students at Kent State University protesting the war. As the young people were running away, they were fired on. Four students died, nine were injured. In solidarity to the horrific tragedy, four hundred and fifty campuses around the US temporarily shut down. *But the war did not stop.*

He turned to her. "Even if I got this old thing running, it probably won't last. Let's put these in my truck."

"Then what?" she demanded. "You drive me home?"

He picked up the Nixon placard. "Mind if I carry this one?"

Vera blinked a few times before she understood. "You're going *with* me?"

He looked at her. "I was over there in that war for two years. I still can't believe I survived. I don't want others to go through that." He took a breath. "Let's get these loaded and go."

It was a peaceful march until two hours later, when the army called a halt to the protest. They didn't use their guns, but they used tear gas, and arrested anyone who resisted.

Miguel grabbed Vera's hand and pulled her into an alley. She fought him. To her, they were cowards to hide, but Miguel was too strong for her.

"I need to help. I need to stay with them."

His arms were around her and they held her tight. "You need to choose your battles," he said. "Don't try to win the whole war in a day. Don't blow up a bridge and kill people in the explosion. Chip away at it slowly. Do you understand me?"

Her face was pressed into his chest and she nodded.

The shouting stopped, the tear gas cleared and Miguel released the strength of his hold on her. "Know where to get some barbecue around here?"

In spite of herself, Vera smiled. The Kansas cure for everything: beef. Thick, succulent, tender beef. "Sure," she murmured. It was rather nice to be held against him. She could feel his heart beating against her cheek.

They walked to his truck and got inside. "So when's the next one?" he asked.

"Next what?"

"You can lie to the others but not to me. When's the next protest, meeting, riot or whatever else you plan to stick your nose into?"

"You don't have to get involved in this."

Miguel pulled his shirt out of his jeans to expose his right side. There was an ugly scar just below his ribs. It was round, as though he'd been punctured with something. "Four days after Kent, eleven students at the University of New Mexico who were protesting the war were bayoneted."

"And you were one of them?" Her eyes were wide. At his nod, she looked away, out the window. "Next Friday."

He drove for a while and they were silent. "How did the old cellar hold up over the years?"

She gave a one-sided smile. "I've had to do some work on it but it's good. It's where I, uh, do things."

"Like make your signs? Write angry letters? Generally cause chaos?"

Her smile broadened. "Yes. You can't go to any of them with me. Gabby needs you." She was teasing.

Miguel groaned. "I'm afraid to be alone with her."

"She might get you pregnant?"

Miguel wasn't laughing. "When Rafe and Forey aren't there, she takes a shower, then walks around in just a towel."

Vera frowned. "That's kind of serious."

"You don't need to tell me. I lock my bedroom door. Tell me about you and Hatten. He still as full of himself as he was when we were kids?"

"I see you're still jealous of him."

"He was born rich, starred in high school sports, had girls hanging off him and boys competing to be his friend. Even when his leg was broken, little Kelly used to risk punishment just to take animals to him. Adam Hatten is a person without problems. So, yeah, I guess I am jealous. Enough about him! What did little Kelly grow up like? You said she's getting married to some guy named Paul. Forey and Rafe *only* talk about Gabrielle, so tell me everything that's going on in town."

Vera was frowning over his description of Adam. Was he actually a person with no problems? Was that possible? "She's pretty," Vera said, and there was love in her voice. "Kelly is sweet and innocent and wasted on a guy like Pauly." The last was said in anger.

"Go on," Miguel said. "Tell me more."

She did.

CHAPTER EIGHT

YOU ARE GROWN UP, KELLY TOLD HER-self. *You're an adult. There's no shame in going to a dance alone.*

She reminded herself that she'd probably know everyone there. She'd grown up with them, attending school, church, fairs, weddings, everything with the same people.

But never *alone*. If Pauly didn't go with her, or Vera or her mom, there were girlfriends. They'd laugh together and make fun of the boys. But now everything had changed.

When Kelly walked in, she stopped by the door and looked around. The dance was being held in the high school audi-torium. It had high ceilings and a big stage at the end. Local musicians, meaning anyone who wanted to sing or play an in-strument, were on the stage. The far wall had tables of food, with half a dozen women watching over everyone.

Kelly thought, *I don't want to do this*, and turned to leave. But her worst fear happened as Celeste Wigman saw her and came running.

"Kelly! I can't believe you're here. All by yourself. Alone. That must feel awful. Everyone in town feels so bad that you were left behind by your boyfriend. Just stay with me and I'll see if I can find *someone* who will dance with you."

Kelly closed her eyes and swallowed. She wanted to hit Celeste. But she'd found out in kindergarten that doing so got her into trouble. It also got her in trouble in the first, second and third grades. Every time a weeping Celeste said, "I forgive her," all the adults smiled and Kelly wanted to hit her again.

Celeste grabbed Kelly's arm and pulled her through the center of the dancers. "Make way!" Celeste said loudly. "I have a lone female in desperate need of companionship."

"I'll dance with her," Harvey Edwards said. He'd tried to kiss Kelly in the eighth grade. She'd pulled out the lizard she had hidden in her shirt and let it flick its tongue on Harvey's cheek. Harvey had never bothered her again.

"Go home to your wife," Celeste said, and kept pulling Kelly.

Tommy Leselles came too close and said, "I'll do whatever you want."

Celeste gave Kelly's arm a strong tug and pointed. "Here," she ordered. "Sit there while I try to find a decent man who'll have you."

Kelly knew she'd been assigned to the wallflower bench. It was empty, just her. She looked around at the couples dancing. A few people waved but they didn't come over to say hi. She knew it wasn't real, but she put her left hand up to her hair. She hoped the big diamond would flash so brightly it blinded them.

She had on the red minidress her mother made. It had long sleeves, a mandarin collar and a skirt that was midthigh. Black pantyhose and black shoes with block heels completed the outfit. Robbie was at their house when Kelly was first trying it on. "It looks like a *Star Trek* uniform," he said.

"It's not that short!" Kelly said, but the damage was done. Her mother lowered the hem by two inches.

Why did I come to this thing? she wondered. Celeste was on the right side of the room, talking animatedly with a guy from high school. Kelly knew he had the IQ of a snail, but the strength of an orangutan, so he was great on the football field and therefore popular.

Kelly stood up and started walking. If she left quietly, no one would notice her. She'd go home, or better yet, go to Dr. Carl's clinic and—

"Want help escaping?"

She looked up to see Tony Pullman. He and his family had moved to Kansas when Tony was a senior. He was a year ahead of Kelly, so she didn't really know him. He went off to college somewhere, then returned to help his dad in the family's used-car business. Tony always drove the most fabulous cars, and he was very good-looking.

"I just—"

"Here comes Celeste." He had his hand on the lever of a door that led to the outside.

"Go!" Kelly said, and seconds later they were outside in the cool night air.

She started to walk along the side of the building, toward her car, but Tony stopped. He stepped under a tree. "That moon is beautiful," he said.

She couldn't see it from where she was standing, so she went under the tree beside him. The moon really was exceptionally pretty.

"Has Celeste always been jealous of you?"

"I don't know if that's the reason, but she's always disliked me. Maybe it's because I tend to smack her in the face."

He gave a low chuckle. "Yeah? You sound like my kind of girl."

Kelly didn't like the way he said that. The music from the auditorium was muffled, sounding far away. There was no one else around. "I think I better go back inside."

Tony caught her arm. "Stay awhile. I've always wanted to get to know you, but your sister is like a guard dog." When he pulled her a step closer to him, she could smell the liquor on his breath.

She twisted her arm out of his grip. "I need to go inside. People will wonder where I am."

He grabbed her wrists and pulled her closer. "No one will notice. Even if they do, Celeste will lie. That wimpy boyfriend of yours is gone. Don't you want a little male company?"

Bending, he tried to kiss her, but Kelly turned her head away, then gave a sharp downward pull of her hands. She got free, but he threw his leg behind her and she fell, landing hard on the ground on her seat.

"I like you down there." Smiling, he took a step toward her.

Suddenly, there was another man behind him. He had a black Stetson low over his face. He spun Tony around and hit him in the jaw. Tony stood still for a split second, then fell back against the tree and slid down. He was unconscious.

Kelly, still on the ground, looked from Tony to the man, who tipped his hat back. "Adam," she said.

He held out his hand to help her up. "Let's get out of here before he wakes up."

"Maybe we should call an ambulance."

"Thanks for the vote of confidence but I didn't hit him that hard. He's just so drunk he went down." Adam went to the school door, ready to open it.

"No, thanks," she said. "I've had all the party I can stand. I think I'll go home."

"Good idea." He opened the door a bit, saw one of his high school buddies and gestured for him to come outside.

When Tony groaned, Adam took Kelly's hand and they ran around the building to the front, where all the cars were parked. There were several couples outside, most of them kissing, some talking.

Kelly ducked down between cars, then tugged on the leg of Adam's jeans. He got down beside her. "Right. Can't be seen together. Gossip. So what do we do now? Crab walk to our cars, then go home? By the way, do you know where Vera went tonight?" he asked. "I called her office but no one answered."

"I have no idea."

"My legs are beginning to cramp." He stood up, then immediately crouched back down. "Celeste is going around the cars looking for someone."

"Me." Kelly sounded fatalistic. "She's always after me."

Adam peeked up over the car. "She's getting closer. Stay here. I have an idea."

He stood up. "Celeste!" he called. "You're just who I wanted to see."

"Me?" She sounded shocked and very pleased.

"Yeah, you. You remember Tony Pullman from high school?"

"Oh, yes."

Kelly could almost feel the wind from Celeste's fluttering eyelashes. Adam Hatten and Tony Pullman. Two knockout men acknowledging her existence.

"He's looking for you."

"Really?" Celeste said. "Where is he?"

"Inside somewhere," Adam said.

"Maybe you'll help me find him." Her voice was seductive.

When Kelly gave a snort of laughter, Adam stuck his leg out and nudged her to be quiet. "I think he just wants to see *you*," Adam said.

Kelly heard Celeste take a step closer. The trunk of the car was between her and Adam, but it looked like she was moving around it. Kelly gave a sharp tug on Adam's jeans.

Adam shook his leg at her.

"Are you all right?" Celeste asked.

"Just a leg cramp."

Celeste took another step toward him. "I could massage it for you."

Kelly had to put both her hands over her mouth to stifle her laugh.

Adam yelled, "Tony!"

"Where?" Celeste asked.

"Damn! He just went into the dance. Who was that girl with him? Kelly, maybe."

"I better go." Celeste ran between the parked cars.

Adam didn't look at Kelly, just put his hand down to help her up. "What a brat you are!" he said.

"Oh, Adam," she said in falsetto. "How big and strong you are. Please let me massage your legs or anywhere on your body."

He tried not to smile but couldn't stop. "If you go home, what will you do?"

"I don't know. Study. Watch *Bonanza*. Regular Saturday night."

"I have a TV," Adam said. "And a fridge full of food."

"Any ice cream?"

"Four flavors."

Kelly sighed. "I'll meet you at your house. Ten minutes."

"You're on!"

Kelly got to Adam's house right after he did. He held the door open for her. She didn't tell him that she hadn't been inside the house in years. He'd probably ask why. She made jokes about Robbie, but he was much too handsy for her taste. She wasn't exactly afraid of him, but she didn't allow herself to be caught somewhere alone with Robbie.

On the other hand, Adam was like her brother. After he married Vera, that's just what he'd be. "I always forget how masculine this house is," she said. "All stone and wood. Even the pillows are corduroy. Did your mom have anything to do with this place?"

Adam smiled. "If Dad said, 'Do it,' Mom did."

"Which is why you want Vera. She's the same way."

That was so absurd that Adam laughed. He opened the fridge and pulled out a plate of chicken.

"What's this?" Kelly was looking at a rectangular machine with a window in the front.

"It's an Amana Radarange. Dad got it. It heats food in minutes."

"It makes the food radioactive?"

"Probably." Adam was serious. "But the good news is that it makes your body glow green. No need for a flashlight."

Kelly worked to keep from laughing. "Maybe I'll be able to see in the dark like a possum can. Show me how it works."

They heated the chicken Adam had bought and Kelly filled plates with salads. They took their food and drink into the living room. The TV was in a cabinet, the huge and heavy body set deep inside. Adam turned it on with a remote control.

"Fancy," Kelly said. "Mom and I argue about which one of us has to get up to change the channel."

"Let me guess—Vera does it."

"Yes, if Mom and I argue very loudly Vera will do it for us."

He laughed. The theme music to *Bonanza* with the burning map, so familiar to all Americans, came on and they settled back on the big couch, plates in hand. The show had been on for thirteen years, and it was rumored that it was soon to end.

"I miss Adam," Kelly said.

"That's nice, and I appreciate your saying that."

"Not *you*. Adam Cartwright." The actor had left the show years before.

"I know." His eyes were twinkling. "He was your favorite?"

"Sure. What about you?"

"Hop Sing. He can cook. And Hoss. Sweet man."

They watched the show about the father and his sons running the vast Nevada ranch. At the break for ads, Adam didn't look at her as he quietly said, "I miss these American comforts. I miss being near people I've known all my life."

"But you're leaving soon."

"I'll be with Vera, so things will be different."

He sounded sad.

"There's no Radarange in your little African village?"

"There's no running water. No indoor toilet."

The show came back on, but Kelly didn't look at the screen. Her intuition was that Adam was saying something serious. Maybe he didn't want to leave home.

"Once Vera leaves here, I'm not sure she'll ever want to return. She's angry about pretty much everything. She reads all the newspapers and watches all the news shows."

"I know," he said. "Vera comes with the world attached to her ankle."

"So what are you going to do?"

"When I was in Africa, all I could think about was how different it would be when Vera got there. But now..." He was silent for a while and Kelly didn't break in. "Hey!" he said. "Why are we talking about me? You're the problem."

She knew he wanted to change the subject, so she didn't push. "How am I a problem?"

"At that dance you were the center of interest."

"Me? That's ridiculous. No one even noticed I was there."

"That's a joke, right? When I went in the front door, all I could hear was your name. People were speculating whether or not you are now single. I wouldn't be surprised if they were laying bets."

She held out her left hand. "While I'm wearing this thing?"

He took her hand and held it up to the light. "You don't like this ring, do you?"

"No. It's too gaudy and I have to take it off to work. It snags on things."

"Like sheep's uteruses?"

"Exactly." She was smiling.

Adam let go of her hand. "The problem is that we know Vera won't leave if you aren't settled. So you have to go to all the—"

"Oh, no, you don't! No more lone dances for me. Celeste is—" She broke off.

"A major bitch?"

"Yes, she is."

Kelly put her empty plate on the stone-topped coffee table. "I need to go." She nodded to the TV. "Little Joe isn't my idea of a dreamboat. And I have to get up early tomorrow. Cages to clean. I'll help you clear."

"No need to. I'll stick these in the dishwasher." He stood up.

She walked to the front door, Adam behind her. "Would you help me remind Vera of something? On Friday at two o'clock she's to meet me at the bridal shop in Lenexa."

"Vera's going with you?"

"It was either her or Mom and Forey. They'd start crying and I'd blab the truth."

"You could go alone or—" He broke off at her expression. "I get it. Wedding dress. Girl thing. Maybe Celeste could go with you two."

"You are so not funny." She opened the door. "Just remind her, that's all. I will, too, so maybe she'll show up."

He frowned. "I'll get her there. Don't worry. But maybe all this is too much. Maybe we should—"

"Tell the truth? No, thanks! I figure this is practice for my own wedding. I just need a groom."

"That's the hard part. You're so ugly, with no talents. I'm sure no one will want to marry you."

"I knew my dress should be shorter! But Robbie said I looked like something off *Star Trek*, so…" She shrugged.

Adam groaned. "For once I agree with my baby brother. That dress is plenty short enough."

"Tony thought so."

"Go home. Behave yourself."

Kelly was backing toward her car. "Mind if I ride Xander tomorrow?"

"He'd love it."

"Good night and thanks for dinner. And you owe me ice cream." Smiling, she got into her car and drove away.

Adam stood in the doorway for a while, watching her car lights disappear into the dark. He went back to the living room, got their plates and glasses, then cleaned up the kitchen. Before he'd lived in Africa, he'd been one of those men who left all household matters to women. After his mother died, they'd had a cook/housekeeper. "A sexless wife," Burke had called her.

But in Africa, Adam had learned how to take care of himself. Cooking and cleaning had been things he'd learned how to do. The women had teased him that he needed a wife to help him. Adam always said, "She'll be here soon."

As he stood in the kitchen and looked around, he thought how easy the appliances made everything. How convenient his life was here. The first time he'd walked away from it had been in anger. He'd had all he could take of Burke Hatten's rules and demands and endless criticism. But all that anger was gone now and he was looking at things differently. That deep need to get *out* was fading.

"But Vera is worth it," he said as he went up the stairs to his bedroom. He frowned as he passed Robbie's empty room. Where was he?

Adam read for a while, then went to bed at midnight. Robbie still wasn't home. Tomorrow he'd talk to his brother about his late nights.

And it will do as much good as when Dad talked to me, Adam thought.

Early Sunday morning, Adam got up, dressed and checked to see if Robbie had come home. His brother was fully clothed and sprawled crosswise on top of the bed just like Adam used to do. How Burke had yelled at him!

Adam was about to do the same to his brother, but instead he closed the door and went downstairs, then outside. The air was crisp and cool and very clean. He saddled Jagger, told Xander that Kelly was going to visit him, then rode to the big barn.

When he'd left Kansas, there had been four full-time employees on the farm. Robbie had gleefully written that their dad had to hire two men to do all the work Adam did.

This morning Jess and Tom were at the barn loading up one of the pickups with fence posts and posthole diggers.

They greeted each other and the men dutifully asked about Africa, but they were more interested in local news. And sports. Lots of sports. Jess and Adam had played football together in high school.

For Adam, it was great to talk of such familiar things with people he knew well. He knew Jess's and Tom's parents, their aunts and uncles. Tom had a pretty cousin who had caught Adam's eye more than once. Tom was married with a baby on the way, and Jess was engaged.

"Like you," Jess said. "Is Vera driving you crazy about dresses and bridesmaids? Are you two gonna do it before or after Kelly and Paul?"

Adam just smiled in answer.

"When I got married," Tom said, "we argued about the cake. I wanted chocolate and she wanted lemon."

"So what did you get?" Adam asked.

"Lemon," Tom and Jess said in unison.

"Don't try to win over the bride," Tom said. "Give her whatever she wants."

"Good to remember," Adam said.

They worked on the farm all day, moving cattle to a different pasture, repairing fences, and they fed all the animals. At the end of the day, Adam felt better than he had in quite a while. The next day, he did it all over again. Then the next and the next.

CHAPTER NINE

VERA WAS INSIDE THE CELLAR. THAT'S what she called it, but technically it was an old basement. In 1958, a tornado had lifted the house and dropped it a hundred yards away. Without a foundation, the house had collapsed. The basement, with its linoleum-covered floor as a roof, was intact.

The family whose house was destroyed sold the land for a pittance to Burke Hatten, and for years it just sat there. The land needed to be cleared for grazing, but no one ever got around to doing it. Grasses grew over the old foundation and people forgot about it.

When Vera was eight, she found it. As she often did, she had been searching for a place of peace, where she could read, write and think without being bothered by the chores her mother assigned or Kelly's endless packs of animals.

Vera had managed to pull the old door up and went down the rotting stairs. There was little light, but she could see the old furniture and the books on shelves. There was a TV that an animal had built a nest in.

She told no one about her find. She knew that if she did, it would be forbidden to her. The old floor overhead was falling apart. One time she sneezed and two rotten boards fell down. Vera knew she should get out. It could collapse at any moment.

But she didn't leave. She just made sure she didn't sneeze anymore.

The next year, Adam broke his leg and Miguel came to spend the summer in Mason.

After a month with Miguel, Vera showed him the cellar. She held her breath. Would he be afraid? After all, it smelled bad, it was dark and the ceiling often rained down dirt and mud.

But Miguel had loved it! And he was the one who talked Burke Hatten into giving them some two-by-fours and nails. They'd lied and said they were building cages for Kelly's animals, so he'd been generous.

They did "repairs" but they were limited in know-how and strength. Instead, they learned where to step so they didn't bring the roof down on them. They pooled every penny they had and biked into town to the dusty old thrift shop. They bought candleholders and framed pictures and books and anything they thought they could use.

After Miguel went back home to New Mexico, Vera didn't go to the place as much. It had lost its appeal.

But when her father got ill, and all responsibilities fell onto her, Vera needed a place of her own.

One rainy night, she ran to the cellar, lifted the old door and went down the steps. It was too dark to see anything, but she knew where everything was. She collapsed on the damp sofa.

When she woke the next morning, she was shocked at what she saw. It was a disaster! The ceiling was ready to come down on top of her. However, the old concrete walls were good.

She tiptoed up the stairs, glad to get out alive, but the place stayed in her mind. She'd been left with the care of her mother and her little sister and nowhere to escape them.

Vera knew that for her sanity she needed a place where she could hide. She needed relief from endless criticism. Her mother didn't approve of what Vera read, the letters of protest she wrote, what she talked about. "No husband wants… You should…" were terms Vera heard constantly.

It hadn't been difficult to hire a couple of men from Lawrence to do what she wanted. They arrived with a backhoe and tore off what was left of the so-called roof. They removed all the rotting furniture, but she saved the thrift-store items she and Miguel had bought. The men put on a flat roof.

"This will leak," they said. "First big rain and this place will fill up like a swimming pool."

"Then I'll bring my swimsuit," she'd said.

The men shook their heads at her, then did their best with tongue-and-groove boards with asphalt shingles over the top. When she told them to dump dirt over it all so the plants could grow back, all they said was "Better not run any cattle over this."

Vera was glad when they left and was pleased that she'd managed to keep the place hidden. Her great triumph was when she hooked up electricity that she got off one of Burke Hatten's fences. If his workmen saw what she'd done, they never told anyone.

Now she was at her big table, made from sawhorses and two cheap, flat doors, when she heard footsteps on the stairs. That had never happened before and her hair stood on end.

As soon as she saw the black boots, she knew it was Miguel.

Bending, he looked at her. "I expected to see a sunken hole in the ground."

He was the only person on earth she was glad to see in her space. "I had it fixed."

He came down the stairs and looked around. There was an

old bookcase on the far wall. He picked up a rock off the top. "I found this by the barn."

"You painted that bookcase."

He ran his thumb over the peeling paint. "I think it's ready for a new coat."

"I like it as it is."

He went to the table and looked at her sheets of poster paper. Together for McGovern. Another Woman for McGovern. McGovern Will Stop the Killing!

There was a poster that had something drawn on it, but he couldn't tell what it was. He looked at her, puzzled.

"It's supposed to be a peace dove," she said.

"It looks like a ghost with one eye."

She handed him a pencil. "Then you do it." She knew that Miguel was good at drawing and watched with a smile as he quickly sketched a big dove.

It was when he held up the sign that he saw the list of names. He put the poster down and went to them. There was a scroll hanging on the wall, with rolled silk fabric at each end. He didn't ask, but he was fairly sure the fabric was Vietnamese in origin. On the paper were the names of young men and women, their birth dates next to them. Their death dates were next.

"I knew him," Miguel said softly. "He lives just a mile away."

"Lived," Vera said.

"And him. And her." Miguel looked at Vera.

"Susan. She was in my high school class. She had some quick training in medicine, then was killed on her second day there. She was an only child."

Miguel went to the bottom and saw the empty space. "Left blank for more names?"

"Yes." She looked back at the signs. "McGovern promises to end the war but I don't think he'll win. Most people want Nixon. They think he's more of a *man* than McGovern. They think—"

Miguel covered the space between them in two steps and put his hands on her shoulders. "You must try to keep more names off your scroll." He looked into her eyes. "Don't lose courage."

She stepped away. "Right. Do what I can."

"We," he said. "When's this rally?"

"Friday. I got the afternoon off. It's in Wichita. I have to—"

"I'll drive you. You and Gabby can ride in the back."

Vera's eyes widened.

"Just kidding. I'll have to come up with a story about why I'm to be allowed out of her sight for a whole afternoon."

"Still bad?"

"It gets worse every day. I, uh, hinted that I was taking on outside jobs to make money to buy her a ring. Forey is hoping for a double wedding in the fall."

"With Kelly?" Vera was frowning. "Is that still on?"

"As far as I know."

"Would you mind helping me paint? I need to go to work and I want these to dry."

He looked up at the ceiling. "Only if you tell me how you managed to remodel this place. Did Adam help you?"

"He doesn't know this exists. Nobody in Mason does. I hired two guys from Lawrence to do the work. They said it'll flood like a swimming pool."

"I guess you have a suit, don't you?"

"That's exactly what I said!"

For a moment they smiled at each other. Vera's crinkly-curly hair was coming out of its ties and surrounding her narrow face. The shadows on Miguel's face made him look darker. The slant of his cheekbones was almost a cut.

Vera broke away first. "I think we should use more red."

"Good idea."

They got busy painting.

By Friday, Adam was ready for a break from the farm. Or maybe it was that he missed Vera.

They'd spoken on the phone every night, but that wasn't the same as face-to-face.

He put on nice trousers—no bell-bottoms for him—and a freshly ironed shirt (thanks to Vera's mom) and drove to the Plaza. He wanted to see Vera, but also wanted to find a way to remind her about her appointment to go with Kelly to choose a wedding dress.

As he drove into Kansas City, he thought of his second reason for going. He needed to go to the apartment his father kept. He thought about how he could give all the contents to charity, then sell the place.

Maybe he'd use the profits to finance a clinic for Kelly. He had a feeling that she wouldn't agree to his help when she saw him get out his checkbook. But maybe if the money was from an apartment that Adam hated... It was possible that some good could come of it all.

But first he had to go *see* the place. Walk into it. See the big secret his father had kept for so many years. What would he find? He imagined a red velvet swing. Gold tassels. Black silk bedsheets.

The vision brought him to what he really wanted. He was going to do whatever he could to get Vera to go with him when he first entered that apartment. He'd coax her with lunch, then offer to go with her to meet Kelly. Later, he'd casually suggest that she go with him to Burke Hatten's love nest.

If he played his cards right, maybe he could get Vera to spend the night there with him. Maybe making it his own "love nest" would take away some of the sting of finding out about his father.

The plan made him smile. He parked in a covered lot on the beautiful Plaza and walked to Vera's office. She was the only one there and she was shoving papers into her dad's old briefcase. She barely glanced at him.

"Got a meeting?" he asked as he kissed her cheek.

"No. I mean, yes. In Wichita. I have to leave now."

"But you have—" He cut himself off. He couldn't say that she was supposed to meet Kelly at the bridal shop. There was no way he could explain how he knew that. "You don't have any other appointments today?"

"Canceled them all." She gave a quick glance out the window, then grabbed another paper off her desk.

Adam saw the tail end of a silver truck that he didn't recognize. A man's truck was as distinctive as he was. "Getting a ride from someone?"

"Yeah. Carol Miller."

"She drives a truck like that one?"

"Of course not! Why are you grilling me?"

Adam took a step back. "I came here to surprise you. Thought maybe we could have lunch."

"Can't," she said as she closed the briefcase. "Maybe Sunday we can do something."

"Sure. Sunday. If you can spare the time."

Vera closed her eyes for a moment. "I'm sorry that I can't drop everything and go out with you. If you'd called beforehand, I could have saved you the trip." She put her hand on his forearm. "On Sunday, let's go to the cabin. We'll..." She gave him a look of invitation.

"Great idea." His voice was cool. "On Sunday, we'll get it on."

Vera grimaced. "I can't stand here and argue. I have to *go*."

She hurried out the door just as Adam again saw the end of the silver truck go by. There was a deep dent in the back. He wished he'd seen the driver.

He plopped down in Vera's big desk chair. What was going on with her? He felt like he'd been brushed off as though he were of no consequence. It was like she'd dumped him. Adam's eyes widened at that thought. "Kelly!" She would get to the bridal shop and no one would be there to meet her. She'd be trying on wedding dresses *alone*. Even he knew that was no good.

As soon as Kelly saw Adam, she knew something was wrong. Since Vera wasn't with him, she figured that was part of his problem. But Kelly had had a lifetime of Vera not being where others wanted her to be. Vera could walk into the woods and disappear. Vanish. Poof! Gone. No one, not even their father, had been able to find her.

Kelly got out of her car and stood for a moment looking at Adam. He was wearing his Burke Hatten face.

Vera always snapped at her when she said that but it was true. Adam often acted like a clone of his overbearing father.

Right now, Adam was scowling as he stared straight ahead. He looked like he wanted to rip someone apart.

Not fair, Kelly thought. *She* had the right to be angry. *She* was the one whose almost-husband had run away. *She* was the one being forced—well, persuaded, anyway—into pretending that everything was all right.

When Adam turned and saw her, he faked a smile.

Wish I had a photo of that, Kelly thought. From the tip of his nose up, his face was scrunched in anger. From the nose down, he was smiling. It was a physically impossible facial expression.

"Don't tell me. Vera isn't coming."

"She's very busy. She—"

"She forgot, didn't she?"

Adam nodded. "Yes. How about if we skip this and get something to eat?"

"No, Mr. Selfish. You're going to help me find a dress for *your* bride."

"But—"

"You're already in a bad mood, so this couldn't make you feel worse."

He blinked a few times, then gave a genuine smile. "That's true, but I know nothing about wedding dresses."

"And I do? I'll model the dresses and you try to imagine which one Vera would like best."

"Something in silver would be my guess," he mumbled.

Kelly quit smiling. "What happened?"

"Nothing. I got..." He smiled at her. "Dumped."

Kelly laughed. "I assume you mean for the day." He nodded. "Maybe we should start a club. We'll call ourselves the Dumpettes." They started walking toward the pretty shop.

"Why are you smiling?" he asked. "I thought you'd be miserable. Having to pick out a wedding dress for somebody else isn't what I'd think a girl would want to do."

"I was very unhappy until I saw you. We can't both be miserable at the same time."

"So we take turns?"

"Yes," she said seriously. "We have to."

Smiling, he opened the door for her.

Inside the shop, a tall, thin woman introduced herself as Miss Evie and she took charge. "You'll try on several dresses," she said to Kelly. "But you won't tell him which one you choose. Leave some surprises for the day."

"He's not—" Kelly said.

"And she's not—" Adam said.

They stopped talking and just stood there, looking embarrassed.

Miss Evie looked from one to the other. "Honey, I know so many bride secrets that nothing shocks me. Tell me what the problem is so I can dress you."

Kelly took a breath. "He's marrying my sister, but she won't pick out a dress, so I'm going to get one for her."

"Okay," Miss Evie said. "As bridal secrets go, that's pretty mild."

"Oh?" Kelly said. "Who else has a bigger secret?"

Miss Evie smiled. "Let's just say that I've had to let out a lot of waistlines and the groom knows nothing. Now, let's talk about what your sister likes."

"Simple, plain," Kelly said.

"Cheap," Adam said.

Miss Evie led the way to the back of the store to two long rows of white dresses. "Take a look to see what you like. I'll make us some tea."

As Kelly went through the dresses, she kept thinking, *What would Vera like?* Kelly passed by lace and beaded tops, strapless and scooped-out necklines.

Finally, she chose two dresses she thought might appeal to her sister. There was no silk, no satin or anything shiny. One dress had long sleeves, a ruffle at the bottom and one around the neck. It was Nebraska prairie.

"It's a bit long for you," Miss Evie said.

"Vera is taller than me and has less…"

"Curves?" Miss Evie said. "Then let's try these."

By the time Kelly got into the first dress, they were thirty minutes into their hour-long appointment. Adam was on the couch and nearly asleep. Seeing Kelly in the plain dress didn't make him fully wake up.

"Yeah, she might like that," he said.

There were three more like it. One was high-waisted with Renaissance sleeves. Very modest. Another had a skirt made of layers of ruffles. It swallowed Kelly.

As she took it off, she told Miss Evie, "This is harder than I thought."

"Trying to be someone you aren't always is. Would you do something for me and try on a dress that would fit you?"

"There's no reason for me to do that. It's my sister who needs— Oh." She was looking at the dress Miss Evie was holding.

"This just came in and no one has tried it on. It's your size."

The short-sleeved top was lace that was as delicate as a spider's web. Under it was a pale ivory gauze. The skirt was white silk as fine as the breath of a butterfly.

"Is that real?" Kelly asked. "I'm afraid to touch it."

Smiling, Miss Evie gathered up the skirt to slip the gown over Kelly's head.

It fit perfectly. Due to her job, Kelly mostly wore jeans and loose-fitting shirts. Her mother had made her some dresses that were nice, but this gown was… "I'm afraid to move," she whispered.

Miss Evie practically shoved her out of the dressing room. "I want to see if anything will wake that young man up."

"Adam? But he's my brother-in-law. Or will be. Why should he even notice?"

Miss Evie didn't reply as she led Kelly into the waiting room. Adam was dozing on the couch.

"Well?" Kelly said loudly. "What do you think of this one?"

Adam sat up, then did a double take. "That's nice," he said.

"It is, isn't it?" Kelly did a full circle. "I've never felt anything like this." She was smoothing the skirt.

Adam stood up and was looking at her, silent.

"What do you think?" Kelly asked.

"I don't think Vera would wear that," he said softly.

Kelly sighed. "I don't, either." Turning, she looked at herself in the mirror. "But *I* would. I'd wear this to my wedding."

Miss Evie looked from Kelly to Adam and back again. "She does look lovely, doesn't she?"

Adam didn't seem to have blinked for the last three minutes. He just nodded, then sat back down. Kelly went back to the dressing room.

Miss Evie came out with one of the long-sleeved, long skirt dresses Kelly had first tried on. "Do you think your fiancée would like this?"

"What? Oh, sure. Whichever one Kelly thinks is best."

Miss Evie sat down beside him. "May I make a suggestion? The last dress is new. It won't stay in the shop for long. When Kelly does get married, she may not find one quite so well suited for her. Perhaps you'd like to—"

"I'll take them both," he said. "My checkbook is in my truck. Wrap them up while I go get it."

"Wise decision."

"But don't tell her," he added as he went out the door.

"Of course not," Miss Evie said, smiling broadly.

Adam waved goodbye to Kelly as she got into her car. Then he headed out to the highway. He stopped at the crossroads. Should he go north to the Plaza and at last see his father's apartment? Or south to home and put it off for another day?

He looked in his rearview mirror. No one was behind him, not even Kelly. He hadn't asked her what she had to do next, but she usually went to Dr. Carl's. She didn't like to be away from her animals for long.

Adam sat there for a few minutes, trying to decide what to do. When she didn't show up, he turned his truck around and went back to the dress shop. Kelly's car was still there.

He parked his truck and walked to her car. She had her head down on the steering wheel and he could tell that she was crying. He opened the door. "Move over."

She started to protest but then scooted across the wide seat.

Adam got in, moved the seat back, started the car and drove. At the crossroads, he didn't hesitate. The last place Kelly needed to go was home. They'd all ask umpteen questions about her red eyes. He turned north toward the apartment.

"It's your turn to talk," he said.

"It's nothing. I just—" She took a breath. "Damn Pauly! Why did he do this to me? I don't understand. If he didn't like me, why didn't he say so years ago? *Years!* Now everything is messed up. I can't see my future."

Adam didn't reply. He knew she had more to say.

"My life should be settled now. You know what I mean? *Settled.*" Adam nodded.

"Vera's going to find out the truth. She'll feel so sorry for me that she won't leave. Will she stay until some man who actually *wants* me shows up? That could be a long time."

"*All* the men want you," Adam said.

Kelly waved her hand. "I mean a man worth having. Not lecherous Tony. Not creepy Tommy. They're the only ones left in Mason. In high school we girls picked out the ones we wanted and staked our claims. June Gilbert laughed at one of Bill Sanders's jokes and his girlfriend, Sue Terrance, went after her with a nail file."

"Did anyone get hurt?"

"No. Sue was too vain to wear her glasses, so she missed June's face. Sue hit the wall and the nail file broke off in her hand. She had to have stitches."

Adam did *not* laugh. It made his stomach hurt by holding it in, but he didn't let it out. "You're young and—"

"Tell my mother that. She's going to make my life one long

date. Every man who passes through Mason will be invited to meet her lonely, unmarried daughter. The daughter who works outside the home. Who chose a *job* over a husband and children." Kelly looked at him. "My mother will have talks with me about my eggs drying up. She thinks I'm a tadpole."

"You mean a frog that lays eggs and...?" He trailed off at her look.

"I'm *her* tadpole and I'm to make lots more tadpoles."

"Ah. I get it. You know, dating isn't the end of the world."

"Says the man who's been with the same woman since elementary school. *You* like change about as much as I do!"

"I did go to Africa to live. That's a big change." He sounded defensive.

"You only went because Vera wanted to, and because you and your dad fought so much."

"How did this become about what's wrong with *me*? You dating is the problem. I have some cousins in Pennsylvania. Want me to fix you up with one of them? Or two?"

"You're not funny. Where are you taking me?"

"Uh..."

"To your dad's apartment." She narrowed her eyes at him. "You wanted to take Vera, didn't you? That's how you found out she wasn't going to meet me at the bridal shop. You felt sorry for me, so you showed up, then slept through all the dresses."

"I, uh..." He started to defend himself but stopped. "That's pretty much exactly what happened. And now I've kidnapped you, my second choice, to go to the apartment with me. I can't bear to go alone."

"How cowardly of you."

He pulled into the parking lot of the apartment building, turned off the engine and looked at her. "You have a real talent for turning everything you're angry about into being *my* fault."

Kelly blinked a few times, then smiled. "I am good at that. But then, so much of it *is* your fault. You were the last one to talk to Pauly before he left. Maybe you paid him to go."

Adam's eyes widened. "Why would I do that?"

"Because you want to buy that strip of land Pauly owns? Or Vera told you to get him away from me? You always obey her."

Adam could feel himself getting angry, but then it all left him, and he sighed. "I just wish she'd sometimes obey *me*. You know anybody who owns a silver truck? There's a dent in the left side of the bed. In the back."

"No," Kelly said. "Why?"

"It was hanging around Vera's office and she kept looking out the window. Maybe it was a coincidence that the truck went by a couple of times just as she was trying to get away. It's probably my imagination. Anyway, I don't want Paul's land or any of the other reasons you can come up with. I didn't pay him to leave you."

Kelly sighed. "I know. It's silly to be so upset because I don't know my future. No one does."

"You're not upset. You're angry because some guy who isn't worthy of you walked out and left *you* to clean up *his* mess. His mother, your job, your mother, Forey and Vera and me. One monumental act of pure selfishness and he changed several lives. I think you have every right to be in a rage."

Kelly sat there looking at him. "Wow. That's insightful. And all true. Thank you."

"You're welcome and you can pay me back by going to that apartment with me. I'm scared of what I'll see in it."

"Let's go!" Kelly said. "The way I feel right now, if Burke Hatten's mistress is living in it, I'll tear that female dog apart." She got out of the car and slammed the door behind her.

"I didn't think of that," Adam said aloud. "*Living* there?"

Kelly knocked on his window. "Come on. I may deflate

at any minute and you'll have to face her alone. Without me there to protect you."

"With a nail file?" he mumbled. Adam got out of the car, but he was very slow doing it.

When they saw a doorman in the lobby, Adam almost left. He took two steps back, but Kelly grabbed his forearm. He still didn't move. She linked her arm around his and pulled.

"How'd you get so strong?"

"Pulling colts into the world. Come on!"

The door opened and the doorman smiled at them. "You must be Mr. Hatten's son. You look like him. We were so sorry to hear of his passing."

Adam just nodded.

"Thank you." Kelly dropped his arm. "This is Adam and I'm Kelly Exton, his sister-in-law. Or will be soon. We'd like to see the apartment."

"Of course. It was cleaned yesterday. Enid did it for no charge. She said Mr. Hatten was always generous to her."

"I bet he was," Adam mumbled as they got on the elevator and the door closed. "This looks to be a very nice place. For my father to conduct his, uh, business?"

"Quit being so gloomy. Just *stop* it!"

He looked at her with a bit of a smile. "Planning to put a choke collar on me?"

"It could only help," she muttered.

When the door opened, Adam took a breath. They were on the top floor. An antique table with a lamp was in front of them.

Kelly got off the elevator and waited. The doors almost closed before Adam stepped out. She held out her hand and he put the set of keys into it.

There were only four apartments on each floor and it was easy to find the number on the key.

She unlocked the door and went in first, then halted. Maybe because Adam had made up his mind about the place, she had imagined red and gold, something garish.

Adam came to stand beside her and the two of them stared in silence at the living room. *Elegant* was too mild a word for what they saw.

The whole front was floor-to-ceiling windows and doors out to a terrace. The views were of the beautiful, Spanish-style Plaza. The room was done in winter white: the walls, the two couches, the long curtains. There were two chairs upholstered in pale blue. The rug was pale blue and white. A fireplace framed in white marble was at one end. Two matching, round-front chests flanked it. A coffee table was of white marble. An antique dining table was off to one side.

"Not what I was expecting," Adam said.

"Those curtains are silk," Kelly said. "And I've seen cabinets like those in museums."

Adam walked beside the couch to the open doorway. The bedroom was as lushly elegant as the living room. It was decorated in white and pale blue-green. The adjoining bathroom was ivory marble with a gray vein. The walls were a matching gray.

"It's beautiful." They left to see the rest of the apartment.

Off the living room was a kitchen with tall white cabinets and Formica countertops in light gray. A laundry room was at the end.

Just off the front door was a little powder room with wallpaper of spring flowers.

Kelly opened a door she thought was a closet and found a second bedroom. It was done in soft lavender and white. A little bath was at one end and a walk-in closet at the other. Inside were stacks of linens and a shelf full of boots.

"Those belonged to my father," Adam said. "Have we seen it all?"

"I guess so. But who lived here? Or stayed here? Where are the clothes?" she asked.

They went back through the apartment to the master bath. There was a narrow door they'd missed and Kelly opened it. Inside was a long, narrow clothes closet and it was packed full. Men's clothes were half of one wall, women's on the other half, divided by a tall stack of drawers.

"There *was* a woman," Kelly said.

Adam pulled out a pink blouse and lifted the collar. On the underside was a purple stain. "I did this. Welch's grape juice. Robbie drank his and wanted mine. I jerked the glass out of his reach, and it splashed on Mom. She and Dad were going out to dinner. She never wore this again and I thought it was my fault." He pulled out a red dress. "Dad gave her this for Christmas. She said she could never wear it."

Kelly took it from him. "Why? It's beautiful. Oh. I see. The neckline is rather low."

Adam was moving the hangers and looking at the clothes. "Birthdays, Christmas, anniversaries. Mom always said she was going to return whatever Dad gave her."

Kelly hung the dress up and looked at the other side of the closet. A shelf held three boxes covered in light blue leather. "Mind if I open them?"

It was Aladdin's Cave. Necklaces and bracelets sparkled from the lids and tiny drawers opened to show earrings and brooches.

"'Too rich for me,'" Adam said. "That's what Mom always said. Everything Dad gave her, we never saw again." He picked up a pair of earrings. "I remember these. I was ten or eleven when Dad gave them to her. I thought they were really pretty and Mom wore them all day. But later, when I asked her to wear them to church, she said they were gone. I thought she meant she took them back to the store."

Kelly stepped out of the closet and into the bathroom. "You know what this place is?"

"A den of secrets?" He sounded disgusted.

"A kid-free sanctuary, that's what. A place of peace. How did they get away with it?"

"They went on overnight trips to business meetings. They went away to buy things for the farm but returned empty-handed. I remember after one trip Robbie said, 'You didn't buy *any* ponies, Dad?'"

They went back into the living room, but they were now looking at it differently.

"I can't imagine my father in this room. The house in Mason with its stone and wood suited him. Not this."

"Maybe they made a deal. He could build the house exactly like he wanted. In exchange, he'd buy her an apartment and she could make it how she wanted. That way they didn't have to fight over a compromise."

"Actually, that sounds like them."

Kelly sat down on a couch. "Personally, I love this place."

He sat on the couch facing her. "Your animals would tear it up."

"I'd leave them at home with the kids and the sitter."

"That's what happened with us. We had about four live-in sitters over the years."

"Please don't tell me you resent your parents for being gone."

"The opposite. I'm not sure I could have survived my father without the breaks we got when he went away."

"I bet your mother knew that. Maybe this apartment was

for you, for your sanity. To keep peace between you and your dad."

Adam stretched his arms across the back of the couch. "Whatever it was used for, I like it. It feels good in here."

"I agree. There's a calmness about it that I like."

For minutes they sat in silence, looking about the room. Kelly wondered if it was the lack of color or the absence of harsh surfaces, but it was a soothing place. "I have to go home."

"Me, too, but my truck is at the dress shop."

She stood up. "I'll give you a ride back. Dumb of us to leave it there."

"I didn't trust you to drive." He stood up.

Remembering her tears made her turn away and they didn't speak as they went downstairs. The doorman bid them good evening and they went to Kelly's car. Adam drove.

They were out of the parking lot when he spoke. "Do you really not know where Vera goes?"

"Really and truly. I thought she'd tell you."

"And I thought we'd see more of each other. Is there..." He hesitated. "...someone else?"

"No, of course not. She's done nothing but work since you left. She takes care of the farm, her job, and that's it. She never goes to any of the social things that other people go to."

"No dances or hayrides?"

"I would know if she did."

"But she does disappear."

"Mom said she thinks Vera hides out in an old hunter's cabin that's hidden in the trees. She just wants a time of peace."

"I can understand that. When I get home, I have to deal with Robbie and his sulking. It's like he thinks I'm his father but I have no authority."

"He'll be worse when you leave," she said quietly.

"I know that too well. Let's talk about something good. What do you have planned for the weekend?"

Kelly sighed. "Mom wants me to choose flowers for my wedding. I don't know what Vera would like."

They had reached his truck. He turned off the engine and looked at her. "Which would be worse? Telling everyone the truth or continuing with the lie?"

Kelly twisted the engagement ring on her finger. "I don't know. I never seem to have time to *think* about what to do. If it weren't for fear of losing my job, I'd tell everyone that Pauly left me behind."

"Are you *sure* that would get you fired?"

"Absolutely."

"Are you hungry?"

"Very."

"Let's go get something to eat and talk about this."

"I can't. Mom will be expecting me at home. And shouldn't you call Vera and tell her where you've been all day?"

"I don't think I will," he said in a way that made her look at him.

"Are you angry at her?"

"I'll just say that I'm not happy. I'll take you to Stroud's for fried chicken."

"Ohhh," Kelly said. "I can't resist that."

"Then follow me."

"Ha! I'll beat you there."

Smiling, Adam watched her drive away. He got into his truck and saw the two big pink boxes on the floor. He didn't know why he'd bought the dress Kelly liked. Maybe to cheer her up. He wanted to wring Paul's neck. He'd been so cold when Adam talked to him, so unconcerned about what he was putting Kelly through. Him and his stupid trees. Adam had a mind to run them over. It would serve him right. Kelly was so well liked in town that if he told the right people, they might actually do it. Adam wasn't sure what about that thought gave him an idea, but it did. If only Kelly would agree.

He caught up with her outside Stroud's. It was a short, plain building, opened as a barbecue place in 1933. During WWII, they switched to chicken, and since then they hadn't changed a thing.

They sat down at a table covered in a red-and-white-checked cloth. Since Stroud's didn't start cooking until food had been ordered, they had a while before they ate.

"What are you working on this weekend?" he asked. "Anything exotic? Wounded goldfish, maybe?"

"I have the weekend off. Mrs. Carl's sister is visiting, and having no help gives Mr. Carl an excuse to hide. And it's good for me, too. When Mrs. Carl's sister is there, she pays less attention to me. Every cookie she bakes—'Just for you, Kelly'—makes me feel like Hansel and Gretel and the witch fattening them so she can eat them."

"So now you have two whole days of freedom. What are you planning to do with it?"

She gave him a look of disbelief.

"Right. Wedding plans."

"What about you?"

"I decided that I'm going to spend the weekend in the apartment. I'm going to have two days of not worrying about my brother or what the hell Vera is up to or about Africa or... anything. You have something you'd like freedom from worrying about?" His tone was teasing.

"Nothing, really," she said. "Just a few whys are in my mind. Why my boyfriend ran away from me. Why my sister has put her life onto *my* shoulders. And why I disappoint my mother in everything I do."

"Nothing important, then. So stay with me."

Her eyes widened. "In the apartment? For the whole week-end?"

"Yes. But with a rule—no talking about *them*."

Kelly laughed. "The rulers of our lives." She thought for a moment. "I can't do that."

"Tomorrow we could look for a place to open your own veterinary clinic."

Kelly looked like she was going into a dream. "I couldn't run it by myself, but there was a guy I went to school with who I think would like a job. He's older, a widower. And Linda Conlan could run the office. She hates her boss and she's smart. I tried to get Mrs. Carl to hire her, but Linda is too pretty, so..." Kelly trailed off.

"I see you haven't given this idea any thought."

"A little bit, maybe."

Their plates of chicken were put before them. Big bowls of green beans, mashed potatoes and gravy were set on the table. And a beer for Adam and iced tea for Kelly.

"I plan to eat every bite of this," she said.

"Please do. Go on, tell me more about your plans."

"That's it." The chicken was divine: crunchy outside, soft, hot and delicious inside. "I haven't thought more about it except that it's all impossible."

"No, it's not. As soon as we find a place, you'll be free to tell the truth to everyone."

"And you get to tell Vera that she is going to have a big wedding whether she wants it or not. And she gets to wear a dress you and I picked out for her. Plus—"

Adam groaned. "Stop! You're scaring me. Are you going to stay or not?"

"I have no clothes, so I'd have to go home and pack. I can't imagine the questions I'd get. My mother would be horrified. 'You and Adam are what!'"

He gave a half smile. "You know there'd be no impropriety and you're close enough to Mom's size that everything is there. Tell your mother you've been offered a weekend seminar with Dr....?"

"Hollander. He's the world's leading expert on the reproduction system of...?"

"Cows, of course," Adam added.

Kelly hesitated. "You don't mind? I wouldn't be in your way? You might want to be alone."

"I need a distraction. Let's go to a movie tonight. I haven't been to one in years."

"Me neither."

"You and Treeboy didn't go on movie dates?"

"We were both too busy and I needed to study and work. I managed to cut a year off my school. Why are you looking at me like that?"

"So what movie do you want to see?"

"I have no idea what's on," she said.

"Vera mentioned one called *The Godfather.*"

"Heard of it, didn't see it."

"Let's get a newspaper and see if it's still playing somewhere."

It was early Sunday morning and Kelly was stretched out on the white silk couch in the living room of the beautiful apartment. She had on a pink satin blouse and flowing trousers of black tussah silk. She wasn't sure, but she had an idea the clothes cost more than she made last year.

Whatever, they made her feel pampered, as though she was in a fairy tale, dressed by tiny birds.

She looked around the apartment—how pretty it was, perfectly decorated. No muddy boots anywhere. Unlike at home, no magazines or newspapers were lying about. No buckets full of anything.

Closing her eyes, she thought of the time she'd spent there.

On Friday, while Kelly called her mother, Adam bought a newspaper and checked the movie listings. They found *The Godfather* still playing in an obscure theater in downtown Kansas City. It was a dirty place, with a sticky floor, and the back rows were packed with teenagers making out. The popcorn was drenched in a greasy substance that had no relation to butter, and the Cokes were half water.

But the movie made up for the unpleasant surroundings. She and Adam watched intently. When the man found the horse's head in his bed, Kelly nearly threw up.

"It's not real," Adam whispered as he squeezed her hand. "*Not* real!" She wasn't sure he was right but she wanted to believe him.

When the movie was over, they sat for a while, letting it digest in their minds. In the car, they talked over every scene of murder, betrayal and the struggle for power.

When they got back to the apartment, it felt like home. Adam insisted that she take the master bedroom. "So you can be near the closet." He was teasing, but she didn't mind.

The next morning they both got up early and planned their day. Kelly said no to looking for a building for her clinic. "It doesn't make sense to drive all the way to Ottawa, then back again. I never get to see the Plaza."

"I could use some new shirts," he said. "And do you own anything that hasn't been peed on?"

"Of course I do. I have—" She stopped and thought. "Actually, no. But don't get out your checkbook. I'm not a charity case."

"Never thought you were."

They went out for breakfast, as there were no groceries in

the apartment, then strolled around, pointing out the beautiful cupolas, fountains and statues on the Plaza. At ten, they went to a men's store and Kelly chose half a dozen shirts for Adam. He was more interested in where they'd have lunch.

They went to two other stores and bought Kelly three shirts and some new jeans. Laughing, with full shopping bags, they stopped for Kansas barbecue.

It was a short walk back to the apartment and they dropped the bags in the living room. Adam found a Frisbee in a closet, so they walked to the beautiful Loose Park and tossed it back and forth.

Adam hadn't remembered how animals were attracted to Kelly. Every dog not on a leash ran to her. The ones that were restrained pulled in her direction. Squirrels ran out on branches to look down at her.

As he watched her tumbling about with the dogs, Adam held the Frisbee and laughed. He stopped when two hippies with so much hair on their heads and faces that their eyes could hardly be seen came up to her.

"Get lost," Adam said.

"Hey, man!" one said. "Nobody can own anybody. Come with me, pretty girl. I've got something in my van that you'll like."

"And what would that be?" Kelly asked. "My—"

"Officer," Adam said loudly. "Nice to see you again."

The hippies ran, but one turned back and made a gesture of smoking, thumb and forefinger together.

Kelly laughed but Adam didn't.

They left the park at about four and that's when the only bad thing happened. They were on the Plaza when Adam saw a man he'd gone to school with. He knew Adam and Vera as a couple. If he noticed Kelly, he didn't recognize her.

For seconds, there was panic. What should they do?

Kelly fixed it by walking past them and going into a store. It seemed like she was just another shopper, with no connection to Adam. Inside, as she looked through the racks of merchandise, she often glanced out the window. She could tell that the man was trying to get Adam to go somewhere, but he was saying no.

Kelly left the store, and without a look at the two men, she started back toward the apartment.

Adam caught up with her before she reached it. "Sorry about that. We played football together and he wanted to go over old times."

Kelly didn't reply.

"You okay?"

"Sure. Do you mind if we go back and…do nothing?" She shrugged.

"That would be nice," he said. "I'll keep watch for any critters following us." Kelly didn't smile.

For the rest of the day, they stayed in the apartment. They went through the books his parents had collected. "I had no idea my dad was interested in space exploration," Adam said.

Kelly found a big book on the animals of the Amazon and settled down with it.

Adam went out and got them burgers and fries and malted milks for dinner and they watched TV and ate. It was late when they separated to go to bed.

This morning, as Kelly looked about the pretty room, her mind full of memories of the last two days, she knew she'd never had a better time in her life. The apartment, Adam, their time together, had been pleasant to the point where she wasn't sure it was real.

Which was why she knew she had to leave. She had to go away and never, ever return. She heard the shower turn on, so Adam was up.

She got her own clothes from the closet. With a sigh, she hung up and folded the beautiful clothes. "Thank you," she whispered, meaning Mr. and Mrs. Hatten. "I had a truly wonderful time."

As she went back to the living room, Adam was coming out of the guest bedroom. He had on jeans and nothing else. "Got any plans for today?" he asked.

He seemed to be oblivious to his appearance, but Kelly observed he was mostly muscle, mostly naked.

"I have to go. There's an emergency at the clinic," she said. *What an adept liar I've become*, she thought.

"I'm sure someone else can handle it."

"No, just me." She grabbed her handbag off the hall table and left. She didn't bother with the elevator but ran down the stairs to her car.

"I have to fix this," she said to herself as she pulled out of the parking lot. "I have to make things right. I have to stop the lies, stop the…" She blinked back tears. "I have to stop wanting what belongs to other people."

All the way back to Mason, she strengthened her resolve about what she had to do.

When Kelly got home, the house was empty. She knew her mom and Forey always went to church together, and no one ever knew where Vera was.

Kelly went to her bedroom, thinking how she had to tell Dr. Carl about Pauly, knowing that tomorrow she wouldn't have a job. Everything was coming apart. She fell across the bed and began to cry.

She'd spent her life building her future, and now it was crashing down.

The next thing she was aware of was her mother's arms

around her. Forey, almost a second mother, was beside them. Four arms were holding her.

"It's awful," Kelly cried.

"What did he do to you?" Forey asked.

"I... He..."

Nella handed her a tissue and Kelly sat up. "Only a man can make a woman cry this hard. Who and what?" She wasn't allowing her daughter to not answer.

Kelly could only tell them part of the truth. "I... I'm not engaged." The women sat there stone-faced. It was not what Kelly had expected.

"Did Mrs. Carl buy this ring?" Forey asked.

Kelly nodded as she blew her nose. "How?"

"How did we know?" Forey asked. "People in love say goodbye to each other. Paul left without even seeing you."

"I don't understand," Kelly said. "You've been baking cakes and choosing flowers for the wedding."

"And we've had a lot of fun doing it," Nella said.

"Maybe Vera can use it in the fall," Kelly said. "She and Adam can—"

Nella groaned. "I can't see your sister walking down the aisle in a white dress."

"She'd wear red just to annoy people," Forey said.

"Or purple. With a fringe." Nella held her daughter's hand. "You lied to keep your job, didn't you?"

Kelly nodded. "I'll be fired."

Nella and Forey looked at each other. "Probably. Honey, we'll figure out something."

Kelly wanted to tell them that Adam offered to help her open her own clinic, but she didn't dare mention him. It would lead to too many questions.

"At least you didn't buy a dress," Forey said.

"No, of course not." Kelly couldn't look them in the eyes.

Nella stood up. "You need to go to Dr. Carl now and tell him."

"And return the ring," Forey added.

"I don't think I can," Kelly said.

"Rip the bandage off. It'll hurt for a while. Then you'll start to heal," Nella said.

"The problem is Mrs. Carl," Forey said.

Nella grimaced. "That woman dotes on her son. No wonder he's like he is."

"Pauly isn't bad," Kelly said. "He's just—"

"He hurt my daughter," Nella said. "I'd like to roast him over an open flame. I'd like to—"

"Okay!" Forey said. "We get it." She looked at Kelly. "Just so you know, I agree with your mother, but Paul is in the past. We need to get the truth out in the open so we can start the repairs."

"Maybe I can get a job in KC or maybe Saint Louis," Kelly said. "They—"

"No!" Nella and Forey said in unison.

"One of my girls is hell-bent on leaving the country," Nella said. "I'm not losing *both* of you."

"I need a job," Kelly said. "Vera won't leave if I have no way to earn money. Our little farm can't support us. I have to—"

Nella frowned. "Don't worry about a job. Forey and I are going to start a business."

Forey barely got her wide-eyed expression under control. She tried to look like she knew what her friend was talking about. "Tell her about it."

"Cakes," Nella said. "We'll sell cakes. And pies."

"Yes, a bakery. We've been looking for a place to open a bakery," Forey added.

"So you see," Nella said. "Things will work out. We just need to get started. Get up and take a shower. You'll feel better. Then put on clean clothes, and we'll drive you to the clinic."

All Kelly could do was nod. She headed to the bathroom. Nella and Forey went to the kitchen.

"A bakery!" Forey said. "Are you out of your mind?"

"Maybe, but I had to say something. That woman is going to fire my daughter. I *know* it! No one in town likes her."

"But at least Kelly got away from Paul. He's too strange for her. For any woman. Those dreadful little trees of his."

Nella sat down on a stool. "Oh, Forey, what am I going to do if I lose both my daughters? Vera is so anxious to get away that I expect to find a note from her. 'Gone to Africa. See you in a few years. Love, Vera.'"

"Adam won't let her do that. He'll…" Forey sat down on the other stool. "I don't know what Adam will do."

"He used to be such a reliable young man. As solid as his father."

"But they fought and…" Forey shrugged.

Nella sighed. "Maybe I shouldn't depend on my daughters so much. That cherry cake you make is really good."

"Oh, no! I don't have time to run a shop." Forey paused. "I like those apple turnovers you make."

"Wouldn't it be funny if we used those little apples from Paul's orchard? What's that word he loves?"

"*Organic.*"

"Mr. Gresham wants to retire," Nella said.

"None of his kids wants to live in Mason and run a diner."

"The kitchen in his diner isn't bad."

"I bet we could get the place cheap."

Kelly came out of her bedroom. She had on a denim skirt and a white cotton blouse. She looked as happy as someone facing execution. "Let's get this over with."

★ ★ ★

Kelly was in the back seat of her car, her mother and Forey in the front. Kelly was doing her best to look on the bright side of her life. After she confessed the truth, all the lying could stop. She could start looking for a new job. She needed to have something waiting for her when she graduated in September.

Of course she couldn't open her own clinic. She was too young, too inexperienced. She still had so much to learn.

But at least she could look Vera and her mother in the eyes. She wouldn't have to say she had to go somewhere when she was really spending the whole weekend in an apartment with her brother-in-law-to-be. *What* had she been thinking!

The women were talking about recipes and opening the Mason Bakery. "People won't have to drive all the way into Ottawa to get doughnuts," Forey said.

Kelly shook her head. She often rode Xander into Ottawa. It was very close.

At the thought of the beautiful horse, tears almost returned to her. She'd have to stay away from him. *Be professional!* she told herself. But that meant she'd only see Xander if he was ill.

The women parked in front of Dr. Carl's clinic. Kelly looked over the front seat, thinking that it might be the last time she was there.

"You want us to go in with you?" Nella asked.

Kelly looked at her mother and gave a weak smile. "No, I'll be fine."

"We'll wait for you," Forey said.

"You don't have to. I…" Kelly quit talking. The women were going to wait and that was that. "Okay," she mumbled. "Thank you."

Kelly got out of the car and headed to the clinic, but she didn't go in. She knew what Dr. Carl would say. He couldn't care less if Kelly married his stepson or not.

The house was next door and Kelly could smell cookies baking. She knocked and Mrs. Carl told her to come in. She was taking trays of cookies out of the oven.

"You're just in time. These are a new recipe—lemon poppy seed. You'll have to have some. Sit down and I'll get you some milk."

Kelly didn't sit. Instead, she took off the engagement ring and put it on the table. "I'm sorry," she said quickly. "I lied. I'm not engaged to Pauly. He didn't ask me. He doesn't want to marry me and I'm sorry. I'll leave. I'll get a job somewhere else. I—" She couldn't say any more. She ran out the door.

Mrs. Carl caught her before she got away. Kelly braced herself for the anger of the woman.

But Mrs. Carl put her hands on Kelly's shoulders. "I'm the one who's sorry. Please come inside. It's too hot out here."

Kelly didn't move. "But I'm not marrying your son."

Mrs. Carl looked at her. "I knew it was too much to hope for, so I'm not surprised. I did everything I could to get you two together, but you can't change people." She slid her arm around Kelly's shoulders and led her back into the house. Mrs. Carl picked up the ring. "I knew I was pushing too hard with this, but I was trying anything I could think of." She put the ring in her pocket and cookies on a plate, poured two glasses of milk and sat down at the table across from Kelly. "Now tell me everything."

Kelly was in such shock that she had difficulty speaking and she was cautious. She told a sugarcoated story of Pauly's abrupt announcement that he was leaving.

"But he did give you the ring."

"No. Adam Hatten did."

"The young man who's planning to marry your sister?"

Kelly nodded.

"How interesting," Mrs. Carl said.

Kelly looked at her sharply. What did that mean? But Kelly didn't want to explore that. Her number one concern was her job. "I'm not sure I can work here," she said tentatively.

"I admit that this is a blow to me, but if I fired you, my husband might divorce me." She was trying to make it sound like a joke, but Kelly had seen too much about the couple to not know there was truth in her statement. Maybe a deal could be made. Mrs. Carl had always found it impossible to fit in the little town.

Kelly munched on a cookie. "My mother and her friend Mrs. Montoya are thinking about opening a bakery. I bet they'd love to sell these." As she'd hoped, Mrs. Carl's eyes showed interest. "They're even thinking of buying apples from Pauly because his are organic. No pesticides used."

"That's why they're full of bug holes," Mrs. Carl said. "I keep telling him there are sprays made, but he won't listen to me."

"I bet he'd be pleased if you used his apples in those muffins you made last week."

Mrs. Carl was blinking at her. "My husband says I pay so much attention to my son because I don't have enough to do. I don't like those church get-togethers. Too many people! And I despise all the animal-related things Carl goes to."

Yet you married a veterinarian, Kelly thought.

"Do you think your mother and Mrs. Montoya would let me help with their bakery?"

"I think they'd love to have you involved." Kelly crossed her fingers and toes. And here she'd thought she'd be able to stop lying.

There wasn't much else to say, so Kelly left. When she got back in the car with her mom and Forey, she said, "You want the good news or the bad news first?"

After Kelly told them, the women complained all the way

home about having to include Mrs. Carl in their proposed business, which they weren't even sure they were actually going to do.

As for Kelly, her life was back on track and she couldn't stop smiling.

Nella saw her daughter's self-satisfied smile in the rear-view mirror. She looked at Forey. "So who should we set my daughter up with for dates?"

"Oh, no," Kelly said. "*No* dates!"

Forey ignored her. "That nice young Tony Pullman comes to mind."

"He attacked me!" Kelly said. "If—" She couldn't say that Adam had rescued her.

"If what?" Nella asked.

"Nothing. I need a rest from men."

Nella gave her daughter a stern look. "I think you need to stop hiding behind four-legged, furry creatures and start looking at your future. When I was your age—"

"I know!" Kelly said. "You were married and had two kids. I am an old maid who works and—" She saw her mother's eyes in the mirror. "Okay, but I get to approve of them. No blind dates."

The two women smiled as they pulled into the driveway. "Why don't you go ride Xander?" Nella said.

Kelly didn't answer.

Vera tossed the tree branches aside, lifted the door and went down the stairs into the old basement. Miguel hadn't arrived yet. There was an anti–Vietnam War rally planned in Omaha that weekend and she'd managed to come up with a fairly plausible reason of why she would be out of town.

But the truth was that no one was paying attention to what she was doing. *Good!* she thought. All attention was on Kelly.

She had at last rid herself of Treeboy, as Adam called him, and everyone was happy about it.

Vera'd had a good laugh when she heard that sweet Kelly had made a cutthroat deal with Mrs. Carl. Kelly got to keep her job but Mrs. Carl would share in the business that Nella and Forey might be starting. So far, the three women were quite indecisive about how to begin or if they should.

Vera volunteered to ask Adam to make a deal with Mr. Gresham for them. She'd thought it would be easy when she proposed the idea to him. Adam, usually so willing to help anyone at anything, had snapped, "No!" then went to one of his horses and began wiping it down.

Vera had been shocked. "Why not? They need help. They have no idea what they're doing and Mr. Gresham is a wily old coot. He'll flatter them and they'll end up baking for him for free."

Adam's eyes were on the horse. Vera thought this one was named Xander and it was the one Kelly liked to ride. Vera stayed well away from them. "What is your problem? You've been in a bad mood all week."

"There's nothing wrong with me. Except Robbie is driving me crazy and there's too much paperwork and too many animals to take care of. When are we leaving the country?"

"Not for a few months." She was frowning. "Call Kelly. She can take care of the animals. I think she'd like a break from textbooks and baked goods. The women want her to taste everything. Mrs. Carl—"

"I'm not going to call your sister." He glared at her. "You're dressed up. Where are you going?"

"To work. How long do you think you'll be in this bad mood?"

"Until I get out of here."

She started backing away from him. "I'm going out of town for the weekend. Do you mind?"

"Mind that you have a *good* weekend? Why would I begrudge you that? I hope everyone has great weekends. And weekdays. I'll be fine here by myself. Just me and my little brother, who believes I was put on earth to make his life miserable."

Vera had reached her car. "Uh, okay. I'll see you on Monday."

"Sure." He brushed the horse so hard that the animal turned and nipped at his shoulder.

"You really should let Kelly do that. She—" Vera broke off at the look Adam gave her. "I'll see you in…" She didn't finish, but got in her car and drove away. At home, she stayed only minutes before she drove on back roads to the cellar where Miguel was meeting her. Usually she walked, but she couldn't leave her car at home while she was supposed to be gone.

Vera was thinking so hard about Adam that she didn't look at Miguel when he came down the steps. When he pulled the door down into place, she turned to him.

"What happened?" he asked as soon as he saw her face.

"Nothing."

He just stared at her.

"Okay. I sort of had a fight with Adam. I don't know what's going on with him. All week long he's been angry."

"And we can't let that happen, can we? Adam the Great and Good. Aunt Forey says he's going to solve all the problems about this stupid bakery idea the women have and—"

"What's wrong with starting a bakery? Do you think all women have to be housewives? That they can't work outside the home? They have to—?"

He narrowed his eyes at her. "I don't deserve that. I'm saying that *these* women have never had an outside job. They don't understand that they have to be there even when they don't want to be. Why does everyone think Adam can make some brilliant deal? They could get a lawyer."

"Adam knows the people involved. When we were kids we used to eat at Mr. Gresham's place. We used to—"

"Could you give me a break from Adam Hatten for one minute? Do you have your suitcase with you?"

"You sound like you're jealous."

Miguel turned away, grabbed a heavy load of the posters they'd made, then went back up the stairs. She'd hidden her car under trees in the deep shade. With a few tree branches leaning against it, it was well camouflaged.

She picked up the last of the placards and her big denim bag, and climbed up to the surface. Miguel was already in his truck, engine running. She put the signs in the back under the tarpaulin cover and closed the tailgate.

Miguel didn't look at her when she got in beside him. "Looks like it's going to rain here. I hope it's dry in Omaha," she said.

He put his arm across the seat and backed onto the dirt road. "Why don't you ask Adam to make it stop? He seems to be second only to God on this earth."

"Are you going to be like this the whole trip?" she snapped.

"Probably. But then, I'm not perfect like Adam Hatten is. I have things in my life that I can't control."

"And you think Adam doesn't? What's your *real* problem? Is Gabby pestering you?"

Miguel took a moment to answer. The rain was starting to come down and he turned on the wipers. "Yeah. They're all on my case. Aunt Forey wants Gabby to be part of this bakery idea. And…" He looked at her. "My dad wants me to return home. My—" He swallowed. "My youngest brother just got drafted."

Vera reached out and took his hand. "I'm sorry. I don't know how to do more to stop this war. Maybe I could—"

He held her hand tight, his other one on the steering wheel. "I know. We're both doing what we can." The rain was pounding on the roof and Miguel used his sleeve to wipe the fog from inside the glass. "Couldn't we talk about something else?"

Vera reached down to her bag and withdrew a book. *The Drifters* by James Michener. "It's about a young man who runs away to escape the Vietnam draft."

"It sounds like what I need to hear right now."

"He and his friends go to places like Mozambique and Marrakech and Pamplona."

"Like you and Adam are going to do." Miguel's jaw was clenched.

"Yes, we are," Vera said firmly. "If you can't handle that, then—"

"Read the book!" Miguel said. "We have hours. Wait! Is anyone in there named Adam?"

"I doubt it. But if you want to hear that name, we could stop somewhere and buy a Bible."

For a second, Miguel looked angry. Then his eyes sparkled. "Read me something I haven't already read a hundred times."

Vera laughed and the bad humor between them was gone.

As she began to read aloud, the rain came down harder. She used a cloth she found in the glove box to help Miguel keep the steam off the windshield.

They were still an hour from Omaha when the truck started to rattle. "That's bad, isn't it?" she asked.

"Very bad. We have to stop." The rain was so hard they could see just a few feet ahead of them. "I can't pull over to the side. Somebody will run into us. Are there any towns nearby?"

"It's the Midwest. We farm. It's miles of plants and cows."

"Right. We need to look for a place where we can get off the highway." They saw the sign at the same time. Sunflower Cottages. One Mile.

He looked at her and she nodded. "The rally isn't until tomorrow. Think you can fix the truck in time to get us there?"

"If it doesn't need parts, yeah."

He turned onto a side road with trees thick on both sides. The truck rattle was getting louder.

Through the rain, they could see four little white houses, separate from each other. The middle one had a pink neon sign that said Office Open.

"I'll go in." He turned off the engine, then ran through the downpour into the office. Minutes later, he returned with a key on a big plastic sunflower and tossed it to her. "We got the last cabin. It's at the end, down the road." He started the truck. "If anyone asks, we're married."

Vera knew that even though it was a time of "free love and hippies," their parents' generation tried hard to stop what they saw as immoral. Nearly all rural motels insisted on seeing a marriage license before they would allow a couple to stay. "Tomorrow they'll want proof."

"I'll show them my bayonet scar and my discharge papers. I think they'll forgive a vet."

With a grimace, Vera agreed. The same generation that believed premarital sex was a sin thought it was perfectly fine to send their young people off to die in a senseless war. They wouldn't like to know that Miguel got his scar while protesting the war.

He stopped at a pretty little white cabin. "I'll open it up. Then you come." He ran to the door, unlocked it, and she ran inside.

"I'll get our suitcases."

"And the signs," Vera said.

With a nod, Miguel ran back into the rain.

It took him four trips to clean out the truck bed. The tarpaulin had leaked badly and everything was soaked.

When Miguel held the two suitcases up, water dribbled out of them. "I was going to buy a new cover, but Uncle Rafe said his was 'as good as new.'"

"It probably was in 1954." She picked up one of the signs. The poster board was so wet it curled around the fence stake they'd stapled it to. But that didn't matter, as the slogans they'd painted on them had been washed away.

"A fireplace! And wood!" Miguel said. "Thank heaven. You didn't happen to bring any food, did you?" He knelt down to arrange the logs.

"I'm a Kansas girl. Of course I have food. My mother believes that if a person misses a meal, he'll drop dead. She jammed my bag full of all sorts of delicious things." She hesitated. "You're sopping wet."

"I am. Get me some dry clothes out of my suitcase, will you?"

She smiled at his joke as she opened the suitcases and pulled out wet clothes, then spread them across the furniture so they could dry. There wasn't much in the room: a couch, an armchair, a plastic-topped table with two metal chairs. Part of one wall held a single-counter kitchenette. And there was a bed. A solitary bed covered with a pretty quilt.

Vera went to the bed, pulled off the quilt and held it up to him. "I promise I won't look."

"In that case, I'm not taking anything off."

Vera felt herself flush. She tossed the quilt onto the couch. "Suit yourself." She got her denim bag, set it on the table and began pulling out food.

Miguel got the fire started, then began unbuttoning his

shirt. As he peeled the wet fabric from his skin, she did her best not to look. She failed.

His skin was the color of honey, with a little hair on his chest. He was lean and muscular. She was sure he knew she was watching him, but he didn't turn to look at her. Instead, as though he were alone, he slowly undressed.

When he slid his jeans down, Vera gave up her pretense of unpacking food and watched him. He was sideways to her, facing away.

Under his jeans, he had on white briefs. His legs were muscular from a lifetime of farmwork. Slowly, he rolled down the wet briefs. When he was nude, Vera could feel her heart pounding.

He still didn't look at her, but reached to the side, picked up the quilt and wrapped it around his beautiful body. Only then did he turn to her.

Vera knew what his eyes were saying. He'd always been clear that he was attracted to her.

She broke the contact. "I'll heat up—" She had to clear her throat. "The soup. I'll heat it for us."

"Good." Miguel sat down at the table.

They ate in silence. They were on slices of Nella's pie when Miguel said, "I've been meaning to ask you something. Why don't you wear your engagement ring?"

"Don't have one."

He smiled. "The Great and Wondrous Adam hasn't shelled out thousands for a ring yet?"

"Actually…" She was pushing her piece of pie around the plate. "He's never asked me to marry him." At Miguel's silence, she looked up.

He was staring at her. "Repeat that."

She waved her fork about. "It's an understanding between us, that's all. After Kelly—"

"I know! I've heard it a thousand times. After Kelly graduates, you and Adam will go back to Africa or Marrakech or wherever the Hatten money takes you."

His growing anger didn't perturb her. "That's mostly right. But one of my clients is a reporter. He's just local but he knows things. We've talked a lot. I plan to become a reporter. I'll tell the US about foreign situations. I wouldn't be living off Hatten money. And the other thing is that I don't plan to get married. Ever."

Miguel leaned back in the chair, letting the quilt fall to his waist, exposing a lot of bare skin. "Aunt Forey thinks you and Adam are getting married in the fall, before you leave the country. She and your mom are planning the cake."

"Too bad no one asked *me*," Vera said. She was looking at him over her glass. She lowered her voice to a whisper. "Adam told me that when he was in Africa, he wasn't faithful to me."

Miguel's handsome face showed shock. Then he smiled in an inviting way. "It's nice to hear that Hatten has a flaw. You want to sit by the fire for a while?"

"I'd love that," Vera said. "And you'll share your quilt with me?"

"That would be my fondest wish."

They smiled at each other.

CHAPTER TEN

One month later

KELLY PUT DOWN HER TEXTBOOK AND looked at her watch. She had to be at Dr. Carl's clinic in an hour. She stretched out on the bed, hands behind her head, and looked at the ceiling.

Everything was going well. Her mom and Forey couldn't stop praising Adam for stepping in and working out a deal with Mr. Gresham. It turned out the man didn't want to retire. He enjoyed seeing people every day, and he loved bossing around the two waitresses and the cook. He just didn't have many customers.

Adam suggested he buy a new glass case and fill it with whatever Nella and Forey felt like baking. And maybe Mrs. Carl would add to the supply.

Getting the old man to agree to that part of the deal had been easy, but it had taken three days for him to agree that the women were to be paid the bulk of the sales price. Only when a diner in Ottawa told Adam what they'd be willing to pay did Mr. Gresham agree to the deal.

"Adam was wonderful," Nella said to Kelly. "I think Robbie is a lot like him." That was an unsubtle hint to her daughter to start dating the younger brother.

Kelly had excused herself and gone to her room. In the last

month she'd been on four dates, all arranged by her mother, all to hometown boys.

On the first date, as they left the restaurant, the guy told Kelly to get into the back seat of his big car. When she asked why, he said, "I'm just trying to save you from the gearshift." She demanded that he take her home.

Another guy spent the evening telling her how she'd snubbed him in high school. He told in detail how her lack of attention had caused him great pain. She honestly didn't remember him.

Number three talked about what their life would be like after they got married. He wanted Kelly to promise that she would quit work as soon as she got pregnant. She smiled. "I won't be having *your* baby, so my job is safe."

The fourth one was the worst. He was allergic to dogs. And horses. And cats. "Did you wash your hair? I'm wondering because you're making me sneeze," he said. Kelly handed him her napkin to blow his nose. When he came up from four sneezes in a row, she was gone.

Other than the dates, everything was the same with Kelly, but not so with anyone else.

Forey was at the Exton house all day and cooking not just baked goods but soups and stews and side dishes. It was enough to feed a city. From the amount sold at Mr. Gresham's diner, it was certainly enough to feed the town of Mason.

They were so busy that only Kelly remarked on the fact that Vera was gone every weekend. "So is Adam," Nella said, and then she and Forey giggled like schoolgirls.

Kelly went into her room and shut the door. *Good*, she told herself. Adam and Vera were spending whole days together. They needed to do that. Get to know each other all over again.

Part of Kelly was angry, but the larger part told herself that *she* was the one who'd made a big deal about the time she'd spent with him. But the truth was nothing they'd done had been out of line. Adam went to the bridal shop with her because Vera had stood her up. He went to meals with Kelly because he was hungry. They'd watched TV together because it was convenient.

She came up with a reason for everything they'd done together. But still, she remembered how good she'd felt at his apartment and when they went shopping. How they'd laughed together.

She sat up on the bed. "Kelly Exton," she said aloud, "you need to find a boyfriend. A *real* one. Maybe I should advertise in the paper. Maybe I should—" She looked at her watch. Thank heaven it was time to go to work.

As soon as she got there, Betty handed Kelly a note.

"I can't read this," Kelly said.

Betty looked sympathetic. "You should've had Miss Wilson for first grade. She could have taught you how."

"What?" Kelly was blank for a moment. "I can *read*. I just can't read your handwriting."

With a look of disgust, Betty took the paper. "It says 'Montoya Farms.'"

"What do they need?"

"How would I know? I'm not a veterinarian."

With an eye roll, Kelly went to Dr. Carl's office. His door was open. "What's going on at the Montoya place?"

"Lame horse. Go now before the pet owners start coming in."

Kelly went to the door. "Can we do something about Betty?"

He looked serious. "Why would I want to? She can read. Maybe she would tutor you."

"You're so not funny."

"You find someone else and I'll hire her."

"That's a deal." Kelly packed her medical bag and went to her car. As she drove, she thought about how she hadn't seen Miguel since he'd returned to town. She remembered the summer Adam had broken his leg. Mrs. Hatten had asked the other kids at school to visit Adam so he wouldn't be bored. But only Kelly and Vera did.

And Miguel, she thought. He and Vera had hit it off well, and Kelly had often seen them running through the woods together. At first, they'd shared what they saw and did with Adam, but by August they rarely visited.

Kelly had felt so sorry for Adam being there alone that she'd taken some animals to visit him. But when she got there, she saw that Mrs. Hatten was having a ladies' party. Kelly knew that grown women made a silly fuss about poop. They were scared it would touch their pretty things.

So Kelly climbed up the trellis and entered Adam's room through the window. It was to be a onetime event, but he'd been so pleased by her entry that she kept on arriving that way.

They always had a great time! He got his mother to order some books on animals, and he and Kelly used to take turns reading them aloud.

It all ended when Adam got well. He went back to school and back to being a big-shot sports king. Kelly was beneath his notice. He wasn't going to admit to his friends that he'd spent time with a kid reading about the habits of elephants and cheetahs.

It took a while to realize that he wasn't going to say more than hello to her in the halls. And that's when she told everyone that she didn't like him. When he came to their house to see Vera, she made sure she said something snotty to him.

She drove down the Montoya driveway and there was Miguel smiling at her. He was tall, broad shouldered, muscular, and his face was gorgeous.

"Look what the scrawny kid grew up to look like," she muttered. "Miracles do happen." Smiling broadly, she picked up her bag, then got out of the car and held out her hand to shake. "It's good to see you again."

"You can't greet me like that!" He put his arms around her and twirled her around, then kissed her cheek enthusiastically.

When he put her down, she was blinking at him.

He had his hands on her shoulders and was looking at her, nearly nose to nose. "So Vera's little sister grew up. And without a coating of feathers and fur."

Kelly laughed. It was a family joke started by her father. He'd said that Kelly would grow up to have feathers and fur. "But I want mermaid scales," she'd said, her lower lip trembling in disappointment.

"You look great." Miguel slipped his arm about her shoulders and they started toward the barn. "I'd ask about your family, but Aunt Forey keeps us informed of every detail. You got dumped and now they've been pimping you out to every unmarried guy in the county. Is that right?"

"Exactly right. Want to hear what I've been through?"

"I want to hear every word."

She told of her four awful dates and was pleased when he laughed at her stories. *Delicious laugh*, she thought.

When they got to the barn, he led the horse to her, then got out his tools. He expertly lifted the horse's hoof and began using a knife to scrape away dirt and gravel.

"Tell me about you," Kelly said. "What have you done since you were here last time?"

"Grew up some, but not too much. Went to school for a while, served a two-year tour in Vietnam."

Kelly drew in her breath. "Vera used to participate in protests but Mom made her stop."

"Did she?" He kept his head down. "I think I've found the problem."

Kelly went to the hoof and used her own tool to scrape. "It's an infection. Probably got a cut, then didn't heal. Antibiotics should fix it. How are the other hooves?" Their heads were nearly touching.

"I think they're okay, but let's check to make sure." He stepped back to watch her clean the area and swab it.

She stood up. "Let's look at the right front. We can—"

"Miguel!" came a woman's voice from outside. "Are you in here?"

"Holy hell," he said under his breath, then looked at her. "It's Gabby and you're way too pretty. She'll be jealous and she'll make my life miserable. And yours." He grabbed her hand and pulled her toward the ladder that went up to the loft. "Go!" he practically growled.

With Kelly's work, she was used to having to do things quickly. Angry animals weren't polite. She scurried up the ladder in record speed, Miguel right behind her.

Once they were up, he went across some bales of hay, then pulled Kelly's hand so she rolled across to him. She was on her stomach, wedged against the bales, and Miguel was practically on top of her. He put his finger to his lips for her to say nothing.

They could hear footsteps below them. "Miguel! I know you're in here. I'll find you. You can't hide from me."

When they heard her climb the ladder, Miguel put his arm across Kelly's head and they stayed as low as possible. Kelly couldn't see her but Gabby seemed to look around the loft. If she came up to the floor, she'd find them. That would be embarrassing and very awkward.

Kelly could feel Miguel's breath on her cheek and his heart

beating against her body. She kind of hoped Gabby would stay there all day.

But alas, they heard her go down the ladder, then footsteps heading out. Kelly started to get up, but Miguel whispered, "Not yet."

Seconds later, Gabby returned. "Miguel!" she shouted angrily. A full minute later, they heard her leave.

He rolled off Kelly and onto his back. "Sorry about that. If I were a real man, I'd face her."

Kelly rubbed his cheek. "Hmm. Scratchy. Feels like a man to me."

Laughing, he sat up. "Would you like a Coke?"

"Love one."

He shoved a bale aside to reveal a big metal cooler. "I try to put some ice in it every day." He pulled out a bottle of Coca-Cola, used an opener on the wall and handed the cold drink to her. "I have sandwich makings in here. And fruit."

"No, thanks."

He opened a bottle for himself, leaned back against the wall and motioned to her to join him. She sat beside him and looked across the loft as she drank. "You hide like this often?"

"Yes. Here or somewhere."

She took another drink. "I assume you know that Forey and Mom think you're going to marry her."

"Oh, how I know that!"

"Didn't I hear that you've been going to school?"

"It's a lie I spread around," he said. "I spend the weekends away, true, but I go to motels or trailer parks. I camp out in a tent."

"That's sad. Maybe you could—"

"What are you going to do about dating?"

"I don't know. Maybe I should be like Vera and find a guy to spend the weekends with. Sex, not love."

"What?" His voice was low.

"I meant that I was offered sex in the back seat of a Buick, but—"

"No. The other part. About Vera."

"She and Adam spend every weekend together."

"You're sure of that?"

"Of course. Who else in this county would be up to her standards? Adam Hatten is smart and educated and—"

"Yeah, yeah, we all know that."

"I thought you liked Adam. When we were kids, you and he—"

"Go out with *me*."

"What?"

"You heard me," he said. "This Saturday, go out to dinner with me. I won't leap on you and I'm not allergic to anything."

She looked at him. "Will Gabby allow you out?"

He gave a one-sided smile. "She'll throw a fit."

"Last time I saw her, she looked pretty strong."

Miguel picked up her hand and kissed the back of her fingers. "I'll protect you."

Kelly raised her eyebrows. "I would love to go. Thank you for the invitation." They smiled at each other.

Her encounter with Miguel cheered Kelly up immensely. Even Dr. Carl noticed. "What are you so happy about?"

"Just glad to be alive."

"In that case, you can clear Mrs. Johnson's poodle's anal glands."

"Be glad to," Kelly said.

When she got home, the house was awash with cooking smells. Beef mixed with cherry pies and bread baking. With their first paycheck, the women had purchased an eight-foot-long oak table. The kitchen was now so packed it was hard to move around it. The women were talking of tearing out a wall so the kitchen and living room were one big open space. Everyone at church was telling them that would be a bad thing to do. They said, "You need privacy" and "Who wants to see the mess in the kitchen?"

Kelly stood at the end of the table. It was heaped with so much food that it looked like a painting of an ancient Greek orgy. The women were so busy they didn't notice her.

In a voice that was barely a whisper, Kelly said, "I'm going on a date with Miguel."

Forey was the first to react. Her potholder-covered hand held a sheet of cookies just out of the oven. "You're doing what?"

Nella looked at her friend. "I said I added citron to the mix." Forey put the cookies down and looked at Kelly, eyes wide. Nella turned to her daughter. "What did you say?"

"On Saturday I'm going out to dinner with Miguel."

It took the women a moment before they could digest what she'd said. Then they erupted like twin geysers. They ran around the counter and began hugging Kelly.

"We'll be sisters," Forey said to Nella. "United forever."

"Our families will be one."

"Wait a minute!" Kelly said. "It's just a date. We're not getting married. And what about Gabby?" The women went back to their cooking.

"He's not that fond of Gabby," Forey said. "And of course you'll fall in love with him. He's the nicest, kindest young man in the world."

"And quite beautiful," Nella said.

"He gets that from my sister's husband. He is worthless as a moneymaker but oh so good-looking! They have *many* children."

"I can understand that!" Nella said.

"I'm still here," Kelly said. "And I am not going to marry someone just so you two can believe you're sisters."

The women stopped moving and looked at her. Their faces were serious. "Is there *anything* wrong with him?" Nella asked.

"Well…" Kelly remembered being smashed against the bales of hay, Miguel's strong body against hers. "He… Uh… And I…"

"Exactly," Forey said. "My nephew is irresistible."

"Maybe not quite that, but certainly…" Kelly didn't say any more, as the women had stopped listening. Besides, what could she say? She tended to agree with them. Actually, she deeply and truly *wanted* to agree with them. Maybe Miguel could take her mind off Adam. Off the forbidden attachment to her sister's husband-to-be.

Kelly went to her room, closed the door and opened a textbook. By ten, she was asleep and smiling. At last, she had a solution to all her problems.

The next morning, Vera was late getting up, but she didn't have to be at work until ten. Last night she and Miguel had worked on campaign posters until midnight.

As they kissed goodbye, she'd been amenable to a quickie on the sofa, but he pushed her away. "What's wrong with you? You've been quiet all night."

"Just thinking, that's all," he said. "Are you packed for Africa?"

"As a matter of fact, I am. Are you going to start on me again? I'm leaving—"

"Don't say it! With Adam in the fall."

"Why are you doing this? I've never lied to you."

"True," he said. "You've been completely honest with me. Sex with me but you leave with *him*."

Vera didn't back down. "Do *you* want to leave the US and live in Africa?"

His voice lowered. "Vietnam was more than enough for me. I've earned being home."

"Well, I don't want to stay here! Since I was a kid I've—"

"I know what you are and what you want!" He was shouting. "I was here with you when you were a kid, remember? Even then all you could talk about was how you were going to save the whole world."

She was glaring at him. "Has something happened?"

"No. Everything is exactly the same. Things will change only if I *make* them happen."

"What does that mean?"

"Nothing. I'm going home."

She watched him go up the stairs of their underground hideaway. When she heard him drive away, she knew that something had deeply upset him. Usually he gave her a ride back to her house. Frowning, Vera got the flashlight and left. On the walk home, she tried to figure out what was bothering him so much, but she had no answers. The question was whether he was so upset that he'd stop…stop everything. Their weekends together were becoming her whole life. Rallies, protests, sit-ins were just a part of it all. She told herself that they were helping the world and what did it matter if there was a bit of sex now and then? That it was glorious, life-affirming sex that left them fulfilled and satisfied was a by-product. "Like sweat in an athletic contest," she'd told him. He'd said she was ridiculous, and then he'd rubbed his sweaty face on her bare breasts.

As Vera dressed for work, she thought about their nights together and last night. She didn't usually allow other people's moods to bother her, but Miguel's did.

She left her room and already the house was full of cooking smells. Nella and Forey had covered half of the new table with their food. "Why are you two smiling so big?"

"Kelly is going out with Miguel," Forey said proudly.

"She's what?" Vera's eyes were wide in shock.

"Kelly and Miguel," Nella said. "It's a perfect match. I can't believe we didn't think of it before."

"That's because there was Gabby," Forey said.

Nella sniffed. "I didn't want to interfere, but Gabby isn't exactly—"

"Stop it!" Vera said. "Tell me how all of this happened."

Nella spoke first. "Kelly had to go to the Montoya Farm for—" She looked at her friend.

"One of our horses was lame," Forey said. "I think it was Belle. Or maybe it was—" She broke off at Vera's look.

"We don't know exactly what led up to it," Nella said, "but Miguel asked Kelly on a date. I think they're a lovely pair and—"

"When?" Vera demanded. "When and where?"

The women looked at each other. "We have no idea."

"They should go to Stanton's," Nella said.

"We'll make a reservation for them," Forey said.

"And we will prepay. We'll send a bottle of wine to the table."

"*Two* bottles." Forey was snickering. "I want grandkids."

The two women laughed together, oblivious to the anger on Vera's face. She grabbed a sweet roll and her handbag, and went to work. "Damn you, Miguel," she repeated all the way to the Plaza. "Damn you to hell and back!"

At six that evening, Kelly was rummaging through her closet. There were four dresses on her bed.

Vera gave her usual quick knock, then entered.

Kelly took one look at her sister and knew something was wrong. "What happened?"

"Nothing. Just idiots at work. Can't make up their minds. So what's all this?" She motioned to the clothes.

"I'm just trying to figure out what to wear."

"Since when do you care about clothes?"

Kelly's face lit up. "I'm going on a date. A *real* one."

"Oh, yes. I heard something about that. Forey's nephew, isn't it?"

"Yes. Miguel. You've seen him since he got back, haven't you? He's very handsome."

"Is he? I didn't notice." Vera turned away from her sister.

"That's because you're in love."

Vera turned around, her face like a storm cloud. "In love? I hardly think— Oh. Right. Adam."

Kelly laughed. "Yes, of course, Adam. The man you spend every weekend with. Don't look so surprised. We figured out where you disappear to."

Vera didn't reply. "So you're going out with Miguel. When did he ask you?"

"Yesterday morning. He had a lame horse. Then Gabby showed up, and—"

"Didn't Forey say those two were engaged?"

Kelly picked up a blue dress. It had been washed many times and was faded. "I had this dress in college. *What* am I going to wear?"

"Gabrielle? What about *her*?"

"He doesn't like her. She follows him and he hides from her. Oh, Vera, it was such a nice time. I mean, it was kind of awful because we were hiding, but it was still good. Miguel and I were lying side by side in the hay. He keeps Cokes in a cooler and he kissed my hand. And he handled the horses very well."

"He sounds perfect," Vera said softly. "I..." Vera didn't seem to know what else to say. Abruptly, she left the room and closed the door behind her.

The minute she was alone, Kelly flopped across the bed. She'd been worried that Vera would see through her act. Kelly had gushed so hard about Miguel to keep from hearing Vera talk about Adam. If Vera started confiding about the cute little inn or wherever she and Adam stayed, Kelly thought she might lose it. She'd cry or scream. Probably both.

She rolled over as a hanger was sticking her. The dress on it was green with white polka dots. It looked like something a fourteen-year-old would wear.

Her mother had said they were going to Stanton's in Leawood for dinner. She'd never been there but she'd heard it was quite elegant.

Kelly was struck by an idea that made her smile. If there was one thing Mrs. Carl was good at other than baking, it was shopping. She went to the hall phone and dialed the house number.

Mrs. Carl answered. "Hello, Kelly. He's right here. I'll get him."

"No!" Kelly said. "It's you I want to talk to."

"Oh?" She sounded pleased.

"I have a date on Saturday night. It's at Stanton's and I need a dress. And shoes and new underwear and pantyhose and... All of it. Would you help me? Please?"

"Oh, Kelly, yes, I would love to. We'll go in the morning, and maybe on Saturday we could do something with your hair. And of course there's the makeup. I know the aesthetician at Estée Lauder. She'll do it all. I'll pick you up at 9:45 tomorrow. Kansas City awaits us. And Carl will pay for everything. I have to go. I have soooo much planning to do. Good night, dear. See you tomorrow." She hung up.

Kelly looked at the phone. "What's wrong with my hair?"

She put the receiver in the cradle, went back to her room and closed the door behind her. "I'm going to fall madly in love with Miguel," she said aloud. "That will give everyone what they want."

It was only later, as she was falling asleep, that she thought it was odd that Vera hadn't told her about Adam. Was everything all right between them?

Of course it is, she told herself. They were as solid as a mountain. They'd been inseparable most of their lives. Well, maybe that one summer Vera spent more time with Miguel than Adam. But they were just kids then, so that meant nothing.

It's going to work out perfectly, she told herself as she fell asleep.

Vera heard Kelly's call to Mrs. Carl. She waited until the light under Kelly's door went out. Then, ignoring her mother's rule that a girl *never* called a boy, she dialed Adam's number. He had an extension in his bedroom and he answered right away. "Did I wake you?" Her voice was low.

"No. I haven't been able to sleep lately. What's going on?"

"I was just thinking that we haven't seen each other in days, so we should make a date."

"Sure. Why not?" He didn't sound enthusiastic.

"Feel like getting dressed up? We could go to Stanton's in Leawood. I hear the food is great."

"I've been there. It's very fancy with not much on a plate. How about Arthur Bryant's?"

World-class barbecue. The thought of it made Vera's mouth water. "Not this time. I'll meet you at your house at seven on Saturday."

"I'll pick you up and—"

"No!" she almost shouted, then looked at Kelly's door. The light didn't come on. "If you come here, Mom and Forey will drill you with questions about where you've been and what you've been doing."

"Anything but that!"

She frowned. "Where *have* you been spending the weekends?"

There was a moment of silence. Then Adam said, "If I have to divulge my secrets, then so do you. I hear there was a big anti-war rally in Omaha."

"You don't have to tell me. See you on Saturday and wear that black suit and the blue tie."

"Why do I feel like you're up to something?"

"I have no idea. See ya." She hung up before he could ask anything else. Vera didn't want to reveal her secrets, but she was left with questions. *What is Adam doing on the weekends? And is it with someone?*

On Saturday, Miguel called and said he'd pick Kelly up at seven. He said her mother and his aunt had made a reservation at Stanton's. "But if you'd rather go somewhere else, we can. We could get ribs."

"Not a chance," she said. "The dress Mrs. Carl had me buy is silk. *Real* silk."

He chuckled. "Then we'd better not risk getting barbecue sauce on it."

Kelly was smiling. "I don't know… The dress *is* red." She'd never done much flirting in her life. She'd tried it on Pauly, but when he didn't react, she'd stopped. Hearing Miguel's intake of breath made her think she should do it more often.

When she hung up, her mother and Forey were standing there smiling at her. "Don't look at me like that. It's just a date."

Smiling even broader, the women went back to the kitchen. It took Kelly an hour to get ready for her date. Mrs. Carl had insisted she spend the whole morning in a beauty parlor. She'd protested until Mrs. Carl said, "Kelly, dear, they may have to take a threshing machine to those eyebrows of yours."

After that comment, Kelly sat in the sticky plastic chair and let them do to her whatever Mrs. Carl told them to do.

Looking at herself, she had to admit that maybe there was better shampoo than whatever was on sale. Her hair was soft and shiny. Or it was soft under what had to be a whole can of Aqua Net? Her hair had been set in rollers and she'd had to endure a long time under a dryer so hot she was sure her scalp was blistered. When she complained, Mrs. Carl said, "Beauty takes pain, but your result is worth it."

Pleased by the compliment, Kelly had said no more. Her usually straight hair had big, soft curls. It was very pretty.

As for the dress, it was more revealing than she had ever dared before. It was a halter top and she hadn't even known how to put it on. From the waist were two long scarves that Mrs. Carl tied at the back of Kelly's neck. Below the tie was nothing but bare skin down to her waist.

"My bra is showing," Kelly said.

"Girls your age invented bra burning. You should leave the thing at home."

"But..." Kelly started, then thought, *Why not?* Vera often wore skimpy clothes. But then, she didn't have much on top to show. "Fried eggs," Vera would say with laughter. Bra size was not something she considered important. "Okay," Kelly said.

Mrs. Carl smiled broadly. "You're the daughter I always wanted."

"If my mother hears you say that, she'll shove you into the oven and roast you."

"Oh? Like a fairy-tale witch?"

Kelly couldn't keep from laughing at her insinuation. Nella

and Forey had not been overly welcoming to Mrs. Carl in the baking endeavor.

Kelly took one last look in the mirror and gathered her courage before she went into the kitchen.

Usually, by this time, Forey had gone home, but both women were waiting to see her.

Their full minute of silence at the sight of her was gratifying. "You look like a girl," Nella whispered.

"I always look like a girl," Kelly shot back.

"She means you don't look like a tomboy," Forey said.

When Miguel knocked, the women went to answer the door, and let him in.

Miguel looked great. His dark hair and eyes were accented by the dark suit he had on. "You are beautiful," he said.

"Thank you," she said demurely. She picked up the little black bag that matched her high heels. Mrs. Carl had found both of them for her.

They went out to his uncle Rafe's car—no truck for this date—and he held the door open for her. On the drive to the restaurant, they kept stealing glances at each other.

"You really do look beautiful," he said. "I've never seen you in anything except jeans and T-shirts."

"Let's just hope that tonight no one needs a calf delivered or it'll all be ruined."

"If that happens, I'll do the work while you stand back and give me directions."

"That sounds good." She took a breath. "How was Gabby tonight?"

"No one had the courage to tell her where I was going."

Kelly frowned. "Poor woman. She could have been told that it's just a date."

"Really? But I brought an engagement ring with me. It belonged to my grandmother." At Kelly's look of shock, he laughed. "Just a joke. Did your mom and Forey, uh…make plans?"

"I think they reserved the church for us. Is October the fourteenth good for you? It's a Saturday."

When he stopped at a light, he looked her up and down. "I will definitely be there," he said in a way that made her blush.

The first thing they saw when they pulled into the parking lot was Vera's Chevy. It was pumpkin orange and it was sitting below a streetlamp.

Kelly felt the air leave her. "Mom did this! She sent Vera to make sure that I don't do anything awful." She threw her hands up. "Mom believes I'll sit with the chair back between my legs or something."

"Vera isn't exactly a queen of good manners."

"Then she's here to make sure you don't pounce on her virginal little sister."

"Virginal?"

"I'm not, but that won't matter to Vera and my mother." Anger was rising in her.

"You want to go somewhere else?"

"And have the police called on us? *You* would spend the night in jail." Kelly frowned all the way into the restaurant. She and Pauly had never really gone on dates. Not like other kids in high school. But then, Kelly was always working at the clinic. And he was with his little trees.

By the time she and Miguel reached the front door, Kelly had decided to tell Vera to go away, that she was too old to need a chaperone. She could handle herself. She could—

To Kelly's horror, both Vera and Adam were standing in the foyer. Kelly tried not to notice how good Adam looked. He wasn't beautiful like Miguel but bigger and more…more *man* looking, she thought.

Vera saw Kelly's expression. "Uh-oh. Looks like no one told you this was to be a double date. Maybe we should leave."

Adam was looking at Kelly. "I'm hungry, so let's just do this."

Kelly glared at him but he didn't seem aware of it.

Miguel took Kelly's arm. "We'd love to have you sit with us, wouldn't we? And Kelly is so beautiful I want to show her off as my date."

Vera had on a flowered cotton dress that had seen better days. She'd tried to pull her hair back but it was escaping its bonds. "My little sister does look great, doesn't she?" Vera was so loud people turned toward them. "But then, she's so *young*, of course she looks good."

Kelly looked at her sister, puzzled. "I am just ten months younger than you. Months, not years."

"Ah, but experience ages one," Vera said. "Shall we be seated?" She took Adam's arm and went into the dining room.

"She's acting very strange," Kelly said.

"Her? Adam was glaring at you like he wanted to bawl you out. Did something happen between you two?" Miguel asked.

"Absolutely nothing! But if he gives me any trouble I'll remind him that he and Vera spend every weekend together. I saw a matchbook on the floor and it was from a hotel in Omaha. Adam has no right to criticize *me* about anything when he—"

Miguel's face had gone pale. "Bringing up something like that is fighting below the belt. Maybe you should pretend that you don't know about that. Certainly not mention it." He took a breath. "For your sister's sake."

"For her, okay, but Adam had better be nice."

It took a while to get settled at the table, place their orders and open the first bottle of wine. When Kelly took a sip, Vera said, "Be careful of that. You aren't used to it."

"Stop acting like Mom," Kelly said under her breath. Their appetizers came right away.

"So, Miguel," Adam said, "what are your plans for the future? Will you get married and still live with Rafe and Forey?" He leaned forward a bit. "And what about Gabrielle?"

Kelly spoke before Miguel could. "Not that it's any of your business, but Miguel has no obligations to Gabby. That whole marriage thing was made up by Forey with help from my mother. Miguel is free to marry whomever he wants."

Adam was calm. "I'm sure he is. I was more concerned financially." He looked at Miguel. "You'll need a house. Can you afford that?"

Miguel's expression was dark. "What I have I've earned. I don't depend on Daddy's money to give me everything."

"But a girl like Kelly needs things. Animals, for one. She—"

Kelly leaned across the table. "We're on a *date*. We're not engaged! You're the one who goes away every—" She stopped when Miguel put his hand on her forearm and squeezed hard. And he was right. She'd been about to remind Adam of his illicit weekends with Vera.

Kelly tossed her napkin on the table. "I'm going to the restroom." Before anyone could speak, she quickly walked to the back. Once she was in the little alcove, she leaned against the wall. She knew she was making a fool of herself, but Adam's insinuations had made her angry. Actually, just the sight of him made her furious. For a whole month, she'd worked hard to avoid him, but tonight she'd been caught off guard. She'd been looking forward to spending an evening with Miguel, an unattached man. Then to have Adam show up and—

Suddenly, he was standing in front of her. "I have to go," she said.

"Please," he said. "Talk to me for a minute. Tell me what I did wrong. Did I ever do anything that was too aggressive?

Out of line? I seem to have made you hate me and I don't understand why."

Kelly took a breath. "You did nothing wrong. You were perfect. You are kind and you listen and you're generous. There is nothing wrong with you."

He was looking at her as though he was in pain. "Then why have you avoided me?"

"What you and I were doing was *dating*." Her voice was rising. "Movies, TV nights, shopping. We even spent the night together!"

They were interrupted by a cough. "Uh, I hate to bother you, Adam. I can see you're, uh, busy, but I'd like to talk to you. Monday, maybe?"

"Sure." Adam's eyes never left Kelly.

"Here's my card," the man said. When he didn't take it, the man slipped it into Adam's shirt pocket. He looked from one to the other. "I'll let you two get back to it."

"Who was that?" Kelly asked.

"A coach I know," Adam said. "You and I weren't dating. We are friends, that's all."

She tightened her lips. "Okay, so let's go back in there and tell everyone what we did together. Let's get it all out in the open and see what people say."

When he didn't reply, she lowered her voice. "Adam, you're *taken*. You're temporary."

"And Miguel is permanent?"

She threw up her hands in exasperation. "Before tonight, I spent an hour with him, that's all. But everyone is marrying me off to him. It's bizarre."

Three men came out of the restroom, laughing, and one bumped into Adam. He was shoved against Kelly.

"Sorry, man," the guy said.

"It's fine." Adam didn't move away from Kelly.

"I can see that it is," the man said, and his friends laughed with him.

"Watch yourselves." Adam sounded threatening.

"Adam!" Kelly snapped.

He looked at her and she glared back. He was still up against her. "Oh. Right. Sorry." He stepped away. "Xander misses you."

"I miss him, too." She was softening toward him. Maybe she'd been too harsh. "We better go back."

"The apartment is the same as when you were there," he said.

All Kelly's good thoughts left her. "You and Vera didn't mess it up on your wild weekends?"

He looked astonished. "What are you talking about? We—"

Turning, she walked away. She didn't want to hear what he had to say.

As soon as Kelly left the table, with Adam just steps behind her, Vera turned to Miguel. Her eyes were furious. "You asked her out just to get back at me, didn't you?"

Miguel smiled. "I have no idea what you mean. Kelly's single and so am I. We're a perfect match. We would unite our families."

Vera lowered her voice. "You two would be horrible together. You're too angry for her. You've been through too much bad in your life. Kelly wouldn't know how to handle you when you think people are shooting at you."

He blinked at that.

"Didn't think I knew about your nightmares, did you?"

He picked up a piece of bread and buttered it. "I think you underestimate your sister. You should see the way she handles horses. She calms them down. *Tames* them."

Vera shook her head. "Kelly doesn't need *more* work to do.

She needs someone who will look after her. She's not like you and me."

"And what are we like?"

"We're the same and you know it. We fight for things with our words and sometimes with our fists. Most people have an anchor inside them that grounds them, but you and I…" She trailed off.

Miguel's eyes were intense, like a fire was inside them. "There is no us. *You* are taken."

Vera leaned back in her seat. "And you are anchored *here*. In this place."

They sat in silence, looking at each other. They had insurmountable obstacles between them.

CHAPTER ELEVEN

WHEN KELLY GOT HOME, SHE WASN'T surprised to see her mother waiting for her. "How was it?" Nella asked breathlessly.

"Interesting. The food was good."

Nella gave a sigh of satisfaction. "I knew you two would hit it off. Did you see that I left the porch light off? Kisses in the dark are sweeter than in the light."

Kelly willed her face not to turn red. This was not something she wanted to talk to her mother about. She smiled and said, "Yes, they are."

Nella seemed pleased by that.

"I'm pretty tired. I think I'll go to bed."

"Of course. I'll see you in the morning. How about strawberry waffles for breakfast?"

"Excellent," Kelly said, then went to her room and shut the door. When she saw herself in the mirror, she thought how different she'd looked before the date. She'd seemed younger, certainly more hopeful, then.

Now she was just confused. Perplexed and puzzled. *What the hell is going on?*

The whole date felt like she'd walked into the middle of a movie and she'd never figured out the plot. Adam had treated Miguel like he was an enemy, while Miguel acted like he knew something no one else did.

And then there was Vera. Usually she was calm. But tonight she'd looked like she was ready to kill someone. It was just that Kelly never could figure out *who* she wanted to murder.

As for Kelly, she ate and drank and said little. Mainly, she stayed out of whatever was going on among the others. *No wonder I love animals*, she thought. *They make more sense.*

She turned away from the mirror. When she had trouble undoing the halter knot of her dress, her bad temper made her want to use scissors on it, but she didn't. She managed to strip down and put on her bathrobe. When she opened her bedroom door, she saw her mother on the phone. She was whispering, so it had to be a call to Forey.

Nella stopped talking as Kelly walked to the bathroom, but when Kelly was out of sight, Nella started again.

Kelly leaned against the door. She wanted to forget that this night had happened.

Tomorrow she'd skip church and go clean out cages. Better animal waste than facing Vera, Adam and Miguel again. Or answering questions about what the double date had been like.

She turned on the shower over the tub, got in and washed her hair. It took three shampoos to get all the hair spray out. She stepped out and wiped the steam off the mirror. With her wet hair slicked back, she again looked like herself. Well, maybe her eyebrows were better, but still the same.

"What in the world is going on?" she said aloud, but there was no answer.

When Robbie bounded down the stairs, he was jolted to see Adam sitting in a chair and drinking beer. It was eight thirty on a Sunday morning. He looked bad. He had on dress pants and a white shirt. His suit jacket and tie were slung over a chair.

"You look like crap. Did you sleep last night?"

Adam didn't reply.

Robbie went to the kitchen and poured himself a bowl of Cheerios and added milk. Back in the living room, Adam hadn't moved. Robbie sat on the arm of a chair across from his brother. "So what's wrong with you?"

Adam took so long to speak that Robbie almost left. "Where are you going?"

"To church."

"Since when do you go to church without someone threatening you?"

"Since I started sitting next to Lisa Chandless."

"The preacher's daughter?"

"Yeah. And before you ask, it's just her. She won't have anything to do with me if I go out with other girls."

"I'm glad someone is having luck with women."

Robbie made a scoffing sound. "No one will believe that! Vera's family knows you spend every weekend in bed with her."

Adam looked at his brother in surprise. "I haven't been alone with Vera in over a month. What she does on the weekend is her own business."

Robbie looked shocked. "But you're not here and she's not at home. Where are you two going?"

Adam was silent.

Robbie got up. He wasn't going to beg his brother to share a confidence.

"I spend my weekends at the apartment on the Plaza."

"The one Dad kept in secret from Mom?" Robbie was frowning.

"It was a secret from us. From you and me. It was their private place."

Robbie put down his empty bowl and slid down into the chair. "They needed to keep a secret from *us*?"

"You should see it. It's like something out of a 1930s movie, all sleek white silk. When they told us they were going to cattle auctions or wherever, they were probably going there."

It took Robbie a moment to digest this. "And now you're using it. So who are you cheating on Vera with? Anybody I know?"

Adam gave his brother a look of disgust. "I go there alone. I need time to think about my future. I spent years living in an African village. Then I came back here and found out that my life had been plotted out for me. Everyone knows what I'm going to do next. From the wedding to flying back to Africa. I thought maybe Mom and Dad's spirit could help me."

Robbie was blinking at him. "I never thought you had any problems."

"What an idiot thing to say."

"Any problems other than me, that is. It's always been you and Vera. So if you're there, what's *she* doing when she goes away for the weekend?"

"I have an idea but it's private."

"She hasn't *told* you?"

"She knows I wouldn't approve."

Rob was taking this in. Never before had he and Adam talked as equals. Even when they were kids, it was always Adam the Wise and Robbie the Screwup. "Why don't you ask Vera to spend the weekend at the apartment with you?"

"No!" Adam nearly shouted. "I mean, Vera wouldn't fit in there. She'd start talking about some massacre that happened a hundred years ago. She told me about one and I was sick to my stomach for a week. She..." He took a breath. "None of this matters. I just need some time to think. I'm fine. Really."

"I can tell that you're doing well. You're drinking in the morning and you look like crap. Did something happen last night?"

Adam snorted. "It was just a double date. Nothing special. Vera and me, with Kelly and Miguel."

Robbie frowned. "Miguel with Kelly? He's going to marry Gabby. The whole town knows that."

"*He* doesn't seem to know it. He had his hands all over her last night. They're not right for each other."

"Why not? Miguel is a good guy. He's smart and a hard worker. He'll probably inherit Rafe's place."

"I'm sure he's a paragon of virtue. They should make a statue of him and put it on the Plaza. Better yet, build a church around it. We could light candles at its feet."

With every word, Robbie's eyes widened. He'd never seen his brother like this. He didn't even know Adam was capable of such fatalism. Robbie stood up. "I have to get dressed to go to church. I think you should go to the apartment and stay there tonight. Maybe you'll get some help from the spirits of Mom and Dad. Whatever you need to do, *do* it. Just don't sit here and get drunk. I'm going to church to meet the lovely Lisa."

Robbie waited until Adam was standing up before he hurried up the stairs. To tell the truth, he did *not* like this Adam. He wanted his bossy, domineering brother back. How could he be a rebel if there was no dictator to rebel against?

When he heard Adam start his truck, Robbie let out a sigh of relief. So who had ripped his big brother up? Vera? She could cut anyone apart. Miguel? He was a great guy. Always calm. He once told Robbie that Vietnam had shot all the anger out of him. Was that true?

The only other person there last night was Kelly. Pretty,

sweet Kelly, who was followed everywhere by critters. No one could be angry at Kelly.

So *what* had turned Adam into someone who drank beer on a Sunday morning?

Robbie didn't think he'd hear Lisa's dad's sermon this morning. He was going to think about how to fix his brother.

As Adam drove from Mason to the apartment on the Plaza, he thought about what Robbie had said. What *was* Vera doing on the weekends? His guess was that she was going to those anti-war rallies. Those things often turned violent and she could be hurt. Killed even.

He had a vision of standing at Vera's grave site and trying to explain why he hadn't stopped her from going. "She wasn't spending the weekends with me and I suspected that she was involved in the protests, but I..." What excuse could he give? That he'd spent two days a week free from dealing with the problems of his life? He didn't want to think about selling a place his family had owned for generations. He certainly didn't want to think about what his little brother would do without constant supervision. Truthfully, in the last weeks, Adam had had so many problems to hide from that he hadn't thought much about Vera.

He let that sink in. For a whole month he had hardly thought about the woman he loved. The woman he was planning to spend his life with.

The person he had thought about most was Kelly. How she'd loved the apartment and had fit into it. Shopping, movies, TV, shared meals. And...and Kelly in that wedding dress. It was still in the box. He'd shoved it on a top shelf in a closet and his only thought had been that he'd never again open that box.

At the apartment, he parked in the underground lot and

took the elevator up. He was glad he didn't have to talk to anyone.

Once inside the apartment, a peace settled over him. *Is this how my parents felt?* he wondered.

Kelly and I could— He cut himself off from that thought.

He peeled off his clothes and got into the big shower. The hot water felt good as it hit his back.

He still didn't know what had made him so angry last night. He'd told Kelly they were just friends, so he should have been glad to see her with a man like Miguel. He was certainly better than Treeboy.

But there was something about the way Miguel kept touching Kelly that made Adam's fists clench.

His hands were on her neck, her bare shoulders. Worst was when his hands were out of sight. That damned dress Kelly had on was naked in the back.

And Miguel was bragging about his war wounds. He— Adam turned in the shower, letting the hot water hit his face. Wait. That wasn't right. It was Vera who'd said the wound wasn't from the war. So how the hell did she know that?

He got out of the shower and dried off. He hadn't brought any clothes with him, but he had the new ones he'd bought. The long walk-in closet was still full of his parents' clothes. Adam had squeezed in a few things of his own. He pulled on a pair of jeans, then reached for a new shirt. Instead, he took out one of his father's shirts. It fit.

For a moment, Adam allowed regret to overtake him. The last time he'd spoken to his father had been in anger. They'd fought over... At the moment, Adam couldn't remember what that particular argument had been about. But then, Adam and his dad had always fought.

I wanted to be the boss, he thought. *I wanted to actually be what everyone said I was.*

He closed his eyes. "Being an adult isn't as easy as I thought it was going to be," he said aloud.

He left the apartment to go to the Plaza and bought a thick Sunday newspaper, walked around a bit, then went back. But he couldn't settle.

As he looked around the beautiful living room, he knew he had to stop hiding. There were problems in his life that had to be solved and he needed to get started on them. The first one was Vera's safety.

He drove back to Mason and went past Vera's house. There were two cars there: Nella's and Forey's. It looked like both Vera and Kelly were out. Vera had been home last night for the dinner, so where was she now? He hadn't thought to check the paper for news of upcoming protests. For all he knew, she'd gone to Saint Louis. It was only about three hours away.

Adam thought about going home, but instead he went to the local barbecue place and got ribs and Cokes. His next job called for food. He needed to apologize to Kelly.

But first, he had to find her. The vet clinic was closed on Sundays and Dr. Carl took care of any overnight animals. Adam wasn't sure where Kelly would be but he had an idea.

He parked his truck off the road, grabbed the bag of food and walked to the frog pond.

She was sitting on the ground, surrounded by wild ducks. With any other human, the creatures would be running away, but not with Kelly. Her medical bag was open beside her, she had a duck on her lap and she was doing something to its foot. The other ducks were nudging her legs, walking quickly around as though they were nervous, or some were being still and watching.

Kelly was talking to them. "He will be fine. It's just bumblefoot and you caught it early. I'm glad you brought him to me. There! Now it's clean and I put antiseptic on it. I'm going to bandage it and I want you to leave it on. Got that?"

Adam was sure a couple of ducks nodded their heads.

She put the injured duck on the ground. "I know it's a lot to ask, but please keep him out of the water for the rest of the day." She watched as they all waddled off, the bandaged duck in the middle. They did not get into the water.

Adam was smiling at them and didn't realize Kelly had seen him. She certainly didn't look happy at his intrusion. He held up the bag. "Peace offering."

She didn't reply.

"It comes with an apology." Still no reply.

"And I'll apologize to Miguel and Vera and promise to never again be a jerk." There was a tiny flicker of a smile on her lips.

"What's in the bag?"

"Ribs." When she nodded acceptance, he grinned, went to her, handed her the bag, then sat down about six feet from her. "Think he'll stay out of the water?"

"I hope so. If not, I'll have to put him in a cage for a few days." They spread the food on white papers and started eating.

"Do you have a reason for searching for me? Last night wasn't enough?" Kelly asked.

Adam grimaced. "I really am sorry."

"You should be! Asking Miguel if he could afford a house was too much."

"I just—" He decided it was better not to try to defend himself. "You're right. So what did you do last week?"

Kelly sighed. "The usual. Sewed up four injured dogs. Castrated a couple of things."

"Ouch!"

She gave him a look that said he deserved it. "I did a C-section on a four-pound Yorkie. The puppies were too big for her to deliver."

"I'm impressed." He wiped his hands and mouth. "Do you know where Vera goes on weekends?"

She just blinked at him.

"I pieced together that people think she and I are in some motel together every weekend, but we're not. I told you that I've been staying at the apartment."

"But I thought you meant that Vera was with you."

"Nope. Just me. Hiding from everybody."

She nodded at his honesty. "So where is my sister going?"

Adam took a moment to answer. "I think she's participating in anti-war protests."

"Like at Kent?" Kelly whispered. "Where the soldiers shot the students?"

"Yes, like Kent and all the other places."

Kelly looked out at the water. "That sounds like her. She told Mom she'd stop. But she's sneaking off and still going. When she's free of Mom and me, she'll do it in the open. You're going to have your hands full with her in Africa."

"I know," he said. "With Vera there, it won't be a quiet village life. She'll go after the tribe's chief. She'll—" He quit talking.

"Yes, she will." Kelly paused. "We're jumping to conclusions. Maybe she's doing something else on the weekend."

"Like what?"

"Maybe she's taken on an extra job to earn money. She'll need a plane ticket. New clothes. Or maybe she wants to buy Mom a new car. There are lots of possibilities."

"Do you believe any of those?"

"No," Kelly said. "Only something she shouldn't be doing needs to be kept a secret." She was quiet for a moment. "So what do you plan to do about it?"

"Me?" Adam sighed. Of course it was *his* job. "I'll find out what she's up to for sure. Then I'll… Any suggestions?"

"That don't involve rope and chains?"

"Right." He leaned back on his arms and looked at the pond. "You going on a date with Miguel again?"

"Probably. You planning to show up on all of them?"

Adam stood up. "No. I think it's time I stop trying to rule other people."

"Robbie will be glad to hear that."

"Except for him. He's half in love with the preacher's daughter."

"Lisa is nice. I hope it works out for them."

"He's too young—" Adam cut himself off. "Maybe he's not too young. I need to go. I have too much to do and…" He looked at her with longing in his eyes. "You were right about us. That we had to keep it secret shows that it wasn't good. Sorry I was so…" He shrugged. "I wish you and Miguel the best. Forever." Quickly, he walked away.

Kelly watched him go. "It was one date," she said in frustration. "Just *one*." A duck was at her feet. "And it wasn't even a very good date."

She cleaned up the area, then went to the clinic.

CHAPTER TWELVE

IT WAS LATE FRIDAY AFTERNOON AND Kelly was in the clinic having just removed stitches from a bulldog's belly. "The wound looks good," she said.

She watched the smiling owner lead the dog away.

Dr. Carl came in. "Are you okay? All week you've seemed a little glum."

"I'm fine," Kelly said. "Doing really well."

"Hot date this weekend?" When Kelly didn't answer, he said, "Sorry. I don't mean to pry. It's just that people keep asking me about you and Miguel. Seems you two are doing some serious dating. You've been seen together everywhere."

Kelly took her time washing her hands. "I've seen him every day this week." She tried to sound as cheerful as possible. When she saw that Dr. Carl was about to ask more questions, she looked at her watch. "Oh! Is it that late? I have to go." She practically ran outside and got into her Jeep.

Everything is great, she told herself. Everyone said she and Miguel were such a cute couple. She let out her breath. She needed to quit lying.

Kelly drove slowly. She wasn't eager to go home to her

mother's incessant questions. Forey would probably be there, too, and they'd be cooking vats of whatever. Sometimes, when the women were using tall spoons to stir giant pots of soup, Kelly thought they looked like witches.

What the women were conjuring was a love match. Well, actually, a wedding. It was like they had a single goal in life and that was to have an autumn wedding. For somebody. Didn't seem to matter for whom.

"I'm only thinking about you," Nella told her daughter.

"I know!" Kelly said. "Because I'm unmarried. Being a veterinarian doesn't matter. It's just if I can snare a man and produce lots of kids."

The look Nella gave Kelly made her hair stand on end. "I'm sorry," she whispered.

"You should be," her mother snapped, then turned to go back to the kitchen. "Maybe you should spend less time with Vera and listening to her ideas."

"I don't spend *any* time with her," Kelly said too softly to be heard.

Instead, she was spending lots of time with Miguel. One afternoon they went to see Pauly's orchard. She was surprised at how much Miguel liked the place.

"I've tried to get Uncle Rafe to branch out from just cows, but he won't listen. He lectures me about Kansas beef, then tells me the plot of every episode of *Rawhide*. I think he cried when that series was canceled."

"I loved that show!" Kelly said. "Cattle drives to get to Kansas City. I had such a crush on Rowdy. I wonder if that actor, Clint Eastwood, will do anything else. Sometimes actors just disappear. They—" She broke off at his look. "Sorry. What were you saying?" She thought, *He's not Adam, so there's no TV talk.*

To hide her embarrassment, Kelly pulled weeds while she

listened. Miguel asked questions about Pauly's plans for the future, but she didn't know the answers. She moved the dirt around the trees to stir up bugs, and Pauly's chickens followed her everywhere, pecking and pecking.

She and Miguel went out to dinner twice, always to big, loud places no farther away than Ottawa.

Each time, people she knew stopped and asked her questions about their animals. Ticks and worms were favorite topics.

Kelly suggested to Miguel that they go to a movie, but he said no. She suggested a small, quiet restaurant in Lawrence where they wouldn't know anyone. Miguel said no. She said they could go swimming at the lake, just the two of them. He said he'd rather go to a public pool.

"Where kids are screaming?" she'd asked.

"Where there will be a lifeguard and safety," he said.

They'd spent most of a week together, but for all their privacy, they could have been in an airport.

Neither was there any intimacy. At the double dinner, Miguel had made several hands-on moves toward her, so she'd thought he'd…well, try things. But he'd never so much as kissed her.

It wasn't easy to return from a date and have her mother waiting for her. Nella warned Kelly about men getting too "fresh."

"Save yourself," Nella said. "Hold back. As tempting as going the, uh, full way is, it's better to wait."

"I will wait," Kelly said. *And wait and wait and wait*, she thought.

Today, as she drove home, she dreaded seeing Miguel again. He was very nice, lovely to look at, but there just wasn't any passion in him. Not for her, anyway.

She slowed down to a crawl. The odd thing was, Miguel hadn't asked her out for the weekend.

Wasn't Saturday night supposed to be date night? Dinner, dancing, kisses in the moonlight?

But there'd been no invitation from Miguel.

Kelly pulled to the side of the road to wave a tractor to go past her. He was speeding along at fifteen miles an hour. But then, he probably had somewhere he wanted to go.

The motor died on her car, and as she started to turn the key, a movement caught her eye.

Through the trees she saw something yellow move. This morning Vera had put on her favorite yellow dress. Kelly watched, but didn't see it again.

Probably a coincidence, Kelly thought, then put her hand back on the key. But she didn't start the engine. Instead, she got out, made her way through the trees and saw the yellow again. It was a person but she couldn't see who. If it was Vera, where was she going?

Kelly stayed behind, only catching glimpses of the bright color now and then. When the figure stopped, she moved closer. There was a little mound of dirt and she stretched out on her stomach, then slithered forward to watch.

It was Vera, standing still in an area of wild undergrowth. It was like primal forest.

After a minute, Vera lifted some wilted tree branches off the ground and tossed them to the side. She bent down, then pulled. Like something out of a science fiction movie, a door rose out of the ground. Vera went down what seemed to be stairs, then pulled the door closed over her. She was gone.

It took Kelly a moment before she got up and went to the door. When she was close, she could see it, but not easily. The wood had so faded that it was the exact color of the forest.

Kelly wanted to pound on the door and demand to be told what Vera was doing down there. But she knew that demands didn't work with her sister. Order Vera to do/say/reveal something and she would attack. Kelly knew she'd end up apologizing for daring to intrude on Vera's private space. Never mind that Vera was probably involved in something dangerous.

Kelly turned away and headed back to her car. No, she wasn't foolhardy enough to tackle her big sister alone. But she knew someone who wasn't intimidated by Vera.

The last place Kelly wanted to go was Adam's house. *Which is absurd*, she told herself. They were going to be family, which meant they would spend lots of time together. *When he and Vera aren't traveling the world*, she thought. But then, considering how Kelly had come to feel about Adam, it was better that they would be gone.

Adam must have seen her drive in because he was standing at the door when she got out. "Kelly," he said in an odd way. It sounded as though she was the person he most wanted to see in the whole world. He stepped aside to let her in. "Are you okay?"

She hadn't realized she was shaking. She didn't want to look too deeply into *why* she was trembling. Being alone with Adam or catching Vera? "Vera," she managed to say.

Adam looked at her in concern, then opened a cabinet, poured a clear liquid into a tiny glass and held it out to her. "Drink this in one gulp."

She didn't think about what she was doing, just threw back the drink. Then she started coughing. "What was that?"

"Tequila." He ushered her to the big leather couch and sat her down. "Now tell me what happened. Has Vera or anyone else been hurt?"

"No." The drink was relaxing her. "I saw where Vera goes. When she was a kid, she used to disappear. No one could find her. Mom always wanted to call the police, but Dad said she'd be back." Kelly looked up at him. "I think Dad *knew.* He must have seen—"

Adam sat down beside her and took her hand in his. His big, warm hands. "Kelly," he said slowly, "tell me what you saw."

She told him everything in detail, and described where she was.

Adam leaned back against the sofa. "I think there was a house there. A tornado took it." He looked at her. "When I was a kid, the men used to say the place was haunted. I think that's why Dad never did anything with that piece of land. He just let it grow."

"They probably heard sounds from Vera. You have to see the place! It's flat. You can walk over it and not see it."

Adam was frowning. "By now that floor should have rotted. My guess is that Vera repaired the door and the roof."

"How? When?" Her head came up. "And *why?*"

Adam's jaw was clenched. "I don't think she did all that just for a place where she could read *Little Women* in peace, do you?"

"No," Kelly said. "You think...?"

"Yeah, I do." He got up, went to the phone in the corner and picked up the receiver.

"Are you going to call Vera?" Kelly sounded afraid. "She'll be really angry that I ratted on her. She'll—"

"If I thought she'd tell me the truth, yes, I'd call her. Before I confront her, I need more information." He dialed a number, listened to the ring, and it was picked up. "I need to talk to Coach. Tell him it's important. This is Adam Hatten."

He looked at Kelly. "This is the KU head coach we saw that, you know, night. If there's any protesting going on, he'll know about it. He keeps close tabs on his players to make sure they don't get into trouble. Hi, Coach!"

Adam listened. "Yeah... Yeah... Sure... Okay." He turned

his back to Kelly and lowered his voice. "No, I haven't decided yet. I told you that I'll tell you on Monday. I have a question. Have you heard of any anti-war protests going on this weekend?" He turned back to Kelly. "Or civil rights demonstrations?" He raised his eyebrows.

Kelly nodded. Vera protested any and all injustices.

Adam was quiet as he listened. "I see... Yes... By Monday at three. I promise. I do understand what an honor this is. And, Coach, thank you." He hung up.

"So?" Kelly asked.

"There's an anti-war demonstration in Lawrence tomorrow. Word is that people will start gathering at noon." He took a breath. "It's being said that the police are on alert. One brick thrown and some trigger-happy kid cop could fire. Then..." He didn't finish.

"What are we going to do?"

"*You* will stay here. I'll deal with this."

"How will you do it?" She batted her lashes, trying to look as young and helpless as possible. Let him think she would stay home and calmly wait while her sister left town to face bullets. Sure she would.

"Vera will probably leave midmorning and I plan to be at her hideout when she does. I want to catch her with her pants down, so to speak. I want her to have a placard in her hands so she can't make up some lie about what she's really doing."

Kelly's eyes widened. She'd always assumed Vera and Adam told each other the truth, confided in one another. But it looked like Adam knew Vera really well. When she didn't want someone to know what she was doing, she didn't tell. If they insisted, she lied. "A different version of reality" is what Vera called it.

"Okay," she said. "I guess I better go home."

"Stay and I'll grill some steaks. We can watch TV and—"

"No!" she said. "I mean, I should leave."

"Of course. You probably have a date. Robbie says you and Miguel are going strong."

"We're not—" she began, then stopped. "He's a great guy. We went to Pauly's orchard and Miguel loves the place. I think he's going to get his uncle to plant some fruit trees. When Pauly gets back, maybe he and Miguel can be friends."

"You can have dinner parties." Adam's tone was *very* unpleasant.

"I have to go."

"Maybe you shouldn't drive after that drink. I'll take you." He put his hand on her forearm.

She jerked away from him. "I can assure you that I'm fine." She just wanted to get out of his house, away from being alone with him.

He stepped back. "I'll call you tomorrow and tell you what happened."

"No need. I'm sure when Vera is caught, she'll explode. Mom won't need to turn on her gas burners. She can just use Vera's rage to heat the pots."

Adam laughed. "I've missed—" He didn't finish. "Okay, then I'll see you in church on Sunday."

She left his house and drove away quickly. As soon as she got home, she called Dr. Carl and said she wouldn't be at work until noon the next day.

"If you and Miguel want to spend all Saturday together, that's okay," he said.

"Uh, no, we don't need to." Kelly figured that, by noon, Vera would be in such a fury that Kelly didn't want to be around it. As for Miguel, she had no idea what he was doing and she didn't really care. She'd heard there was a fair three counties over. He'd probably want to go there. Anything rather than being alone with Kelly.

★ ★ ★

At nine the next morning Kelly was doing her best to walk silently through the forest. It was an impossible task. Just as she'd thought he would be, Adam was stretched out on his stomach on the little rise, the same place she'd been when she first saw Vera's hideout.

"Did you learn stealth from an elephant?" He didn't look up but kept his eyes on where the door was.

"A buffalo taught me. Nice guy. Too bad about what I had to do to him." She stretched out near him. "So what's going on?"

"I shouldn't tell you."

"And I should knock on the door and tell my sister she's being spied on. Family loyalty, that sort of thing."

Adam rolled to his side to face her. "Last night I went down into the place."

She turned toward him. "What did you see?"

He grimaced. "This wasn't an overnight deal. Vera had the roof that used to be the floor of a house replaced. I can't imagine how she did that in secret."

Kelly shrugged. "You know Vera."

"I'm beginning to think I don't. Why did she feel she had to keep this secret from *me*? There were things in there from when we were kids. I think she's been using this place for years but she left *me* out of it. She—"

Kelly cut him off. "Did you see any signs of what she's doing?"

Adam turned onto his back. "Oh, yeah. I was right. The place looks like it's set up for underground rebels fighting a war. She has a big table where she paints posters. Anti-war slogans are everywhere." He shook his head. "She's done a lot to the place. She stole electricity from my fences. There's a big old couch. It's comfortable for her to spend the weekends there."

Kelly could tell that he was angry but he was also sad. He and Vera were meant to spend their lives together, but she'd kept this huge secret from him for years.

"What's your plan?"

"She arrived about twenty minutes ago. She was as loud as you, but then, she feels secure that her secret is safe. I was careful to leave no sign that I'd seen her den."

"You want to surprise her." Kelly was torn about protecting her sister. But protection from what? Outside danger or Vera's right to privacy? "Mom will be upset when she finds out about this."

Adam stood up. "I don't plan for anyone to know. I'm going to bulldoze this place. It's a hazard. Half a dozen cows walk across it and they could fall in. Or riders on horseback." He looked at her. "I guess it would be useless to tell you to stay here."

"A total waste of breath."

He gave a half smile. "Okay, then, but let me go first."

"Of course, master."

He gave a snort and shook his head. "Just be quiet. I'll do the talking." She pantomimed locking her lips and throwing away the key.

They went to the door, standing side by side, looking down at it. "As soon as I open the door, she'll see the light, so we need to move quickly."

Kelly nodded and they both took a breath. Adam threw open the door and practically leaped down the stairs. She was half a step behind him.

At the bottom, they stopped.

Vera and Miguel were on the big couch. They were both naked, Vera on top. Their eyes were closed in the ecstasy of sex. They were going at each other hard, their skin slapping together so it echoed through the underground room.

Adam and Kelly were too shocked to move.

Vera opened her eyes and saw them. She was like a deer in headlights and froze. "I'm…" she whispered, but seemed unable to say anything else.

Miguel, his hands on Vera's bare hips, rolled his head back to see what she was looking at. Given their circumstances, it was hard to believe, but his lips curved into a smile. He was glad they'd been discovered.

Vera grabbed her shirt off the floor and held it over her naked breasts. "Adam, I—" She didn't finish because he went up the stairs in two bounds.

Kelly stood there, her eyes on Miguel. So now she knew why he'd not made a pass at her. But he had on the double date. Looked like that display had been for Vera. "I think you two should get dressed," she said, then ran up the stairs after Adam.

Adam was getting into his truck.

"Move over," Kelly said. "You are *not* going to drive."

He didn't argue but slid across the wide seat, then stared out the window as though he weren't quite alive.

When she drove toward his house, he said, "I can't see Robbie right now."

Kelly turned the truck around, then headed north. The apartment would be the best place for him.

Neither said a word during the drive. When she pulled into the underground garage, she turned off the engine and leaned back in the seat. For minutes, they didn't move, just stared at the concrete block wall.

Finally, Kelly got out of the truck, went around and opened Adam's door. "I have to figure it all out," he said softly. "Africa, everything."

"I know you do. Come on and I'll go up with you." She

didn't mention it, but she didn't know how she was going to get home. Should she call and ask someone to come and get her? Vera, maybe? She didn't laugh at her silent joke.

Adam got out of the truck like he was an old man. She couldn't imagine what a blow this was to him. How could Vera *do* this? And Miguel?

Kelly directed him to the elevator and they went up. He got his key out but couldn't seem to get it into the lock. She took it from him and opened the door.

She told herself she should leave, then do what she must to get herself home. But Adam just stood there. She did a push-pull to get him to the beautiful white couch, then made him sit down. "I'll make you something to drink and..." She had no idea what to do in a case like this.

In the kitchen, she opened the refrigerator. It was fully stocked with beer and barbecue.

There were vegetables in the bottom. It looked like Adam had been telling the truth about spending weekends there.

All while Vera had been with Miguel. If Vera and Miguel were together, why did she allow her sister to go out with him? Vera must have known that Kelly was going on a fake date.

How could Vera do that to me? Kelly thought. Her sister had been so sympathetic about Pauly dumping her, but then Vera had let Kelly go out with a man Vera had laid claim to.

And she still had Adam. Vera had *two* men!

Kelly looked around the pretty kitchen, remembering the days she'd spent there with Adam. It was the most perfect time of her life.

But she'd given it up for Vera. Out of love and respect for her sister, Kelly had left before anything serious could happen. And all the while Vera had been banging Miguel.

Kelly had a glass in her hand. It matched the beauty of the apartment. A work of art with delicate etching around the lip. She didn't realize she was holding it tight until the fragile glass broke in her hand. She just stood there, staring at the broken pieces. Blood ran down her arm but she didn't move.

She had no idea she was sinking down until Adam grabbed her and pulled her up. He moved her to the sink and ran cold water over the cut.

"Why didn't you call out?" he asked. "It's a wonder I heard the glass break."

Kelly didn't say anything while he cleaned the wound and declared it wouldn't need stitches. He dried her hand, got a bandage from a drawer and taped it.

When he finished, he put his hand under her chin to lift her head. "I know you're angry, but it's going to be okay. Don't be mad at Vera."

She pulled away from him. "I'm not."

"I've known you too long not to know when you're furious. Quite often, it's directed at me." When she didn't smile, he paused. "You can talk to me. Better me than raging at your sister. She'll tear you apart and—"

"I'm not angry at Vera. I'm angry at *me*. I'm jealous. Just old-fashioned *jealous*. What's so great about Vera that the two most eligible men in Franklin County are mad about her? Sex, sex, sex. She gets lots of it. But I get Pauly and there was nothing. Of course, there was the offer for the back seat of a Buick and I can't forget a near rape by Tony Pullman. But why doesn't a decent man want *me*?"

Adam stood in silence, staring at her.

"Right," Kelly said. "It's better that you don't tell me the truth, that I'm too tomboy, or too..." She waved her hand. "Who wants a girl ducks like?" Adam was still silent. "I better go." But he caught her arm. When she looked at him, he wore an expression she'd never seen before. She took a step backward.

"You think you aren't desirable? I should get a Medal of Honor for keeping my hands off you."

She stopped moving. "But you never—"

"No, I didn't, but I'm going to."

Kelly's eyes widened. "Adam—" He pulled her into his arms and kissed her. Deeply, passionately kissed her.

Between masses of schoolwork and a boyfriend who never showed much interest in her physically, his kiss was a new experience. A glorious, wonderful experience.

Adam held her at arm's length. "Stay here or go. But know that if you stay, you're going to get that up-against-the-wall you're so curious about."

Kelly's eyebrows rose. "My car isn't here."

"I can take you—"

"It looks like I'm staying."

One moment they were in the kitchen and the next her back was against the dining room wall. She had no idea how her jeans came off but they did. They fell to her ankles. She gave a little kick but they stayed on, like a rope binding her feet.

Adam put his foot over them and lifted her. Her legs went around his waist, his bare waist. He entered her with the pent-up force of months of longing.

Kelly gave a little noise of shock.

"Okay?" he asked.

"Oh, yes. Yes, yes, yes."

Minutes later she felt his release, but not her own. She just felt that she wanted *more*.

Adam knew. He made a sweep of whatever was on top of the dining table and set her down on the edge.

"Uh-oh," she said as things clattered to the floor.

Adam didn't comment, as he was too busy removing her shirt. His mouth was on her breasts, his tongue on her skin.

After the dining table, he carried her to the big bed, and it was there that Kelly felt the release that Adam had.

He rolled off her and they lay side by side.

"I had no idea." She looked at him. "This is new to me. Now what happens?"

"We shower, then we eat so I have the energy to do it all over again."

Kelly jumped out of bed. "Let's go!"

He heard her turn on the shower. "I have unleashed a monster," he said with a smile.

That evening Adam got around to calling his little brother. Robbie picked up on the sixth ring. There was music in the background.

Immediately, Robbie started to defend himself. "It's just a few friends. It's not a real party. We won't break anything or—"

"It's okay," Adam said. "It's your house, too."

"Are you drunk? Or did you drop some acid?"

"Sort of," Adam said.

"What's going on? Vera's called about fifty times and Miguel came by. He said he has to talk to you. Life or death. He looked bad. Has something happened?"

"Yes. Lots of things. What kind of truck does Miguel drive?"

"Silver Chevy. Why?"

"Dent in the back?"

"Yeah. He said Gabby hit it with the tractor. On purpose. Forget that. What's going on with you three?"

"Four," Adam said. "There are now four of us."

"You and Vera, Miguel and Gabby?"

"No, not Gabby." Turning, he saw Kelly. She'd put on a

black negligee. It was semitransparent and there was a tiny red bow between her breasts. "I have to go. Something's come up."

At the double entendre, Kelly giggled.

"That's a woman!" Robbie said. "Is Vera there with you?"

"Yes. No. Keep the music down, light booze, no drugs, and I better not get a call that you're in jail. I'm going to be too busy to bail you out. I'll see you…whenever."

"Wait! What about—?" But Adam had hung up. *If it isn't Vera with him, who is it?* Robbie shrugged and went back to what was becoming a large, loud party.

It wasn't until Sunday afternoon that Kelly and Adam actually talked seriously. They were lying in bed, side by side.

"What happens now?" she asked.

"I thought we answered that question, but if you need a reminder, I'm happy to oblige." He rolled toward her.

Kelly put her hand up. "I mean, will you and Vera get back together?" He moved to his back and said nothing. "I understand. I was just rebound sex. It's always been you and Vera."

"Don't be ridiculous," he said. "Vera and I are done. And you and I are…" He waved his hand as though it didn't matter. "I have something to tell you. Remember that double date from hell?"

"The one where you were angry at Miguel?"

"The one where the bastard kept touching you. What were you thinking wearing a dress like that? He was all over you."

"All that stuff about Miguel being able to afford a house was about *me*?"

"Yes," Adam said. "It was."

"Oh."

"But anyway, remember when you and I were in the back and I was begging you not to be angry at me and you were telling me to go rot?"

"That's not how I remember it, but I do know what you're talking about."

"The man who stopped us is the head coach at KU. He offered me a full-time coaching job. It starts in the fall."

"But you're going to Africa and…" Kelly trailed off. A vision of Vera and Miguel naked came to her. "Have your plans changed?" she whispered.

"I didn't realize it, but they changed as soon as I saw Robbie. He needs a home. He needs supervision."

"Of course he does."

He turned to look at her. "Kelly, I know this is sudden and maybe I'm too quick in asking, but you and I… I mean, maybe we could become an 'us.' You know, dating, that sort of thing. Take your time thinking about it but—"

"Yes."

"You're sure?"

"Absolutely, positively, completely sure."

He smiled. "Maybe with time you'll get over your doubts and—"

"Do shut up," she said as she kissed him.

CHAPTER THIRTEEN

One month later

KELLY WAS CLIPPING THE WINGS OF A sun conure parrot. The poor thing had flown at a window and nearly broken its beak. If it had escaped, it would have died on the first cold Kansas day.

She clipped carefully. Too long and it was useless, too short and the wings would bleed and maybe not heal. The owners, a mother and daughter, were watching her with a nerve-racking intensity. The bird was a much-loved pet.

"There!" Kelly let the bird jump onto the girl's hand. The child's smile was worth it all. The pretty little bird nuzzled his head against the girl's cheek.

"Thank you," the mother said, and they left.

Kelly washed her hands and cleaned up the room. *Not long now*, she thought. In just six more weeks she and Adam would be married and moving into his house and the apartment in Kansas City. They'd decided to keep that place their secret, just as his parents had. Robbie knew about it but he had no interest. He was leaving for college soon and he was looking forward to it. His romance with Lisa was still going strong and they were vowing to get married soon. Adam was trying to get his little brother to wait until he graduated, but no one believed they'd hold out that long.

After that first weekend Kelly and Adam had spent together, she'd been sick with worry about how everyone, especially her mother, was going to take the news.

She didn't have to worry. The day after they'd been discovered together, Vera and Miguel sat down with Nella, Forey and Rafe, and told them the truth. Later, Nella and Forey told Kelly the story in such detail it was almost as though she'd been there.

First of all, Vera said she and Miguel had been in love since they were children. "What about Adam?" Nella asked her daughter.

"I love him, too."

Nella's eyes had widened.

"No!" Vera said. "Not like that. Adam and I..." She waved her hand. Vera wasn't a person who felt a need to confess her innermost feelings. "Let's just say that I choose Miguel and leave it at that."

"The wedding?" Forey had hope in her voice.

"No wedding," Vera said. "Sorry."

"You're still going away?" Nella asked.

"Yes. To Africa, Afghanistan, wherever the world leads us." Vera stood up. "Now that that's settled, I need to go to work."

"But what about Adam?" Nella asked. "Have you told him that you're leaving him?" She sounded close to tears.

For the first time, Vera looked a bit guilty. "He knows about Miguel and me, but no, he and I haven't talked about things yet."

Through all of this, Miguel didn't say a word. He just sat there with his head hanging low and Rafe's eyes seemed to burn into his scalp.

"I tell you," Nella told Kelly later, "it's a wonder that boy's hair didn't catch on fire."

"Because of Gabby," Kelly said.

"Right. Poor Gabrielle," Forey said. "Miguel led her on. He let her believe they were going to get married. He even hinted that he was buying her an engagement ring. And there he was, in love with Vera. That poor girl. She's thinking of going back to her parents in Mexico."

"And Rafe," Nella said. "He is *not* happy with Miguel."

The turmoil caused by Vera and Miguel was such that Kelly and Adam kept quiet. Kelly didn't want to say anything for fear people would blame her for the breakup. Not Adam but *her*. The woman was *always* blamed. Like the man was an innocent victim.

Adam had a baser reason for keeping things quiet. "I want both of them to drown in guilt. I was worried about Vera being hurt in one of her protests, but she was in bed with someone else."

"She's still in danger," Kelly said.

"No longer my problem." Adam walked away. He was more angry than he'd admit.

They spent a second weekend in the apartment but Kelly didn't have as much fun as the first time. "I don't like sneaking and hiding," she said. "Unless you're ashamed of me. Is that it? I'm your interim girl? Something to occupy you until you find a replacement for Vera?"

Adam laughed at that. "Interim Girl? Sounds like a comic book character." He began kissing her neck and Kelly forgot about whatever she'd been saying.

The next Friday morning everything came to a head in a very public way. Kelly had gone with her mother and Forey to deliver boxes of pies and muffins to Mr. Gresham. They'd entered by the back door.

Vera, who was working hard to avoid the sad-eyed looks from her mother, had stopped for coffee.

Miguel and Rafe entered minutes after Vera, and Adam and Robbie came in through the side door.

The restaurant was packed with people, all of whom knew each other. And they all thought Vera and Adam were still together.

It was the first time Adam had seen Miguel since the day in the underground room. The three of them looked at each other across the restaurant.

Kelly set down her box of apple muffins and moved closer to Adam. If he was going to hit Miguel, she wanted to be ready to stop him.

Vera looked defiant; Miguel seemed to be ashamed; Adam turned red with anger.

The people of Mason sensed that something was going on and they froze, food on the way to their mouths.

Adam turned to Kelly. "I think we need to end this."

"Adam! No!" She grabbed his forearm.

But Adam didn't go after Miguel. To Kelly's shock, Adam swept her into his arms and kissed her. Miguel looked at Vera, and in the next second, they, too, were kissing.

There had to be a new word for the silence in the restaurant. If they'd been on the moon it couldn't have been quieter. Outer space was a rock concert compared to the restaurant.

It was Mr. Gresham who broke it. "So now I'm running a kissing parlor?" he said loudly. "Nobody does any work?"

The two couples broke apart. "We switched," Adam said to their audience. He was holding Kelly's hand tightly. "Any questions, ask Vera. She's good at making up stories." He led Kelly outside to the parking lot. "Happy now?" he said.

She figured she should say something about the way he'd done things, but the truth was, she didn't really care. She was grinning. "I have to go to work." She got into her Jeep. "You need to tell people about your new job." She glanced at the door to the restaurant. Her mother and Forey were coming out. "And you have to answer bunches and heaps of questions. See ya!" She didn't give him time to reply but drove off quickly.

That afternoon, for the first time, Adam showed up at the clinic. He was frowning. "It was a day of questions. Part two of the Spanish Inquisition. Nella and Forey grilled me, stuffed me with food, then interrogated me some more. The only thing missing was a spotlight in my face and guns on their hips."

"Oh?" Kelly was giving a litter of puppies their shots. "Were conclusions reached?" When he didn't answer, she looked at him.

"Yeah," he said softly. "They were."

It was a week later that he asked her to marry him. "I know it seems soon but we've known each other all our lives and—"

"Yes," she said. No other words were needed. Her mother and Forey were going to get the autumn wedding they'd dreamed of.

In the following weeks, Adam and Kelly had twice sneaked off to the apartment together.

"I'll have to get a dress." She was looking at the ring Adam had given her. It was unlike the one Mrs. Carl had bought. The diamonds were set in a way that they didn't snag on things. She could wear it even while she was working.

"About that." Adam got out of bed and returned with a large box.

"Is that the dress we chose for Vera?" She couldn't keep the disappointment out of her voice.

"I thought you liked it." He opened the box.

When she saw the gossamer-thin gown that she'd liked so much, her eyes filled with tears. "You bought it for me?"

He smiled smugly.

"But you've *seen* it!"

"I've seen a lot of things of yours but I still love them."

Smiling and crying, she opened her arms to him.

CHAPTER FOURTEEN

MIGUEL WAS HOLDING A POST IN THE hole he'd dug and pushing dirt in with his foot. The job needed two people, but since Vera and he had openly become a couple, he'd tried to not ask for anything from anyone. There were too many questions. "When did you two…? What did Adam say? How's Adam handling all this?" It always seemed to be about Adam Hatten.

He'd tried to talk to Vera about how he felt, but she wouldn't listen. "It is what it is. You can't feel guilty because you do or don't love someone."

"It's a matter of ruining lives. Gabby—"

"So marry her!" Vera snapped. "Marry her, have a dozen kids, live in a two-bedroom house on Rafe's ranch and lead the most normal life there ever was. It's your choice."

Miguel never had an answer about what he wanted. All he was sure of was that he and Vera had loved each other since they were kids. Her adventurous spirit and his down-to-earth personality meshed. He imagined that their life would be Vera getting into trouble and him rescuing her.

Only once had he tried to talk to her about the reality of

their future. Would they have children? A home? Miguel had always liked planting things and watching them grow.

Vera's answer had been puzzlement. "How can we haul a pack of kids around the world?" He didn't want an argument, so his reply had been kisses.

As he held a level to the fence post, he asked himself what he really did want in life. When Rafe said hello, Miguel jumped. "I didn't hear you drive up."

Rafe nodded toward the horse tied under a tree. "Since you're so good at running off, I thought I'd come quietly." He spoke in Spanish. He took the level and held it against the post while Miguel filled the hole. "Gabby is going back to her parents."

"I know." Miguel's voice was soft.

"Are you sure about you and Vera?"

"I love her. Like breathing. And it's been that way since we were kids."

"Yeah, I understand that. But she plans to go to Africa."

"And I'm going with her." Miguel sounded defiant.

"After you got back from Vietnam, you said you never wanted to leave this country again. You said Maine was too far away for you."

"Love changes a person."

"Does it?" Rafe asked. "Does it change your entire personality? Forey and I always wanted the same things. Just a quiet life in the country. I don't think our marriage would have lasted if one of us suddenly decided to move to another country that has a different language, a different everything. Adam said he didn't even have indoor plumbing in Africa. He said—"

Miguel stood up straight, his face angry. "The days of having to hear about the glory that is Adam Hatten are over. I'm done with that."

"And you won the prize?" Rafe said. "You won *his* girl? Did Vera ever really want to be Mrs. Adam Hatten? Or was he her ride to Africa? Did she just change drivers?"

"I'm not going to listen to any more of this." Miguel's fists were clenched at his sides.

Rafe stepped back. "You're like a son to me and I just want you to think about things. I'll back you in whatever you decide. I'll..." With his shoulders drooping like a man who had failed, he went to his horse and rode away.

Miguel worked until long after sundown, then went back to the house. It wasn't a pleasant place. Rafe looked like he'd aged twenty years. Gabby rarely raised her head. She put food on the table, then sat down to eat without looking at anyone.

Forey was the only one who was happy. When she was there, she talked about nothing but the wedding. "You should see Kelly's dress! It looks like it was woven by hummingbirds."

"They're aggressive little beasts," Rafe said. "Ever get hit by one of those beaks? They can pierce you."

Forey ignored him. "Nella and I tried to get Kelly to choose the cake but she said she wanted animals on it. Lions and giraffes and elephants. Can you imagine? On a wedding cake?"

"Maybe *she* should go to Africa," Gabby said, then jumped up so quickly that her chair fell over. She ran from the room.

Forey and Rafe looked at Miguel as though he was supposed to fix the girl's unhappiness.

But what could he do? Tell Gabby he was sorry he'd led her on? What he'd really done was not make it clear that there was nothing between them and never would be. If he was honest with himself, he'd admit that he'd *liked* being pursued. At the time, the woman he loved had been planning to marry someone who wasn't right for her. It was good to feel that someone wanted him.

Miguel tried to put logic into all of it. Adam and Vera were too much alike. Both of them were bosses.

Adam and Kelly were a much better match. As long as she had her animals and probably a few kids, she would be happy to leave everything else to Adam.

Unlike Vera, who wanted to change the world.

And I will be the follower, Miguel thought.

He'd been spending a lot of time at Paul's fruit farm. The man who'd been taking care of it wasn't doing a good job. Weeks ago, Miguel had sent a postcard to Paul asking if it would be all right if he spent some time there.

That had started a correspondence between them. Paul was traveling with some like-minded young men and said he was learning a lot. He'd be returning with boxes of cuttings and seeds.

Since Miguel wanted to be anywhere except his uncle Rafe's place, he began to prepare some beds for the new arrivals.

Miguel tried not to think about the fact that he wouldn't be there to see the trees planted. Vera wanted to leave the country the day after Kelly's wedding.

He thought about the most recent argument he and Vera had had.

"At last, I'll get to do what I've wanted to do for my whole life," Vera had said. "No more being chained down by land and cows and..." She waved her hand. "All things to do with a *farm*."

She'd been wildly excited that she had a job with Joe Harding. "He wants you and me to go to Tibet with him." Vera's eyes were like headlamps. "Isn't that wonderful?"

"Yeah, great," Miguel said.

"*What* is wrong with you?" Vera had nearly yelled. "I thought this was what you wanted to do. You've been involved in the protests and you said you wanted to do it on a global scale. But now you seem reluctant."

They were in the cellar. It wasn't the same now that outsiders knew about it, but it was the only place they had. He turned to her. "What if I said I don't want to live in Africa? That I don't want to leave Kansas?"

"Is that what you *are* saying?"

"If Kelly and Adam marry, they'll live in his house and your mother will be alone. Paul isn't going to run your family's farm, so what if you and I move in there instead? I have some ideas about farming that Uncle Rafe says are too progressive."

"Is that what you want to do?" She was whispering.

"I'm thinking about it. Would it be too horrible to stay here?" He took her hands in his. "To have children and see them grow up?"

"No," she said softly. "I guess it wouldn't be."

"I'll go with you wherever you want. I can't lose you again." He turned away. "I need to go. I have to—" He couldn't think of anything he had to do except *think*. He needed to put everything together and sort it out. What to do with his life? He didn't like Rafe being so upset with him. Didn't like feeling that he'd lied to Gabrielle, that he'd toyed with her for his own amusement. He didn't like how he'd misled Kelly.

Miguel thought he was becoming someone who wasn't *him*.

For the next week and a half he avoided Vera. She called, even stopped by the house, but he stayed away from her. He worked from before daylight until long after. He dug holes at Paul's place and even spent a couple of nights sleeping in his shed. It seemed that Paul had had the same idea because he'd fixed it up with a cot and a hot plate.

Guess Paul needed a place to think about his problems with Kelly, Miguel thought.

After days of being a ghost to everyone, Miguel knew he

needed to go home. He had to face the guilt that was being piled on him. Face all the misery he was causing.

But he missed Vera. He needed to talk to her. Maybe they could go to a protest and that would put life back into him.

Her car wasn't in the driveway and neither was Forey's. Miguel gave a sigh of relief at that. Being bombarded with questions like what shade of pink would be best for Kelly and Adam's wedding was not something he could deal with.

The front door was open. As always at the Exton house, the smell was heavenly.

"Miguel!" Nella said. "How good to see you."

"You look happy. Figure out the flowers for Kelly's wedding?" He was teasing.

Nella took a deep breath and pointed out the window. "There. *That's* why I'm happy."

There was an old oil barrel in the yard and it was smoldering. It looked like they'd burned something. "Cleaning up?"

"Not *me*. Vera."

He didn't understand. "You got her to clean her room?"

"No." Nella seemed to be bursting with pride. "*You* did. You made Vera burn it all."

He looked at her. "What did she burn?"

"This morning Vera burned everything. Books, maps, even letters. She said, 'It looks like I'm not going anywhere.'"

Miguel was staring at Nella in astonishment.

"I said, 'Do you love Miguel that much?' She said that yes, she did. Oh, Miguel, you *did* it. My daughter is going to stay here. She isn't going to run off to China or wherever. She's staying *here*. In Kansas. Oh, but it will be perfect. Of course you two will live here with me. And when you have children, we can add on to the house. We'll build a mother-in-law apartment for me so I won't interfere in your lives. But I'll still be here to babysit. I hope my grandchildren have your cheekbones. And I hope none of them get Vera's hair. It has always been impossible to manage. I told her—" Nella stopped and looked at Miguel. "Are you all right?"

"Did you say those things to her?"

"I've been saying all this for her whole life. She just wouldn't listen to reason. Not until *you*. You have made her see sense. It was so smart of you to give her a choice between you or... or the world."

"And she chose me," Miguel whispered. "Where is she?"

"Work, I guess. I told her she needed to start thinking about linens. She'll need new ones for the wedding."

"Linens? Wedding?"

"You don't seem at all right. I thought you'd be happy about this, especially since you're the one who got her to give up her ridiculous ideas. Did you know that she'd arranged a job in...in... I don't know where. Someplace I'd never heard of."

"Tibet."

"Yes! That's it. If you ask me, you dodged a bullet on that. Who wants to go someplace no one has heard of before?"

"Vera does," Miguel said softly. "It's her dream. Her life."

"Not anymore," Nella said. "She's given that up. Of course Kelly will be Vera's maid of honor. Who will be your best man at your wedding?"

But Miguel didn't answer. He was already out the door.

CHAPTER FIFTEEN

VERA WENT TO THE BREAK ROOM AND poured herself a cup of coffee. Her hands were shaking so badly that she could hardly hold the cup.

I'm doing the right thing, she told herself. She couldn't leave her mother alone. Kelly would go to Adam's, so Nella would be alone.

Vera tried to calm herself. Everyone knew that love was the most important thing in the world.

And with Miguel she had that love. Deep love. She should be grateful. She should...

She took a breath. *Should* seemed to be the number one word in her life right now.

When she went back into her office, Hank said, "Some guy called and left a message for you. I don't know why he called *me*. He—"

"Who was it?"

"Mike somebody."

"Mike? You meant Miguel?"

"Yeah. That's it. He said to meet him at three p.m. and that you'd know where."

Vera looked at her watch. If she left now, she could be there at two thirty. She and Miguel really needed to talk. She'd tell him she was staying. Then he'd hold her and make her know she'd made the right decision.

By the time she got to the cellar, she was smiling. Her plan to travel the world had been a fantasy. She had romanticized it. The truth was that all she knew and loved was here and that's where she should stay.

The door over the cellar was closed. She threw it open and ran down the stairs. What she saw was déjà vu, only from a different perspective.

On the big couch Miguel and Gabrielle were both naked. Having sex.

Miguel didn't look up when Vera pounded down the stairs. But Gabby did. The look of triumph in her eyes was like a soldier who had just won the war. She smiled at Vera, then picked up Miguel's hand and put it on her large breast.

Vera leaped up the stairs, then ran all the way home. She packed a single suitcase, kissed her mother's cheek and said, "Tell Kelly goodbye for me." Vera left the house before Nella could say a word.

Adam answered the phone at his house and listened. When Kelly came into the room, he held out the receiver to her. "It's your mother and I can't understand what she's saying, but something bad has happened."

"Tell her I'll be there in minutes."

Adam drove her there.

Nella was outside, waiting for them. She fell onto Kelly, crying hard. She was incoherent. Forey was standing in the doorway.

"What happened?" Adam asked.

"Miguel," Forey said. "He…"

"What?"

"He was in bed with Gabby and Vera saw them." Forey lowered her voice. "Vera packed a bag and left. Nella said she's gone to Thailand."

"Tibet," Adam said. "Has anyone talked to Miguel?"

"No. He's disappeared. Gabby is…" Forey looked up. "She's very happy."

"I bet she is."

"I don't understand this," Forey said. "Miguel never liked Gabby."

He turned to see Kelly and her mother. Nella was still crying. She left her daughter and went to Forey, and they went into the house.

"You heard?" Adam asked Kelly.

"Enough. He gave her freedom," Kelly said. "He let her go." There were tears running down her cheeks. "I think we just saw what true love really means."

"Poor Vera," Adam said.

"And poor, poor Miguel," Kelly added. They went into the house together.

CHAPTER SIXTEEN

Mason, Kansas
1996

KELLY SENT VERA AN EMAIL.

> Miguel is in a bad way. He needs you. Come home
> immediately.

Others might be in awe of her famous sister, but Kelly
wasn't. Eighteen months ago, something bad had happened to
Miguel and his beloved daughter, Caitlyn, but no one knew
what.

Whatever the reason, Caitlyn had abruptly broken up with
Adam and Kelly's oldest child, Jared.

He'd begged Cait to tell him why but she refused to even
talk to him, much less see him. The next morning Caitlyn
was on a plane to Florida to stay with her mother, Gabrielle.
When she returned a year later, she was a different person:
subdued and quiet. She didn't go out much.

Since she returned, her home—the old clinic, as people in
Mason called it—had become as quiet as a monastery. Miguel,
Paul, Seth and Caitlyn ran their business, Heritage Harvests,
from the building that used to be the vet office.

Miguel wined and dined clients and traveled when necessary, while Paul and Seth stayed in Kansas and took care of the trees. They'd always called Caitlyn their "satellite hub." From an early age she'd coordinated everyone. She knew what Seth was doing in the office, what Paul was doing with the trees and where her dad was as he sold their products.

Cait had gone to KU in Lawrence, often driving in with Adam. He'd been made head coach a few years back and he looked after anything Cait needed. That she and his son Jared had paired off in elementary school had been a happy bonus.

As Jared and Cait got older, Kelly said, "Now I understand why Mom was so fierce in wanting grandchildren. So do I!"

"They won't have fur," Adam had said seriously.

"But they *will* crawl," she'd answered, and they'd laughed.

All their happiness and plans for the future had ended when Cait broke up with Jared. He was a grown man but he came home crying and collapsed in his mother's arms.

"Why?" was all he could say. "Why, why, why?" He never got an answer.

Kelly had interrogated Paul. "You owe me," she'd said. "You led me on for years and didn't tell me you were gay."

Pauly sighed. He'd explained it all many times. "I didn't *know.*"

"Yes, yes. You didn't know for sure until you went off to Ireland with a bunch of guys. I get it. But you still owe me. What happened to Caitlyn?"

"By all that's holy, I have no idea. Only she and Miguel know and they're not telling."

"It was something bad," Kelly said. "I know she and Jared were in love but now she'll hardly speak to him. He's too young to have his heart broken."

"I agree," Pauly said. "And I've asked. Seth has asked, but we get no answer."

"What's she going to do?"

"She does her work but there's no heart in it. Seth and I offered to send her to Europe for the summer. We thought a change of scenery would help. Know what she said?"

"I can't imagine."

"That it was no use. She couldn't change her life."

"Her *life!*" Kelly said. "That's dramatic."

"Personally, I'd like some drama. It might end the misery that has descended over our happy home. Cait and Miguel go off together for hours, days even. Sometimes they disappear and we don't know where they are. If Mom were still alive, Cait would talk to her."

When Mrs. Carl had been told that her only child was gay, she'd been surprisingly understanding. If she was upset, she kept it to herself. However, when Paul told her that Gabby was pregnant from one time with Miguel, Mrs. Carl had stepped in. With the force of a Kansas tornado, Mrs. Carl took over. She told her son—didn't ask—that Miguel was going to become a partner in Pauly's business. Then she hired a lawyer to arrange for Miguel to get full custody of the baby. But Gabby didn't fight them. She just wanted enough money to start a new life without the burden of being a single mother. In the end, Gabby went to Florida and baby Caitlyn stayed in Mason with her father. And Mrs. Carl.

There was never a more doting, adoring honorary grandmother. Everyone in Mason thought Forey would be jealous, but she said, "Love is multiplied, not divided."

When Kelly's letter reached Vera, telling what was happening, Vera wrote back, saying, "I bet she read that on a greeting card. I'd put money on it that Forey is jealous as all hell. But at least Miguel got what he wanted."

All these years later, Vera was still angry, still bitter over Miguel being with Gabby. Kelly had written her theory—

that Miguel had done it to give Vera her freedom—but she didn't believe it.

Or maybe Vera didn't want to believe it. Maybe she needed the tie between her and Miguel broken.

Whatever had been done and why, the result of Vera's years of nonstop traveling was that she had become a famous reporter. She went anywhere on any assignment. More than once she'd dressed as a man and infiltrated sites forbidden to women.

She wrote about it all with great feeling. Not just cut-and-dried news but the tears and laughter of those involved.

For years Vera had worked with the seasoned news reporter Joe Harding. He taught her everything she knew.

Eight years ago he'd stepped on a land mine. He heard the click and knew what was going to happen. He looked at Vera. "I love you, kid," he said before he died in the violent explosion. The book Vera wrote about Joe won her a Pulitzer Prize.

Vera had returned to Mason only once, for Nella's funeral. Even then, she'd only agreed if Kelly swore that Miguel wouldn't be there.

Kelly didn't know if Vera hadn't forgiven him or if she still loved him so much that she might be tempted to stay in Kansas. Truthfully, Kelly didn't think her sister knew, either.

So much had changed since Vera left. Miguel's life was his daughter and selling organic fruit to groceries across the US. He had expanded the business greatly. Paul had fallen in love with Seth Murray and wanted to stay home with him, so Miguel did the traveling.

When Caitlyn was four, Dr. Carl died after being kicked by a horse that was in pain. Adam then built Kelly her own veterinary clinic on Hatten land.

Paul had inherited Dr. Carl's place, and he remodeled the old clinic to use for his business.

It seemed natural that the people involved in Heritage Harvests would live together. Paul and Seth moved into the house. They bought a cute little cottage, moved it onto the property, and Mrs. Carl lived there. For a couple of years, Miguel and Caitlyn had lived in a trailer on the land. When an old schoolhouse came up for sale, Miguel bought it, moved it onto the property and made it into a home.

Caitlyn grew up surrounded by four loving adults, plus Forey and Rafe, who visited often.

But everything was different now. The happiness, the joy, even the love, seemed to have vanished.

And no one knew why.

Kelly told Adam, "If something isn't done to fix this, it's going to get worse."

"It's not our business," he said.

Kelly glared at him.

"My mistake. What can we do?" he asked.

"*We* can do nothing. Vera is going to fix this since it's *her* fault."

"How is—?" he began, then stopped. "Oh. Right. She loved Miguel, but he didn't want to leave. He didn't want to hold her down, so he…"

"Right. Went to bed with Gabby and knocked her up. *All Vera's fault!*"

"Think your famous sister will see it that way and come home?"

"If she doesn't, I'll go get her. Wherever she is."

Adam tried to hide his smile. He'd learned that for all his wife's cuteness, with her big blue eyes, she was made of steel. If Vera knew what was good for her, she'd do what her little sister wanted. "Will she stay in our guest room?"

"She's going to have the whole house."

"Oh?" Adam's eyes widened in surprise. "And where are we going?"

"You and I are going on a trip."

"What about the clinic?"

"I have someone to take over for me and Caitlyn is going to help him."

"Is this animal therapy?"

"Sort of. Do you want to go somewhere hot or cold?"

"Galápagos is hot, right?"

Kelly grinned. Rampant wildlife. He knew the way to her heart.

CHAPTER SEVENTEEN

AS CAITLYN FINISHED PACKING HER SUIT-case, she looked around the hotel room to see if she'd missed anything. She'd spent the last three days in Lincoln, Nebraska, going to elementary schools to talk about organic foods. She'd shown them fruit from the Heritage Harvests orchards and from the grocery store.

She held up her family's small, asymmetrical apples and pears. "These are what your grandparents ate," she told the students. Then she showed the big, shiny ones from the grocery store. "And these are what you buy." Of course she had to deal with the fact that the kids liked the look of the big, perfect apples better than the ones Caitlyn had brought with her.

She understood because she had the opposite experience. She'd grown up surrounded by gnarly trees hanging with delicious fruits. Mrs. Carl did the grocery shopping and the cooking, so she didn't know that what she ate was different.

But one day her honorary uncles, Pauly and Seth, took her to a city grocery.

In the fruit section, Caitlyn started screaming in fear. It took a while to calm her down and find out what she was so upset about. She'd seen the big red grocery-store apples in a Disney movie. The evil witch poisoned people with them. Caitlyn thought the perfect apples in the display were poisoned and all the people in the store were going to die.

The story went into family legend and there was rarely a family gathering where it wasn't told.

Just as Cait closed her suitcase, the phone rang. It was her uncles, each on an extension phone, something they always did. They didn't bother with an introduction.

"Kelly's substitute vet came," Pauly said, "and we put him in the trailer. He didn't bring much."

"He looks good," Seth said. "Not beautiful like Adam or your dad, but pleasant. He's built like a prizefighter. Solid."

"But he never smiles, and he wouldn't come to dinner." Pauly sounded shocked and a bit insulted.

"He closed the door and kept us out."

Caitlyn smiled. Not coming to dinner and locking them out would devastate her uncles. They loved to know everything about everyone. "And?" she encouraged.

"He has no pets," Pauly said. "Kelly would be appalled."

"We were told that he yelled at Betty Lewis."

Caitlyn frowned at that. She'd heard gossip about Mrs. Lewis being "unusual," but she'd dismissed it because of her son. Caitlyn had gone to high school with Taran and he was a great guy. He was really smart and was on the cross-country track team. He said that minds and bodies worked together. *His* certainly did. If Jared hadn't been— She cut off her thoughts. She could not, would not, and refused to, think of Jared. He was the past. Gone from her life. Forever.

"We can hardly wait for you to get home," Pauly said. "Maybe you can make Dr. Jones smile."

"I doubt it." Caitlyn was beginning to see where they were going with this. "And I don't intend to try."

"But maybe you can save Betty," Seth added. "After all, she is Taran's mother."

Caitlyn rolled her eyes. They knew that she'd always liked Taran. This was blackmail. Old-fashioned, down-and-dirty *blackmail*. Their breezy, happy talk had a devious purpose: they wanted Caitlyn to fix whatever was going on at the clinic.

Some people rescued animals. Her uncles rescued people they thought were being abused in any way.

"Look at us," Seth said one night at dinner. "We know about discrimination. We're not allowed to legally marry, but who's more married than us?"

Miguel had spoken up. "I agree. Why should just us straight guys be miserable?"

Caitlyn started to reply to them, but what could she say? That she'd fix it? That's what they wanted, but Kelly's clinic wasn't something she knew much about. On the other hand, what possible reason could the new vet have for being angry at Mrs. Lewis? If she was like her son, she was perfect. "I better go," Caitlyn said. She wasn't going to let them talk her into taking on a new job. "I'll be home soon." She hung up.

As she checked out of the hotel, she left bags of fruit at the desk. She labeled hers Good and the grocery products as Tasteless. "No subtlety in our Caitlyn," Uncle Pauly often said. She smiled at the thought.

She put her case in the back of her Jeep. As she started the engine, she thought about what her uncles wanted her to do and grimaced in defeat. Okay, she'd stop by and see what was going on. But that didn't mean she *wanted* to do it.

Thirty minutes into the drive, she was growing angry. All she wanted was to be at home. No strangers, no things happening that would turn her world upside down, no one asking her endless questions about why she'd done what she did. Just quiet and peace. *Home.*

She did *not* want to think of a prizefighter of a stranger living in the old trailer just a few feet from her house. Why had the uncles agreed to that when Kelly suggested it?

"You can show him around Mason," Kelly had said.

Well, that's fifteen minutes, Caitlyn thought.

Was it the man's idea to live so near other people? If it was, then why was he refusing a dinner invitation? Why did he—? She drew in her breath so sharply that she nearly swerved off the road. Maybe he didn't want to go to dinner with them because he didn't approve of Seth and Pauly. Maybe this Dr. Jones was homophobic!

By the time Caitlyn pulled into the parking lot of the Mason Veterinary Clinic, she wasn't in a good mood.

Cooper opened the file drawer to put away a card recording his treatment of a Hatten horse.

Since he'd been in Mason, he'd been trying to deal with Betty, the woman who supposedly ran everything. She said she'd worked in the vet office for thirty years, first for Dr. Carl, then for Kelly. It seemed that no one bothered putting "Doctor" in front of Kelly's name.

He told himself that if the woman had been there that long, she must know what she's doing. He hadn't protested when she'd dumped the whole filing system out on all three exam tables. For two days, every table had been covered with cards and drawers and markers.

When a woman brought in a Pekingese that the owner said was feeling bad, Coop had no exam table. Betty said, "Use the desk. I'm busy."

Coop bit his tongue. He really *needed* this job. For years he'd had his own clinic with Leo, his best friend. They'd met the first day of college and rarely parted. They were best men at each other's weddings. The two families traveled together.

It had all ended in one explosive nightmare of an evening. Coop's wife, Rilla, took the stance that it was all his fault. "What was I supposed to *do*?" she'd demanded. She'd been wearing a blue silk robe that he had bought for her. Behind her, under the sheets, Leo was wearing nothing.

The next day, Coop left the state. Lawyers handled dividing the business and the divorce, while Coop took a job in Wyoming. But that hadn't worked out. His bad temper was too much for the small town. One night he got in a fight with three men. While it had felt good at the time, the resulting stay in the hospital wasn't good. The sheriff suggested that Coop take his temper somewhere else. "It was fists this time. Next time, it might be guns."

When he was released from the hospital, Coop went back to his apartment and called one of his former professors. After the man's obligatory "I'm sorry about..." Coop asked him if he knew of any jobs available immediately.

"Actually, I do. There's a job in tiny Mason, Kansas, in a clinic owned by a woman vet. She used to have a partner but he passed away. If you behave yourself, it might lead to a permanent job."

"I'll take it," Coop said. "Will you recommend me?"

His former teacher hesitated. "Yes, based on when you were in school. I think I'll keep my mouth shut about what's happened since then. Did you really—?"

Coop didn't let him finish. "Yes. Whatever you heard, I'm sure I did it. Let me know about the job."

So now Cooper was in Mason and doing all he could to "behave." That meant not getting involved with any human. He was quite annoyed about the little trailer he'd been told was where he was to live and he planned to fix that as soon as possible. But with an empty bank account and no assets, new housing wouldn't be easy.

Card in hand, he was looking through the drawer marked *H* but he didn't see "Hatten."

He opened the drawer labeled *B*. A header read Blue. Subfiles were Robin's-egg Blue, Midnight Blue, Sky Blue, Peacock Blue. There were labels for twelve hues.

Puzzled, he pulled out a card under Gray-blue. It was for a wolfhound named Rab and listed the shots the dog had had. Flipping through the cards, he saw that horses, turtles and goldfish were categorized by color, all seeming to be a shade of blue.

He opened other drawers. Red, Green, Purple. There were four drawers for Brown, two for Black. "What the hell?" he muttered.

The front door opened and in came Betty. He had no idea why she'd left the office in the middle of the day. She was in her fifties, with iron-gray hair and a shapeless body. She had an air of confidence about her that seemed almost regal. He'd already learned that she believed she was in charge.

"What have you done?" Coop didn't yell. He was calm as he held up the card.

"I organized the system properly." She sounded as though he was stupid for not seeing that.

His teeth were clamped together. "By *color*?"

"Yes, then name. If the dog is black and named Schooner, you can find it right away."

Coop swallowed. "The owners' names. Where are they?"

Betty gave him a look of disbelief. "This is a hospital for *animals*. Not *people*! Animals come first. Didn't you learn that in vet school?"

He felt his temper flaring. "I learned that turtles are not *blue*!"

"Hmph!" she said. "You should have told Kelly that you're color-blind."

"I am not color-blind!" he shouted. "I am a licensed veterinarian and I need to be able to find information quickly."

Betty looked at something to the side, then backed up to the wall, her eyes wide. "Does Kelly know you're a violent man?" she said in fear. "Please don't hit me."

"I've never hit a woman in my life!" He took a breath to calm himself. "You took over all my exam tables because you said you were reorganizing the files. I let you do it because I thought you knew what you were doing." He was having to work to not shout at her. "This is going to take me days to fix. I ought to—"

"You ought to what?" said a female voice. He hadn't heard the young woman enter through the side door. She was about five foot seven and quite pretty. She had dark brown hair, skin like sunlit honey and blue eyes. Eyes that were flashing fire at him.

She put her arm around Betty's shoulders. Minutes ago, Betty had been defiant and aggressive. Now she was squeezing out tears and looking helpless. Her shoulders sagged like an old person. "Go home," the young woman said. "I'll take care of him."

"Oh, Caitlyn, thank you." Betty's voice was trembling. "If I'd known he was like this, I would have brought Taran to protect me." She looked at Cait with the eyes of a wounded puppy.

"Do you need help getting to your car? Should I call Taran to come and get you?"

Betty sighed. "I think I can manage." She patted Cait's arm. "You're such a good girl. Maybe you could come to dinner. I know Taran would love to see you."

"That would be very nice."

Cait waited until Betty was out the door before she turned back to face the doctor. "Well?"

Coop was still in awe of Betty's act. "That woman…" He couldn't think how to explain all she'd done in just three days.

"Betty Lewis is a well-respected member of the Mason community. But you are…" She didn't complete her sentence.

"I am what?"

"Not wanted here. I'll call Kelly and she'll get someone else."

"She'll do it from South America? That should be easy."

The front door opened. It was a woman with a poodle. "Oh. Cait. Are you working here now?"

"No, Mrs. Lexton, I am not."

"But she is helping today." Dr. Jones looked at Cait. "Would you please get the card for Mrs. Lexton and bring it to the exam room? I'd like to check on previous treatments."

"I do *not* work here," Cait said, then turned to Mrs. Lexton. "Maybe you should come back tomorrow."

"Oh," Mrs. Lexton said. "But tomorrow we are leaving town and Lady has something in her paw. She's been limping. Could I use your phone to call my great-grandmother and tell her we'll be late for her birthday party? It's her ninety-fourth, so I'm sure she won't mind. She'll have many more."

Caitlyn muttered, "More emotional blackmail."

"What was that, dear? How's your dad?"

"He's just fine. But my uncles may be dead meat." The doctor and Mrs. Lexton were looking at her. "Okay," Cait said. "I'll get the card. Go!"

As Coop opened the exam room door, Mrs. Lexton stopped by him. "She's a darling girl, isn't she?" she said. "And she's not married. I don't believe you are, either, are you?"

"Definitely not!" He waited until the woman was inside, then turned to Cait. "Bring the card in as soon as you can. I need it right away."

She gave him a look that let him know he was pond slime,

then turned away and went to the cabinet where Kelly kept her meticulous records. She told people they went back to the 1950s. "Every cat, dog and pet rat in Mason is in my files," Cait had heard her say many times.

She opened the *L* drawer. There was a divider that said Lavender. Cait knew no one in Mason by that name. Where were the alphabetical names? In the *R* drawer were labels for shades of red. Red-brown had a card for a fox. Female named Vixen, owned by Seb Allen in 1964, died in 1971. If the animal was deceased, why was it in the current files? And why wasn't it under *A* for Allen?

Caitlyn opened all the drawers. There were lots of colors, with many variations. Orangey-yellow?

Was that real?

Dr. Jones opened the exam room door. "Could I have Mrs. Lexton's card, please?" His voice was so sweet it's a wonder his teeth didn't instantly rot and fall out of his mouth.

Caitlyn glared at him. "I can't find it."

His tone got even sweeter. "What was that?"

"I can't find it!"

Mrs. Lexton came to the door. "Caitlyn! Are you all right?"

"I'm fine," she said.

Mrs. Lexton went back into the exam room to her dog.

The doctor stood in the doorway, smiling so smugly that Cait wanted to throw something at him. "Try the Blue drawer, or Silver-blue." He looked into the room at the dog. "Or maybe Gray. My color-blindness hinders me."

With her jaws clenched, Caitlyn opened the *B* drawer, and under Blue, she found Silver. Lady was right after Killer, one of the Hatten bulls. How could a bull be classified as silver-blue? Cait didn't ponder the question. She removed the card and held it out to him.

But the doctor didn't walk across the room to get it. He waited for her to come to him.

When Caitlyn got to the door, she smiled at Mrs. Lexton, then turned to the doctor. "You are a pile of steaming dog poop," she said without losing her smile.

"You could always call Betty and have her explain her filing system. Maybe she'll bring Taran, as you seem to be enthralled by him. Is he as smart as his mother?"

"Drop. Dead." Turning, she smiled at Mrs. Lexton. "When you get back from your trip, bring Lady to see Kelly. For a *real* exam by a *real* doctor."

Cait had had enough! As she shut the front door behind her, she heard Mrs. Lexton ask if he was a fully qualified vet or not. By this time tomorrow, everyone in Mason would doubt his credentials. "Serves him right," Cait muttered as she got into her Jeep. Let him deal with his own problems! She had hers.

It was a day and a half before Caitlyn was called to account about Dr. Jones. Even though he lived in the trailer just a few feet from her house, she'd managed to avoid him.

Caitlyn went to what the town still called "Gresham's" for lunch, and that's when Forey caught her. Mr. Gresham had sold the place when Cait was just a kid. Six months later, he'd died. "Couldn't stand doing nothing" was the Kansas verdict that everyone understood.

Nella and Forey had continued to cook for the new owner, but each year they did less. One afternoon, Nella said, "I think I'll take a nap." She didn't wake up.

After Nella's death, Forey's loneliness was something people could feel. No one, not her husband or her faraway daughters, could replace her friend. She still cooked, but not much. She had just delivered a batch of cookies to the diner when she saw Caitlyn. She sat down across from her.

"You've ruined his reputation." There was no need to tell who "he" was.

"Me?"

"Everyone in town is making fun of him. He's all alone and he can't find anything in that office. Mrs. Babshaw's cat fell against a threshing blade, but Dr. Cooper couldn't find the tools he needed to sew the poor thing back together. They searched the office and found nothing, so someone called Betty. She was so angry that she refused to tell what she'd done with the tools. Pauly was the one who got her to tell, but I don't think he did it nicely.

"Anyway, Betty had put the surgical instruments in the old microwave in the back storage room. She said she didn't pick the new microwave because she needed it to heat her soup for lunch. She didn't want the new one contaminated. Do you know why she put the tools in the old one?"

"The microwave would sterilize them?" Cait said.

"That's exactly what she said. Never mind that the metal would blow up."

"I bet she wrote where the instruments were on a card and filed it under *S*."

Forey's eyes widened. "You're right. *S* for sterilization, I guess."

"No. For the color silver. I don't know anything I can do to help the man. I have a full-time job. Call an employment agency in KC and get a professional."

"We tried that. They said they would put an ad in the paper, then interview people, and in a couple of weeks they'd have someone. And they wanted a percentage of the year's salary up front. It was thousands. Dr. Cooper said—"

"Let me guess. He said this was Kelly's problem and she's on an island off South America."

"You sure seem to know a lot about what's going on."

"I just use logic, that's all."

"And that's what poor Dr. Cooper needs."

Caitlyn looked hard at Forey. "Who put you up to this?"

Forey looked back at her just as hard. "Those two."

Cait knew who she meant: the uncles. "*Why* are they pushing me toward this man?"

"They're not! The man has nothing to do with this. Pauly and Seth are shoving you out of the nest. They're trying to get you to leave home. You and your dad are... You know."

"We're happy at home. Why is it bad for Dad and me to enjoy our time together?"

"If you were flying off to Disney together and laughing yourselves silly, we'd be happy. But you and Miguel disappear for days at a time and we all know you sit in silence. We know you don't talk to others or to each other."

Cait didn't answer because Forey was right. "What am I supposed to do?"

"Help this man."

"I don't like him."

Forey blinked at that. "That's bad. Maybe we should have listened when Betty said she was afraid he was going to hurt her."

"After I saw what she did to Kelly's files, I can see why he was angry."

"Caitlyn." Forey's eyes were pleading. "The one thing we all agree on is that this man cares about animals. Like Kelly does. That's probably why she hired him."

Caitlyn felt like a general at war finally admitting defeat. There was no way she was going to win. The whole town knew she was good at organizing. She'd been running Heritage Harvests since she was a kid. In college, her weekends had been filled with balancing accounts and making sure orders were completed.

Maybe it would be good for her to get away from fruit that had bugs that couldn't be sprayed. It might even be good to see people other than the men who raised her. "I'll see what I can do," she said softly.

"She's going to do it!" Forey said loudly.

The collective sigh that came from the other diners, all of whom had been listening, made the paper napkins flutter.

"My pigs aren't feeding," Ralph Carmichael said. "I *need* a vet."

"And my hens aren't laying," Abbie Sears said.

Caitlyn stood up. "The problem with all your animals is pesticides. If I fix this guy, I better see lots of orders for organic windfall fruit for your animals."

There were several silent nods. Cait left the diner and got into her Jeep. Before she headed to the clinic, she went home.

As she knew they would be, the uncles were waiting for her. Forey had called them. They followed her into her house and she brewed them a pot of organic, good-for-you, herbal tea.

Pauly began. "When Kelly asked us to put him in the trailer, of course we inquired about him. He used to own a clinic in partnership, but one day he walked out. We don't know why. He sold his half. He went to Wyoming, but he left there, too."

"He seems to move around a lot, doesn't he?" Seth said. Then they were silent.

"What are you dying to tell me?" she asked.

"He was married and got a divorce," Pauly said.

"We're not sure, but we think that's why he sold his partnership and moved away," Seth said.

"The end of love affairs causes people to do drastic things," Pauly said.

They gave piercing looks to Caitlyn. She knew they were urging her to tell them why she'd broken up with Jared. Giving her the opportunity to spill all was a daily thing. And Cait saying nothing was also their daily routine.

Seth sighed. "We need to introduce him to people."

"No, we don't," she said. "After working all day, he probably likes being alone. He doesn't want to go drinking and dancing and looking for a new wife."

"You seem to know a lot about him."

She narrowed her eyes at them. "I know nothing about him and I want to keep it that way. I have to go. Dad is waiting for me."

The uncles knew Cait didn't have an actual time to meet her father. She was telling them that the Q-and-A session was over. She followed them outside and watched them walk away. The cottage where Mrs. Carl used to live was now Cait's house and she had to pass the trailer to get to her father's house.

When Mrs. Carl died, it had taken all of them a long time to adjust. She'd been a true force in their lives. Sometimes her bossiness had nearly driven her son crazy, but Pauly didn't know what life was like without her. She'd been accepting of his sexuality, and she had adored Seth.

Most important, Mrs. Carl was the reason Cait was with them. The men said that was worth all the eccentricities the woman had.

After her death, her house stood empty for months. If Cait hadn't seen a bird fly in and out of the chimney, the little house might have stayed closed forever. Left as a shrine to Mrs. Carl.

It took a family meeting before they got up the courage to unlock the house and enter. They'd prepared themselves for grief. Miguel said they were being ridiculous, but they knew he'd loved Mrs. Carl. He might cry the hardest.

But entering the untouched house was like seeing her again. It was a feast of "Remember when she—?"

They cleared the birds out of the chimney, made some decisions about what to give away and who wanted what as a keepsake. They were at the door, about to leave, when Caitlyn sat down on the old sofa and said, "Does anyone mind if I move in here?"

She was actually asking her father if he'd be okay on his own. He smiled. "I think it's time you had your own place."

Pauly looked at Miguel. "And you can have a live-in girlfriend."

"As soon as I find a woman who'll put up with me, I'll do that."

It was an old joke. Miguel was a *very* handsome man. His cheekbones were still sharp and the gray at his temples only added to his appearance. Every unmarried female in the county had let him know she was available, but he usually turned them down.

There had been a few girlfriends over the years. One had stayed for four years and Cait had liked her. She made pancakes in funny shapes and helped Cait with her clothes and hair.

But like the others, she left. Cait heard her tell Miguel, "There's something missing. I don't know what it is, but it's not there. I'm going to leave while I'm still young enough to find the real thing."

Twelve-year-old Cait held her father's hand as they watched the woman drive away. "Will you make me dinosaur pancakes?"

"No," Miguel said. "How about an apple named The Cait?"

"There are already three of them. I'm going to miss her a lot." She looked up at him. "A whole lot."

Miguel sighed. "How can I bribe you to forgive me for losing her?"

"A week off from school so I can help the uncles in the nurseries."

"And you'll still do the bookwork?"

"Yes."

"You got it." He bent and she jumped on his back for a piggyback ride. They never spoke of the woman again.

Cait found her dad where she knew he'd be. When he'd moved the old schoolhouse onto the property, he'd built a long gazebo. Part of it had a roof to shield against the rain, and the rest was covered with grapevines. In the summer, it's where the two of them hung out.

Miguel was on a chaise with one of the several newspapers he read every day. He subscribed to six. "I like to know what's going on around the world," he said.

"And who's reporting it," Uncle Seth said.

Caitlyn had asked what that meant but no one would tell her.

Miguel didn't look up as his daughter stretched out on her lounge. "How bad did they torture you?"

"Aunt Forey, the uncles or the whole town?"

Miguel chuckled. "Did they win?"

"Completely. Looks like I have a new job. That means you and the uncles will have to do my work here."

He gave a genuine laugh at that and put down his paper. "Like we could do it! It looks like you're going to have two full-time jobs. For a while, anyway. You wanna tell me what happened?"

She told him about Betty's filing system.

"So what do you plan to do about that mess?"

Caitlyn sighed. "Those files have to be dumped out and completely redone."

"Who better than you to do it?"

"I…"

"What?"

"I don't like him. He's bossy and…" She waved her hand. "Something about him makes me angry."

"Maybe that's good," Miguel said.

For a moment they looked at each other. Maybe anger was better than the nothingness they usually felt.

"I guess so. I think I'll go to the clinic tonight when no one is there. I'll dump all those thousands of cards out and put them back in the proper order. At least she didn't rewrite them."

"Maybe you could put them on the computer."

Cait groaned. "That would take weeks. And new software. Besides, maybe Kelly wouldn't want me to do that."

"Kelly would love it and you know it."

She looked at her hands for a moment. "I have a favor to ask of you."

"Name it."

"I need a key to the clinic. I don't want to ask *him*."

Miguel nodded. "You want me to ask Jared for a key, don't you?"

"Would you?"

He sat up and swung his feet to the brick floor. "I'll go now. While you make dinner."

"That's a deal."

Miguel took his time driving to the Hatten farm. The sprawling wood-and-stone house hadn't changed much since Kelly married Adam.

He didn't want to see Jared. The poor boy was so sad that it hurt to look at him. If Miguel knew anything in life, it was what a broken heart felt like. And he knew that, once broken, it never truly healed. It might mend a bit, but that wound couldn't be repaired.

Three times Jared had asked Miguel, "Why?" Of course he couldn't answer. He and Cait had agreed to say nothing, but his silence was also pride. Miguel didn't want to tell the truth any more than Caitlyn did.

He was concerned for his daughter. "This pain, this misery, will fade," he'd told her. "It doesn't seem so now, but it will recede."

"I can't believe that," she'd cried. "You, Jared, everyone. It hurts too much."

"It doesn't matter," he'd said. "Not to me, anyway. What about to you?"

"No," she'd whispered. "It means nothing."

That first night, he'd tucked her in bed as he used to when she was a child. They'd both wanted to return to that time of innocence.

"Jared?" she'd whispered.

"He'll be all right," Miguel had said. "I know what he's feeling and he *will* survive."

As Miguel looked at the big house, memories came back to him. He'd hated Adam Hatten. He had what Miguel wanted. Not the money or the admiration of the town, but Vera. The woman Miguel had loved since he was a child had belonged to someone else. And now he had even more.

He started to ring the doorbell but he heard the crunch of gravel and turned toward it, bracing himself for poor, sad Jared.

Miguel froze. Vera was walking toward him. She had her head down, her hands full of papers, and she was frowning in concentration as she read.

She looked good. Older, but still lean and lithe. She had on shorts that showed her long, beautiful legs. Her hair had escaped its bounds and was a crinkled mass around her head. Like him, there was gray in it. Vera wouldn't waste her time coloring it.

"Nobody's home," she said, but didn't look up. "They won't be back for weeks. Leave a message and I'll—" She looked up and saw him.

The last time they'd seen each other, Gabby had been on top

of him. Both of them naked. For a split second, he saw what he used to see in her eyes: passion, desire, a need for him. Love.

It was gone in a flash, and emptiness replaced it. Not love, not hate, not even dislike. Just blank. "They aren't here," she repeated.

"I know." Miguel's voice seemed to crack. "Caitlyn needs a key to Kelly's clinic."

"That guy she hired has it."

Miguel swallowed. Is this the way she looked at people she interviewed? No judgment about their heinous crimes? "I know. But Cait..." With a shrug, he turned away. "I'll get it from him. Sorry to have bothered you." He had driven Cait's old Jeep and he went to it. His hands were shaking.

"Wait," she said.

He didn't move, certainly didn't turn toward her. He heard the front door of the house open, then the gravel crunching as she came toward him. She was on the other side of the Jeep and he looked at her.

"Here." She tossed him a set of keys.

He didn't catch them. His heart was beating too hard to control his hands. Bending, he picked them up from the ground. When he stood up, she was gone and the door to the house was closed.

Miguel managed to drive home. Cait had dinner ready, a skillet full of seasoned hamburger meat and a pile of warm tortillas.

"You want the works?" she asked. "I have tomatoes, lettuce, cheese and—" She looked at him. "Are you okay?"

"Stomach upset. And headache. I'm going to lie down."

"Maybe if you ate something you'd feel better."

"Take it to him. I need to sleep."

"Okay," she said. "But if you get hungry—" He had already shut his bedroom door.

★ ★ ★

Cait's plan was to fill two bags with food, put one on the doc's doorstep, give a quick knock, then skedaddle away in her Jeep. She'd take her food to the clinic and start on the files.

But the doc thwarted her. He wasn't hidden safely away in the trailer but was outside and came around the corner just as she put a bag of food down.

She came face-to-face with him. "I, uh, was leaving you something to eat. My dad wasn't hungry, so—" She shrugged, not wanting to explain. "I have to go. I need to—" She wasn't going to tell him where she was going or what she planned to do. She turned away.

"Is that your dinner?"

She stopped and turned back. He was looking at the bag in her hand. "Yeah. I have to go." Again, she turned away.

"How about if we eat together?"

Cait frowned. Was he hitting on her? She didn't look at him, just raised her hand in a wave. "I'm too busy tonight. Maybe another time."

"What if I drive us to the DQ and we get Cokes and ice cream?"

With an expression of horror, she whirled to face him. "Have you been spying on me? Stalking me?"

He seemed unperturbed by her anger. "Your dad left the door to your Jeep open just now and a wrapper blew out. I assumed it wasn't his. He doesn't look like a DQ kind of guy. More of a steak from an animal that he brought down himself. With a penknife."

She couldn't suppress a smile at the image of her father and relaxed her shoulders. "Guilty. The wrapper is mine." She looked around. "But I warn you that if you tell my uncles, I'll get Betty Lewis to come clean the trailer. You'll never find anything ever again."

He feigned a look of fear. "She would put kitchen utensils in my bed."

"And your shoes in the fridge."

"I don't want to think where she'd put the toilet paper." They looked at each other for a moment, smiling.

"Okay," she said. "Large Cokes and huge ice-cream cones, but tell no one."

When he grinned, Cait thought he was rather attractive. She'd only seen him when he was scowling or smirking.

There wasn't a question as to which vehicle they'd take. His car was a four-door sedan, cheap and old.

She didn't mind letting him drive. The two bags of food were at her feet. She searched for conversation. "So how do you like Mason?"

His answer was a look that said, *What do you think?*

Her face reddened a bit. "Right. You haven't had it easy."

He changed the subject. "How are you related to Seth and Paul?"

"I'm not. At least not by blood, but they helped raise me. Uncle Pauly's stepfather owned the whole property. You know that the business office used to be his vet clinic, don't you?"

"I had no idea. I'd like to know what's what. Would you mind explaining things?" He was at the drive-through for the DQ. "What do you want? A large Coke? We can get dessert later."

"I shouldn't. They're not healthy, but a tall vanilla cone covered in chocolate that cracks off in sheets… I can't resist those things."

Smiling, he ordered their drinks for starters, handed them to her, paid for them, then drove to the side and parked.

"Let me pay you back," she said.

"Just tell me what I've walked into here and that'll repay me in full."

She told him about Kelly and Paul being childhood sweethearts. "Then he went away to Britain and realized he was gay. But by that time Kelly knew she was in love with Adam, who was about to go back to Africa with Kelly's older sister."

"I think I'm sorry I asked. Who is Jared? I keep hearing his name mentioned."

Cait took a breath, but said nothing.

"Did I say something wrong?"

"He's Kelly and Adam's oldest son. They have two younger boys. Jared and I were…together, I guess you'd say."

"But you're not now?"

"No. What about you? I heard you were—" She didn't finish.

"You can say it. Divorced. Yes, I am. Does everyone ask you to explain exactly what happened in your breakup and why?"

"Oh, yes! They drive me crazy about it."

"But it's no one's business but your own."

"Exactly! You ready for ice cream? I need to go to work." She drew in her breath; she hadn't meant to say that.

He was looking at her. "Your uncles expect you to work at night?"

She couldn't think of a quick lie.

He opened the car door. "I'll go get us ice cream while you think of an answer that is close to the truth but covers what is actually one great whopping lie." He closed the car door.

Blinking, she watched him walk away. She hadn't planned to tell him she was going to the vet clinic so he wouldn't interfere. But actually, if two people worked on Betty's chaos, it would be faster.

He came back with two identical cones, handed her one, then got into the Jeep and closed the door. He didn't look at her.

She bit into the chocolate. It cracked satisfyingly. "I'm being punished for not helping you."

He bit his chocolate but he still didn't look at her. "What does that mean?"

"I've been told that I wasn't fair to you, so I have to reorganize Kelly's files. Dad wants me to put them on a computer."

"Good idea."

"That would take more hours than I can spend."

"Set up the program, then add as needed. Within a year, all the current files will be on there. Let Kelly hire a kid to enter the old stuff."

She picked a piece of chocolate off her cone. "Not a bad idea."

"Right now, I need an assistant."

"I'll ask the uncles and Aunt Forey to find someone."

"Who is Forey?"

"She's Dad's..." Cait thought about it. "...adopted mother, I guess. Dad is from New Mexico, but he spent his summers with her and Uncle Rafe when he was a kid, then came back here when he grew up."

He turned to her. "What about your mother?"

"You do ask a lot of questions. Where'd you grow up?"

"Northern California. And no, I've never surfed. I like mountains."

"Like we have here in Kansas?"

He smiled. "Your black soil that grows anything makes up for the lack of height. Think we could work on the files together?"

She was down to the ice cream. Soft and cold. "This isn't a...you know, a pickup, is it?"

He hesitated. "When you broke up with your boyfriend, was it bad?"

"It was my worst nightmare."

"Multiply that by a thousand and you'll imagine a small part of my divorce. I'm not ready to risk something like that again."

He seemed to have more to say, so she waited.

"However, I could use a friend. This town hasn't exactly been welcoming. And Betty Lewis has said some unpleasant things about me."

Caitlyn winced since a lot of it was her fault.

"I've heard enough gossip to think you and I have been through some of the same thing. I'd appreciate it if what I tell you doesn't get out."

"Ask anyone," she said. "I don't blab what's told to me."

"That is exactly what I've heard. 'Caitlyn has secrets.'" He took a breath. "One day I came home to find my wife in bed with my friend and business partner. Within months, I lost everything—my business, my best friend, my marriage." He hesitated. "And every penny I had. I'm broke. I really need this job for as long as it lasts. And maybe later..."

She had finished her cone. "Kelly is going to need someone full-time. My guess is that she wants to see how you fit in with the town and with her beloved animals."

"How do you think I'm doing?"

She felt blood rush to her face. Thanks to her, he wasn't doing well at all. As Forey said, people were laughing at him. He was a man who couldn't even find what he needed to be able to sew up a cat. Caitlyn was the reason he might lose his job. She'd never before done anything like that to anyone and it didn't feel good. She was ashamed of herself. "I think I owe you. I'm sorry. I was planning to spend tonight reorganizing Kelly's files."

"Yeah? Betty will have a fit."

"No, she won't because I'm going to fire her."

"You're going to discharge Taran's mother?"

She knew his sound of shock was fake, but still... "He and I are *not* a couple. I hardly know him. We were in some classes together in high school, that's all. And I've seen him at a few town events but not many."

Coop pantomimed taking a notebook and pen out of his pocket and making a list.

"It's not like that." She was laughing.

He faked putting the notebook away. "Okay, no Taran the Great. What about Betty the...? What is she?"

"The Infallible. Never made a mistake in her life, but she's always wrong."

As he started the engine, he laughed and it was a nice sound. "Mind if I help you reorganize the files? By the name of the owner, right?" He pulled onto the road.

"We need to establish search bases. Name, dates, types of treatment, even the animal's name."

"And color," he said seriously. "I really want to see the Hattens' blue cow."

"I spent half my childhood at the Hattens' and never saw a blue cow." She'd meant it as a joke but a vision of her and Jared in a sunlit field came to her.

He glanced at her. "If you start remembering, so will I. Want me to tell you about my *wedding*? The cake had pink roses on it and there were two little girls carrying baskets of flower petals. And—"

"No!" She put her hands over her ears. "I can't take it." She put her hands down and looked at him. "We must do our best to forget the past. Move forward."

"Does the future include a job for me?"

"Of course. And a town."

"And a house, I hope. No offense, but that trailer..."

"Hey! Dad and I lived in it for the first three years of my life."

"That makes sense since it's the size of a playpen. I can almost touch both walls. If I wore a hat, my head would scrape the ceiling."

"Why do you think Dad bought the schoolhouse? The rooms are two stories high."

"I bet it's nice inside."

"It is." They had reached Kelly's office.

"I'll unlock it," he said, and got out.

She stayed in the Jeep and watched him. *Maybe Forey was right*, she thought. Maybe she was pulling into herself. Since her breakup, it had become just her and her dad. They were too isolated.

Caitlyn had a vision of herself in the future and she was alone. She couldn't marry, of course, but there were other things she could do. Maybe she'd be like Kelly's famous sister, Vera. She was on the news often, and was known globally as a major do-gooder. And look at her. She'd never married, never had kids. Caitlyn wondered if Vera had ever been in love.

I'll ask Dad, she thought. Maybe he'd met Vera Exton. Maybe he knew what she was like and what had led her to a life of helping others.

Dr. Jones had unlocked the door and turned to her.

Maybe I can take him on as a project, she thought. *I'll get him involved in the town. When Kelly returns, everyone will say she should keep him.*

The idea that there were other things to do in life made her smile. She got out and went inside.

CHAPTER EIGHTEEN

CAIT HAD SPENT HER LIFE WITH MEN, SO working with Coop, as he told her to call him, seemed natural. But still, it was extraordinarily easy. They agreed on every aspect of what to do.

Their first thought was to rearrange the contents of the drawers while making a minimum amount of mess.

"Betty covered all three exam tables," he said. "I assumed she knew what she was doing."

"Pompous know-it-alls project that image."

He looked at her and it was like mind reading. They knew what they had to do. "Floor or tables?"

"Floor!" Caitlyn said. "Unless you'd rather not do all that bending."

"Try me."

They dumped the hundreds of cards into a pile, then started twenty-six categories by the first letter of the last name of the owner.

She stood back and looked at the piles. "This does need to be put on a computer. I'd want to be able to search how many dogs were dewormed in 1991."

"That would help us find out if they were eating something that was infected. Know any high schoolers who could do the data entry?"

"I know the principal and maybe he could give extra credit for the job."

"Good idea," he said. "But *you* set it up."

The way he said it made her feel good.

They went back to the boring task of separating hundreds of cards.

Cooper started the conversation. "I was at the diner and I kept hearing that a woman named Vera was back in town. I didn't pay much attention until I heard it was Vera Exton they were talking about. Did they mean the Pulitzer Prize–winning journalist?"

"Yes. She's Kelly's sister."

"Wow. I'm impressed. Does she come home often?"

"The only time she's been in Mason since she left in the seventies was for her mother's funeral."

"Uh-oh. Is that caused by one of those small-town feuds?"

"Not at all. Kelly meets her sister somewhere in the world every year. Sometimes with the family and sometimes just her and her sister."

"Right. You would know because of Kelly's son." He stopped and looked at her. "Sorry. I didn't mean to step out of bounds. I don't usually get involved in gossip, but I do go to the diner, and people talk. I swear, when they were talking about Vera Exton, they were extra loud. They seemed to want to make sure I heard them."

"That's probably true. We are proud of her."

"So tell me what she's like."

"I have no idea. I've never met her."

"Was your dad living in Mason when she was here?"

"Yes, but I doubt if he knew her. He's never spoken of her.

But then, Hattens and Montoyas weren't exactly in the same social whirl."

"But you must have heard some gossip."

"Why all these questions?"

"I admire her work very much. Her reporting is honest and forthright, but she tells the human side of everything. She seems to be afraid of nothing. That book she wrote about Joe Harding… I shouldn't say it, but I bawled." He was looking at her, waiting for her to reply.

"I only know what I've been told. Kelly adores her, and I know Adam and Vera were friends."

"Oh, yes. You said he was going back to Africa with Kelly's older sister. I didn't put the Exton name together. Was it the Peace Corps?"

"I think so." She didn't feel a need to elaborate on that connection. Mason was already sounding like a soap opera. "I think Vera was different. I guess you'd say she never really belonged here. Kelly said her sister had always wanted to leave. As soon as Kelly got her vet license, Vera left Mason and didn't come back until she had to. She was more involved in the world than in little Mason, Kansas. Somebody told me she was shot once."

"In 1987. Thirty-first of July. At Mecca. The Saudi police opened fire against demonstrators. She was one of the wounded and helicoptered out of there. I read that when she was young, she demonstrated against the Vietnam War. That would have been when she lived here."

"I don't know about that. It was well before my time."

"The gossip machine didn't tell you?"

"No, which means she probably didn't do it unless she somehow managed to keep it a secret. But that's not possible in this town."

"Even though I've heard that 'Caitlyn has secrets'?"

He was teasing but she didn't like it and her frown told him so.

"Sorry. Overstepping again." He stood up to look at the neatly stacked cards. "That's the last of them. We can put them back in the drawers now."

The reorganization had taken hours. It was dark outside and Caitlyn knew she should say good-night and wish him luck, but she didn't feel tired. "So where's this storeroom where Betty hid the surgical instruments?"

"That door." When Cait started toward it, he said, "No! That is a cave of chaos. I'm afraid there are snakes in there."

"Kelly would never mistreat an animal. More likely it's full of I-may-need-that-someday items." She opened the door, then stood there in shock.

Coop stood beside her. "It's not really my business to tackle this. I just need to search through it for supplies. Of course, someone could ask Betty where she put what."

"She gets fired, then she's going to help you? I don't think so."

"I'll drive you home. Then next weekend I can—"

Cait removed a box from a shelf. On the bottom were leather straps so old that they had cracked. But on top were new boxes of sterile gloves.

"I need those!"

She put the boxes in his arms. "Know where the trash bags are?"

"No idea. I worry that Kelly might kill me for rearranging her stuff."

"You think she never asked *me* to do this? Ha! I made Jared help me organize his parents' garage. His dad said I did such a good job that Jared should—" She cut herself off.

"Should marry you?" Coop asked softly.

"Yes." There was pain in her eyes.

"Too bad. I could help you plan your wedding. Don't get a chocolate cake or a red velvet one. They stick in people's teeth. The guests get drunk and they're grinning and showing off their red and black teeth. Place begins to look like a horror show. You get scared. Like really, really afraid."

She smiled. He had lightened the ugly moment. She grabbed another box. Under a muzzle big enough for a camel was a box of paper surgical gowns. They had to be twenty years old. "I'll give you a nickel if you can find some trash bags."

"My week's salary," he murmured, and left to search.

It took hours and they ended up with nine bags full of rubbish. Cait had found a big black marker and labeled the boxes. Coop made a list of what was there. They could add it to their data bank and keep track of how much they had and what they needed to buy.

It was nearly dawn when they finished. Cait flopped down in one of the chairs in the waiting room, Coop across from her.

"Tired?" he asked.

"Exhausted."

"Let's go home."

The way he said it made her smile. "Gladly. We can—" She was about to suggest breakfast but the phone rang. She looked at her watch: 4:42 a.m. "This isn't office hours and it's Sunday."

Coop's face was serious. "Could be an emergency." He picked up the receiver and said "Yes" about eight times. "I'll be there as soon as I can... No, but I have someone here who can tell me." He hung up and looked at Caitlyn. "On the drive home, you can tell me where the Fredericks place is."

"It's—" Caitlyn began, but stopped. "I'll go with you."

"You don't need to. I can..." He smiled. "Okay. Help me gather things. Just so you understand, it's possibly a rabid raccoon."

"Who was on the phone and what did they say?"

"Celeste Wigman Schneider. She said—"

"Oh," Caitlyn cut in. "That woman is always hysterical. She's had three husbands and her kids are constantly in trouble. What were they doing at that old house in the wee hours of the morning?"

"Being threatened by an insane raccoon was what I was told. Do you know everyone in this town?"

"Pretty much. Tell me what you need." They gathered what Coop thought he might need, both for capture and testing. He grabbed his bag of surgical instruments.

Minutes later, they were in her Jeep and heading toward the old homestead. He asked about it. "Built in the 1800s, I guess. It's been falling down for years. Kelly said it was a make-out place when she was a kid."

"Is it still?"

"Yeah, it is. Adam did some repairs but it was years ago. He said he didn't want the roof falling in and killing his future players. He's the head coach at KU."

"And the ruler of Mason, from what I hear. I've heard 'Ask Adam' a dozen times. Doesn't he have a brother who gets into trouble?" When Cait didn't answer, he glanced at her. "Did I put my foot in it?"

"No." Her voice was quiet. "Adam had a younger brother, Robert, called Robbie. He was killed in Vietnam."

"I'm sorry about that. That war seems so long ago but it still affects people. Did he—?"

"There!" Cait said loudly. "That's it."

The sun was up enough that they could see the old house. The pink dawn light looked good on the gray siding. The house was perfectly symmetrical, with tall windows and a wide front door.

"It's quite beautiful," he said. "Who owns it?"

"Adam. Or maybe Kelly. Their lands have merged. Or

maybe they're separate, I don't know. But I do know that Heritage Harvests land butts up against this."

He parked in front of the house and turned off the engine. "If I asked you to stay in the car, what would you do?"

"Say yes, then stay right here."

She was so insincerely sincere that he laughed. Then he grabbed blankets from the back. "If you can, throw that over him. Do *not* try to capture him, hold him, touch him or—"

"Got it!" she said as she stepped down. "Too bad I'm not Kelly. She'd sit down on the grass and the critter would crawl onto her lap." She was looking at him.

"Nope, not me. I'm not magical. Just a grown-up kid who can't stand to see an animal in pain. Now, no more talking. Listen and watch."

They separated, going around the house, each carrying a blanket.

Caitlyn heard the sounds first. She waited until he came to her side, then pointed under the old house. He got down on his stomach, a small flashlight in hand, to look in the crawl space.

He stood up. "She's under there and I think I see the problem. I'm going under and will get her out."

"If the animal is rabid, maybe you should call someone."

"*I* am the one they'd call." He was smiling at her. "I'm going to tranquilize her and bring her out. I think she's injured."

"But…" Caitlyn began, then stopped. "Tell me what to do."

"Just wait here and be ready with the blanket."

She got down on her stomach and watched him snake himself under the old house. The floor was a foot and a half off the ground and there were old cans and bottles, rocks and millions of spiderwebs under there.

He was talking softly, soothingly, to the animal, calming it, reassuring it.

Then suddenly there was a tussle. The animal screeched and Coop moved backward, but he didn't come out.

Caitlyn waited. It was too dark to see much and she didn't want to disturb the mood with her questions.

It seemed like a long time before he came back out and in his arms was a blanket-wrapped bundle. He peeled it back to show her the sleeping raccoon.

"She has an injured foot and a couple of babies under there. My guess is that she thought her kits were in danger, so she protected them. Let's go inside so I can check her out."

It didn't take Coop long to sew up the cut on the sleeping raccoon's leg. Caitlyn stayed close and handed him whatever he asked for from the supplies. She was a good assistant and he knew it wouldn't take much to train her. *Too bad*, he thought, *she's wasted on a bunch of fruit trees.*

When it was done, he took the mother raccoon outside and put her back under the old house. He wanted her to wake up near her kits.

After he scooted out, he took a few minutes to walk around the old house. If it were restored it could be a beauty. Whoever had built it had money. There were some details on the windows and along the roof that took taste as well as money.

When he went back inside, he saw that Caitlyn had fallen asleep on one of the old mattresses. At least her head was on the clean blanket he'd given her.

She looked good lying there and for a moment he had a vision of snuggling up against her.

Spooning. It had been a long time since he'd felt the closeness of human contact. Not sex, just touch with someone he liked.

Abruptly, he turned away. It was light enough that he could see the inside of the house. It had a big living room with a fireplace. The mantel was gone but a visit to an architectural salvage yard could fix that. Cait was in the dining room, which had tall windows looking out to the back. The walls were covered with graffiti.

There was another sitting room that would make a good home office. The kitchen was along the back. Falling-down cabinets made the room quite ugly. Rat droppings were everywhere.

There were two staircases, the wide one in front and the narrow, steep one out of the kitchen. He took the skinny steps up. They weren't stable. If they weren't repaired soon, they'd collapse.

There were six bedrooms upstairs, but two of them were small. Servants' quarters. They would make good bathrooms.

He spent a few moments looking out the windows. He wasn't sure but he thought there had once been a manicured garden. Someone who knew about plants might be able to figure out what the original owner had installed.

He went downstairs and was putting away his instruments when Caitlyn woke up.

She sat up, blinking. "Sorry. Didn't mean to flake out on you. Did you put her back under the house?"

"Yes. She'll wake soon."

"Then tear off her bandages?"

"Probably. You ready to go?"

"Sure, but I'm starving. I have emergency food in my Jeep. Interested?"

"Very much so."

They went outside and he put his equipment in the back while Cait opened a metal cooler. Inside were so-called health food bars, packages of jerky and bags of trail mix. Bottles of water were at the side.

He pulled out jerky, trail mix and water. "Are you always prepared?" he asked.

"Sometimes I go somewhere and I want to stay."

He could tell that she was holding back information. "Anytime you want someone to talk to, maybe a stranger who isn't involved, I'm here."

"Thanks." She looked at him in speculation. "I'm beginning to think you might be an asset to Mason."

"I'm not sure about that." He gestured toward the house. "I like this place. Just before I left, my wife and I were looking at houses to buy. I liked the old ones but she wanted modern. We..." He let out his breath. "You ready to go?"

She didn't move. "You should buy this house."

"I told you, I'm broke."

"I bet I could work out a deal. Heritage Harvests will buy the property. I think it's about three acres. We'd put in an acre and a half of fruit trees, then lease the house and the remaining land to you. Nothing down, but you pay the land tax. The deal would be that you restore the house to what it used to be. Nothing modern. No demolition."

"How long a lease and who pays for restoration?"

"Ten-year lease, you pay for supplies and labor. If you don't buy the house in that time, it reverts to Heritage Harvests, and they'll reimburse you for whatever you've spent for the remodel."

"The appraisal price now and in this condition would be less than it would be if I restore it."

"Get the appraisal now and I'll see that you have four years to buy it at that price. Year five and it's reappraised."

He smiled. "You are a fixer as well as an organizer, aren't you?"

"I like being needed. Heaven knows my dad and uncles need me."

"What about your mother?"

Cait was silent.

"You don't have to tell me."

But he had confided in her. "You know those fairy tales where a kid grows up and finds out she or he isn't actually related to their family?"

"Sure."

"That's my mother and me." Cait hesitated. "I was a mess after Jared and I broke up. I went to Mom in Florida. I didn't know her very well, but I'd always been curious."

"Let me guess. You didn't fit in."

"Not at all. She got married not long after I was born and she had two boys, my half brothers. She and Dad never married." Cait paused. "They were a family."

"And you were an outsider."

"Yes. I'm Kansas through and through and they are a whole different culture. Different language, different everything."

"How long did you last with them?"

"A month at their house. Then I got a job at a big nursery and rented a tiny apartment and..." She shrugged. "It was good for me to be alone. I needed it."

"But you came home."

"Dad..." She took a breath. "He needed me. And the uncles tend to let unpleasant things go. They believe they'll fix themselves."

"Meaning that Cait will show up and fix it all. And besides, by then you were sick of being alone."

She smiled. "That's true. You know what my uncles did to make *sure* that I returned?" She didn't wait for an answer. "They quit telling me the news in Mason!"

"Who was dating? Scandals and triumphs? Births and deaths?"

"Exactly! They went from six-page letters about everything going on in Mason to half a page about the damned fruit trees."

"Totally wicked of them. What did your father write?"

"Just business. What was selling and what wasn't. No gossip at all."

"So you had to return to find out about the people you love."

"Yes, I did. What about you? You left your town. Do you miss your friends?"

"I'm not like you. You love many people. I cared only for two."

He didn't have to say which two people. "But you must have met people in your practice. Plus lots of wormy dogs and injured wildlife."

"That's true, but not one of them wrote me a letter saying he missed me."

"What about your parents? Siblings? Cousins? School friends?"

He chuckled at that. "You *are* Kansas. My parents were workaholics and I rarely saw them. No siblings. No cousins that I know about. I was a loner in school."

"I'm beginning to understand about you with the animals."

"Yup. Lots of them. I had a lazy nanny who left me alone with my pets while she read romance novels. Thousands of them! I used to help her hide them from my mother."

"Where are your parents now?"

He shrugged. "Traveling. Spending all the money they earned while I was growing up. Sometimes they send postcards. Remind me to give them my new address."

"You know what I think? You *need* us. You need busybody Mason, a place that makes you feel like you *belong*. And I need to help you with it. By the time Kelly returns, you'll be so deep in this town and the people that she'll have to keep you. I'll even find you a girlfriend."

"Are you volunteering?"

"Me? Heavens, no! I'm not… I mean, I can't…"

"I got it," he said. "For whatever reason, you're off-limits. So what does Mason have to offer in terms of girlfriends?"

"Pure Kansas health and vitality. Good morals and a great sense of humor. You can't do any better than us!"

He smiled. "And here I'd heard that California girls were—"

Cait snorted. "Wimps! Raised on tofu and bean sprouts. They don't even know what a burnt end is."

He was laughing. "Sounds good to me. I think I'd like something that would take my mind off my past."

"A Kansas sunflower will do that," she said. "I could stand a few sunflowers in my life."

For a moment they looked at each other, smiling.

Cait looked at her watch. "Dad is going to file a missing person's report on me. We need to go."

It was early Monday morning and Miguel was driving Cait's Jeep, with her beside him. They'd been in Ottawa getting supplies and were now heading toward Hatten land. They'd been told that cows had escaped and were endangering Heritage Harvests trees. Strong fences were important in Kansas.

If necessary, they would have to get a couple of Hatten horses and start herding. But then, with both Kelly and Adam away, the horses probably needed the exercise.

Cait had spent the whole morning telling her father every detail about the Saturday night and Sunday morning she'd spent with Dr. Jones. She was talking at lightning speed as he listened, mostly in silence.

"And he might buy the old Fredericks place and restore it. I came up with a lease-purchase deal that I think the uncles will like but maybe you can help talk them into it. Oh! And I said I'd get him a date or two. And—"

"Dates! Did he ask you to do that or was it your idea?"

"Um. Mine. But he's kind of lonely."

"*He* told you that he's lonely, so *you* said you'd fix him up?"

"Don't make it sound bad. It was very nice. We'd spent the whole night together and… Stop it!" She was looking at his raised eyebrow. "You know exactly what I mean. We were cataloging. Then he sewed up a raccoon. Don't let me forget that I need to call Mrs. Schneider and tell her to keep her kids at home. At least during the night."

"Celeste always was a pain. She used to drive Kelly crazy."

They were at the stoplight on Main Street and Miguel glanced at his daughter, but then he looked across her and his eyes changed to something Caitlyn had never seen before.

She whipped her head around. What in the world was he looking at?

Just a few feet from her, driving the truck next to them, was Vera Exton and she was staring at Miguel. Cait looked back and forth from one to the other. Their expressions were so intense, so, well, intimate, that she felt herself beginning to sweat.

Her dad didn't break eye contact with Vera, but when the light changed, they both floored their gas pedals. The trucks seemed to leap forward in a surge of speed and energy that made Caitlyn gasp.

She held on to the door armrest. Holy crap but they were still looking at each other, not the road.

The trucks were doing forty, fifty, then fifty-five. They were in the downtown of Ottawa. Not a place for speeding! Cait thought she might start whimpering in fear.

Vera broke the spell. Suddenly, she slammed on the brakes, did a turn that laid rubber and went down a side street.

Caitlyn's heart was pounding as she looked at her father.

He seemed to be calm as he slowed to the speed limit and took the road toward the Hatten place.

As far as Cait could see, he wasn't going to mention what just happened. "You know her," she whispered. "*Know* her. As in the Bible. You and Vera Exton."

Miguel frowned. "It was a high school thing. Not important."

"You didn't return to Kansas until after you graduated from *college*. Everyone knows Vera was going to marry Adam Hatten, but he ran off with cute little Kelly. People said Vera was so heartbroken that she fled to the Middle East with that man who was killed."

"Joe Harding."

"But *what* was going on with you and Vera?"

His silence showed that he had no intention of answering.

Caitlyn was wide-eyed. "What about you and Mom…? If you and Vera were an item, how did I get made? Did you…?" She drew in her breath. "Did you cheat on Vera? While she cheated on Adam? Did Kelly—?"

"Caitlyn," he said sternly, "I'd like for you to stop this."

"Mom said—"

"We both *know* what your mother told us!"

That made her stop talking.

They had reached the Hatten land and Miguel turned off the engine. They sat there in silence, looking out the windshield.

Caitlyn spoke first. "Have you seen her since she arrived?"

"Just for a couple of minutes. We didn't talk."

She put her hand on his arm. "I'm sorry for whatever happened. You and Mom and Vera Exton. It must have been awful."

He turned to her and smiled, but it didn't reach his eyes.

"It worked out well. Vera got to leave Mason and help save the world, your mom got a family and I got you. Everyone is happy." He stepped out of the truck.

Caitlyn watched him walk away. His words were good but the pain in his eyes was something she'd never seen before. It hit her that she'd never really thought about tragedies in her father's life. It had never occurred to her that there was a lost love in his life. Or that her father knew all about broken hearts.

Maybe this is what it means to be grown up, she thought. For a long time, all she'd thought about was her own anger and hurt about her and Jared. But today she was seeing her father as someone who possibly knew a great deal about pain and maybe about sacrifice.

Was *she* the reason he'd given up a woman he loved who he obviously *still* loved? The irony of it all weighed on her. If he and Vera had only known the *truth*.

CHAPTER NINETEEN

WHEN THEY GOT HOME, CAIT REALIZED that seeing her dad's face when he looked at Vera Exton was bringing her back to reality. His look and his little death-defying stunt in the truck. He was living proof that love could hurt for a lifetime.

Whatever had happened between her dad and Vera, Cait never, ever wanted to be in that much pain and certainly not for that long. Breaking up with Jared had been bad, but sometimes, deep down, she felt relief. She'd known him all her life. There'd never been any surprises. She knew what he was going to say before he spoke. Even his lovemaking— She made herself stop that train of thought.

With Coop, everything was new and fresh. Too new. Too fresh. And way too exciting!

If her life were different, yes, she'd go on a date with him. For a moment, she let herself imagine living in the beautifully remodeled Fredericks house. With him. There'd be animals and lots of fruit trees and...

She took a breath. It couldn't happen.

She called June Sanders, who everyone knew was the best

gossip in town, and told her Dr. Cooper Jones was a really great guy. "He's funny and interesting and is looking for a place to settle down. Yes, he's divorced, but he's ready to start dating."

"Thanks for the tip," June said, and hung up.

Miguel was standing nearby. "Sure you want to give him up?"

"Yes," Cait said. He waited for her to say more but she didn't. *I wouldn't do that to him.*

She made another call, this one to Forey, and Cait spun a story about Dr. Jones's loneliness. "I think maybe he loves animals as much as Kelly does, but he has no one to help him in the office." Her voice was rich with sadness. When her father raised an eyebrow at her, she turned her back on him.

"What a good idea!" Cait said. "Yes, call KU and see if you can find some help for him. I'm sure he'd appreciate it... Love you, too." She hung up.

"You're burning your bridges," her father said.

"Doing what I must." She quickly left the room.

The next day at breakfast, Forey called to say she'd found a receptionist and two veterinary students to help in Kelly's clinic. "You really lit up the town by saying he was ready to date. The girls are tossing names in a hat to see who gets him first. Even Louise Peverel entered."

"She has three kids and she's ten years too old for him!"

"You lost the right to judge when you threw him back into the water," Forey said tersely.

Caitlyn rolled her eyes as she listened. "Heather Winters? She's good. Very good." Heather was a beauty and smart and likable. She was a wife waiting to happen. Cait could imagine Coop and Heather living in the restored Fredericks house. It would be a perfect marriage, with three perfect children, and a perfect...

"What?" she asked. Forey repeated that Heather and Dr. Cooper were going out to dinner on Saturday night.

"Good," Cait said. "I'm sure they'll have a wonderful time." She hung up.

Miguel was reading one of his newspapers. "Did any of you girls consider letting Dr. Jones make his own decision about who he wants to date?"

"Don't be ridiculous," Cait said. Before he could say anything else, she said, "Have you been reading those newspapers all these years just to keep up with Vera Exton?"

Miguel put the paper in front of his face.

"People in glass houses..." She left the kitchen.

Caitlyn did her best to avoid Coop. It wasn't easy since he lived so close, but she knew when he left for work and when he returned. She managed to be on another part of the property whenever he appeared. After a couple of near misses when she pretended not to see him, she spent the night in her old bedroom in her father's house. The next morning, when Miguel saw her in his kitchen, he didn't say anything. But his knowing look made her face turn red. However, her embarrassment didn't make her go back to her own house. It was too close to Coop's trailer!

She did talk to the uncles about the house deal she'd outlined to Coop and they liked it. "I have some ideas about restoring that old place," Paul said. "It could be magnificent."

But Coop never spoke of it to them. They said that twice they'd tried to bring it up, but he wouldn't listen.

"Maybe he wanted *you* with the house," Seth said.

"We spent just a few hours together." Caitlyn was frowning.

"Sometimes it takes only minutes," Paul said.

"This is *not* a romance," she almost shouted. "It's a business deal. A way for a man to buy a house. That's *all!*"

When the uncles looked at her in silence, she made a sound of frustration. "How about if we go out for barbecue tonight?" Paul said. "That will make you feel better." He was offering Kansas penicillin.

With a toss of her hands in surrender, Caitlyn walked away.

During the week with her father, Caitlyn only mentioned Vera once. It was at night, the TV was off and they were both reading. John Grisham for Miguel; Amy Tan for Cait. "Have you been to see her?" she asked.

Miguel didn't look up. "I figure she came back here to stay at her sister's empty house to give herself peace to write something. I won't bother her."

Cait nodded, but she didn't believe that. Vera Exton traveled the world. Surely a cabin in a forest or a hut on a beach would give her more privacy than being in a big house in a small town that was full of people she'd grown up with, every one of whom was eaten with curiosity. Caitlyn had no doubt that the residents were ringing Vera's doorbell constantly.

But if her father didn't want to face the past, Caitlyn understood that.

On Sunday morning, the house phone was ringing before Caitlyn got out of bed. She stumbled to it.

"He's horrible!"

It was a woman's voice but Caitlyn didn't recognize it.

"He was sullen and sulky. Never said a word but his eyes spoke volumes. All night long, he glowered at me. Like an evil cartoon character."

"Heather," Caitlyn said.

"Yes, it's me. Your *former* friend. You wanted to get rid of him, didn't you? He probably fixated on *you*, so you dumped him on *us*."

"No!" Cait said. "That's not true. Dr. Jones is a great guy."

"You don't even call him by his first name. Really, Cait,

what you did is unforgivable. We *trusted* you. Believed you, and you dumped that sulking man on us. He made me feel awful, like I was ugly and stupid and a predator! I'm telling *everyone* what you did!"

"But I didn't—" Heather had hung up.

"Trouble in paradise?" her father said, yawning.

"I'm going to kill him. Just plain rip him into pieces. He has *ruined* me in this town. I didn't do anything to deserve this!"

"Except for pimping him out."

Caitlyn narrowed her eyes at her father. "If you think—"

The front door opened and in came the uncles. Unlike Caitlyn and her dad, they were dressed in crisp, clean clothes, carrying a basket of bran muffins fresh out of the oven. "We saw your light on and thought you'd like these."

Paul looked from one to the other. "What's going on?"

"Nothing!" Cait snapped.

"Heather Winters called and she had a rotten date with the doc and now she's mad at Cait," Miguel said.

"But that girl is Mason cream," Seth said. "I dated her mother for years. Although I thought we were friends but she threw me aside in a very unpleasant way."

"Wonder why?" Miguel said under his breath.

Paul was looking at Caitlyn. "Your name won't be fit to mention around this town."

"Quite the pariah," Seth said.

"I'm going to go over there and tell him what I think of him," Cait said.

"Oh," Seth said. "Take him some muffins."

"I'd like to give him some big, perfect red apples. From the grocery!" She stomped down the hall to her room and slammed the door.

"Hmm," Paul said. "The witch's poisoned apples."

Seth looked at Miguel. "Your daughter appears to be in love with the new vet."

"Even I figured that one out." Miguel yawned again.

"Does she know?" Paul asked.

"She hasn't a clue."

"I bet she thinks there'll be nothing after Jared," Seth said.

"Probably."

"Have you tried talking to her?" Paul asked.

"No."

"Think you could—?"

"No."

"But it might help if you—"

"No!" Miguel said. "And I forbid you two to say a word to her about this. Am I understood?"

The two men gave silent nods. They knew when he was being serious. He didn't allow anyone to do what he thought was bad for his daughter.

"So what's on for today?" Miguel asked.

"Nothing much," Seth said. "One of the workmen said he saw a light in that barren Hatten field. The one south of the river. He said the light seemed like it came from underground."

"Might be a spark from an electric fence," Paul said. "I've never understood why Adam hasn't done something with that field. But he never lets anyone touch it."

"Let's buy it," Seth said. "It'll be fertile from years of no use. Let's go look at it today and—"

"No," Miguel said softly. "That place is dangerous. An old well is there. That's why Adam keeps it fenced off. I'll go look at it."

"We'll all go," Paul said. "After Caitlyn finishes yelling at Dr. Jones, we'll have a picnic over there. Maybe he'll go with us. We can—"

"No!" Miguel was loud. "Stay away. I'll do it!"

"Okay." Paul spoke gently, like he was talking to an angry animal. "No picnics. You can go by yourself."

Miguel nodded.

Seth put the basket of muffins on a table. "We'll go to the Nelson-Atkins today," he said. "That's always a treat." They were backing out of the house.

"We'll see you, uh…"

"Later," Seth said.

"Yes, later."

They left quickly.

CHAPTER TWENTY

MIGUEL WAITED UNTIL HE'D SEEN CAIT-lyn storm toward the doc's trailer. For all her protest, she had certainly taken time with her appearance!

With a sigh, Miguel knew what he had to do. There was no more putting it off. Like he knew anything in the world, he was sure that the "underground light" was an invitation to him. Vera was in the old cellar and waiting for him.

Like his daughter, he dressed carefully: jeans, a denim shirt, boots. It's what Vera liked and, right now, what she wanted was what mattered to him.

He took his time getting there and he parked his truck under the trees where no one would see it.

He hadn't been in the cellar since the day he took Gabrielle down those stairs. There were so many bad memories about that day that even now, many years later, they still made his stomach turn. Vera's face with its hurt and disbelief, her horror at the betrayal, would always stay with him.

As young as he was then, Miguel hadn't thought past what he saw as his "ultimate sacrifice," an act that put him above sainthood. He had thrown away what he wanted most in life to give Vera her freedom.

While that had worked hideously perfectly, he hadn't for a second considered Gabby.

Later, she'd screamed at him, "You used me!" She'd bawled him out in two languages. She talked of his ancestors, his vanity, his lack of a true job, etc. But every direction she took led to one place. Miguel absolutely, positively *had* to marry her. *Had* to. There was no choice in the matter.

Rafe had backed her up. He was in total agreement. But then, he wanted them both to stay with him.

But Forey didn't agree. In fact, there was something in her manner that made Miguel believe he shouldn't "make an honest woman" of Gabrielle and marry her. So he didn't.

When Gabby said she was pregnant, it started all over again and he knew he had to give in.

She was going to be the mother of his child!

But by that time, Mrs. Carl was in Miguel's life and she'd stepped in. "I don't like her," she told Miguel. "If you marry her, she'll ruin your life and your child's."

"But it's my baby," he'd said. "I can't leave my child."

"You won't have to," Mrs. Carl said. And she arranged everything.

Miguel had had little time to think about what he'd lost. But at night, alone in his bed, he yearned for Vera.

After he had custody of Caitlyn, he would hold his child and whisper that Vera should have been her mother. When one of Cait's first words was "Vera," he stopped all audible references to her. He kept Vera inside, hidden away. His only contact with her was what he read in the media and through Kelly. After every visit with her sister, Kelly and Miguel spent an afternoon together. He relished the anecdotes she told him, memorizing each one. There was a hidden safe in his bedroom.

It didn't contain riches or deeds. It was packed full of photos and memorabilia from twenty-plus years of loving Vera Exton.

At each of their meetings, Miguel asked the same question: "Did she ask about me?"

Kelly, always kind, brushed over her "no," then said she'd made sure Vera heard about him and saw photos of him and Caitlyn. Vera never commented on the pictures, never asked for more information. But when Cait was four, a local photographer had taken an especially good snapshot of father and daughter. The love between them seemed to glow from the picture.

"It disappeared," Kelly told him. "I looked all over the hotel room, under the bed and even behind the nightstand. But that picture wasn't there." She looked at Miguel. "I think Vera took it."

After that, he made sure Kelly always left with a professional portrait of him and his daughter. But no more went missing.

If nothing else, the annual photo shoots made him keep in shape. Horse riding, workouts in the fancy gym the uncles had set up and turning down desserts had kept him lean and hard-bellied.

He pulled up the door of the cellar and went down the stairs. The last time he'd been on those stairs, he'd felt that his life was over.

Vera was standing to the side, but he didn't look at her. Instead, he glanced around the place.

Kelly had told him that she'd fixed it up. She said she was using it to attract Vera back home. "She needs to know there's a place here where she can hide from us."

The inside was all new and rather posh. He was glad to see that the infamous couch was gone, as was Vera's big table where they'd made the posters. It was still just one room, but against the back wall was a bed and in front of it was a seat-ing area. There was a cabinet with a fridge, a hot plate and a toaster oven.

Without looking at her, he said, "It's as fancy as the cabin where you and Adam used to go."

She sighed. "You're still jealous of him."

"Of course I am. And you fell in love with Joe Harding."

"I did." She sounded happy about it. "He replaced the father I lost too early. He was also an alcoholic who loved all women. He had every sexually transmitted disease there is."

Finally, he looked at her. She looked good. News photos didn't do her justice. Her hair was still wild but she'd tied it back so it was almost presentable. "You didn't put that in your book."

"I was being kind to his wife and kids. And saving his image in the world."

He sat down in one of the chairs and she sat across from him. It was an awkward feeling, so close but so far apart. "Kelly's kept me up to date on you."

"I assumed so. She and I became friends, true friends. It was no longer big sister, little sister. When I was shot, she came and stayed with me."

He nodded, looking at her. The silence between them was heavy. "You're still angry at me."

"Why shouldn't I be? Nothing has changed. *You* chose what I would do with *my* life."

Miguel was calm. "Your mother said you burned everything because you weren't going to leave. You were going to give up your life *for me*. Would you have been happy being a Kansas housewife? Kids and cows? Being a travel agent? A life of seeing people go and do while you stayed here?"

"I—" The anger left her. "No. I would have been miserable. I would have made *you* miserable."

"And our children."

"You could have gone with me."

"You didn't ask me to go. You assumed I wouldn't leave here." She narrowed her eyes at him. Her mouth was a hard line. "Okay, so maybe you did ask. Sort of. And maybe I did say no."

"You're happy here. You have your daughter. Kelly says you two are a perfect pair. You got what you needed."

"And so did you."

"So why am I here now?" Her anger was returning. "Kelly told me I had to return for you, that you were in a very bad way."

He didn't say anything.

"Kelly thought your daughter and her son were going to get married. The whole family came apart when she dropped him. I got about twenty letters that were tearstained. I could hardly read them. Kelly said—"

"Cait and Jared are first cousins," Miguel whispered.

"—that Jared was suicidal. He—" She halted. "What?"

"Robbie Hatten." Miguel could hardly be heard.

"What are you saying?"

"That summer, Robbie was sneaking around with some woman. It was Gabby. She got pregnant."

"He was a kid!"

"Old enough."

Vera stared at him in silence, trying to comprehend what he'd just told her. "Kelly doesn't know."

"No one does. Just Cait and me and Gabrielle."

Vera's voice softened. "So Caitlyn isn't...?"

"She isn't my biological daughter," he said. "We always wondered what ancestor gave her the blue eyes. And her skin tone is so light and..." He looked away. "I should have guessed."

"I'm so sorry. Adam..."

When he turned back, there was fire in Miguel's eyes. "She's Adam Hatten's niece. He always got everything, didn't he? You, then my daughter."

Vera was beginning to recover from her shock. "Tell me about Caitlyn. How did she find out?"

He took a moment to get himself under control. "Cait never had much contact with her mother, but when she was thinking about getting married, they began exchanging letters. Maybe Cait felt she needed a mother then, and—"

"Of course she told her about Jared."

"Right. Gabby flew back here to tell me the truth." He grimaced. "The bitch! When I think of all she put us through! That summer, she was banging the Hatten kid while trying to get *me* to *marry* her!"

"She could have used birth control but she didn't. She…" Vera thought for a moment. "My guess is that it was the act of a desperate woman. If she got pregnant, yours or Robbie's, she could probably get one of you to marry her. She wanted to stay in the US any way she could."

"And I played into her hands when I used her to…to…"

"I know. You used her to make me leave. Kelly told me why you'd done it, but I didn't believe her. I told Joe what had happened but he didn't say anything. About a year later, we were being shot at by a bunch of drunken soldiers. They didn't want us there. Joe said, 'So this is what that guy gave up his life to give you?' It was just the one sentence but it made me see the truth. I wanted to call you and tell you that I knew."

"I wish you had."

"No. It was better this way. If I'd called, I would have taken away *your* freedom. You got your daughter and you didn't have to marry Gabby. And thanks to my leaving, you got the opportunity to have a real life. A normal one." She glared at him. "That you didn't take it was your fault, not mine."

Miguel gave a half grin. "Marry someone else? Some pretty blonde girl who adored me? Who would braid Cait's hair? We'd have a couple more kids? Boys, maybe? I could teach them to ride horses. How to barbecue beef."

By the time he finished, Vera was smiling. "Now that I'm here, I can see the impossibility of that. You have a temper. You need someone to hold it down." For a moment they stared at each other in silence. "So now what?" she asked.

Miguel didn't move but his body and face changed. "That bed looks nice." Vera's mouth twitched. "Clean sheets."

"I've always liked clean sheets. Actually, they turn me on."

"What a coincidence. I feel exactly the same way."

In the next second, they were on each other. Mouths and hands moving with years and years of suppressed lust. The sheets were well used.

CHAPTER TWENTY-ONE

CAIT KNEW COOP WOULD BE HOME. BUT then, he wasn't exactly adventurous. He didn't spend his evenings in a bar. He came home after work with a bag of takeout—he never seemed to cook—and didn't go out again. Except for one night. She woke when she heard his old car go out and she didn't go back to sleep until he returned three hours later. That afternoon she went to Gresham's and found out that Dr. Coop had delivered a breech calf.

"He did a good job," June Sanders's husband said. That was high Kansas praise. Last night with Heather was his only evening out for anything social.

Not that Cait was keeping track. Not that it was any of her business. Certainly not that she cared.

But what he'd done to Heather *was* her business. Outsiders never seemed to understand what it was like to live in a small town. Those people were separate even from their next-door neighbors. In Mason, no one was separate from anybody else. What he'd done to Heather was going to directly affect Caitlyn.

She *had* to fix this!

Outside his door, she stopped and took some deep breaths. She needed to stay calm, reserved. She knocked on his door.

No answer.

She knocked louder.

"It's open," came his voice.

Trying to remove her frown, she entered. The door opened into the tiny kitchen to the right, a two-seater banquette to the left. Past it was what passed for a living room with an old couch and a chipped coffee table. Beyond that was the bath and bedroom. When she was a child, her crib had been in the living room.

Coop stepped out of the bathroom, wearing only a white towel around his hips. It looked like pulling calves at 3:00 a.m. kept him in shape. "Did you run out of hiding places?"

Ignoring his question, she turned her back to him. "Everyone is angry at me! You were horrible to Heather." She heard him moving about. Then he came to the kitchen.

"I'd offer you coffee but I don't have any. Your uncles left me six kinds of tea. Want some?"

She turned to face him. He had on a pair of sweatpants that hung down low. No shirt. He wasn't a very hairy man. In fact, he was just exactly as hairy as she liked. She started to tell him to put on a shirt but she could imagine his sarcastic look.

"Why did you do it?" She sat down on the plastic seat under the window. There was a tear along the back. She and Jared used to use the trailer for privacy. They tore the seat when they—

When she looked at Coop, he seemed to be waiting for her to give him her full attention. He was leaning against the counter. "Out with it."

"What you did last night may be the way you treat people in California, but here in Kansas, we're *nice*. Heather said you sulked and sneered, that you refused to even *talk*. Why would you do that to her?"

He filled a teakettle with water, put it on to boil, then turned back to her. "She had researched me. Like I was a prize bull she was considering buying."

Cait shrugged.

He filled two mugs full of hot water, put them on the table, then opened a box full of assorted tea bags. "Lemon? Milk?"

She shook her head no.

"When I agreed to a date, that's what I meant. A few drinks, some laughs, conversation." He dunked his tea bag in his mug. "But right away I saw that your friend was a brooding hen. Three dates with her and she'd expect a ring, with marriage four months later. She'd get pregnant on her wedding night, if not sooner."

What he was saying was exactly right, especially about Heather. For all that she was beautiful, etc., she wasn't *married*. Her high school boyfriend had run off with a girl from Saint Louis. Heather had something to prove to everyone.

But Cait would have swallowed her tongue before she said that. "Well, what did you expect? You're a catch. You have a job and potential. You're not ugly. And the whole town knows you want to renovate the Fredericks house and stay in Mason." When he raised his eyebrows, she said, "The uncles aren't known for keeping secrets."

"You people got to know each other growing up. If I'm supposed to marry the first one I date, how do I get a choice?"

He said it all so seriously that it took a second to realize he was joking. Maybe. "Three," she said just as seriously. "That's the limit. Three different girls, then you choose one of them."

"I see. What if I go to four?"

"Then you're a male slut. Not a good name. We'll say you're just playing around, toying with women's emotions."

"That sounds like it would take away my status as a 'catch'?"

"Yes." She leaned back in the seat. "What am *I* going to do? Everyone thinks I know that you're a jerk and I was trying to get rid of you. Heather is furious with me."

"Should I buy her an engagement ring so they'll forgive you?"

"Couldn't hurt." She looked at him. "You're not sorry in the least, are you?"

"Your friend is lovely to look at, but she's not very smart, is she? I bet she'd agree with Betty's filing system."

Cait's lips twitched.

"Anyone ever put Heather and Taran together?"

"Oh, no, you don't. I have dibs on him."

"So he asked you out, did he? Betty invited you to dinner this weekend? What color food do you think she'll serve?"

"You really are a despicable man."

"Heather agrees completely." He stood up. "Let's go get some food and take it out to the Fredericks place. I'd like to look at that house more closely. Maybe make a floor plan. Hey! With all your fruit tree experience, I bet you know about plants. You can redo the garden."

"I don't know anything about garden design."

"You have to know more than me. I'd probably put the plants in upside down."

"We need to talk about money."

Coop groaned. "Some Sunday date."

"I am *not* a date!" She was serious.

"Right. In Kansas, dates are a prelude to a walk down the aisle."

Cait sighed. "Taran and I will have a cake full of strawberries. My dress will be—"

"Okay," Coop said. "We'll talk about money. I have none." He opened the trailer door. On the step was a pretty basket that appeared to be full of food. "This could only be from your uncles." There was a note on the side that said, "We're off to the KC Zoo. Thought you two might like this." He turned to Caitlyn. "This was nice of them."

She was frowning. "*Too* nice!"

It didn't look like she was going to go with him. "Help me make a floor plan of the house and I'll buy you a DQ cone."

She hesitated.

"*Two* of them."

"We need paper and a tape measure and—"

"All of it is in my car. I bought everything yesterday."

She nodded and followed him out the door. "You need a different car."

"I'll put it on my list of things to buy as soon as I get some money."

Vera and Miguel were in the cellar and in bed together, as they had been for most of the last three days.

Smiling, he rolled off her. "We're not kids anymore. I need rest." He was quiet for a moment, then said, "Have there been many men?"

"Yes. Lots. I have a little red notebook where I list them. I don't put in their names, just the places. I'm trying for sixty countries. I'm up to fifty-seven."

"I deserved that."

"What about you? Lots of women?"

"Only four."

"Oh." She sounded defeated. "Just four."

"What does that mean?"

"That they were long-term. Marriage material, right?"

"Sometimes I felt that Cait needed a mother."

"But nothing for you?"

He knew she was being sarcastic but he was honest. "I tried

to feel something for them, but I couldn't." He took her hand in his and for a while they were silent.

"What happens now?" he asked.

"I promised Reuters I'd go to India in September, then maybe Cambodia. Nepal is—"

He looked at her.

"I know I'm avoiding the issue. Since you have a history of deciding my life for me, why don't you tell me what I'm going to do?"

"Retire. Stay here with me. Cait will marry her vet and give us a dozen grandkids." With each syllable, Vera's look of horror increased.

"Okay," he said, "so you leave and I stay. I'll send you photos of us." He paused. "Guess my grandkids won't look like *me*."

"And I won't have any children or grandchildren, so we're even."

He smiled. "I never could get any sympathy from you."

"Why don't you go with me?"

"And do what? I'd be useless. I'd just follow you around. I'd be Vera Exton's—"

"Boy toy?"

"I rather like that idea. Or maybe I could get the press to call me your Man of War."

Vera snorted. "Good luck on manipulating *us*."

His eyes sparkled. "I thought you liked the way I manipulated you."

She started to respond in an appropriately teasing way, but she looked into his eyes. "What's worrying you?" She didn't let him answer. "No. Wait. It's your daughter."

"Yes," he said. "She's been through a lot. The Hatten family is angry at her about Jared. They pretend that they're not but we feel it. And Jared! He has no idea what's going on."

"Did you even consider telling them the truth?"

"No," Miguel said. "They have enough. They don't get my daughter, too."

"Robbie..."

"Yeah, right. His death was hard for everyone. He barely got off the plane before he was—"

"Shot," Vera said, and her whole body tensed. "If only we'd protested the war more. Louder. I should have led a march on DC. Organized a—"

Miguel pulled her head to his shoulder. "Yes, we all should have done more, but we can't go back."

For a while they were quiet, remembering those days of rallies and sit-ins and violence. Sometimes Miguel's bayonet wound hurt as much as when it was new.

Vera spoke softly. "Adam would like to know that something of Robbie exists."

Anger shot through Miguel. He got out of bed and pulled on his jeans. "Then Cait would be taken over by the Hattens? They'd take her on vacations around the world? Maybe Adam would give her a yacht for her birthday."

Vera sat up, the sheet up to her arms. "Come on! Get real. They aren't that rich."

Miguel pulled on his shirt. "What about Jared? He's supposed to sit next to his *cousin* at meals? His former girlfriend?"

Vera was frowning. "How intimate were they?"

"Not 'all the way' is what Cait said."

Vera didn't reply but her raised eyebrows said it all.

"I don't want to talk about this anymore. I am *not* going to give my daughter to Adam Hatten."

"What does Cait say?"

"She agrees with me."

"How convenient," Vera said. "I bet you told her what

you want. Then she had the choice of breaking your heart or obeying you."

He narrowed his eyes at her.

Vera smiled. "I'd forgotten that look. I bet it scared your four women, didn't it? It is downright frightening. Dark eyes, that gorgeous honey-colored skin of yours. Yes, quite intimidating."

Miguel gave her a look of disgust. "I had forgotten what you're really like."

"Poor you," she said.

He couldn't contain his laughter. "Okay, you've made your point. You want me to tell Adam that he has more in his full life." He waved his hand. "I have to go."

"Me, too."

"Writing something?"

"Yes, always, but I'm also trying to find a photographer to go with me. They're a bunch of lazy scaredy-cats. They—" Her eyes widened. "You could do that job."

"Oh, no. Not me. I have too much to do here. And Cait *needs* me."

"Does she?"

"Stop it! I'm not one of your peons you can order about."

"Never thought you were. You stayed here while I went away. And that worked out really well, didn't it? You exude happiness."

Miguel closed his eyes for a moment. "The problems now are temporary. I have a life. People need me. Pauly and Seth need me to—" He stopped, as the way she was looking at him was making him angry.

"The man I knew fought for what was right. But I'm sure staying here and making sure Cait doesn't blab your secret to the Hattens is a worthwhile life goal."

"I never—" He was too angry to speak coherently. With a look of anger, he left.

Vera leaned back in the bed. Now, *that* was the Miguel she knew. And loved. She lay there for a while, smiling. Then she got up and dressed. There was somewhere she needed to go.

Cait was holding the clipboard and writing down the measurements that Coop gave her. "Your new employees couldn't be that bad," she said. "Aunt Forey said they were all highly recommended."

"They're kids. You know what they did when the toilet paper roll was empty? That's eighteen feet, six inches."

She wrote the number on the sketch of the rooms. Later, they'd put the plan in the computer. "I hate to hear."

"They pulled a roll out of the cabinet and set it on top of the holder. Fourteen and a half feet." He closed the tape.

"Because Mom always put the paper on the holder for them."

"Right. Only in this case, *I* was supposed to do it."

"Their dad. How cute."

He looked at her in speculation.

"What's that look for?"

"If *you* ran the office, you could—"

"No! Absolutely not."

"But I need—" At her look, he stopped talking. For a few minutes, he measured and she recorded the numbers.

When they took a break to drink the bottles of organic, no-sugar-added juice the uncles had included, he asked about her life. "Are you planning to always live in your little house? Always work at Heritage Harvests? I get the idea that you don't really date anyone."

Part of her wanted to tell him to mind his own business. But they were becoming friends. True friends were something no one could afford to lose. "I don't know. Sometimes I think of going off with Vera Exton."

His face showed his surprise. "Is that the kind of thing you always wanted to do?"

"No. Not really. It's just a thought. To do something important appeals to me."

"I think that what she does may be a calling, like becoming a preacher. I can't see you in, say, Vietnam unless maybe you went on a quest to find the grave of the youngest Hatten kid."

Cait looked at him in shock. "Why did you mention him?"

"I don't know. Mention of Vera made me think of Vietnam and that led me to... What's wrong?"

"Nothing. In Kansas, we take death and war very seriously." She stood up. "Let's finish this and get out of here."

Coop didn't know what he'd said wrong, but it seemed to be important and it made him curious. Was she upset at the doubt he'd cast on her and Vera Exton? Or was it the mention of Robbie Hatten that bothered her?

Whatever it was, he was going to see if he could find out.

CHAPTER TWENTY-TWO

CAIT DIDN'T BOTHER TO KNOCK ON HER father's door before she entered his house. He was in the living room and, as he always did lately, he scurried to hide the books and papers he was looking at. If it were BC—Before Cooper—she would have asked him what he was doing. But not now. Cait had too many of her own problems to snoop into anyone else's.

"You mind?" She had a folder full of papers the uncles had handed her and she needed to sort them.

Miguel nodded toward Cait's favorite chair. "Go ahead. I'm, uh, reading." Even his hesitation sparked no interest in her.

Tonight was the big party for Vera Exton. It was at the Hatten house and most of Mason was going. Why not? Free beer and the Jack Stack restaurant was catering. It was a Kansas dream come true.

Cait and her father had been invited but they'd turned it down. Miguel told Caitlyn she should go. "Your doctor will be there."

"When isn't he there?" she'd mumbled.

Miguel put an arm around her shoulders and gave a hug of understanding. "Hattens take whatever they want."

Usually, when he said something like that, she disagreed. But this time she didn't.

Since Kelly and Adam had returned from their trip, Coop had disappeared from Cait's life. For weeks after their afternoon measuring the Fredericks house, she and Coop had become, well, almost inseparable. At least that's what the uncles called it.

If there was one thing about Coop, it was that he didn't give up. He wanted Cait to help him at the clinic and he didn't quit asking until she did. Every evening, he found a reason why they should share a meal, watch a movie or discuss something he considered important.

And important to him meant keeping his job. He wanted to impress Kelly when she returned. "Should I paint the place?"

"I think redoing the files will do it."

"We put them back the way they were. She won't see anything different."

"I'll tell her," Cait said. "And she'll see the closet."

"*You* did that, not me."

"Okay, Eeyore, I'll tell her everything you did. And I'll make sure she hears from everyone in town about how you've sewn up animals and pulled them into life, and all the other things you've done."

"Thanks," he said. "I couldn't do this without you."

The way he smiled at her was so warm that she blinked at him. "Why do you *really* want me in the office?"

He just kept smiling.

"Heather?"

"And Leslie and a couple of others."

Cait smiled back. "Just be yourself and they'll go away."

"Thanks for the vote of confidence. What do you want for lunch? Besides DQ, that is?"

Friends, she thought. Over the weeks, that's what they'd become. They could talk about anything.

Well, she hadn't confided in him about her connection to the Hatten family. Hadn't told him about her and Jared. And she'd told no one, not even her father, what had happened when she visited her mother. But then, she planned to take that secret to her grave.

One night as Cait was in bed, half-asleep, she thought, *If this were a movie, this is the part where they'd play music.* Some fabulous melody, composed by Carter Burwell, of course, would play while the film showed her and Coop together.

Sleepily, she went over all the scenes that would be shown.

The KC Zoo had called him and asked if he knew anything about large animals. He'd answered yes before they told him how large.

He called Cait. "KC Zoo wants me to check out an elephant. Wanna go?"

She was out the door before he finished his sentence. It was a glorious experience!

She went with him on several of his calls. She helped hold a snake that had swallowed a toy windup mouse. The motor was still running.

But it wasn't one-sided. Coop had spent two weekends helping pick bugs off the fruit trees. They dropped them into buckets of soapy water.

"*Sure* you don't want to spray these trees?" he asked.

"Be quiet!" Cait hissed. "Or I'll sic the uncles on you. They'll lecture you until your ears bleed."

"I'm picking! I'm picking!"

Forey had been pleased to see them together. She wanted

to unite Cait with the Hattens, but if that wasn't to be, Coop was a good second. "He *is* Kelly Hatten's partner."

"We hope he's hired," Cait said.

Forey had given her a look to not be absurd. She put on a big picnic for a couple dozen people.

Rafe wasn't in good health but he was pleased to sit to the side and watch everyone having fun.

"It may be my imagination," Coop said, "but have all the titans of Mason industry been invited?"

Cait laughed at that, but due to hard work and a lot of common sense, there were several prosperous people in Mason. Some of them owned businesses in KC. "Forey wants them to meet you so they'll call you when they have an animal problem."

"Me instead of the big shots at the giant Ottawa clinic?" She laughed again, but then, Coop often made her laugh.

As Caitlyn thought of those weeks, she could almost hear the music playing. There would be balloons and cute dogs and children with ice-cream cones. Or maybe Cait would have the ice cream. Give the kids four-inch-wide lollipops.

The difference between her vision and the movie scene was that the made-up ones always ended with love. And maybe a ring. Movie music scenes were *always* deeply romantic.

But with Coop and her, there was none of that. He'd never come close to making a pass at her. Had never made an off-color remark, or even a suggestive hint.

"I might as well be a boy," she'd muttered more than once.

One time, her father heard her. "I like him even more," Miguel had said.

"But—" Cait stopped at her father's look. She couldn't very well tell him that she wanted Coop to at least try to kiss her or more.

If it were a movie, the music would stop when a plane carrying Kelly and Adam Hatten arrived in Kansas City.

Kelly had been pleased with everything Coop had done. Cait, standing in the background, smiled proudly.

"I couldn't have done it without Caitlyn," he said. "She organized and cleared and—"

"Thank you." Kelly glanced at Cait, but there was no warmth in her eyes. But then, Caitlyn had dumped her son without giving an explanation. Kelly's words and her cool look were a dismissal. Cait picked up her bag and left.

That had been over a week ago and she'd rarely seen Cooper since then.

Miguel said, "He's been swallowed by the Hattens. Get used to it. It happens often."

Caitlyn gave herself pep talks about how silly she was being.

As a friend, she should be glad he was meeting new people. Glad he was being accepted in Mason.

Yesterday, the uncles told her they were working on buying the old Fredericks house. "So we can lease it to Dr. Cooper. It was such a good idea you had."

"Aren't I clever," Cait muttered, then walked away.

She'd seen Heather at the grocery and she told Cait she'd misjudged Coop. "I saw him at the Hattens' and he was really nice. Jared likes him a lot. They— Oh! Sorry, Cait. I better be going. I'm meeting them—" She waved her hand. "You probably don't want to hear that. 'Bye."

"Yeah, 'bye." Cait tossed broccoli in the basket. "Jared and Cooper as friends. Perfect."

When Cait got to her Jeep, she resisted the urge to cry. It's not like she and Cooper could ever be a couple. Not a *real* one. He was the type of man who wanted, needed, a family. He'd already been married. That his wife had cheated wasn't his fault. Coop had complained of his date with Heather, that she wanted marriage and kids. But now that he had job security, was going to have what would be a beautiful house and was occupied in town, maybe things were different. Maybe now he liked Heather's desire for home and family. It's something that they might have in common.

CHAPTER TWENTY-THREE

THREE DAYS LATER THERE WAS A TOR-nado warning; the sirens went off, and Caitlyn was terrified. Where was Cooper? He was from California, so what did he know about tornadoes?

She called the clinic but no one answered. Of course not. The warning sirens were screaming, so they were taking shelter. They weren't sitting by a phone hoping the roof wasn't lifted off.

She tried to remember if she'd heard anyone complain about a sick animal. Hoof-and-mouth? Anthrax? Swallowed anything? Nothing came to mind. *Where can he be?*

The answer came to her. The Fredericks house, of course. The uncles said they often saw him there. No purchase deal had been made, no papers drawn up, but Coop often went there.

Alone? she'd wondered when told of his visits, but she didn't ask.

Now was not the time to think of that. She ran to her Jeep. There was the urgency of finding Coop, but she also didn't want her father or uncles to see her. If her dad saw her getting into a vehicle when a tornado was coming, he'd… She didn't want to think of what he'd say, but the words *stupendous stupidity* were sure to be part of his bawling-out.

The sky was dark and Caitlyn drove with her face as close to the windshield as she could get it.

She couldn't see the tall funnel but that meant nothing. They could turn on a dime.

She was concentrating so hard that she didn't see the big black truck until she almost hit it. She swerved hard and went into a deep ditch. Her forehead hit the steering wheel. Then everything was a daze.

"Caitlyn!" a man was shouting at her. "Caitlyn!"

She thought it was her father and turned with a smile. "Hello."

He opened the door and she just sat there. In the next moment, he was pulling her out.

Cait looked up to see two vehicles, both at forty-five-degree angles, in a ditch that she knew led down to a creek. "I don't know where Cooper is," she said.

"He's at my house and safe. Your dad is out looking for you. Pauly called me in a panic because no one could find you."

It was Adam Hatten. She could hardly hear him over the noise of the wind.

"We have to go now!" He grabbed her hand and they began running. He led her across a field, the one that her uncles wanted to buy for their fruit trees.

The tree branches overhead were bent nearly double. She heard a loud crack, then watched as Adam tossed a broken branch aside to expose a weathered door flat in the ground. He lifted it to expose stairs that led down into darkness.

He went down the steps, then held his arms up to her. She took his hands and went down until they reached the floor.

"Stay here while I turn on the lights."

She heard him move along the wall. Then a switch flicked and the lights came on. Adam ran up the stairs to pull the door closed and the noise was greatly reduced.

She looked around. It was a big room of what looked to be the basement of a house, and it was quite nice. Someone was taking good care of the place. There was a living room, a kitchenette and a bed against the back wall. Except for the absence of a bathroom, it was a nice apartment.

Adam was standing to the side, watching her, seeming to be waiting for her questions or, more likely, to ask her questions.

Caitlyn wanted to run back up the stairs. A tornado couldn't be worse than being alone with Jared's father. He was sure to ask her questions that she did not want to answer.

"Are you all right?"

"Fine." She felt her forehead. There was a lump but no blood. "It's just a bruise. I've been hit on the head by apples harder than this."

He was looking at her as though trying to decide if she was telling the truth.

"I better go. Dad will be really worried. I should—" A crash above their heads made her stop.

Adam ran up the stairs and she watched him try to push the door up but it didn't move. "I think a tree just fell over the door. We'll have to wait to be rescued."

"Who's going to do that?" Cait asked. "No one knows this place exists." Adam raised an eyebrow.

Since it was clean and well kept, it certainly was known about. "What is this place?" Adam didn't reply. "I'm all grown up. If you secretly meet someone here—"

"I should be offended at that, but it's so ridiculous that I'm not." He was looking at her with the same coldness in his eyes that his wife had. "I guess you *are* grown up. And adults can handle the truth. This hidden place is where your father and

Vera used to meet in the seventies and where they meet now. But they think no one knows."

Cait kept her expression as neutral as she could.

"You don't look surprised."

She wasn't about to tell of the breakneck ride down Main Street. Her father and Vera, with eyes locked as they raced. No, she wasn't surprised. "I don't know the details."

"Vera and Miguel. One of the great love affairs of all time."

"But how did my mother figure into that?"

"You asked for the truth. Gabby was a means to an end. Vera was so in love with Miguel that she was going to stay here in Mason. Your dad went to bed with Gabrielle to force Vera to leave the country and do what she was meant to do. Sorry to say it, but there was never any love between your parents."

Cait well knew that. What shocked her was Vera Exton. Her reputation was that nothing hindered her. "The famous journalist was going to give it all up for the man she loved? For my father?"

"Yes. They used to hide out in here. There was a big table over there where they made posters protesting the Vietnam War. They marched together."

It wasn't easy hearing that her father had kept such a big secret from her. "Coop asked if she did that, but I didn't know."

"No one in Mason did, but Vera never knew fear. Or your dad. He was stabbed with a bayonet in a rally that turned violent."

Cait looked away. She knew about the scar on his side. When they went swimming he would make up stories of how he got it. Ogres and unicorns often played a part.

"Maybe if we'd all helped in those protests, my brother would be alive now."

He was talking about Robbie. She turned to him. "I'm sorry about your brother." She took a breath. "What was he like?"

For a moment, Adam looked away. "He was a smart-ass, devil-may-care. He did what he wanted when he wanted to do it. But he was likable. Very, very likable." Tears were starting in Adam's eyes. "My little brother never had a chance to live." He looked at her. "Sometimes Kelly gets mad at me and I have no idea what I did wrong. Did my son do something to you that he doesn't know he did? Why did you break up with Jared?"

"We never had an argument. We agreed on everything."

"Is that bad?"

"No. It was great."

"Then why? Please tell me. Whatever it was, I'll keep it our secret. Was it another girl? Was he flirting? Or was it something more serious? Whatever it was, you can tell me."

"No, no. There was nothing bad. Jared is a good person. He never did anything bad to me."

"Then *why*?"

Maybe it was that Adam had revealed a great secret to her, or maybe it was that she was sick of holding in the truth. Maybe it was hearing how her father had fought against that useless war. Whatever the reason, she couldn't hold it in any longer. This secret was causing too much pain to too many people. "Jared is my cousin. My *first* cousin. I can't… I couldn't—"

"Miguel and Gabby aren't related to my family. They—" Adam's eyes widened as he realized what she was telling him. "Robbie? *He* is your father?"

"My mother knew she was pregnant when she went to bed with…" Her chin came up. "With my father. *Miguel* is my father."

Adam nodded. "Of course he is. But Robbie…" He was thinking. "Yes, back then there was a woman he was seeing. I never asked who it was. I just got angry when he stayed out all night. I guess it was…"

"My mother." Cait took a few breaths. "She didn't tell anyone. At least not until she had to. When she heard about Jared and me, she came here and told us."

Adam took a moment to digest this. "Miguel gave Gabby every penny he had to get custody of you."

"I know. And Mrs. Carl did, too. I've always loved hearing the story of how they wanted me so much."

"Why didn't Gabby come to me? I would have—"

Instant anger came to Cait. "You would have paid even more for me?"

Adam was calm. "Yes, but it wouldn't have been like that."

Cait released her anger. "Maybe she knew that Dad would give his whole life to me. You had Kelly and would have more kids and…" She took a breath. "With Dad, I am one of one, not one of many."

"I don't like that idea, but I understand it." Adam paused. "Your father hates me."

Cait didn't disagree.

"He must have been ripped apart when he was told."

Cait swallowed. "Yes, he was."

Adam was quiet for a moment. "He must think I have everything he ever wanted. He's loved Vera since we were children, but when we were adults, she and I were…" He didn't finish.

"People say they thought you two would marry. I never heard a word about my dad and Vera."

"Few people knew. They found this place and kept it a secret from everyone, even me. They came back to it when they were adults."

"And that was when you and Vera were a couple?"

"Today it's called friends with benefits. Everyone in town was asking when we were going to get married."

"But there was Kelly," Caitlyn said.

"Yes." Adam smiled. "It's funny now but it wasn't then. Kelly and I were falling in love but we held back. We didn't so much as touch each other. And meanwhile, Miguel and Vera were—" He looked at Cait and shrugged.

"Doing the dirty in their underground love nest?"

Adam smiled again. "Exactly! But when Kelly and I found out, we made up for lost time."

"Especially since her boyfriend had been Uncle Pauly. I can't imagine that there was anything dirty between them."

Adam laughed. "Kelly was—" He cleared his throat. He wasn't going to say more about that. "So what happens now?"

"Nothing!" Cait said. "Nothing *can* happen. No one needs to know. I don't want this town gossiping." She glared at him.

"I have to tell Jared and Kelly."

"You can't—" She knew it was useless to say no to that. And actually, she'd feel better if Jared knew the truth. She nodded.

"Kelly will want to tell you about Robbie. She says she never wants him to be forgotten. She put together three photo albums of him. She asked people around town for stories and she wrote to the young men he'd met in basic training." He paused. "I guess she skipped Gabby."

"Yes," Cait said softly. "I'd like to see all of it. But—" She stared at him.

"I understand. Miguel isn't to know."

Cait swallowed. "He *will* know. Dad will take one look at you and me in here together and he'll know I told you. He'll—"

"I'm a good liar," Adam said. "And I'm brilliant at keeping secrets."

"After you share them with your whole family?"

He chuckled. "You got me there. But people I love are in pain. I have to stop the bleeding."

"I know what you mean."

There was a pause between them. "So tell me about you and this doctor. Is it serious?"

"Not at all. We're just friends. We—"

"Caitlyn!" came the frantic voice of her father from outside.

"I'm in here," she shouted, then turned to give Adam a look of warning.

He made a zipper movement across his mouth. When they heard a chain saw cutting into the tree that was over the door, Adam put his arms around her. "You're my niece." There were tears in his eyes. "Robbie's daughter. You can't imagine what this means to me. I—" He cut off when they heard the door hinges creak.

Adam stepped away from her and in the next second he was yelling at Miguel for taking so long to find them. "Did you sit in your living room and wait for the weather to clear up before you came looking for us?"

Since the rain was pouring down hard, that didn't make sense.

Miguel, water cascading down his face, said, "I was *never* looking for *you*. Cait?" He held out his hand and she took it and went up the stairs. Her dad led her to his truck; they got in, and he started the engine.

"What about Adam?" she asked.

"He can get in the back. Or walk. It's no matter to me."

Caitlyn turned away so he wouldn't see her smile. They passed the two vehicles that were halfway down the embankment to the overflowing creek. Tomorrow they'd pull them out with the tractor.

CHAPTER TWENTY-FOUR

"*WHAT* ARE YOU SO NERVOUS ABOUT?" Miguel asked Cait.

"Nothing," she said. It was three days since the tornado. It had struck west of them and hadn't been too bad, a few trees down but no houses. To Cait's mind, the damage had been inside, not out.

"If it's the doc, why don't you go see him? Make up an excuse of having too much food or too much…" He waved his hand. "Or you could tell him the truth, that you miss him."

"That's *not* my problem," she said softly.

Frowning, he looked at her. "Then what *is* bothering you?"

She managed a weak smile, then said she needed to go do something. She couldn't think what since she'd cleared all the accounts. There wasn't a single piece of paper on her desk.

She quickly left her father's house and went outside, blinking against the sunlight. She couldn't very well tell him that she was afraid one of the Hattens would show up and blab all. It wouldn't surprise her to see Jared ride up on a horse. He'd choose a big black one, as he was good at drama, and tell her he forgave her. Or that he understood. Or that she'd made the right choice but he wished she'd talked to him about it.

Just so it was great and noble. He was a Hatten, so that made him like something out of a romance novel.

But Cait didn't care a fig about any of them. She was deeply worried about her father. *She had betrayed him!* She had told his deepest, darkest secret to a man he considered his enemy. How could she have done that? What was wrong with her?

When her father found out what she'd done, what would he say? Would he disown her? Tell her that if she wanted the Hattens so much she could go live with them? Would he turn his back on her forever? Or would he deliver the killer line: "I'm disappointed in you."

When Uncle Pauly spoke, Cait jumped so high her feet came off the ground.

"What in the world is wrong with you? You and your dad have a fight? I'd think it was Dr. Coop, but since you refuse to even see the poor man—"

Cait cut him off. "Do you have something for me?" He was holding a piece of paper.

He handed it to her. "Forey wants you to go to the grocery for her and deliver it all as quickly as your old Jeep can move. Double pronto."

She looked at the list. Two twenty-five-pound bags of unbleached white flour. Four twenty-pound bags of white sugar. A dozen boxes of brown sugar, both light and dark. "Why does she want *me* to do this?"

"You are asking *me* about women?"

Cait sighed. "I have to…" She couldn't think of what she needed to do.

"Polish your empty desktop? That thing is so clean dust is afraid to land on it. Go! Get those nutritionally murderous items and deliver them. And why don't you stay and talk to

Forey? Tell her whatever it is that's making you jump at every little sound."

"I don't—" His look cut her off. She couldn't make someone who'd changed her diapers believe a lie. "Okay, okay, I'm going."

As she quickly ran the errand, her mind never left her problem. What if...? How would she...? Maybe she should...? All questions she couldn't answer.

She hauled the bags into Forey's kitchen, but Forey was nowhere to be seen. "I got everything," she called out.

The back door opened and in came Forey. Behind her was Kelly.

Caitlyn wanted to scream in frustration. This was it. The showdown. This was when a Hatten revealed all.

Forey began chatting about what she was going to bake. "And Kelly agreed to help me. Wasn't that sweet of her? Are you all right? You look pale."

"I'm fine," Cait whispered.

Kelly raised her head and they locked eyes. In that moment, Cait knew it was going to be all right. There wasn't going to be a huge, horrible fight with everyone screaming at each other. No tears of agony and accusations.

"I'm not getting enough Kansas sunshine," Cait said. "Hello, Kelly."

"Hi," she said. "I've been meaning to thank you for helping Cooper while I was away. He told me what Betty Lewis did to the files."

Forey spoke up. "I can't figure out why you hired her in the first place."

"You try to hire a temp and you'll find that you get what you can." Kelly looked back at Cait. "Thank you."

The last time she'd seen Kelly, there had been a frigid coldness in her eyes. A mother protecting her son. But that was no longer there. Her eyes seemed to be saying that Cait was welcome to whatever she needed.

Cait gave a quick nod of acknowledgment. "I better go. The uncles will come up with an apple crisis and they'll need me." She kissed Forey's cheek, then turned and kissed Kelly, too, like she'd done for her entire childhood.

By the time Cait got to her Jeep, she was blinking back tears. She was nearly home before she saw the box that was on the floor, tucked half under the passenger seat. Instinct told her that Kelly had put it there, and instinct said that Kelly had arranged the whole meeting. "Bet she volunteered to cook with Forey just to get me there," she said aloud. The thought of that sacrifice made her smile. Kelly and Adam and all the Hatten family had been a big part of her life. Her dad had dragged himself to their frequent parties and there were times when he and Adam almost seemed like friends.

At the breakup with Jared, Cait had lost much more than just a boyfriend.

She didn't think about where she was going but she went down the weed-infested drive to the Fredericks house. She needed somewhere quiet and private where she could look at what Kelly had left for her.

With the box in her hands, she sat down on the old mattress under the windows. As she knew it would be, the box was full of information about Robbie Hatten.

Cait took a breath. Her father. Biological. His blood was hers.

Her first shock was how young he was. Dads had lines at their eyes, and skin tanned by years of sun. But Robbie Hatten was a teenage boy and as pretty as a model.

It took hours, but she read it all, studied every photo. It was hard to judge herself, but she thought she had his eyes. They were certainly the same color.

She put the box to the side, leaned back and thought about it all. What if her mother had revealed the truth when Cait was born? Caitlyn would have been raised in the Hatten family. She would have been the daughter Kelly often said she'd always wanted. Raised in that big house. Adam would have acted as her father. Her life would have been full of sports and animals. Adam's coaching job had brought hundreds of big, good-looking athletes through their home. One of them might have been Cait's first boyfriend. Kelly's passion for animals would have introduced winged, clawed, hoofed creatures into Cait's life. Adam said he'd once woken up in bed with a monkey.

Miguel had been there that day and he'd said, "How dare you say that about Kelly!" Everyone had laughed, even Adam.

Most important, she would have always known that Jared was her cousin. She did *not* want to think about how her life would be different if she'd known that.

Instead, Cait thought of her life as it was. The uncles with their fruit trees. Their obsession with organic.

And her father. In spite of all the people who lived close to them, it had always been the two of them. No one had ever come close to breaking their bond. "Just the two of us" had been their motto. Their siren song. Escaping to go camping, horseback riding, spending weekends in some backwoods town in Nebraska, Missouri or their beloved Kansas.

No, she thought. She liked one-on-one better. She was *needed*. And wanted in a way a big family couldn't provide.

But she wasn't the only one involved. If it weren't for her, would her father have left Kansas and joined Vera Exton on her trek around the world?

Back then, it hadn't been long since he'd been to the war in Vietnam. His stab wound had hardly healed. All he'd wanted to do was stay *home*. But she and the uncles knew that in the

JUDE DEVERAUX

years since then he'd come to love to travel. He went to New York every year. Miami. The summer when Cait was eleven, the uncles sent him to England to collect grafts of old fruit trees that were growing in remote areas. He was gone for over two months and he'd loved it.

Did I hold him back? Cait wondered. *Did he stop his own life because of me?*

The thought of that made her sick to her stomach.

I wish I could give that time back to him, she thought. *But you can't redo the past.*

It was getting late and she needed to go home. With a heavy heart, she packed the photos and the pages of stories Kelly had collected and put them back in the box. Standing, she looked at it. If she took it home, someone would see her with it and ask questions.

She went upstairs and shoved the box on the top shelf of one of the tiny closets.

Coop will have to make some walk-ins when he remodels, she thought, then grimaced. Dr. Coop was no longer part of her life. As her dad said, the vet had been swallowed up by the Hattens.

But I wasn't. That thought made her feel the best she had in days. Instead of thinking about what she couldn't change, she was going to be happy with what she had.

By the time she got home, she was smiling. As she got out of her Jeep, a big black Mercedes pulled into the yard.

Oh, good! Cait thought. *A customer*. She hoped it was someone with thousands of acres and they wanted a zillion organic fruit trees. She'd like to be overwhelmed with work.

She was grinning widely as the tinted window went down.

A beautiful woman was in the car. Her face was made up perfectly, but naturally. She had long dark hair that softly curled about her shoulders.

314

"Could I help you?" Seth asked from behind Cait.

"I hope I'm in the right place." Her voice was like liquid honey.

"What do you need?" Seth asked. He was practically purring in the presence of such beauty.

"I'm looking for Dr. Jones."

"There." Seth nodded toward the trailer, and then he nudged Cait to stop gawking and speak. She just kept staring.

"Oh, my," the woman said. "That is rather forlorn looking. It—"

"He's buying a house," Cait blurted. "Beautiful house. A big one."

The woman smiled.

"Is he expecting you?" Seth asked.

"No. I'm his surprise." She paused. "But it'll be all right. I'm his wife." Still smiling, she drove to the trailer.

When Cooper opened the door, he wasn't surprised to see his ex-wife. He'd known she'd show up eventually. He felt that pulse-quickening moment he always experienced when he first saw her, but then, she was always more beautiful than he remembered. He got himself under control.

He didn't speak but he opened the door for her to enter. He saw Seth and Cait standing together and watching them. He dreaded to think what Rilla had told them. Something to establish possession, for sure.

He didn't invite her to the living room, not that it was an actual room, but nodded toward the cheap, plastic-covered banquette seat.

With his arms crossed over his chest, he remained standing and looked at her. "Dumped you, did he?"

For a moment she blinked as though fighting back tears. It was an act he'd seen many times.

But his look told her he wouldn't fall for it anymore.

"She took him back. Forgave him. He told her it was all my fault. She always hated me, so she believed him."

When Coop raised an eyebrow, she had enough conscience to blush.

"You never let me explain. He was always watching me. I knew he wanted me. I'm human. I couldn't resist."

Coop knew that what she was saying was true. If Leo had more than two beers, as a joke he'd start asking what Rilla was like in bed. Coop had brushed it off with laughter, then listened as Leo complained about what a dud his wife was. It had all seemed like drunken barroom talk and Coop never took it seriously. That had been a mistake.

"What do you want?" His jaw was set. Maybe Leo's wife forgave, but he didn't.

"I'm broke." Her eyes were pleading.

"Get a job."

"Doing what?"

"Something in an office with lots of men."

She glared at him, but then she softened. "You and I were good together."

She was looking at him in that way he used to find irresistible. But no longer.

"No," he said. He didn't need to explain what he meant.

She gave him another look, the one that used to make him tear her clothes off. She glanced at the door to the bedroom, then back again. She raised an eyebrow in question.

Again, he said, "No."

Her face changed. It was the look of what he'd come to call "the real Rilla." The calculating one. The one who'd do anything to survive in the manner to which she believed she was entitled.

She looked around the trailer. "What is this place?"

"Free housing while I try to rebuild my finances from the bottom." He'd meant to sting her but she just smiled. Rilla liked to win and her tears and threats had won big in the divorce.

"I thought you had a job here."

He sighed. "I've told you a thousand times that I don't earn what a doctor for humans does."

"I always said that you should have gone back to school."

He didn't fall into her trap of defending himself by saying that veterinarian school didn't transfer to a medical degree. And how was he to support her if he was in school? She had a knack for making him feel less than he was.

"What about the big house you bought? You could sell it and we could go away together."

"House?" For a moment, he was puzzled. Then he laughed. "I don't own any house."

"But that girl said you—" She broke off and looked at him in speculation. "She was defending you. I saw this hideous trailer and she started bragging about your wealth. So is she your newest piece?"

Coop went to the door and put his hand on the handle. "It's time for you to leave."

She didn't move. "Who is she?"

"Rilla!" He opened the door a few inches.

She still didn't move. "Oh, my. Have you fallen in love?"

"Caitlyn is the daughter of the man who owns this place. I'm not going to do anything to piss him off."

She opened her bag, pulled out a tube of lipstick and reapplied it. "You never could hide your feelings. That night when I first met you, I saw everything. You were quiet and shy. You don't go after women, so you get ignored. Leo was beside you and he was the opposite. His eyes were flashing fire, but so was the shiny new wedding ring."

"And he told you we were doctors."

She grimaced. "Yes, he did. I thought I'd hit the jackpot."

Coop moved away from the door. "I guess the joke was on you when you found out I wasn't the rich kind of doctor."

"You had a lot."

Coop looked away for a moment. It was true. He'd had a house, clinic, good salary, a best friend. All gone now. "But it wasn't enough for you."

"*I* wasn't enough for *you*! I knew you were growing bored with me. And there was Leo, drooling whenever he saw me." Her voice lowered. "But I knew that if I had a child, you wouldn't ever throw me out."

Coop turned and looked out the window. And there was the root of it all. He looked back at her. "You came here to try again, didn't you?"

"It was worth a shot. Mother said a man like you always has money hidden away and I—"

He glared at her. "We went through that during the divorce. I have no money hidden away, no property. I'm doing all I can to hold on to this job. I was fired from my other one because I couldn't control my anger." He took a breath. "I want you to leave."

She didn't move. This time when she looked at him, there were actual tears in her eyes, and fear. "I need a place to stay tonight, then plane fare to get home."

"And someone to pay for that flashy rental car? Did you think it would impress me? I owe you nothing."

She was recovering her dignity. "I know that, but I could try." She moved the blinds to look out. "Your girlfriend is still out there. She's pretending to do something to a tree."

"It's an orchard and they sell the fruit and the trees. She's working."

"Maybe I should have a chat with her about our marriage.

There are things about you that she should know. *Important things.*"

For a moment, they stared at each other. "One night. Then you're out of here."

"And the plane?"

He gave a curt nod, and then he left the trailer. He'd had all he could stand.

Miguel didn't see Vera for nearly a week. Seeing Adam Hatten with Cait, the two of them hidden away in the cellar, a place Miguel had always thought of as private, was almost more than he could bear.

He didn't want to tell Vera how he felt because he knew she'd give him no sympathy. She always told him his animosity toward Adam was unfounded. If she was in a bad mood, she said it was "ridiculous."

So he stayed away from her, away from the cellar and all things Hatten.

But Mason was a small town outside another small town. He nearly bumped carts with Vera at the grocery in Ottawa.

As always, his heart did a little jump, but he got it to settle. He gave her a look to remind her that they didn't want gossip going around about them.

After a nod of hello, he turned his cart away.

Vera grabbed his arm. "What the hell?" she whispered.

"Not here," he said quietly.

She let go of his arm, stood full height, shoulders back, and looked him in the eyes. "You either talk to me or I tell this whole store everything, starting with when we were kids."

Miguel closed his eyes for a moment. He knew she meant what she said. He glanced at his full cart. "Give me one hour. I'll meet you there."

Vera nodded, then casually rolled her cart away. Even so, three women were watching them.

Miguel checked out, loaded, unloaded, threw things into the pantry and fridge, then practically spun out in his truck. He didn't want the nosy uncles to ask him what he was up to.

The Hatten truck Vera was using was barely visible in the trees and he parked near it. He jumped up into the back, unlocked his big toolbox, then took out his electric drill and the bag of supplies he'd bought days ago.

At the door to the cellar, he paused. Last time he was there, he'd found Adam with Cait inside.

With his teeth clenched, he pulled the door up and went down the stairs.

Vera was in the bed, the sheet pulled up under her arms. Her hair was down, like a great cloud around her head.

He so wanted to join her that he groaned, but he had something to do first. He didn't look at her as he installed a lock on the inside of the door. It was an old-fashioned, heavy hook lock, like something seen in a medieval castle. The wood of the door would break before that lock did.

When he finished, he put his tools away, then looked at Vera. She dropped the sheet to her waist. By the time he reached the bed, he was naked.

It was quite some time before they were sated enough to be able to speak. Her head was on his shoulder, their legs entwined.

"Think that lock you put on the door is big enough?" she asked.

Miguel didn't laugh. "You don't know what happened?"

"I guess not."

He told her that during the tornado he'd found two vehicles—Adam's truck and Cait's Jeep—together. "I knew where they'd gone. I figured Cait had found the place, but she said

Hatten was the one who knew about it." He was getting angry. "All these years and I thought this place was *ours*."

"Kelly takes care of it."

"I knew that, but I think I believed that *he*…" Miguel didn't finish, as he knew it was absurd. Of course Adam knew. He looked up at the ceiling and was silent.

"What are you *really* angry about?"

He took his time answering. "I think Cait told him."

"About…?" She hesitated. "About Robbie?"

"Yes. There was a light in his eyes that I hadn't seen in years. He was his usual privileged self, giving me hell, but there was something else there."

"And Cait?"

"She looked sad."

"Or was it fear? If she did tell Adam, she'd be scared to death of you and your temper."

"I have no temper. Ask the uncles. I get along with everyone."

"Of course you do."

Miguel groaned. "I hate when you patronize me. Have you heard that Cooper's wife is back in town?"

"Are you changing the subject to avoid what's painful to you?"

He gave a one-sided smile. "She's beautiful. Cait is very upset about it. Not that she's said anything, but she is." He chuckled. "She thinks the two of them are spending the night together in that little trailer."

"But they're not?"

He grinned wide. He had managed to get her off the subject of the glory of Adam Hatten. "Coop's been spending the nights in Cait's room in my house."

"But you didn't tell her?"

"Nope. A little jealousy might light a fire under her."

"You are a wicked man. So what's she say about your photography classes?"

"Haven't told her about them, either."

She shook her head. "So tell me about this new vet. Kelly likes him a lot. Is he worthy of our Cait?"

Those words were music to him. "Our" Cait. The child they should have had. "I think they'll get along well. He's a quiet man and she's a dynamo. She'll lead him to where he's supposed to go in life."

"Like you and me?"

"Yeah, like us. With you leading us both."

There was a tone in his reply that made Vera rise up to look at him. "What are you saying?"

"I... Uh..."

"Yes?" She lay back down.

"I want my daughter to become independent of me because..." He took a breath. "I might go with you."

Vera was silent. It wasn't until he felt her tears on his bare skin that he knew she was crying. His arms tightened around her.

"I've been alone since Joe died," she whispered. "I've tried to replace him but I wear them out. When they leave, they like to tell me off. Their favorite thing to say is that I'm not really a woman. I'm—"

He didn't let her finish, but kissed her to silence.

They made love sweetly and with all the depth of feeling they'd had for many years.

It was later, as they dug into the bags of food that Vera had brought, that she gave him the gift. It was wrapped in blue paper with a silver ribbon.

Inside was a box containing a Nikon F5 with a 20–35 f2.8 lens.

"This camera isn't on the market yet, so it's the absolute latest. I got it from a friend. He didn't want to part with it, but I reminded him that I got him his first job with Reuters and persuaded *National Geographic* to hire him and—"

Miguel kissed her. "You were so sure that you could bully me into giving up my life and taking on yours that you black-mailed a man into parting with his prized possession?"

Vera's eyes lit up. "Yes, I did."

"That's sweet." He kissed her again, then pulled the camera out. It was the size of half a concrete block, and about the same weight. "It's going to take a lot of rolls of film for this baby."

"Yes, it will," Vera said.

"Got a roll or two? I need 400 for in here."

"Listen to you! You're learning so much." When she leaned over the side of the bed, the sheet slipped down to expose most of the back of her.

She came up with a bag full of rolls of Kodak film, then smiled as Miguel loaded one into the big camera. Before she could protest, he took a photo of her, not quite nude, but not exactly clothed.

Laughing together, they spent the next hours talking about what might possibly be their future together.

When Coop woke and looked around, he smiled. He liked being in Caitlyn's childhood room. Her father hadn't touched the place since she'd left it. It wasn't pink and frilly as might be expected, but was done in blue and dark brown. It was like her: sane and sensible. Not silly or frivolous. There were a few posters but mostly there were photos, especially of her and her father. Some of the uncles. There was one picture of a plump woman, a man and two teenage boys who didn't look at all like Cait. Were they the half brothers she said she had nothing in common with?

He saw a high school yearbook and flipped through it.

Cait wasn't in it much. No sports teams, certainly no photos of her as a cheerleader. But then, she seemed to have worked for most of her childhood.

Toward the back was a snapshot of a truck with wooden sideboards and filled with hay. Cait was in it and surrounded by kids, all of them laughing. On the back was a sign for Heritage Harvests.

He got dressed and went into the kitchen. Miguel was already there, a mug of coffee in his hands. On the night Rilla had arrived, Miguel had come out of his house. He looked at Coop, then at Rilla, and had seemed to size up the situation in an instant. But then, from what Coop gathered from gossip around town, Miguel knew lots about women who were exes.

"I have a spare bedroom," he'd said, then walked away.

Rilla had asked who he was. "He's so beautiful."

"He's not rich enough for you."

"Oh." Her disappointment was obvious. "In that case, you don't need to stay somewhere else. I'll take the couch."

He didn't bother to reply. He knew she'd crawl into bed with him. That night, he stuffed clean clothes into a duffel bag and knocked on Miguel's door. The man said nothing, just motioned toward the hall, then went back to whatever he was doing. The next morning when Coop got up, the older man was gone.

It had been that way for the three days he'd been there, but this morning was different. Miguel seemed to be waiting for him.

Coop braced himself. On the surface it must look like he'd been leading Caitlyn on, but was now sheltering his ex-wife. Would threats come? Warnings? From the serious look on Miguel's face, it was going to be bad.

Miguel's look could only be called a glower. "What do you think of my daughter?"

It wasn't what Coop had expected. He'd thought Miguel would tell him to stay away from Cait.

Coop took a moment as he decided to tell the truth, holding nothing back. "A Realtor contacted me about a nice apartment that I could get for a cheap rent. I told him no because *she* lives where there's a crappy old trailer that I can use. Then the Realtor showed me photos of a new three-bed, three-bath house on two acres. Downright cheap and move-in ready. But *she* likes some rotting old house that will take masses of work, so I've been measuring the place and working on my finances. I was offered a job in Dallas. Great salary. But *she* lives in tiny Mason, Kansas, and is tied to the place by tree roots. I told them no."

A smile was peeping from under Miguel's frown. "What about the Hattens?"

Coop looked genuinely confused. "If you want a job and your boss invites you to her home, do you turn it down?"

Miguel nodded in understanding. "And your ex-wife?"

"What can I say? I'm a good guy. I tend to take care of people."

Again, Miguel nodded. "Let me know if you need any help."

Coop's face changed to pleading. "I could use it. I don't seem to be making any progress with Cait."

"Then try harder." Miguel put his hands in his pockets and went down the hall.

"Bastard!" Coop muttered. "If *I* had a daughter, I'd help. I'd—" He didn't allow himself to finish his sentence.

Caitlyn was about to step into her Jeep when a car drove up to her house. She could see that it was three of her girlfriends and she knew why they were there. They were going to give her a hard time because she hadn't seen them in a while. But to be fair to herself, the constant question of *Why did you break up with Jared?* nearly drove her mad.

"Hi," she said as they got out of the car. She was cautious, preparing herself for their questions and their scolding. It was an unwritten law that work wasn't a valid reason for neglecting your girlfriends.

"So how are you doing?" Bobbi asked. "Been busy?"

"Like always," Cait said.

"We were wondering—" April began.

She broke off because Rilla came out of Cooper's trailer. She was wearing a purple dress, one of those that was only a foot wide on the hanger and you had to struggle to pull it up. With it was a huge pink hat and what had to be ten pounds of gold jewelry. It's a wonder she could lift her arm with that chain bracelet. It could be used to anchor a ship. She flashed in the sunlight as she walked toward the big black Mercedes.

"Hello, girls," she said in her silky voice. She slipped into the car with the grace of someone trained in etiquette.

Cait rolled her eyes. Now she'd be interrogated about Rilla. But they surprised her.

"She saw that it was just us females here but she still walked like men were watching," Millie said.

"I think that breaks the girl code," April said.

Cait spoke up. "She has the right to walk any way she wants. She's Cooper's ex-wife."

"Ex?" Bobbi said. "But she came out of *his* place."

Cait shrugged, hoping she appeared to be nonchalant and sophisticated. Let them think that it didn't matter to her.

"How long?" Millie's teeth were clamped together.

"Three days," Cait replied.

For a moment, all four of them were silent as they watched the big black car drive away. "Is *that* what he wants?" Bobbi asked. "He's a body-only man? I thought better of him."

"Me, too," April said. "I had high hopes for him since he turned Heather down flat. We thought it was because he was, you know, for you." She looked at Cait.

She shrugged.

"You spent the whole night with him at Kelly's clinic. We were sure that after that you two were a couple," April said.

"And what Heather said confirmed it. If he didn't want *her*, he must have another girl."

"Heather…" Cait began, but didn't finish. She should tell them what Coop said, but she couldn't make herself do it. Was there any better feeling in the world than having people on your side?

"That ex is quite pretty," April said.

"So what?" Bobbi snapped. "My face is prettier than hers."

They nodded in agreement. So what if she had a few extra pounds below her gorgeous face? "I've got better legs," April said.

They turned to Millie. "We know what I have." She was more than a bit top-heavy.

"You guys are wonderful," Cait said. "The best friends anyone ever had, but men have the right to make their own choices. If he wants her, then he should have her."

"That's crazy talk," Bobbi said.

Cait smiled but the others were serious. "I have to go. Thank you very much for this. You've made my day. Really." She got into her Jeep. "On Saturday, why don't we go barhopping?" That was a Mason joke. There was only one bar in town.

"Sure," Bobbi said, and they stepped back as Cait drove away.

She watched them in her rearview mirror. They had made her feel much better.

For the next few hours she ran errands, then delivered everything to the uncles. She looked at her watch. It was early, so Coop would still be at work. There was one more thing she had to do. The box of photos that Kelly had given her was still hidden in the Fredericks house. She didn't think anyone would see it, but she didn't want to risk it. She needed to get the box and come up with a secure hiding place.

Cait was standing on her toes and trying to get the box off the top shelf. She could barely reach it. It came down in a whoosh, almost hitting her head, but she caught it. Relieved that nothing had fallen out, she went downstairs. She'd left her bag in the dining room on one of the old mattresses. Just as she picked it up, she heard the front door open. She shoved the box at the back of the mattress, then turned.

It was Coop and he looked furious! "What the hell were you thinking? They came into the clinic. Where I work! Every day, I'm doing the best I can to make Kelly think I'm a serious person who wants a job in this town. Then you send half-naked girls to parade in front of everyone."

"I have no idea what you're talking about," she said.

"Those girls. It was embarrassing," he said. "Everyone was laughing at me."

Cait was puzzled. "Half-naked? Who was?"

"I don't know their names. I've never seen them before. Or maybe I have. I don't remember."

Cait was beginning to understand what he was saying. "They really did it?" She grinned. "I have an idea that they were trying to show you that other women have beautiful body parts. They know it's hard to compete when a man wants a woman like Rilla."

He was blinking rapidly. "You think I want her?"

"You *married* her, so, yes, I think she's your type."

"She's every man's type. When I met her she came after me. I was too astonished to ask why. That's all past history."

She glared at him. "Not quite since she's staying with you."

His voice lowered. "I like those posters in your bedroom, and the colors. How long did you last in ballet lessons?"

She grimaced. "That was the uncles' idea. They wanted me to be graceful, but..." She stopped. "How do you know what my room looks like?" When he didn't answer, her eyes widened. "You spent the nights with Dad, didn't you?"

"Not how I'd put it, but I did stay in your bedroom in your father's house."

She turned away so he wouldn't see her smile of relief.

But he knew what was going on. "I didn't mean to lie."

"You didn't. Not really. I just assumed that you and she were... She's so beautiful. She's—"

He kissed her. It wasn't a kiss of kindness or reassurance but one of passion. Repressed passion that had been building for weeks.

Clothes came off and they made love on one of the old mattresses. It was quick and fierce. Later, they fell back against each other, wrapped together.

"What did they look like?" she asked.

"Who?"

"April and Bobbi and Millie."

"I was too angry to look."

"I think your nose just grew about a foot."

He gave a one-sided grin. "When it comes to body parts, I must say that your friends have no competitors. Which one is April?"

"Legs."

"Right. Long, lean, toned, lightly tanned. And her backside! The way it curved. I bet you could bend a nail on it. She must—"

Cait cut in. "Got it. What about Millie?"

"Six-inch cleavage and even that didn't show it all. Quite extraordinary uplift. I'm not sure, but I don't believe she had on undergarments."

"She doesn't need any. What about Bobbi?"

"Very pretty girl. Like an angel. I bet she has a really good personality."

Cait laughed. "I think you did appreciate them."

"I might have if Mrs. Chandless hadn't been there with her schnauzer."

"The Baptist pastor's wife." Cait couldn't hold in her laughter. "My friends will never live this down. And they'll blame me. All my fault." She was laughing hard.

"Get the uncles to send them fruit baskets." He reached under his back and pulled out something. It was a very dirty penny. He tossed it across the room and listened to it spin, then settle. "This mattress..." he said.

"Better not think about it."

"Anyone ever think that the house could be locked?"

"Bolt cutters are in every Kansas teenager's truck. They come in handy for lots of things. Especially locks on empty old houses."

She was running her hand over his chest, something she'd wanted to do since she'd seen him wearing only a towel.

"Then we'll have to fill the house." He rose up on one arm and kissed her. He was ready for her again.

But Cait pulled away. "What does that mean?"

"Kissing? It's usually a prelude to the other part." He bent toward her.

She pushed him away. "To fill the house? You said 'we.'"

With a sigh, he fell back onto the mattress. "Too soon, isn't it? I did that the first time. Made up my mind right away. Isn't there a saying about that? *Marry in haste, repent at leisure.* But this time, I don't think I'm making a mistake."

"This time?" she whispered. "Marry?" She sat up, pulling on her shirt, then her jeans. She didn't bother with underwear. Her sandals went on quickly and she stood up. She looked down at him. He'd pulled his shirt across his hips but most of him was nude. He looked very good. So good that Cait's stomach lurched at having to leave him.

But she had to. "I'm not..." She inhaled deeply. "I don't want to get married. Ever. Sorry I misled you. This was fun but this is it. No more." She didn't give him a chance to reply but ran from the house and got into her Jeep and spun out of the driveway.

Coop fell back against the mattress. He had no idea what the problem was. Yet again, he seemed to have done something wrong but he didn't know what.

It was a while before he saw the bra and underpants she'd left behind. He picked them up. Plain white cotton. As sensible as Cait was. Did he leave them there or give them back to her? When he stood up and pulled on his jeans, he saw the box tucked behind the mattress. He sure hoped it was one of Cait's emergency meals! After the fiasco of the naked parade, he'd been too timid to face the laughter at Gresham's for lunch.

But the box didn't contain food. It was photos and papers. He started to close it but on top was a black-and-white photo of two young men. One was Adam Hatten and Coop guessed the younger one was his brother, Robbie, the one who'd died in Vietnam.

Why was Cait looking at them? He'd been in Mason long enough to have heard of the coolness between Adam Hatten and Miguel. Had she hidden the box in the house so her father wouldn't see them? But why did Cait want to look at them?

He spread the photos out on the old mattress and looked at

them more closely. By the third picture of young Robbie Hatten, Coop saw the resemblance between Cait and the young man. Same eyes, same nose, same little bend in their mouths. There was a picture of Robbie with a woman he assumed to be his mother. They looked very much alike. If Cait were in the photo, people would marvel at the family resemblance. Three clones.

Coop thought about what he'd heard about Cait's mother. *"No one in Mason even knew Miguel and Gabrielle were going together."*

He leaned back against the wall. From what he was seeing and putting together, it looked like the father of Gabrielle's baby wasn't Miguel. He wasn't Cait's biological father.

When had the woman told Cait and Miguel who the real father was? When Cait said she was going to marry Jared? No one knew why Cait broke up with Jared Hatten, including Jared. Coop had heard of the bewilderment of the townspeople. But if Robbie was Cait's biological father, they were first cousins.

Poor Caitlyn, he thought. And poor, poor Miguel.

Coop sat up. This was tragic, true, but why did Cait think this mistake meant she could never marry? Was it some kind of lifelong punishment? It wasn't her fault. She'd done nothing wrong.

He took a breath. Or maybe Caitlyn was being honest and she actually didn't want him.

CHAPTER TWENTY-FIVE

AFTER CAIT SPED AWAY FROM COOPER, all she could think was that she had to have some privacy. She needed to think. In the last weeks the Fredericks house had given her that, but not now. And she couldn't go home. The uncles would see her and they'd invade. They wouldn't mean to, but they'd take over.

As she drove down the road, she suddenly turned and went across the grass. The only place she could think of was the cellar where she'd sheltered with Adam during the tornado. She parked far back under the trees, her vehicle unseen from the road.

She ran to the old door, kicked the fallen branches off it. She ran down the stairs, let the door drop down into place, then ran to the bed. All she wanted to do was be quiet. And to cry.

She curled up on the bed, her knees to her chest, her head down. The release from what she was feeling wouldn't come. There were no tears.

When she heard the door open, her body tightened. *Please don't let it be Dad*, she thought. *Please, please, please.*

She heard footsteps but didn't look up. A light came on, and then a woman's voice said, "Oh!"

Cait didn't look to see who it was, but she knew. The cellar was probably the only true secret in Mason, so the possibilities were limited. It was Vera, the town celebrity. The love of her father's life.

The other side of the bed sank down as Vera sat beside her. "I'm not making a pass at you," she said. "I just feel awful and I need a place to hide from my relatives." She groaned. "Everything in me hurts. My head, my stomach, my ankles. All of it." She adjusted the pillows. "You can't tell anyone that I'm not well. Not Kelly, not Miguel, nobody. They'll think it's some foreign disease and tell me I can't leave again. Kelly will decide I have leprosy. Or the black plague. Smallpox, for sure. Then she'll tell me I have to stay here, that I can't ever leave. You know Kelly, right?"

Cait was still curled up, her back to the woman. "Yes."

"But I bet you don't know the real Kelly! She's capable of locking me in a room. I'll die if I have to stay here. I can't breathe here. But my sister is worse than Mom was. If she thought I was sick, she'd have me put in jail."

Cait rolled onto her back. "My dad...?"

"Miguel! Don't get me started on him! He wants to wrap me in a quilt and put me in front of a TV so he always knows where I am. *Safe* is the only word those people know. I know words like *adventure* and *life*." Vera gave a sigh of exasperation.

Cait turned her head to look at her, but she didn't say anything.

Vera put her hand to her forehead. "Getting Miguel to leave with me is going to be hard enough, but if I don't feel well—" She stopped, then looked at Cait in shock. "Oh, hell! I didn't mean to say that. Pretend I didn't."

"Dad wants to leave with you?"

"Yes."

"He wants to travel the world and...do what? Just follow along behind you?"

"He's taking photography classes at KCAI."

Cait lifted on her elbow. "*That's* what he's been hiding. I saw the papers but I didn't know what they were. I've been so wrapped up in myself that I wasn't paying attention."

"I gave him a camera." She was looking at Caitlyn hard. "You don't mind if he leaves here? Leaves *you*?"

"I think it's wonderful. He's stayed here because of *me*. If I hadn't been on the way, I think he would have eventually gone to you. But he couldn't leave because he had to take care of me."

"Isn't having the responsibility for other people's lives the pits?" Vera said.

"Yes, it is."

"Your dad says he's just waiting for you to agree to marry your hunky veterinarian. But I don't believe that'll be enough for Miguel. I swear, I think he won't leave until you're pregnant. Knowing him, he'll want to wait for the delivery before he gets on a plane. But I—"

Cait let out a howl like an animal in pain. It was an eerie sound that made Vera's hair stand on end. Considering what she'd seen in her life, that was saying a lot.

She grabbed Cait to her, holding her close. She didn't tell her to stop crying, didn't try to soothe her, just let the tears come. When Cait's body went into convulsions, shuddering hard, Vera pulled her closer.

It was a long while before Cait began to calm down. Vera didn't let go but pulled the sheet up and wiped Cait's young face. She was drenched in tears. There was a box of tissues on the side table and Vera handed her a thick pile.

Cait blew her nose. "Sorry," she managed to whisper. "I don't know what got into me. I just—"

"Cut the crap," Vera said. "What is torturing your soul?"

Cait sat up, her back against the headboard. "I can't tell anyone. I…" Vera's look made her stop. "Torturing my soul. Yes, I think that describes it. Dad doesn't know. Jared… He's—"

"I know who he is. Kelly and Adam's sad boy. When I got here, he was looking like he'd lost the meaning of life. But lately he seems to have perked up. I think we can guess what monumental thing he was told that made him feel better."

"You know?"

"Of course. Your dad and I have connected spirits. We don't hide the truth from each other."

Cait sniffed and blew her nose again. "You talk like you write. Very dramatic."

"A hazard of being a writer. Stop dancing around and tell me what's killing you."

"I…" She hesitated. Vera's look was intense and she was waiting. "I was carrying Jared's baby."

Vera's eyes widened. "No, your dad doesn't know that."

"I couldn't tell him."

"You were right not to. Finding out that you're related to the Hattens almost did him in. What happened with the baby? Put up for adoption?" She studied Cait's face. "No. Something else. Abortion?"

"I couldn't do that," Cait said. "It was an ectopic pregnancy and there were complications. I needed surgery. I…" Tears were running down her face.

"Lost it all? All your baby-making equipment?"

Cait was crying into her tissues and could only nod.

"That's tough. Did you tell your veterinarian?"

"Of course not. Men want their own children, but I can't have any. I'm only half—"

"No!" Vera shouted. "Don't tell me that bullshit that you're only half a woman and therefore not fit for any man. I won't hear it. If you knew what I've seen in my life, you'd know how stupid that is."

Cait got off the bed. "I'm sorry I dumped my small-town problems on you. You're used to dealing with the whole world. But even if my problem is inconsequential to your worldly life, I'd appreciate it if you didn't tell my father."

"I will tell," Vera said. "I'm going to tell Kelly and Adam and Jared and that vet of yours. You are *not* going to carry this secret around alone for the rest of your life."

Cait squinted her eyes. "Like you never told anyone about my father and this place? *You* can keep secrets that affect other people but no one else can? You're special because you got a big-deal prize for a book? You wrote about some news reporter but you should have written about my father, and yes, that's what he is. He gave up his whole life for you and for me. No glamour, no bombs exploding, just pure unselfishness. That is *real* sacrifice!" She was shouting.

Vera smiled at her. "That's better," she said. "Anger is what you need. Good, self-righteous anger at the unfairness of life." Her eyes softened. "Why don't you come back here and tell me everything? From beginning to end. Then we can make rational decisions about what we need to do."

Cait took a moment to decide. It was the "we" that got her. To not be alone with this was something she needed. She climbed back onto the bed. Sometimes it was easier to talk to strangers than to people you loved. "Jared and I were always friends," she began.

Vera listened. Outside, the sun went down and Vera still listened. And Cait told her all the things that were jammed inside of her.

★ ★ ★

The next afternoon, there was a knock on Cait's door, but she didn't want to answer it. She just wanted to be alone to think about what to do with her life.

But the knocking continued. Reluctantly, she got up and went to the door. It was Coop, standing there with his hands behind his back. "I can't talk now. I have things to do," she said.

He moved his arms to the front. Each hand was holding a tall DQ ice-cream cone.

Cait smiled and opened the door to let him in. They sat down on the couch, side by side, but not touching. They began on their cones.

"Hear from your girlfriends yet?" he asked.

"I haven't answered the phone, so I'm not sure."

He was crunching a piece of chocolate. "Would it help if I told you I think you're prettier than all of them? Including my greedy ex-wife?"

"Doesn't hurt, even if it's not true."

"You never heard that love is blind?"

She paused with her cone but she didn't look at him. "I think it is. Love has sure blinded *me*."

They were silent as they finished their ice creams. Then Cait leaned back against the couch. It was time to get serious. "I made a deal with Vera. I have to tell you something that no one else knows, not my father, not any friends. I even managed to keep it from my mother and she was there. If I tell you, Vera swears she'll tell no one else."

"I will keep whatever secrets you entrust me with."

"I know you will. I…" The words wouldn't come out.

He said nothing, just waited, giving her time to collect herself. "Jared and I…" She halted. She couldn't say the words.

"Are you trying to tell me that Jared is your cousin?"

She looked at him in shock.

"I found the box in the house. I didn't mean to snoop but I thought it contained food. When I opened it, I saw the photos. You look like him. And his mother."

"My grandmother," she whispered. "A whole different family."

"So you broke up with Jared because of that."

She nodded. "But that's not my problem. I ran off to Florida because I was late. *That* kind of late. I was pretty sure I was…"

He reached out and took her hand. "Children born out of wedlock aren't—"

"I can't have children," she blurted. "Not ever."

"Neither can I," he said softly.

"I'll never be able to— What did you say?"

"I can tell you about the tests, the tears, all of it, but it comes down to the same thing. I shoot blanks. Probably from a childhood illness, not that it matters why."

They looked at each other, their minds working on the repercussions of this news. Cait got up and went to her refrigerator. Way in the back behind the yogurt and the mustard was a bottle of champagne. It had been there for two years. She pulled it out.

Coop was behind her. There was a glass cabinet with champagne flutes inside. He took two out and held them while Cait poured.

When they finished the first glass, they began to laugh. After the second one, they made love on the kitchen floor.

Three days later, Vera and Miguel were sitting in the doctor's office. They were holding hands as Vera was shaking so hard she could hardly sit up.

The doctor opened a folder. "Your tests came back negative. Except for one of them."

Vera, who had faced warlords without showing any fear, began to cry. It was soft but there were tears.

The doctor was smiling. "I loved your book about Joe Harding. A real masterpiece. The ending of that book stayed with me for days."

"Hey!" Miguel said in a way that cut through the niceties.

"Oh, right." He smiled broader. "There's nothing wrong with you. You're pregnant." He shut the folder. "We've got some good OBs here. It's your choice. But that book was great. I bought half a dozen copies and gave them as Christmas gifts. Joe Harding was—"

"*I am what?*" Vera shouted.

The doctor looked surprised at the fierceness of her response. "With child." He glanced at Miguel, who was pretty much catatonic. Frozen. "It happens."

Vera came out of her chair, hands on his desk, and leaned over him. He was seeing the Vera Exton that her colleagues saw, the ones who ran away from her. "I am forty-nine years old. I can *not* be pregnant."

"Age does slow down pregnancy, but research has shown that an active sex life activates the hormones. Have you two, uh, been active?" He was looking at Miguel, who had not moved so much as an eyelash.

"This is not possible." Vera leaned farther over his desk. She was tall enough that her head was near his. Her hair had escaped its bonds. She was formidable looking.

The doctor rolled his chair back. "I, uh… I'll give you some brochures to read." He punched the button on his desk phone. "Get Ms. Exton a bottle of prenatal vitamins and—" He raised his voice. "And come in here now!"

Finally, Miguel reacted. He stood up, took Vera's arm and pulled. She didn't move. She was still looming over the desk, still glaring in threat at the doctor. Miguel got behind her, put his hands firmly on her upper arms and led her out of the office. He didn't let go until he got her into the cab of his truck. He walked around the front and got in beside her.

He didn't turn on the engine. They sat there in silence, staring out the window. "It's not possible," she said. "I'm too old. The baby will have problems."

"Not necessarily," he said. "Maybe not."

She looked at him. "You're glad, aren't you?"

He kept looking straight ahead. "I will do whatever you want. It's your body."

"Did you read that response in a book somewhere? What to say to an angry pregnant woman?"

He turned to her. "I know what you want in life. You *must* go. But this would be my child. I'm not going to have another one."

"And you would stay behind to raise it? Déjà vu? Do it all over again? I'd go off alone and you'd stay here?"

"Yes," he said. "You can go and I'll stay here and raise our child alone. Again." He started the engine and pulled out of the parking lot.

They were almost home when Vera whispered, "I think I know a solution."

CHAPTER TWENTY-SIX

Mason, Kansas
2019

VERA EXTON WAS RETURNING.

The entire town was reverberating with the news. The local celebrity was coming home. To stay. "The town wants to put on a parade for them!" Kelly's voice was trembling with anger. She and Adam were in their bedroom in the apartment on the Plaza.

"I know," he said. "Can you imagine Vera and Miguel standing on some decorated wagon bed and waving to people? I heard they're supposed to ride through Mason tossing flowers out. My guess is that they'll change the parade so it goes down Main Street in Ottawa. Make a real spectacle of it."

"Oh, great! There'll be hundreds of people lining the street. If my sister hears of this, she'll never return. Never!" She flopped down on the bed next to Adam and he drew her into his arms.

"And they've scheduled this parade on Kyle's wedding day?"

"Yes! That hideous Celeste Wigman did this." Kelly never bothered using Celeste's married name. She said it changed often, so how could she be expected to remember them? "She did it on purpose. I swear, you'd think that all Vera has accomplished was due to Celeste. She'll probably set up a table and autograph copies of Vera's book about Joe Harding." When Adam didn't answer, she pulled back to look at him. "Why aren't you giving me one of your pep talks about how everything will be fine?"

"Because I don't think it will be. If Vera hears even a hint that the town is putting on a parade in her honor, she'll wait another year before she shows up."

"Then she'll slip into town and no one will know she's here until they see a light on in the schoolhouse."

Adam kissed the top of her head. "By the way, you did a brilliant job on that."

Kelly smiled in memory. For the last eighteen months, her life had revolved around remodeling what everyone called "the old Exton place." The house and about three acres had been rented for years. Jared had tried to oversee it, but he was busy with the farm and a family. When the tenants moved out, the house was in bad shape. Adam had suggested bulldozing it. The look Kelly gave him answered that! So the house had sat empty for over a year.

When Miguel sent an email saying he was making progress in getting Vera to consider retiring, Kelly had been ecstatic. "He says she's going to write her memoirs," she told Adam. "And Miguel is going to work on a book of his photos."

"That's great." Adam's reply was cautious. He didn't believe Vera was capable of staying in one place for very long. "So where will they live?"

She'd looked at her husband. They'd lived together for so many years that their minds were in sync.

"Your old house," Adam said softly. "And let me guess. You're going to bring it into the twenty-first century."

"Yes, I am." Kelly's eyes seemed to glaze over. It had taken her a while to adjust to retiring from full-time work as a vet.

Turning over the clinic to Coop and moving into the KC apartment had been a jolt to her. It had taken her a while to find things to do. This new project excited her. "Granite and quartz countertops, Bosch appliances, a big stainless sink, a—"

Adam laughed. "I'm sure Vera will use all the appliances to their full capacity. Just in case, maybe you should put a firepit in the back so she can roast pigeons or whatever."

Kelly grimaced. "She'll want to work and that's all. And Miguel will fiddle with his photos. I'll make a bedroom into an office so they can—" Her eyes widened. "Bait! That's what I need. Something that will entice Vera to stay. I'll use the schoolhouse. I'll move the whole building onto the property, then turn it into a work zone. All Vera's books and papers will be there. It'll make her *want* to stay."

"I think that's an excellent idea. You can get Mike involved. I think she owns that house now."

"Perfect." Kelly smiled in contentment. She had a plan!

In the year and a half since then, Kelly had pretty much gutted her childhood home. It had been a bit sad when she tore out the kitchen where Nella and Forey used to cook so many wonderful dishes. To compensate, she kept the big oak table the women had used.

Forey was the one who encouraged Kelly. She was now in her nineties and as bossy and feisty as ever. "Tear it all out!" Forey said. "Open it up. Don't isolate the cook."

That's just what Kelly had done. She'd made the separated living and dining rooms into one big area and had furnished it all in the modern way of grays and white.

"I don't know what you youngsters have against *color*." Forey was frowning.

"Don't worry," Kelly replied. "I've been receiving papers and art objects from Vera since 1974. Everything is in storage units. There are magnificent things in there—African masks, Persian rugs, Chinese embroideries…and my favorite, a cannibal fork from Fiji. You and I are going to fill this house with her treasures."

Forey smiled. "That sounds good."

Adam oversaw moving the schoolhouse. "Poor thing," he said. "This is its second move. It must want to put down roots and stay there."

"Exactly my hope for my wandering sister," Kelly said. She set about her plan to entice Vera to stay by giving her and Miguel a place that was for work only. They wouldn't be distracted by the things that went on in a house. No appliances beeping when the cycle was finished, no doorbells ringing, no deliverymen.

An acre away from the house, near a big oak tree, she had plumbing and electricity installed.

Then Adam and a crew had moved Miguel's old schoolhouse, the place where he'd raised Cait. Kelly left one bedroom and a bath closed off, but other than that, it was all open, with Miguel's little kitchen against one wall. They brought in the old, peeling bookcase from the cellar and all the books and papers they'd been able to save.

When Jared saw it, he frowned. "Maybe they'll want separate offices."

Adam and Kelly had looked at each other and laughed. "It would be easier to separate conjoined twins than those two," he said.

"Certainly less painful," Kelly added. She looked about the big space with its desks, couch and chairs, with a big table at the side. Neither she nor Adam mentioned that it looked remarkably like the interior of the old cellar, but with windows.

When the cellar roof had collapsed in 2002, Kelly had cried. "Now she'll never come home."

Adam held her as he looked over her head at the big hole.

The destruction seemed like the end of an era. Vietnam protests. Miguel with Gabby so he could give Vera the freedom to leave. Then years later, Miguel and Vera hiding out and creating Mike. Michaela Vera Montoya. He couldn't help laughing.

Kelly pulled away to look at him. "What's so funny?"

"That's Mike's real birthplace."

"It is." She turned to look at the big hole in the ground, with the broken roof sticking up. "What are you thinking about doing with it?"

"Fill it in. No, don't give me that look. When that was first used back in the seventies, no one had ever heard of a seat belt or any kind of safety. Times have changed. That place is a hazard. It's a wonder no one fell into it."

"You did keep it fenced. We could—" His look made her realize he was right. "You do it. I can't bear to see it destroyed."

So Adam had taken over the job, first hiring a backhoe to remove the pieces of the roof. The next day, he went down the rotting stairs. The bright Kansas sun showed how bad the interior was. Mold and insects and animals had destroyed nearly everything. He salvaged what books and papers he could, and the bookcase that Miguel had painted. He put what was salvageable in his truck and stored it. The rest he took to the dump.

Once the space was clear, he turned it over to Cait. He knew of her attachment to the place. It's where she'd told Adam that she was his niece. It's where Cait had poured her heart out to Vera about her infertility.

"It's like the ending of time," she said. "Robbie, Vera, Miguel. So many things happened in there."

Adam took a long, deep breath. He was seventy-two years old now, and as much as he fought it, he felt his age. Ending things of his youth was difficult. "You'll plant trees on top of it?"

"Oh, yes," Cait said. "Peaches. Vera told me she likes them and Mike loves them."

Adam knew that if Michaela loved them, that was the selling point for Cait. He turned toward the truck. "Send Jared the bill," he said, and she nodded.

Years before, Adam had decided that he wasn't going to be like his father and hold on to everything until his last breath. Jared was the only one of their three sons who loved farmwork and he had ideas for change. When he wanted to set some acres to "organic marijuana," Adam knew he was at a crossroads. He could follow his instinct and refuse, and thereby alienate his son, or he could step aside. That night, he told Kelly, "Let's go away for a while. I need to talk to Miguel." If there was any person on earth who knew about "life changes," it was Miguel.

They were away for three months; half of that time they'd stayed with Vera and Miguel in a little house that was far from luxurious. Adam put himself in charge of chopping wood for the cookstove and a fireplace. The rest of the time they went sightseeing: London, Paris, most of Italy. When they got back to Mason, Adam and Kelly turned the bulk of the Hatten properties over to their eldest son.

"It's your turn," Adam told Jared. He and Kelly moved into the apartment in town.

At the same time, Kelly put her beloved clinic into Coop's hands. She began volunteering to help at the KC Zoo and she loved giving hands-on talks to elementary schoolkids. As for Adam, he ran a sports program for underprivileged children. He said it was a lot like his time in Africa and he thoroughly enjoyed it.

But now, after all their planning and work of "baiting a

trap," the self-aggrandizing Celeste Wigman just might ruin it all.

"Vera won't come," Kelly said. "She'll never see the office I made for them."

"And they'll miss the miracle of Kyle's wedding." Adam was being truthfully sarcastic.

Kyle was their youngest son. "He's a clone of my brother, Robbie," Adam had often said, always with his teeth clamped together. It was one thing to eulogize his brother, but quite another to have to deal with him in life.

Since high school, Kyle had given his family problems. Girls, cigarettes, fast cars and bets placed on anything were what he liked and indulged in lavishly. Adam had tried everything to make him control himself but nothing had worked.

It was Coop who stepped in. "I think the boy just needs to find his passion."

"Passion is what he has too much of," Adam said.

"Let me try him with animals. Maybe he inherited Kelly's genes."

Adam had started to protest that with Kelly as a mother, Kyle had always been surrounded by wildlife. But Adam was too frustrated to turn down any offer of help.

At seventeen, Kyle had happily packed a bag and moved into the big Fredericks house with Coop, Cait and young Mike. Kyle hadn't been the least interested in sewing up animal wounds, but he did enjoy hanging around Cait's office at Heritage Harvests. One afternoon, he talked a man from Wisconsin into doubling his order for his chain of groceries.

Kyle's easy charm, his likability and his good looks made him a born salesman. Everyone was relieved that Kyle had at last found something he liked to do. However, it hadn't been easy to get Kyle to go to college two days a week. He just wanted to sell things. It was six years before he graduated, but by then he was Heritage Harvests' top salesman. He was a big part of why it had become a massive company. Whereas once *organic* had been an unknown word, it was now used by everyone for everything.

Everyone would have sighed in relief if it weren't for Kyle's flitting from one girl to the next.

Every time he brought home a beautiful, intelligent, interesting young woman for Sunday dinner, they all had their fingers crossed. Maybe he'd settle down with this one.

But Kyle always broke it off.

"What was wrong with *her*?" his mother would demand.

Unperturbed, Kyle would say, "Nothing. She was perfect."

"Perfect" seemed to be his condemnation of a person.

When Kyle turned thirty, everyone quit trying. It looked like he was never going to be a family man.

By then, Kelly had grandkids from her other two sons, so she was content.

Then, when Kyle was thirty-three, he brought Rebecca "Becks" Newcombe home to meet the family. She wasn't like the others. She was two years older than Kyle, widowed and had two well-mannered daughters, aged two and four. Becks had placed second in a Miss Kansas pageant and she carried herself elegantly. And she was a lawyer. She worked at a busy, prestigious firm in Kansas City.

All in all, Becks was a bit intimidating. Beauty, brains, accomplishment. She wasn't like Kyle's other girlfriends, who were just starting out in life. Becks was already there.

The first thing they noticed was that Kyle was nervous around her and he tried hard to please her. The cigarettes were gone. Usually, on Sundays, his eyes were red from a late Saturday night. But not after Becks entered his life.

After the first dinner, Kyle and Adam took her daughters outside to toss a ball around. Kelly looked out the kitchen window to see her son with the little girls clinging to him as he gave them a dual piggyback ride.

Abruptly, Kelly turned to Becks and said, "What are your intentions toward my son?"

Becks was loading the dishwasher. She smiled at Kelly like an equal, not like a girl trying to please someone who could become her mother-in-law. "I think he has great potential, don't you?"

Kelly smiled. They understood one another.

What Becks wanted from Kyle was what he was so very good at. She'd expected him to sell himself. She knew her worth and wasn't giving it away to some guy who, at thirty-three, still liked to party until dawn.

Kyle had straightened up, proved himself to Becks and eventually proposed. When she said yes, he was floating in happiness.

They bought a house in Mason, with the plan that Becks would open a local law office. She was tired of being away from her daughters so much.

Finally, they were ready to have a wedding.

Kyle told his parents, "I want everyone who didn't believe in me to be there."

"You mean the whole town?" Adam said, deadpan. "Or all of Kansas?"

Kelly gave her husband a look to cut it out. "Big or small?" she asked.

It was a redundant question. Kyle liked flashy.

"*How* big a wedding?" Kelly asked. "Are we talking dinner for twenty or fireworks and limitless buffet?"

Kyle's eyes widened. He was as handsome and as charismatic as his late uncle Robbie. "Fireworks! Now, there's an idea. I'll call Becks. She does love a pageant." He hurried out of the room.

Adam was smiling. "It's good you didn't suggest riding in on an elephant."

Kelly groaned. "Don't let him hear that or I'll be calling the zoo and seeing what I can arrange."

Adam smiled in silence. He knew that the idea of saying no to her children went against her nature.

So Kyle's wedding was scheduled for a Saturday, three months away. And it was one of the things that had been used to coax Vera to give a date for her return. Miguel said his wife was dreading it. "She thinks it's the end of her life."

No one brought up the truth. They knew Vera was struggling to keep going. Both she and Miguel were worn out from many years of constant movement, going wherever there was unrest and trouble in the world.

"She won't admit it but our joints are wearing out," Miguel told Kelly on one of their frequent calls.

They knew he was referring to the fact that they'd again been shot at. They'd been lucky that a bullet only grazed the side of Vera's head. "I wasn't close enough to her," Miguel had cried over the phone the night it happened. He was at the hospital. "She didn't react right away. She didn't fall to the ground fast enough. And I couldn't—" He was crying too hard to say more.

"Bring her home," Kelly said. "I'll get her to quit. And I'll give her a place to stay here."

"Yes" was all Miguel could manage to say.

It had taken him two years, but Miguel had at last persuaded her. Kyle's wedding had been what he'd needed to get her to set a date. That and the fact that their daughter was now a grown woman.

"Someday we'll have grandchildren," Miguel said to Vera. "I didn't think I'd live long enough to hold them." He slunk down in a chair. "I want to go home," he whispered.

Vera looked at him. She'd loved him since they were kids. It was time for *her* to make sacrifices. "Yes," she said. "I have some things to do, but we'll be there in time for Kyle's wedding."

Miguel had just nodded.

Kelly repeated her concern to Adam. "Celeste is going to ruin everything."

"So fix it," he said.

"How do I do that? People love a parade, and when they show up and Vera doesn't, they'll be furious. At her! They'll say she's a snob. That she thinks she's too big for little Mason, Kansas. It isn't fair. She won't stay if everyone is angry at her. She'll leave again."

"Then give the people something else!" Adam snapped. "Make Kyle's wedding so big that they'd rather see that. Why are you looking at me like that?"

"You are brilliant!"

Adam didn't smile. "What did I just get myself into?"

"A fair."

"Affair? Whose?"

"No. A fair. Two words. A homecoming celebration. *Everyone* will be returning to Mason. Vera will be just one of them. I'll overshadow Celeste's little parade with a big one, and I'll take the spotlight off Vera. The stars will be veterans and school principals. We'll have a whole float full of past mayors. We'll get all your sports kids who went on to be pros. We'll—"

Adam's head came up. "Mayors? But *I* was the mayor. I will *not* ride on a float."

She waved her hand. "Too bad we don't have those big gold mayor necklaces like they have in England. You could wear one in the parade. I have to go see Forey. She knows who is famous enough to ride on a float."

"Kelly, I will *not*—" He quit talking because she'd left the room. He sighed. "Maybe I'll put a peacock feather in my hat," he muttered, but when he heard Kelly excitedly talking on her cell phone, his annoyance left him. As always, he was glad to see her happy. Whatever it took, he'd do it.

CHAPTER TWENTY-SEVEN

MICHAELA WAS TALL, SLIM, WITH MIGUEL'S cheekbones and a much-subdued version of Vera's hair. She was looking at the necklaces hanging on her closet wall. She and Papi had spent an afternoon using a level to stick little hooks in a row so she could suspend all of them. On the top row were the thin, delicate necklaces given to her by Mom and Dad. They had hearts and circles and lockets containing photos.

On the second row were the necklaces she'd bought or had been given during her summers spent with her "other" parents: Vera and Papi, as she called Miguel. They were brightly colored, usually big and often flamboyant.

"Story of my life," she muttered. "Two of everything." She reached for a gold necklace with a little circle covered in tiny crystals. Conservative and tasteful.

She was so nervous she dropped it and of course the chain tangled. It was magic the way delicate jewelry chains could tie themselves into knots merely by touching them.

As she left the closet, she told herself to calm down. In her bedroom, she took a few deep breaths and looked around. Her house always brought a smile to her.

It was the little house her mom and dad had lived in when they first got married. It used to belong to a woman called Mrs. Carl. That it was on the same property as the Heritage Harvests main office made an easy commute for her mom. It had taken them two years to restore the Fredericks house. People still laughingly said that Michaela's first sounds were of nail guns and electric saws because Cait and Dr. Coop took her with them everywhere. "They don't let that baby out of their sight ever," they said.

And baby Mike had loved it! As she rocked in her little spring seat, she'd laughed at all the noise. The workmen made her a set of wooden blocks that she played with until she was in the third grade. Now they were stacked on a bookshelf. Worn, covered in faded paints and stickers, they were a prized possession.

Next to the blocks was a set of wooden dolls from Africa. The objects seemed to symbolize the two parts of her life: Kansas and the world. From the time she was nine, Mike had spent winters in Kansas with Cait and Coop, who she called Mom and Dad. Summers were with her birth parents, Vera and Papi, in whatever country they were in.

Restrictions were set before the first summer spent away. Vera would have taken Mike with her anywhere, but Cait and Kelly wouldn't let her go where there was danger. The rules they imposed had put Vera's back up. She didn't like agreeing to anyone's orders.

When Miguel stepped in and said he'd have to spend summers in Kansas with their daughter, Vera gave in. For three months every year, they borrowed a house from one of their many friends, and Michaela stayed with them.

Cait and Kelly felt they'd won a war. It was only after Mike returned from her first summer away that the women realized they'd not stipulated things like indoor toilets, electricity and not teaching Mike how to use native weapons. This was discovered when Michaela was suspended from school for three days for using a broom handle to teach spear tossing. One of her "students" had missed the target so completely he'd hit another child in the stomach. Thankfully, it had only resulted in an ugly bruise, but the principal shouted, "It could have been an eye!" Cait and Coop had hung their heads in agreement.

On the drive home, Mike, in the back seat, said, "Lance Pullman is a jerk. He wouldn't do what I said. Then he told everybody it was *my* fault that he missed. He wouldn't last ten minutes in the bush."

Coop had started to laugh but the look his wife gave him made him stop. When he caught his daughter's eyes in the rearview mirror, they knew they agreed.

Mike turned away from the bookcase. She had to get ready to go to what Kelly had named the Homecoming Carnival. It wouldn't be open to the public until four, but since Mike had done a lot of work to make it happen, she was allowed to get in early and Hayes was meeting her there.

She and Hayes Lancaster had been going together for two years and she knew it was time for them to move forward. Would this carnival weekend be when "it" happened? A ring, maybe? Or some commitment to the future?

She'd teased her dad by saying his clinic was better than any online dating service. It was how she and Hayes met.

He grew up in a big house in Brookside, a rich, exclusive neighborhood in Kansas City. After he graduated from a private high school, he went away to an Eastern Ivy League university. When he returned to Kansas, Hayes went directly to a managerial position at an international bank, thanks to his father. He moved into his parents' guesthouse. He'd made Mike nearly swoon when he said he didn't want to buy a house until he had a wife and they could choose it together.

In normal circumstances, someone with Hayes's background and Michaela, from farm country, wouldn't usually meet.

She and Hayes liked to say it was fate that brought them together—that and Hayes not seeing an animal hospital when he drove past it. He'd been on the highway, driving south to Lawrence to meet a client, when a dog ran in front of him. He swerved, nearly missed it, but he saw in his rearview that the dog went down. He stopped and cautiously picked it up, but the animal seemed grateful. There was blood on its side. He wrapped it in his gym towel, put it in his car, then took the exit to Ottawa. Somehow, he drove past their big animal clinic and on to Mason. That day, both Coop and Mike were there. While Coop treated the dog, Hayes and Mike talked, and he asked her out for the next weekend.

It had been a wonderful date. They'd gone to a nice restaurant in Overland Park and had talked for hours.

When she said her biological mother was Vera Exton, his eyes lit up. "My father is a big fan of hers. He says she's the only reporter he actually believes."

Hayes wanted to hear all about Mike's life and she'd enjoyed telling him about her summers in faraway countries. After three months of dating, he invited her home to meet his parents. His mother hadn't been the warmest of people, but his father had been enthralled by everything Mike had to say about her time in distant places.

Since then, she and Hayes had spent a lot of time together and they got on very well. There'd been a few disagreements, as Hayes did have a temper, but she always managed to calm him down. As for her own temper, which everyone said was just like Vera's, she'd learned to keep it under control.

She didn't want to ruin a good thing.

All her family liked Hayes well enough except for her uncles Seth and Pauly. Years before, they'd retired and turned Heritage Harvests over to Cait.

"Now all we want is endless sunshine," Pauly said.

"And checks," Seth added. They'd moved to a pretty villa in the south of France, and Heritage Harvests sent them a fat check every month.

They rarely returned to Kansas, but once when they did, they met Hayes. "He certainly is fancy," Seth said.

"Quite above us," Pauly said.

Cait narrowed her eyes at them. "I think you two should leave Michaela's life to her."

"Wouldn't think of interfering," Seth said.

"Are his shirts bespoke?" Pauly asked. Cait shooed them away.

All in all, Mike was glad they weren't returning for Kyle's wedding. "Too much for us," Seth said over the phone. "But give Vera and Miguel our love."

"Especially Miguel," Pauly added, and they'd laughed together.

So now Mike was getting ready to meet Hayes at the Homecoming Carnival. They'd have hours together before the public would be allowed in. There were only four rides and they were for kids, so no scary roller coaster or sexy haunted house, but there were lots of game booths. Ring toss, fishing for ducks, darts thrown at balloons. She knew how much Hayes liked to win, so he'd love them.

She imagined herself with her arms full of cute stuffed animals and some food on a stick and smiling up at Hayes. They were going to have three whole days together, with the romance of a candlelit wedding in the middle. Waltzing together under the mirrored ball could lead to...

Michaela took a breath. *Being settled*, she thought. No more being torn between her life in Kansas and her life in the world.

No more of people she dearly loved being split in two. She'd have them all in one place. *Settled.* It had come to be her favorite word. A home where she didn't move around. A job. A husband, children. All of it *secure.* She was sure the restless feeling inside her would finally go away.

She'd at last know who she was and what she wanted in life. Peaceful Kansas or the endlessly exciting world? She would know—

Her ringing phone stopped her thoughts. It was her mom. "Did you check on the game booths?" Cait asked.

"I'm about to leave now."

"Good. I'll be there as soon as I can. The florist for the wedding is giving us trouble. I don't think Becks is going to like the color of the roses that are available."

"She'll adjust. She always does."

"To take on Kyle, she'd have to be very flexible. I have to go. I've had three texts in the last four minutes. Mike, dear, is Hayes coming?"

"Yes! I'm meeting him before things open. I think he wants to win a teddy bear for me."

"How sweet," Cait said. "Are you planning to introduce him to Vera?"

"Of course. He's looking forward to it."

"I think you should wait until tomorrow. Give her time to adjust to being here. You know how blunt she can be. She might hurt his feelings."

Mike sighed. "Okay, I'll let him win me a prize, feed him, then send him home. Happy now?"

"Michaela."

"Sorry, Mom." Caitlyn didn't allow her daughter to have an attitude. "You better answer your texts. Maybe they'll say that Uncle Kyle is in jail and the wedding's off."

Caitlyn groaned. "That's not funny. Love ya!"

"Me, too." Mike tapped off. She started on the tangled necklace in her hand, but hadn't made any progress when her phone rang again. It was her dad.

"I'll be late, honey," Cooper said.

"You *have* to be there." Mike's voice was a plea.

"Tell that to Jared. He's got a mare in labor. I'll be there as soon as I can." He paused. "Are you nervous?"

"No, of course not. It's just Vera and Papi."

"Easy, huh? Just don't do *anything* to set her off. You know how Kelly and Miguel have spent years getting her to agree to stay. The least little thing and she might jump on a plane and leave."

"I know. She *is* my mother, remember?"

"You never let me forget."

Mike smiled at that. It was a family joke that Michaela was so much like her biological mother that it felt like Vera was always with them.

"Is Hayes there yet?"

"No, but he'll be here soon. We're going to the game booths early, before they're crowded."

"That's a great idea. I better go before Jared skins me. I'll see you there."

"Or at the airport as her plane flies away."

Coop groaned. "Don't say anything like that to Kelly. Please." Laughing, Mike clicked off.

Just as she got the knot out of the chain and put the necklace on, her phone rang again. It was Hayes. "Hi," she said in the low tone she used only for him, then leaned back against her bedroom wall.

"Hi yourself," he said in the same tone. "I'm on my way. Should be there in an hour or so. Need anything?"

Just you, she thought but didn't say. Hayes didn't like gushy sentiment. "No, nothing. They were setting up the booths last night, and they swore they'd be done by now. Are you planning to toss a ball? Throw rings over milk bottles?"

"Actually, I've got something to show you."

"Oh?" Her eyes were wide.

"I never told you, but in university I was on the archery team. Kyle told me a target has been set up."

Mike dropped her head back against the wall so hard it thumped. "I'm going to kill him," she whispered.

"What was that?"

She stood up straight. "Nothing. Just muttering as I try to untangle a necklace chain. Archery, huh? Did Kyle see you shoot?"

"He did, and I don't mean to brag, but he was impressed. Maybe it's not nice of me, but I'd like to show off for my girlfriend and for your famous mother."

Mike swallowed. "That sounds great. I look forward to seeing you, uh, shoot."

"I look forward to it *all*," he said suggestively. "I'll pick you up at your house."

Her mind raced. "No!" she said. "I mean, I'll meet you there, on the grounds. You know where it is, right?"

"It's not like Mason is a grand metropolis, is it? I'll find it." He clicked off.

Mike put the phone down on the dresser top and glared at the corner of her bedroom. Propped near the door, from where she'd left it after practice yesterday, was her sixty-inch Striker Takedown recurve bow. The canvas case next to it had her initials on the leather flap. Inside were her gloves and arm guard. Her quiver, also initialed, was next to them. Outside her window was her big target, and boundaries had been spray painted on the grass. There was no way she could clear up everything before he got there. She grabbed her equipment and put it in her closet. Too bad there wasn't a lock on the door.

The second summer she'd spent with Vera and Papi was in Bhutan, and she'd tried the national sport of archery. Unlike the other sports and crafts she'd dabbled in over the years, archery stuck. She and Papi often spent long afternoons aiming at various targets, some of them moving.

She'd become rather good at the sport, which Kyle well knew. If he'd seen Hayes shoot and Kyle had still arranged a target, then he must know that Mike's skill level was better. Damn him! It was just his sense of humor to set up an archery field so Mike would be tempted to show off. In other words, she'd beat Hayes at something he believed he was good at. She could almost see Kyle laughing and exchanging money on a bet.

"Kyle is *not* going to win," she told herself. When she got to the archery field and Hayes picked up his bow, she would bat her lashes in admiration and heap him with praise. She didn't want her day, the whole carnival, ruined by a silly archery contest!

CHAPTER TWENTY-EIGHT

WHEN MIKE GOT TO THE FIELD WHERE the carnival was set up, she had a moment of pride. It had been mostly her and Kelly who'd organized it. Her mom was too tied down with running Heritage Harvests to have time; her dad had his clinic, and Adam had half a dozen teams to coach. The others came up with creative excuses, so it was left to her and Kelly. At least Forey had taken care of the food.

Mike looked around with a critical eye. The parking was ample for the few hundred people they expected to show up. With no big rides and no alcoholic beverages for sale, they didn't expect huge crowds.

She saw the vans marked Security with muscular men armed with Tasers standing around drinking coffee. She'd met all of them earlier.

It was Adam who'd insisted on hiring them, and he'd paid for them. "Vera has been enraging people for forty years," he said. "I don't want to risk any problems." He looked at Kelly when he said it, remembering the drunken man who'd once attacked her at a dance.

Mike waved to the guards as she went to the entryway. Adam had had the whole area fenced off.

Four local women were setting up tables, cash boxes and sunshades. People who showed proof that they'd ever lived in Mason got free admission and a purple armband that gave them half price for everything. Any profits from the carnival went to the Mason town council, to be given out to the fire department, police, schools, wherever it was needed.

Mike greeted everyone.

"Excited about your mother coming home to stay?" Mrs. Chandless asked. Her husband's grandfather had been the Baptist preacher back in the seventies. Her husband taught high school science.

"Very much," Mike replied. "A friend of mine, Hayes Lancaster, will be here soon, so let him in for free."

"Oh?" Mrs. Sanders asked. "How will we recognize him?"

Forey had told her that years ago Mrs. Sanders had stolen her husband from Sue Terrance and that was why Sue had been married four times. "Nothing to do with her bad temper?" Mike had asked.

Mike knew she was being teased, and they were all watching her. She gave Mrs. Sanders a smile. "I'm sure you've seen him. Six-two, blond, blue eyes. Probably wearing a sports jacket."

The women at the table smiled. "Oh, yes. The Brookside young man," Mrs. Miller said.

The first place she went was to the food lane, which had been organized by Forey. She knew who in Mason could cook and what they were good at. "That woman can't bake anything," Forey said about Mrs. Dunham. "The last time she made biscuits they were so salty people's tongues curled up. But give her a deep fryer and she's in heaven."

Mike walked along the line of booths. The first one was

barbecue and the smell was divine. Corn on the cob on a grill was next to ice cream, a pie stand, then homemade bread with freshly churned butter.

The next booth was more barbecue. It was manned by the Mason Fire Department and "manned" was the key word. They had on fire pants, boots and aprons. No shirts.

Mike stopped to admire them.

"Can we get you anything?" Bob Fairway asked. His mother, Bobbi, was a friend of Cait's and she was beautiful. She had passed on her looks to her son.

"How about a photo for my uncles?" She held up her phone.

Obligingly, the four men stood side by side and smiled. "No, no. Turn around. Show some skin."

Laughing, the men turned their bare backs to her and she snapped three shots. "Thanks." She walked away, looking at the photos. "Uncles be damned," she said. "I'm keeping these for myself."

She was still smiling when she got to Forey's booth. Forey was wrinkled but her eyes were bright and she moved well. Most important, she could still order people about and get them to do what she wanted, all using her old-fashioned, push-button landline. She was often referred to as TB, for Telephone Bully. She was carrying a cake.

"Let me do that." Mike set the cake on the table with the other baked goods that had been donated by the churches.

"Are you nervous?"

Mike sighed. "Why does everyone think I can't handle my own mother? Is everything ready on *your* end?"

Forey gave a knowing smile. "We ask because you and your mother scare all of us."

"Hilarious."

Forey smiled broader. "Yes, it's all been done. House, office, everything." She tipped her head to one side. "What's bothering you? I can see it in your eyes. Too many texts? Or not enough? Or are you twittering too much?"

"You're a real comedian today. If you must know, I talked to Hayes. It seems that he used to be on his university's archery team. I think he's bringing his own bow today. He wants to show me how well he can shoot."

Forey's smile vanished. "Let him win! Don't do a Vera and step in and be better than everyone else. Do *not* show him that you can outshoot everyone in six states. If you want to keep him, *let him win*. Understand me?"

"That is so last century! Today's men understand that women are sometimes better at certain things than they are. Women can..." Forey's look made her trail off. "I didn't bring my own bow."

"That's a start. Now go away. I have work to do."

With a sigh, Mike turned away.

"I hope you don't pass out," Forey called after her. "Those jeans are so tight they must be cutting off your blood."

Mike turned back and grinned. "Who needs circulation? It took me half an hour to get them on."

Forey shook her head. "Try to be a *lady*. In my day, we didn't—"

"Ha! You want me to believe that you didn't show off *those* knockers? No way!"

Forey tried to look shocked but she couldn't do it. She laughed as she waved her hand for Mike to leave.

When Mike was walking back to the gate she spotted a stranger. The man was scruffy, dirty and wearing ragged clothes. Her first thought was *How did he get in here?* Everyone but workers were to be told to come back later. Even Mason residents weren't yet allowed in.

When he saw Mike, his dirty face seemed to light up and he took a step toward her. If she weren't hurrying to meet

Hayes, she would have stopped and told him he wasn't supposed to be there.

Instead, she frowned at him.

To her annoyance, he smiled back. From the look of him, she expected blackened teeth, but they weren't.

When he took another step toward her, she practically ran. She didn't have time to deal with an overly friendly trespasser. Besides, he looked like he was going to ask her out on a date.

She was almost at the gate when she saw Hayes. He looked scrumptious! All blond and clean and pressed. He was perfect. He smiled at her in a way that made her knees weak. But the best thing was that he wasn't carrying a bow. The tension she didn't know she was holding left her shoulders and she smiled broader.

They exchanged double cheek kisses, then held hands.

"What do you want to do first?" she asked. "Barbecue isn't ready yet, but there's lots on the food tables. How about a cinnamon bun?"

"Too much sugar," he said. "Any bagels? English muffins?"

"I doubt it but let's go see."

They walked to the food tables, and Mrs. Murray, Uncle Seth's grandniece, handed her a fried pie. "I know you love these."

"Cherry?"

"Of course."

She bit into it. "Great. Perfect. Thank you."

"How's my uncle?"

"He and Pauly send their love to everyone, especially to Papi." They laughed together.

Through this, Hayes had been standing back. When they were getting to know each other, Mike had introduced him to people around town. When he said there were too many to remember, she stopped. She saw him look at his watch.

She wiped her mouth with a napkin, then held up what was left of the pie. "These are really good. Want to try one?" A movement caught her eye. Behind them was the dirty, raggedy man. He was staring at them intently. She looked back at Hayes. "Sorry, what did you say?"

"How about we *do* something rather than just stand here?"

"Sure, of course." She quickly finished her pie. When Hayes looked away, she saw that the man was still there. She gave him a fierce glare to leave. She didn't want Hayes thinking he was a representative of Mason.

But Hayes did see him. "Excuse me," he said to Mike.

A security guard had entered the grounds. Hayes went to him and they talked. The guard spoke into the radio on his shoulder and minutes later two more guards appeared.

"Let's go." Hayes took Mike's arm and led her toward the long row of game booths.

When Mike looked back, she saw the three guards go to the scruffy man and start talking to him. When he stepped back, a guard grabbed his arm. The man jerked away, but two guards clamped down on his arms. In the next second, they'd pulled his backpack off and were searching it.

The man looked over the shoulder of one of the guards and gave Mike a look of such anger that the hair on her neck stood on end. She turned away and clutched Hayes's arm hard.

"You okay?"

Mike couldn't keep from glancing back. The man was still glaring at her in anger. She looked away.

"He won't bother you anymore. Security will take care of him. He probably came in for free food, which I understand, but I did *not* like the way he was looking at you."

"Me neither," she said. "But I didn't think you noticed."

"Any man who comes after my girl and I'll see it." He kissed the top of her head. "Let's forget about him. How about a ring toss? Or water guns?"

"All of it." When she looked back over her shoulder, the man and the guards were gone, and she was glad. She wondered if they'd found anything illegal in his pack.

For the next hour, she and Hayes went from one booth to another, and he played each game.

Maybe it was cowardly of her, but she didn't participate in any of them. Usually she tended to be competitive. Okay, so maybe she was a bit Win or Die, but not today. It could have been Forey's warning, or maybe it was just that Mike didn't want anything to ruin this weekend. She had a beautiful dress for the wedding and she planned to dance all night.

Hayes won every game he tried, but then, there weren't many people to play against. Twice she'd motioned to a couple of guys she knew to come and play. One was Betty Lewis's grandson. His father was Taran, and her dad always said he was the main rival for Cait's hand in marriage. "I never dated him," she said. "Wanted to, but didn't."

Mike had gone out with the grandson. She'd come back with the verdict: pretty to look at but dull. He played a few games with Hayes, then left to get barbecue.

"You ready for lunch?" she asked Hayes. "The Mason Fire Department has a rather nice booth." She was clutching three stuffed animals in her arms and had a chocolate-coated ice cream on a stick in her hand. It was her dream come true.

Hayes shook his head. "How do you eat so much and stay slim?"

"Mom says it's because I never sit down. You ready for barbecue?"

He looked at his watch as he'd done every ten minutes for the last hour. He smiled in a secretive way. "It's time to show you what I can do."

Mike's face fell. She knew what was coming. "I'm really hungry and I'd like to—"

"Come on," he said. "You can last a few more minutes. You'll like watching what I can do, I promise."

There was no way she could get out of it, so she nodded.

He led the way through the kids' rides to a gate that hadn't been there yesterday. Mike was beginning to put things together and she had an idea who was behind all this: Adam's bratty son. "Kyle put this in?" she asked.

"He did. He really is a nice guy. When he saw me with a bow, he bent over backward to set up a field for me."

"I'd like to bend him over backward," she muttered.

"What did you say?" He was holding the gate open for her.

"Not a word."

"Why don't you let me carry those?"

The ice cream was gone but her arms were wrapped around the stuffed animals like they were a shield. "No, thanks."

With a shrug, he led the way through a line of trees to a clear spot. It was a place that for some unknown reason Papi called "the cellar." Her mother said that someday she planned to plant peach trees on it but she hadn't done it yet. A big, new archery target had been set up at the end. On the side were two young men. Their clothes, hair and the way they carried themselves seemed to scream "private school." One of them was holding a compound bow. Mike knew it was quite expensive.

"These are friends of mine from school, Bradley and Arthur. And this is Michaela, Vera Exton's daughter."

Mike didn't frown at the introduction, but kept smiling.

Hayes held out the bow to show her. "Beautiful, isn't it? Let me shoot a few. Then I'll give you some lessons."

Mike just nodded.

"I'll hold those for you," Bradley said. She relinquished the plush creatures and went to stand by Hayes.

He lifted the bow, took too long to aim and shot off three arrows. They came quite close to the center of the target. Turning, he smiled in triumph.

"Wow," she said as Bradley walked to the target and removed the arrows. "That's really good. And your bow is certainly beautiful."

He smiled. "Want to give it a try?"

She took a step back. "That looks a bit, uh…"

"I'd like to try," came a voice from the side.

They turned to see the raggedy man standing there. If possible, he was even dirtier.

He hit his ratty old jacket with his hand and dust flew up, and flakes of mud fell away. "Sorry 'bout that but I was thrown to the ground by some overzealous wannabe cops. Seems that someone told the guards I was a known drug dealer." His eyes glittered in anger.

Mike took another step back and looked at Hayes. "I think we should go."

Neither of the men moved. They were facing each other like in an Old West gunfight.

The man held out his hand toward the bow. "I promise I won't shoot you, if that's what you're afraid of."

Hayes's upper lip made a sneer. "I'm not afraid of anything about you."

Mike knew she was watching male egos sparring and she didn't like it. "Don't give him your bow." She looked at the two young men standing to the side. "Could you please get Security?"

The dirty man smiled. "Now we see who the boss is." He turned away.

"Here!" Hayes held out his bow.

The second the man touched it Mike could see he was quite familiar with one.

"Please," she said to Hayes. "Let's go."

The man put his arm through the quiver and took out an arrow. As he slipped it into place, he gave Mike such a look of triumph, of *winning*, that she wanted to hit him.

As she knew he would, he shot three arrows smack into the middle of the target. It was much better than Hayes had done. When the odious man finished, he turned to Mike and held out the bow. "Want to try?"

Behind him, Hayes look defeated. He'd planned this all so carefully, as a gift for her. But this jerk had ruined it.

So much anger filled Mike that she could only see red. A great, ugly cloud of red. The man's stance was a display of triumph. She grabbed the bow, then four arrows out of the quiver.

She and Papi used to have speed drills. She was fourteen before she could beat him, but by sixteen he wasn't even a challenge.

As fast as a human could load, shoot and reload, she put four arrows into the target. They went in a close circle around the three that the man had put into the center.

Anyone who knew about archery knew that what she'd done was more difficult than his shots. In a way, she'd imprisoned his arrows. Caged them in.

She gave the man a look that let him know his arrogance was undeserved, and then she handed the bow to Hayes.

All four men were staring at her, eyes wide.

To Mike's mind, she'd shown up the arrogant, bragging, insufferable man. But when Hayes's expression changed from astonishment to…to… She wasn't sure what it was, but it wasn't triumph. There was no look of *We showed him!* on

Hayes's handsome face. No feeling that they were a pair fighting a mutual enemy.

The only thing she was sure of was that she'd just made a mistake. A huge, enormous mistake.

But maybe she could fix it. She tried to appear helpless as she looked up at Hayes. "He's not worth the bother. Let's go back to the fair."

Hayes took a moment to nod to Bradley and Arthur to take care of his bow. Then he walked away, with Mike close behind him. He went back through the new gate to the carnival grounds. He didn't speak, didn't take her arm.

At the gate, she stopped and looked back. The stranger was standing under a tree and looking at her. There was a lot of hair hiding his face, but it seemed as though he was trying to figure out something.

To her annoyance, he raised his hand and gave her a military salute. A salute from the loser to the winner.

She glared back, then looked to see if Hayes had seen it. No, he hadn't. His face was as cold as a glacier in Antarctica.

He walked past the rides and turned right.

"The food is this way." She knew she was pleading.

"I have some things I need to do. I'll see you later."

Before Mike could say a word, he had slipped around a booth and was out of sight. Her impulse was to run after him, but then what? She'd say she should have told him that she knew how to use a bow and arrow? Or maybe if she apologized and explained her side, that would be enough. She'd say it was them, together, against the stranger.

She ran after Hayes, but by the time she reached the gate, she saw his blue Jag leaving the parking lot.

"Everything all right?" Mrs. Chandless asked.

"He didn't like *something*," Mrs. Sanders said, and they looked at Mike.

"He had an urgent call from home," she managed to say, then turned away. All she wanted was Papi. He would understand. He would know what to do to make things better.

CHAPTER TWENTY-NINE

MIGUEL WAS IN HIS OLD SCHOOLHOUSE
and marveling at what Kelly had done with it. The whole
back of it was now floor-to-ceiling glass, with double sliding
doors. The view was of woodland and an exquisitely pretty
orchard. It was the scene Cait used in her publicity photos for
Heritage Harvests. Now he and Vera would see it every day.

On the west wall, away from reflected light, was his work-
table. It was a slab of maple, reaching from one side to the
other. On it was an enormous video screen, a keyboard below,
and to the left was the big console with storage measured in
terabytes. He didn't have to look to know his thousands of
photos, as well as all of Vera's articles, plus every note and letter, were all there, categorized by date and subject. From the
day he left, he'd sent copies of everything to Cait, and when
Mike reached fourteen, it was all sent to her to store.

On the back wall was a tall cabinet with linen-covered
boxes for his lenses and the camera bodies. Everything was
labeled.

The other side was Vera's work area. Kelly certainly knew
her sister! There was nothing that spoke of technology. The

desk looked like somebody's castoff. The chair's upholstery was nearly worn out.

On the wall above it were things that had good memories for Vera and for Miguel. Kelly had emailed him, asking what items in the storage units were Vera's favorites. "Anything to do with Michaela." He sent her photos of a couple of masks, a bow, two shell necklaces and a photo taken by Miguel of Vera and Mike laughing, lit only by firelight.

All those things were artfully arranged on the wall.

In front of the desk was a fat chaise longue that Miguel knew was the one that had been in Vera's room when they were kids. It was faded and worn.

He turned to his right, to the long wall, and smiled. There was the old bookcase from the cellar, the one he'd painted. It showed its age and weariness from a life hidden underground. He and Vera had bought it together, bargaining to get it for five dollars. At the time, they'd been shocked at the high price.

Books and papers, all curled, rippled and yellowed but dry, had been carefully placed on the shelves.

As Miguel ran his fingertips across them, his eyes teared. He knew they were from the cellar, from that place where he and Vera had spent so many wonderful hours. Where they'd worked on trying to stop a war. *Where they'd created Michaela.*

He wiped his hand across his eyes. He'd told Vera that returning to Kansas was not the end but a new beginning. The look she gave him at his cliché had nearly scared him, but now he smiled in memory. It really was going to be good to be near their daughter every day. And to be close to Cait. He might even help pick apples.

He glanced at his side of the room. More likely, he'd spend his time trying to cajole Vera into writing about what she'd seen and done.

"Who wants to read about *me*?" she'd asked when he told

her she should work on her memoirs. "Other people are the story. I'm just a human typewriter."

"Then write about the blood that was spilled when your keys were punched," he'd snapped. Their argument had dissolved into laughter and lovemaking.

It had taken masses of persuasive talks, anger and a lot of love to get her to even consider giving it all up. There was one point when Miguel began to believe that Vera was trying to get herself killed rather than retire. At last, he'd softly said, "I'm not going to stay." That had done it.

As he looked at the beautiful room, he said, "But how long will it last? How long before she—?" The slam of the front door stopped his thoughts.

"Papi! Are you here?"

He smiled. It was his beloved younger daughter. He'd returned a week earlier than Vera, as she had publishing business in New York, and Miguel had planned to spend the time with his daughters. He'd enjoyed some quality time with Cait, but Michaela was always busy. It seemed that some guy now took precedence over her family. It made Miguel understand why fathers went after their daughters' boyfriends with shotguns.

"I'm here," he called. He could tell by her voice that she was upset and he worked to remove the smile from his face. When she truly needed someone, she ditched the boyfriend and went to her father. That was worth smiling about. "I need to work on letting go," he muttered as she came into the room.

She really was a combination of him and Vera, and he warmed with love for her. "Sit and tell me all."

"Can't sit," she said, and began to pace.

Just like Vera, he thought as he stretched out on her old chaise.

"I did something awful," she said as she paced. "Forey warned me but I didn't listen."

He repressed his smile. Vera never listened to anyone. "Tell me what happened."

"It was so nice. Hayes just wanted to show me something he could do. He wanted to give me a gift. But I ruined it." She looked at him with sad eyes.

"I'm sure it can be fixed. What did he want to show you?"

Her eyes were bleak. "How good he is at archery."

"Oh," Miguel said. "How bad did you beat him?"

"Take a guess."

"You shot rings around him, didn't you?"

She sat down at the foot of the chaise. "That's exactly what I did. I put four arrows in a circle. I surrounded him."

Miguel tried not to smile, but he didn't succeed.

"This is *not* funny."

He got himself under control. "How serious are you with this young man?"

"I, uh, I thought maybe that this weekend there'd be a ring offered."

Miguel instantly sobered. "You're so young and that's so serious." When she frowned, he knew he wasn't saying the right thing. He put his hand on her cheek. "I'm sorry, *querida*. Really, I am. What did he do after you, uh, showed him up?"

"He left. He just walked away. The whole thing was all Kyle Hatten's fault. I want to murder him! Kyle saw Hayes with a bow and arrow and thought it would be hilarious to get Hayes to show me how to use one. Kyle even had a gate installed at the back. Then he set up a target over that old cellar place. You know where I mean?"

"Yes," Miguel said. "I do."

"If Kyle wasn't getting married tomorrow, I'd find him and kill him. Really. One lead-tipped arrow and he'd be gone. *Why* are you *smiling*?"

"Because I'm agreeing with you. There was a time when I could have easily killed Adam Hatten."

She smiled. Her father's "feud" with Adam Hatten was long-standing. Some people thought it was real, but Mike knew the men could spend hours talking.

"The problem now is what you're going to do about this angry boyfriend."

"I thought maybe you'd have some wise advice."

"Find a boyfriend who can outshoot you?"

She just looked at him.

He got serious. "Archery is just one of your many talents. Are you going to try to conceal *all* of them from him?"

She gave him a look that was so like Vera he almost put his hands up in protection. She was about to deliver a zinger.

"I guess I should search for a man who is just like me like you did. *You* married someone with the same temperament as you, the same abilities, the same goals, the same—"

Miguel gave a snort of laughter. "I get your point. Yes, your mother and I do have some differences."

"Like the moon and the sun do."

"So which one am I?" he asked.

"I'm not fool enough to answer that. So what do I *do* about this? How do I make it up to him?"

"You don't." Miguel was no longer laughing. "Let me tell you what I've learned in my many years of marriage. Everything is about pattern. Today you beat him at something, and he got angry. If you go to him and apologize, that will set up a pattern that will last a lifetime. If you two do stay together, you'd have to be careful to never again beat him at anything. If you slip up and do anything better than he can, he will get angry and you'll be expected to apologize. And let me tell you that once one of those things is set up, they're pretty much impossible to break."

Michaela was blinking at him. "Unfortunately, that makes sense. But if I don't fix this, what do I *do* now?"

"Nothing. Let him make the next move."

"So I just wait and worry?"

"No. You do the opposite. You don't worry, and you certainly don't wait around for him. Don't you have a few friends you could have a good time with?"

"The Mason Fire Department?"

Miguel smiled, glad she was lightening up. "Maybe a little less dramatic than that. What does he like most about you? And remember that I'm your father, so PG only."

"Vera."

"What about her?"

"He introduces me as Vera Exton's daughter. His father is a big fan of hers."

"Really?" Miguel's tone told what he thought of that.

"It's not like that. I've always had to live in the shadow of her spotlight."

"And you've never paid any attention to it." Miguel stood up. "I'm supposed to meet your mother at the fairgrounds. Want to join us?"

"Yes. Maybe if I send Hayes some photos of us, he'll—"

"Come running?" Miguel's jaw was clenched.

"You're angry! About what?"

"I think my daughter is worth more than just who gave birth to her."

"He doesn't mean anything bad," Mike said. "Lots of people want to meet her. I can't blame Hayes for wanting to."

Miguel put his arm around his daughter's shoulders and started toward the front door. "Let's go get something to eat. But do *not* tell your mother that your boyfriend is desperate to meet her. And it's better that you don't tell her about the archery battle. And say nothing about Kyle's prank."

"Can I talk about the weather or will that be too controversial for my mother's delicate, fragile sensibilities?"

He opened the door. "All right. Do what you want. Feel free to tell her all."

Mike let out her breath. "No, thanks. No archery and nothing about Kyle's low-down, dirty trick." She looked at Miguel. "Would it be all right if I put itching powder in his tux tomorrow?"

"Hmm." Miguel seemed to consider it. "As funny as that would be and well deserved, you'd better not. But I agree that he should be punished."

"What would be appropriate for destroying my entire life?"

"Tell him it had no effect on you whatever. That should do it."

Mike smiled at that. "Good idea."

Miguel walked her to her Jeep, opened the door for her, then went around to the driver's seat. There was no need to take two vehicles, especially since he *really* wanted to meet this Hayes character.

When they arrived at the gate, everyone gathered to say hello to Miguel and tell him they were glad he was home.

Once he'd said hello to a number of people, they looked around the grounds. Food was to the right, rides in the middle, game booths to the left. "Where do you think she is?"

"With the downtrodden. Wherever she can find a wrong to fight, that's where she is. Look for a placard stapled to a fence post and a gang of angry people following her."

He laughed. "How well you know her. Let's get barbecue first, then go hunting."

"I agree with that!" She led him to the firefighters' booth.

"You're going for half-naked men? Wait! Don't answer that." He handed her a fifty-dollar bill. "Get two pulled pork sandwiches and whatever you want. I'll go get us a vat of lemonade."

She kissed his cheek. "It's for charity." His look told her what he thought of that.

They met again by the rides, food in hand. "You didn't see her?" he asked.

"All was quiet. Maybe she went to visit Kelly. Or—"

A man's loud, angry voice reached them. "You can't do that. Get away from those!"

Miguel and Mike looked at each other. "We found her."

They walked down the lane of games Mike and Hayes had gone through just hours before. She couldn't help looking to see if the scruffy man was hanging around. This time, if she saw him, she'd tell everyone: Security, her father and all the firefighters. She'd do whatever was necessary to get that man off the grounds.

The first person they saw was Jared Hatten. For years, he'd been Mason's most eligible bachelor: good-looking, smart and took his responsibilities seriously. A true Kansas man.

When Mike was in the fifth grade, "Uncle Jared," as she called him, went to Warrenton, Virginia, to look at a horse to buy. He was supposed to be gone for three days, but he stayed a month.

He returned with a wife. Not a girlfriend or a fiancée but a done deal. Immediately, the town prepared to be snubbed. If she was from Warrenton, Virginia, the most elite town in the US, they were sure they knew what she would be like.

But Keely Hunton surprised them. She was small and cute, with curly dark hair, and had an infectious smile. She soon knew everyone in Mason and she put together the most wonderful social events. If she hadn't been out of town, she would have helped organize the carnival.

She and Jared had four children, the first two boys, then

two girls who looked like her. Everyone was glad that at last the sadness had left Jared's eyes.

He and his two sons, eleven and twelve, were standing in front of the booth where you throw darts at balloons taped to a wall. All three of them were blowing up balloons and the youngest looked a bit dizzy.

Behind the counter, on a ladder and removing balloons that were half-filled, was Vera. Her hair was mostly gray now, but it was as wild as always and it was threatening to leap out of the band that was trying to hold it.

Near her was a little man who was yelling up at her. "You have no right! You can't do that! I'll sue you!"

Miguel and Mike paused for a moment to figure out what was going on. He looked at his daughter. "Let's get her out of here."

"Agreed."

Miguel went to the boys and took the balloons out of their hands. "Go get something to eat and charge it to your grandfather."

The boys ran away so fast it was hard to see them.

Jared put down his balloon. "You and my father! Still rivals after all these years." Miguel just smiled.

The man who was yelling grabbed the ladder Vera was on and pushed it. Mike made a leap to steady it.

Jared spoke to the man. "How about if I buy you some lunch?"

The man didn't release the ladder.

"I know where to get beer."

With a grimace, the man let go of the ladder and walked around the counter. Jared looked at Miguel. "She's all yours."

"Always has been," he said. Jared left with the angry man.

Vera looked down from the ladder to her daughter. "Hello. It's good to see you again. Done anything interesting?"

"Not really," Mike said.

Miguel held his hand up to his wife for her to come down and she did. When she was on the ground, he said, "Vera, my darling, what are you doing?"

She dusted off her trousers. "That man was tricking people. The balloons aren't fully blown up so no one can hit them with the darts."

"But if everyone is able to burst a balloon, they'll *all* win prizes," Mike said.

"So?" Vera asked.

"Every two-dollar dart thrown would win a ten-dollar stuffed animal. That's not good economics," Mike said.

"But think of the happy faces of the winners."

Mike took a step closer to her mother. "What about the man who's trying to make a living?"

"You won't win," Miguel said to his daughter.

Vera smiled. "I took care of that problem. I sent Kyle off with a truck and his dad's credit card. He's buying more prizes."

Miguel gave a laugh that was more triumph than humor. "It's not Adam's day. Poor guy."

"Poor Kyle when I get hold of him," Mike muttered.

Vera looked at her daughter hard. "What has Kyle done to you?"

Miguel quickly spoke up. "He had a gate installed in the fence in the back, probably so out-of-towners can get in for free. He messed up what Michaela and Kelly had planned."

"A pair of scissors could cut that fence unless Adam added barbed wire." Vera looked from her husband to her daughter and back again. "I can see that you two are hiding something. Don't worry. I'll find out the truth. I always do."

When she turned away, Mike let out her breath, and Miguel winked at her.

"We came ready for lunch." He nodded toward the food bags on the counter. "How about a picnic?"

"Only if you show me the new gate." She was looking at her daughter with intense eyes and Mike was staring back with an identical glare.

"My two Veras," Miguel said softly, then louder, "I'll do better than that. We'll go to the cellar."

"But it's gone." Vera's voice was heavy.

He put his arm around her shoulders. "What we made there is here. You can tell her all about it. I'm sure she'd love to hear the story."

"You just want me to stop causing trouble."

"Then you wouldn't be the woman I love." He smiled at her and she smiled back.

CHAPTER THIRTY

"IT WAS HERE." VERA WAS LOOKING AT the leveled ground. "A tornado lifted the house but left behind the basement. The floor was the roof." Her tone told of her sadness at the loss.

Michaela was listening to her mother but she was watching her father. He was frowning. It was slight but Mike could see it. She knew what the problem was. Vera was still fighting against staying in Kansas. When Mike was growing up, every summer Vera was supposed to spend three whole months in one place. That had been torture for her. Mike had learned to keep the secret that Vera had never been able to spend the whole time with her husband and daughter. She never left for long, not more than three weeks, but she did go.

When Mike was twelve, Vera had come into the bedroom to tell her daughter good-night. "I'm sorry," she said, "but I have to go. Miguel will be here with you and he'll—"

"I know," Mike said. "Your feet are on fire."

Vera looked startled. "That's exactly what I feel, but how do you know that?"

"Sometimes I feel that way, too."

Vera's eyes widened. "Tell me what you mean."

Mike thought for a moment. "I like helping Mom with the trees and I like Dad's animals. I like Papi's photos and I like the way you're angry about everything. I like *all* of it."

Vera was trying to understand, then smiled. "You don't have just *one* passion."

"Yes." She yawned. "Uncle Kyle only likes selling things."

"But you need more than just one." Vera was looking at her daughter with new eyes. "If you spend too many days with one thing, does your whole body start twitching? Like a motor is inside it?" She smiled. "Do your feet burn?"

"Yes." Mike's eyes closed.

Vera tucked the blanket around her daughter. "Right now, my feet feel like I'm standing on lava and I need to cool them off. Tomorrow morning early I'm flying to Brazil to cover a story."

"Okay." Mike turned over and went to sleep.

That had been years ago and Mike knew that now the ground under her mother's feet was already beginning to heat up.

As for Mike, she'd been quite successful in extinguishing the fire inside herself. Her life was here now. Everyone she loved was here, and switching from one job to another kept the restlessness under control. *Settled*, she reminded herself. That's what she needed and wanted.

"I don't know about you two," Miguel said, "but I'm starving." He sat down on the grass where the cellar used to be. The women sat down with him.

"If Kelly were here, there'd be a perfect little cloth to sit on," Vera said.

They looked at one another and smiled. They had done things they didn't dare tell the people at home. When Mike was older, she and her father had gone with Vera and kept it a secret.

Mike opened the wrapping on her sandwich. "I'm grateful when there isn't any tear gas."

"Snipers for me," Miguel said.

"No dictators!" Vera said, and they laughed. "So tell me what's going on around here."

Mike wanted to groan. That was her mother's journalist voice. Papi called it her get-into-trouble voice.

"The town's mayor is embezzling funds. I hope the money from the carnival isn't stolen. The governor is on the payroll of some contractors who're building skyscrapers with substandard steel. The buildings will probably collapse and kill thousands."

Vera's eyes didn't change. "No abused children?"

"I hear one Mason kindergarten teacher is a brute. She—"

"You two!" Miguel looked at his wife. "Tell her about your new project. The one that's going to keep you so busy that you stay out of people's hair."

Vera's eyes lit with excitement. "Remember Joe Harding?"

"Of course," Mike said.

"About six months ago, his grandson contacted me. He wants to write about what Joe did, who he met, where he went. All of it."

Mike frowned. They hadn't mentioned this before and she was feeling left out. "But you already did that."

"But now things are different. When I wrote that book, the censorship was horrific. I had to leave a lot out."

"And Joe's family was young. You wanted to protect them," Miguel added.

"True," Vera said. "Griff wants to include the more colorful aspects of Joe. To tell what it was like before there was this political correctness. Before—" She closed her eyes for a moment. "Oh, how I want to go with him! To relive everything from the beginning. To—" She looked at her husband's expression. "Okay, I'm going to stay here and Griff is going to send me every word he writes. I'm going to add things and tell more, whatever he needs."

Miguel turned to their daughter. "And he's sending me photos of places as they are now. I wasn't there when Joe was with Vera, but we've been to some of the same places. We'll do some then-and-now spreads."

"That sounds very interesting," Mike said.

Vera was looking at her daughter. "We waited until this was agreed on before telling you. We need your help."

"Me? What can I do? Besides, Mom keeps me busy with the trees, and Dad always has a zillion things for me to do, and—"

Vera smiled sweetly. "If you can't do this, then maybe I will go with him." Miguel looked at his daughter hard.

Mike was still feeling hurt. She sighed. "I'd love to do whatever I can. So where is this guy? What's his name? Gary?"

"Griff. Joseph Griffin Harding. His mother told me he's been fascinated by his grandfather since he was a kid. I wish Joe had lived to see him."

"So when's he coming?"

"Next week sometime." Vera looked in the direction of the carnival. "I don't think he wants to attend some local festival, and certainly not a wedding."

"He sounds like a very serious person," Mike said.

Vera sighed happily. "He is. For the last year he's been traveling through South America. Wherever he went, he filmed and wrote about indigenous people. Not one of those 'see how miserable these people are because they don't own a three-bed, two-bath house.' It's about what we can learn from them. It's going to be a six-part documentary and Netflix has already bought it."

"Wow, that sounds impressive."

Miguel smiled at what his wife was saying. "Griff is a great guy. We've spent a lot of time with him and know him well. He's accomplished a lot. When he got out of high school he spent two years traveling around the US, taking odd jobs and talking to people and filming it all."

"He has a knack for getting people to confess truths to him." Vera's voice was full of admiration.

"He didn't go to college?" Mike took a drink of her lemonade. An ugly feeling was beginning to fill her. Could it be jealousy? "He should have gone to school."

"He did," Miguel said. "After a couple of years on the road, he decided that if he was going to follow his grandfather, he'd be better received if he had credentials. Those degree letters after a person's name mean a lot to some people. He finished university in just under three years."

"That long?" Mike murmured. Miguel looked at her.

"Joe made a lot of friends," Vera said, "so when his son graduated, a man at Sony gave him a job."

"Oh. Wow. Fancy," Mike said.

Miguel raised an eyebrow at his daughter's tone.

Vera seemed oblivious. "His father worked his way up and became a big shot in the company. He set up trust funds for his two kids. Griff decided to use the money for school."

"How wise of him," Mike said.

Miguel narrowed his eyes at her.

"But Griff had only been at school for two months when some guy said, 'What do you know about hardship? You live on a trust fund.' So Griff—"

"Let me guess," Mike said. "After that, he put himself through school on student loans. Just like us commoners. I bet he's paid them off by now."

Vera looked at her in shock, while Miguel's expression was of disapproval.

Embarrassed, Mike stared at what was left of her sandwich. "Kansas barbecue. Nothing like it, is there? It's Kansas all the way."

"Michaela," her father said softly.

Mike had a vision, a wish, that the old cellar roof would open up and she'd fall through. Alas, it did not. She cleared her throat. "He sounds like a great guy. I'm sure you'll have a good time working with him."

When Vera turned away, Mike gave her father a look of *There! Satisfied?*

He didn't seem to be. "We should—" His phone beeped and he pulled it out of his pocket. Vera didn't carry a cell phone but left "all that" to her husband. It was a text. He looked at his wife. "It's Kelly. She's looking for you. This morning she said something about your autographing table. Maybe she wants to know where to put it."

Vera wadded up her sandwich paper and threw it down. "My what? I'll tell her what she can do with her autographing table! I am *not* a damned celebrity!" She stood up. "Where is she?"

"With Forey, I think. She—" He didn't say more because Vera was already heading toward the new gate.

He turned to his daughter. He had on his "dad duty" look. He did this when Mike was too much like Vera. "I'm doing all I can to get your mother to *stay* here. If some kid asking for her help to write a book is what she needs, then you and I are going to give it to her. She…" He turned toward where his daughter was looking.

Mike was still watching her mother. A young man had come through the gate and Vera hugged him in a familiar way that could only be described as *love.*

He had on jeans and a khaki shirt. Her view was obscured by a couple of trees, but he seemed to be nice looking. Not double-take handsome like Hayes was, but good. His body was like those men on adventure-wildlife TV shows who climbed up rocks and slid through caves. Strong and sturdy. He certainly wasn't beautiful and elegant like Hayes was, not that there was any reason to compare them.

"Is that him?"

"Yeah. I hope you're going to be nice to him."

She looked back at her father. "Why wouldn't I be? I imagine he's very interesting since he's done so much in his short life."

"I don't think jealousy has a part in this. Your mother needs—"

"Jealousy? Why are you saying that? I've never—"

"Hello," the man said as he sat down on the grass where Vera had been.

He had dark hair, dark blue eyes and was freshly shaved. Not bad, she thought, but his khaki shirt was pretentious, like he was going on a safari. Not quite right for Kansas. He was looking at her so intensely that she frowned.

"Griff!" Miguel said. "It's so good to see you again. We didn't expect you until next week."

"I was deep in the bayou in Louisiana when Mom called and said Vera was here. I was afraid she'd leave before I saw her, so I jumped in my van and drove. Got here this morning."

He hadn't taken his eyes off Mike. There was something about his voice that was familiar. Since he'd done TV documentaries seemingly since he was an infant, maybe she'd seen one.

It was when he slipped his oh-so-familiar backpack off and put it on the ground that she realized who he was. He was the jerk who'd tried to make a fool of Hayes!

Absolute rage ran through her. *This* was the guy her parents were praising? Raving about his accomplishments? Her mother was planning to *work* with him?

Mike picked up her big lemonade cup. It was half-full. She didn't think about what she was doing but just threw the contents into his face. With a sneer, she got up and walked away.

She was at the gate before either of the men had recovered enough to speak. They were still sitting there, watching her storm away.

"Just out of curiosity," Miguel asked Griff, "did you deserve that?"

"Oh, yes. Totally. I'm just glad it wasn't a hot latte. And I'm really glad she didn't have a bow and arrow." He turned to Miguel with a sheepish look. "For the record, I didn't mean to upset anyone."

"That's okay. With Vera for a wife, I'm used to chaos and drama."

"And her daughter is like her?"

He sounded so hopeful that Miguel had to work not to smile. "Half and half. A tiny injustice will make Vera ready to fight the world, but it takes a lot to rile Michaela." He paused. "I was told about the archery show, but I only heard of Kyle Hatten and the new boyfriend. Where do you come in?"

"*New* boyfriend? She was looking at him like he was the last great hope. He could do no wrong. I thought they were a forever couple."

Miguel was blinking at his tone. He sounded angry, as though he'd been betrayed. "We haven't met him. What's he like?"

"I think it says a lot that she's his girlfriend but he didn't know that she's an Olympic-quality archer."

Miguel leaned back on his elbows. "Maybe so, but my daughter has been taught to keep secrets. What's his personality?"

"He carries himself like he's had everything given to him."

"How were you involved in what happened?"

"I was walking around and I saw a woman who looked like a young Vera and I guessed who she was."

"You should have introduced yourself."

"I tried to but the boyfriend told the guards he *knew* I was a drug dealer. They believed him without evidence. It took lots of ID to get them to believe I was who I said I was. Even then, I had to wait until they did a background check."

"You don't look dangerous."

"Well, uh, to be fair, I was a bit dirty then. And hairy. And maybe too friendly to a pretty girl. Anyway, after that hassle with the guards, I wasn't in the best of moods. I saw her go through the trees and I shouldn't have done it, but I followed them to the archery range. When I saw that he was holding the bow wrong, I stepped in. I'm afraid I let my ego take over."

"I take it you beat him."

"Easily. But then she beat me." Griff was grinning. "Not just won—she slaughtered me. That girl could have worked for Genghis Khan." He turned toward the gate. Mike was gone, but in her anger she'd left the gate open. He turned back to Miguel. "So now what do I do?"

Miguel's face gave away none of what he was thinking. "Depends on your goals in life."

Griff looked serious. "To write about my grandfather with Vera's help. What else could I want?" He looked back at the gate. "She sure is pretty, isn't she? You should have seen her with that bow! She was Artemis come to life. The sun lit up her hair. And her eyes... They were like gold. She—" He caught himself and looked back at Miguel. "Sorry. I mean, she seems really smart and I'd like to work with her. If that's possible. But I guess you and Vera are all I need." He stood up. "I better go. I haven't had anything to eat all day. Where can I get food?"

Miguel was still stretched out on the grass, leaning back on his forearms and looking up at Griff. "Go through the gate, past the rides, turn left. Ask people until you find Forey. Fortunata. Tell her you're my guest and she'll feed you."

Griff was walking backward. "Thanks, and, uh, sorry about what I said about your daughter. And what I did to her boyfriend. I'm sure he's a nice guy. I'll see you later, I guess."

"Meet us at the schoolhouse in an hour," Miguel called after him. "Forey will tell you where it is. We'll start going over things."

"Will do." Griff hurried away.

Miguel watched the young man. He and Vera had come to like him very much. They'd had a lot of talks that lasted into the night. They cooked meals together, confided about their lives. Miguel knew about Griff's past girlfriends, and he'd talked to Griff's family via Skype. A few times, Miguel had told stories about him and Vera. But they'd never said much about Michaela. And by silent mutual agreement, he and Vera hadn't told Michaela anything about Griff.

The closer Griff got to the gate, the faster he walked. *In a hurry to get to Michaela?* Miguel thought. *Interesting that her new boyfriend lied to Security. He used his local ties to get rid of someone who was...what? Looking too hard at his pretty girlfriend?* Miguel got up, smiling. *Artemis, was it? Eyes like gold? Sunlit hair?*

As he cleaned up the area, Miguel looked around. The cellar may no longer exist, but there were other places where young people could meet. He needed to unlock the schoolhouse, then keep Vera busy for a few hours. He didn't want anyone interrupting Griff and Michaela.

He called Kyle. "Are you doing anything today?"

"Becks gave me a dozen things to do. I'll pay you to get me out of them." He paused. "I'll make Dad do them."

"In that case, I definitely have a job for you. I got the idea that you aren't enamored of Michaela's new boyfriend."

"Pompous, know-it-all jerk. What does she see in him?"

"I have no idea, but I'd like you to talk to a young man about her."

"Yeah? You matchmaking?"

Miguel's voice strengthened. "You and your little archery stunt caused a lot of problems to the wrong people. You need to right your wrong!"

"Okay," Kyle said meekly. "What do you need?"

Miguel told him.

Later, just before he was supposed to meet Griff at the schoolhouse, he texted his daughter.

> Vera needs an article she wrote in 1982 about the Falk-
> lands War. ASAP, please.

He well knew that his wife had never written anything about the Falklands.

Fingers crossed, he went in search of his wife and whatever pies Forey had for sale.

CHAPTER THIRTY-ONE

"PAPI?" MIKE CALLED AS SHE ENTERED the schoolhouse. Before she was old enough to travel to foreign countries to be with her parents, twice a year they would return to see her. The old schoolhouse was always kept ready for them. Vera never stayed more than two weeks, but Papi usually stayed for a month. Mike smiled in memory of the good times they'd had there.

When Griffin stepped into the light, Mike's mouth hardened and her fists clenched. All day she'd been trying to follow her father's advice of not contacting Hayes, but it hadn't been easy.

She was the one who usually made the most effort in the relationship, but she knew she was like Vera. Neither of them liked to wait for something to happen.

But Hayes hadn't contacted Mike. And standing before her was the cause of the problem. She turned to leave.

"Wait!" he said. "Please. I apologize. I'm sorry." She didn't turn around but she didn't start walking. "Don't I deserve a trial? At least a hearing?"

She turned to look at him, but her face hadn't softened. "I'm listening."

"My sin was not having showered and shaved, and smiling at a pretty girl. That's all, but those guards were about to call the sheriff and have me arrested. If I hadn't been able to prove who I was, I would've had to spend the weekend in jail. The punishment was far stronger than merited."

She knew he was right but that made things worse.

"If it helps any, I'm here for less than a week. Then I leave and you'll probably never see me again." He looked at her in a pleading way. "But I hope to have lots of correspondence with you about my work."

Mike walked past him to go into the glass-walled area at the back of the house and turned on the big computer. "I never knew your grandfather. I can't tell you anything about him."

"That's okay. Your mother already wrote everything about him that's important."

"The Pulitzer committee thought so, too." She sat down in the chair in front of the screen.

Griff was standing beside her. "All I can add is that Granddad screwed around with young prostitutes. Thirty years ago that was shocking but not now." When he turned to look out the big glass doors, he seemed to be contemplating something. He turned back to her. "I have a secret. Not even your father knows this. I want to write about Vera, too. I want to lead in with Granddad, but then go on to Vera. The truth is that I want to do a bio on your mother."

She turned to him. "She will *not* like that!"

"Don't I know it. I tiptoed around the idea with her, but just a hint and I thought she was going to take a fork to my chest."

"If she thinks you're going to be writing about her, she'll never tell you a word."

He didn't reply, just looked at her.

"Why are you looking at me like that?"

"When I first met your parents, all I heard was Mike this and Mike that. Except with your dad, it was Michaela this and that. They told me you spent every summer with them."

"I did." She was cautious. It sounded like he was leading up to something.

"And the months with your parents were peaceful?"

"Yes."

He took out his phone and began to read from his notes. "I did a bit of research. On the sixteenth of July 2007, when you were ten years old, Vera Exton covered the aftermath of a major earthquake in Japan. Her reports brought tears to the eyes of viewers around the world."

"Sometimes she had to leave."

"But you stayed home in safety?"

"Of course."

"I find that interesting, as Miguel's photos of the earthquake were magnificent. They show real empathy for what the people were going through. I guess you were left with a babysitter."

Mike didn't reply.

"The next year, on the eleventh of June 2008, Cuba announced they were going to change their economic policies that had been in place since 1959. Aren't the old cars there great?"

"They are! And the colors! I thought—" She glared at him. "Are you finished?"

"Almost. Just two more. On the sixth of June 2012, when you were fifteen, England was celebrating the sixtieth year of Queen Elizabeth II on the throne. During that time, Vera and her husband spent two weeks in a castle in Scotland with the Duke of McTarvit. Your father took some excellent photos." Griff held out his phone to show a picture of Mike on a horse, riding beside the duke's second son. "Can you ride as well as you shoot a bow?"

"Give me one now and I'll show you." Her arms were folded across her chest.

"Here's my absolute favorite. In August of 2013, when you were sixteen years old, Vera and Miguel were in Cairo. She was interviewing people in the peaceful, six-week-long mass sit-in as eighty-five thousand people protested the ousting of President Morsi. Your father was photographing it all. At eight a.m. on the fourteenth, the Egyptian military opened fire with tear gas and birdshot. There were also bulldozers and rooftop snipers. Hundreds of people were killed and thousands injured. Among the dead were five journalists. Your mother reported on it all and your father's photos of the violence were shown around the world. It became known as the Rabaa Massacre." He looked at her but she said nothing. "No reply?"

"None. So now what? You blackmail me into helping you do something my mother doesn't want? You promise to keep your mouth shut if I spy and sneak and tell you family secrets?"

He looked surprised. "I hadn't thought of that. Would it work?"

"No."

"Then I guess I won't try blackmail. What I'm really curious about is why all the secrecy?"

She hesitated before answering. "My family is complicated, and there are things that are better not to tell."

"Like people not knowing who your parents are?"

"Everyone in this town knows exactly who my parents are! Vera and Miguel are my biological parents, but Vera has—"

"You call her 'Vera'?"

"Yes. Mom is Cait, Dad is Dr. Cooper and Papi is Miguel. Vera is Vera to everyone. Including me. The four of them came up with a plan before I was born. Mom and Dad couldn't have children, and Papi and Vera wanted to travel, so it worked out. For school and all, legal guardianship was signed over to Mom and Dad. I spent winters and went to school here in Kansas. In the summers Papi found a place overseas and I stayed with them. Simple."

"I see," Griff said. "If Cait and Dr. Coop and, it seems, your aunt Kelly knew you were being hauled into the middle of massacres, there would be legal problems."

She glared at him. "And if they were told now, there'd be family problems. Lots of yelling and tears." Her voice rose to falsetto. "'You lied! How could you do that? We trusted you!'"

Her mimicry was so perfect that he laughed.

At his laughter, her eyes softened. "What are you hoping to find out?"

He pulled a chair up and sat by her. "What I can't find by research. Your mother is a national treasure. I think she deserves a place in history."

Mike couldn't help smiling. She agreed. While he'd been talking, she was searching through computer files.

"What is it you're looking for?"

"Falklands, 1982."

"I've never read that Vera was involved in that."

"But—" Mike began, then picked up her phone and sent a text to her aunt Kelly. The answer came right away. To Kelly's knowledge, Vera had never been to the Falklands. Mike showed the text to Griff.

"Miguel was going to meet me here but you showed up instead. Is it possible your father wanted us to meet? So maybe you'd forgive me?"

"Maybe he wanted to give you a chance to apologize."

"But your boyfriend called the guards and—" At her look, he calmed himself. "Do I get to present my case?"

She shut down the computer and turned to him.

"The minute I saw you," he said, "I knew you were Vera's daughter. You look like her. You even carry yourself like her. There's an air about you that—" He stopped and cleared his throat. "I should have cleaned up first. At least shaved, but I was afraid Vera would leave and I wouldn't see her again. I really am sorry I lost my temper. I hope I didn't do any permanent damage to you and your boyfriend."

Mike hoped so, too, but she knew the truth was that Hayes was angry because *she* had beaten him. If she had walked away after Griff shot, there wouldn't be a problem.

But she'd die before she admitted that.

She and Griff looked at each other for a moment. Mike was the first to turn way. "I guess we could call it even. I shouldn't have been so judgmental and you shouldn't have humiliated Hayes in archery."

Griff bit his tongue to keep from saying that it was *her* beating Hayes that made him so angry. "Yeah," he murmured. "Fifty-fifty. I hope everything between you two is good now."

"Yes, of course it is. Hayes will be at the wedding tomorrow. Kelly put us at a table right by the dance floor."

"That's great. Maybe before or after the wedding I can offer my apology to him. I shouldn't have shown up so dirty. But I'd been filming in a swamp and…" He shrugged.

Mike had always believed that people had a right to dress as they wanted. Because Griff wasn't prep-school clean didn't give anyone the right to… She made herself stop that line of thought. It was almost as though she was on Griff's side.

He stood up. "You know what? I'd really like to see this carnival. It's been years since I attended something like that. Maybe you could show me around."

She glanced at the blank computer screen. So far, the carnival she'd worked so hard on had been a bust. The argument with Hayes, then seeing this man and... She thought of the drink she'd thrown on him.

The truth was, she needed to get over her anger at him. Whether she liked it or not, her parents were going to be working with him. If Mike acted like a temper-tantrum-throwing toddler and refused to deal with him, it would be unpleasant for everyone. She could hear Vera now. "Do you think I've *liked* even half the jerks I've had to work with? And I'm not including the despots I've had to interview. You suck it up and get on with the job!"

Mike didn't want to think how Hayes would view this. Certainly as a betrayal. But her father's advice, to not plead for forgiveness, came to her. For a second, she thought of her and Hayes. Is this what love was? To make yourself over to what the person you loved wanted you to be?

"Are you okay?" Griff asked.

"Sure. I'd like to see the carnival, too." She stood up. "I'll see you there. Lock the door. Strangers are in town today."

Before he could say anything, she was out the door and he heard her Jeep start.

Griff stayed there for a moment, looking around the long, narrow room. It was obvious that one side was for Miguel and the other for Vera. He envied them. All his travels were alone, or with a temporary crew. When the job was over, he went back to his hotel or camp or wherever, alone. Of course there'd been women in his life, but none of them could stand the way he lived. They wanted a man who'd be with them every day. Backyard barbecues. Kids' birthday parties. All the normal things.

When Griff had started researching, he'd assumed Vera Exton's daughter, who'd lived most of her life in Kansas, would be like other women. But when he'd seen the dates that Vera had done dangerous investigations, it hit him that her daughter must have been with them. It had been exciting to think there was a young woman who knew what was needed to get a true story. He began to think that maybe he and this woman could work together.

But that didn't appear to be true. She wanted exactly what other women did. That's why she had a boyfriend like Hayes. Griff could imagine the future between Hayes and Michaela: big house, three kids, cocktail parties on the lawn.

When he'd first seen Mike, he was astonished at the sexual attraction he'd felt for her. He hadn't counted on that. He'd seen a few photos of her but they didn't convey the energy that came from her. Her with that bow! She was magnificent.

But obviously he'd misjudged. She wasn't like he'd hoped. It seemed that all her adventures, the dangers, had made her want to live a different life. One where she knew what was coming from day to day. No surprises. Certainly nothing like what she must have experienced in the Rabaa Massacre.

He left the schoolhouse, locked the door behind him and drove to the carnival grounds. The place was filling up. Loud music clashed with kids yelling and laughing, and there was the smell of popcorn and hot dogs.

When he saw Mike at the entrance table, listening to the women ticket takers, he smiled. He went to stand beside her.

"What do *you* want?" one of the women asked in an unpleasant tone.

"He's with me," Mike said. "He owes me a big lemonade." Griff laughed. "I do. I'll—"

The woman cut him off. "We don't have any lions here."

"It's just his shirt," Mike snapped. "He's not on safari."

Griff smiled at the women. "I don't know about that. You three look like you're in need of taming." Mike rolled her eyes but the women giggled.

"Go on with you," the first woman said. "No charge."

"Thank you very much," he said. "And if a lion shows up, I'm dressed to save you all." He caught up with Mike.

"That was Betty Lewis," she said. "She usually..." Mike didn't finish, as she would have said that Betty usually didn't like anyone but did seem to like *him*. "What do you want to do first? Ride the teacups?"

"I want to say hello to Forey."

"You know her?"

"Are you kidding? She gave me food and information. I'm in love with her. Even though she did ask a lot of questions."

"Like what?"

"All about me. Parents, siblings, did I have any childhood traumas? Been married? Any kids? Do I have a girlfriend now? Am I financially stable? She pretty much went over my entire life."

Mike didn't let him see her frown. Forey hadn't asked Hayes a single question. She'd been very polite to him, but not the least invasive or inquisitive.

When they got to Forey's booth, Mike stood back and watched the women. None were under seventy and they were all flirting with Griff. He said he liked pie better than cake, so he was given a paper plate with three kinds of pie. They waited for him to take his first bite, but he stopped, fork in the air. "I just want to be sure that this fruit is from Heritage Harvests."

"Of course it is!" Forey sounded affronted. The women smiled. A quarter of Mason worked for the company.

"Truly delicious." Griff ate all three slices and the women were beaming at him.

He told them thanks, put a twenty in the donation box and walked away with Mike. "I am stuffed! You Kansans sure know how to eat."

"Healthy begins in Kansas, then spreads across the nation like a sunflower."

He laughed. "I'm beginning to believe it. I saw you playing the games with your boyfriend. Did you beat him?"

"I didn't play any of them with Hayes."

He stopped walking and looked at her. "Why not?"

Her lips tightened. "I didn't want to."

He shrugged. "You aren't any good at them, are you? You only play games where you're *sure* you can win. I understand that." He looked around. "Think I can find anybody here who'd offer me any competition?"

As she walked past Griff, she said, "I'll beat you at *everything*."

Grinning widely, he followed her.

For the next hour, she and Griff battled it out. There wasn't a game they didn't try. He was going to pay for them, but the look Mike gave him made them take turns at paying.

Mike told Griff about Vera on the ladder and Jared and his sons blowing up the balloons. Griff listened eagerly. "That's the kind of story I want to hear. They make her human."

She thrust a stuffed monkey into his arms, along with the four he was already holding. "She is very human. The cellar proves that." She gasped at her slip.

Griff's eyes widened. "What is that?"

"Nothing. Let's get rid of these."

They went to the fire department booth and dropped off the prizes in their donation box. The firefighters teased Mike. "Stay and help us. We'll lend you an apron."

"And I'm to be shirtless, too?" she teased back.

"Of course. It's all for charity."

"Maybe," she said. "I could—"

Griff spoke up. "I can beat you at the ring toss. Let's go."

"Looks like someone's jealous," one of the men said.

"So, Mike, you got *two* boyfriends now? Wanna make it three?"

"I'll tell Charlotte on you. Save me some burnt ends," she said. Laughing, she turned away to leave with Griff. "You aren't really, you know, are you?"

"Jealous?" He snorted in derision. "That would imply ownership."

"I guess it does." With guilt, she remembered her jealousy at the way Vera and Papi had talked about him. "So you're good at ring toss, are you?"

"In Namibia, I was the best."

She smiled in memory. "Oh, those sand dunes in Sossusvlei."

"And that one little tree in front of Big Daddy. Did you climb to the top?"

"Of course, and Papi shot it all. Used his 400 lens. I said he wouldn't need that long, but he was right."

Griff was smiling smugly.

"What does that look mean?"

"Your dad said you knew about photography."

"Dad is Dr. Coop. Miguel is Papi."

"Right. I'll get the hang of it." They were at the ring toss booth. "Pick out what animal you want because I'm going to win it."

"Yeah, well, you pick out the top three and *I* will win them all."

"You're on!"

CHAPTER THIRTY-TWO

WHEN MIKE SAW KYLE HATTEN WALKING toward them, she scowled so hard her eyebrows met in the middle.

Kyle grinned. "This your new boyfriend?"

"I hate you," Mike said.

He reached out to ruffle her hair as he'd done since she was a kid, but she did a half backbend to avoid his hand. "Ah, come on, Mikey. It was just for fun. So how bad did you beat him?"

Griff was standing beside her. "If you mean the archery, she killed both of us. Did you put the target up?"

Kyle was looking at Griff in a sizing-him-up way. Kyle was taller, more handsome, and went through life with the belief that whoever he met was going to like him and they almost always did. He looked at Mike. "Come on. It was just a prank. Ol' Hayes was bragging about his 'artistry with a bow' and I was shocked that you hadn't told him that you with an arrow is a lethal weapon. What was I supposed to do?"

Mike was still frowning at him. "*Not* put in a new gate. *Not* set up a target. *Not* put me in a situation like that."

Kyle grinned more. "You mean when you *had* to show

him up?" He looked at Griff. "Have you learned yet that our Mikey is the most competitive person on the planet? Double-dare her and she'll do *anything*."

"I wasn't going to shoot but—"

Griff took a step forward. "It was my fault. I forced her into it. And really, she was just protecting *Hayes*." He emphasized the name.

"Is that true?" Kyle asked. "I bet the Brookside guy loved being bested by a girl. Did he run away and hide?"

Mike glared at Kyle. "You're a jerk." To Griff, she said, "I don't need you to defend me." Turning, she walked away from both of them.

When she was gone, Kyle turned to Griff. "I'm Kyle Hatten, Adam and Kelly's youngest kid. The late-in-life one."

"And now the groom."

"That's me. Who are you?"

"A friend of Vera and Miguel." Griff hesitated, but there was something about this man that made him feel he could trust him. Or maybe it was that Kyle obviously adored Mike. "I'm here to try to talk Vera into letting me write a bio of her."

Kyle gave a whistle through his teeth. "That'll never happen."

"I'm not convinced."

Kyle put a five down on the counter and the two of them picked up water pistols and aimed. They tied the game.

They put down the pistols and Griff gave Kyle a serious look. "I just found out that a lot of the dangerous places Vera and Miguel went, Mike was there with them."

"Don't let my mother know that or she'll have a fit. But it doesn't surprise me." Kyle nodded to the lemonade booth. They ordered and Griff paid. "You should know that Mike is as good at keeping secrets as her mother."

Griff took his time responding. "I need an assistant for my bio. Miguel said Mike is good with a camera, so I thought—"

"Forget it," Kyle said. "Mike won't leave here."

"Because of the boyfriend?"

"Hell, no! He's just a means to an end. The problem is that the Exton girls always put family first."

"That's hard to believe. Vera's rarely been here since the seventies."

"But she didn't leave Mason until my mother had finished veterinarian school and was able to support herself."

Griff's face showed he wasn't understanding.

"Both sets of Mike's parents will be here in Kansas, and she has a strong connection to us Hattens. Has she told you what she does for a living?"

"No."

"Think of a pinwheel. Every blade of it is a different business of her family. There's Heritage Harvests, Coop's vet clinic, the book Vera and Miguel want to write, my mom's volunteer programs, plus half a dozen more. Mike is the pin in the middle. She's needed by all of them."

"And the boyfriend?"

"I understand Mike's *why*, that she wants to anchor herself here, but no one can understand the *who*. Mike is half Kansas and half places we've never heard of. Maybe Brookside Boy is an in-between creature. Who knows? But I do know that he thinks Mason is full of uneducated yokels."

"I didn't like him but I thought it was just me."

"Must be confusing since you're already half in love with Mike."

"I'm not!" Griff sputtered. "I mean, that's ridiculous. I haven't known her even twenty-four hours. And she can't stand me."

"When I first met Becks, the woman I'm going to marry

tomorrow, she told me she'd rather date an escaped convict than me."

Griff grimaced. "So you stalked her? Wore her down?"

"Hell, no! That would have been easy. I cleaned up my act. I got rid of my Harley, bought a sedan, stopped chasing women, cut the drinking. As for the gambling, *I* am the highest stakes I'd ever played. I bet it all to win."

Griff was looking at him. "I think you want me to win."

"Maybe so. I love that kid like she's my little sister. Ask her how many times I saved her neck when she was growing up. She's as fearless as Vera."

"Any advice?"

Kyle sighed. "None. You're fighting generations of Exton women. Might as well try to move Stonehenge. But I wish you luck." He looked at his watch. "I have to go. Big day tomorrow." He started walking backward. "You'll come to my wedding? I have the most beautiful bride in the world."

"She can't be as pretty as Michaela. That hair of hers! It—"

Kyle was laughing. "I'll get Becks to seat you next to Mike. Brookside Boy will be put at the kids' table."

Griff smiled. "I'll be there with bells on."

"Skip the bells. Suck up to Miguel. It may not seem so, but he's the power behind the throne."

"Good to know. See you tomorrow. I bet your dress is really pretty."

"All French lace. With little pearls." Laughing, Kyle hurried away.

CHAPTER THIRTY-THREE

MIKE WAS GLAD TO GET AWAY FROM Griff, and Kyle was her excuse. In normal circumstances, she'd bawl Kyle out, and then they'd end up hugging. After all, he was a close relative. Sort of. Maybe the bloodline had a disconnect in it, but Kyle's uncle was her mom's biological father. Only the two families knew that. It was one of the rare secrets they'd been able to keep from other people.

The truth was that Mike left the games because she was enjoying herself too much. It had been a lot of fun playing them with Griff. She'd tried hard to win and, when she succeeded, she'd made it known by dancing, cheering, bragging, and he'd done the same. By the end, they were both laughing hard.

She tried to not compare this with the time she'd spent with Hayes. That had not been fun.

She shook her head, trying to clear it. The men were different, that's all.

Suddenly, she wanted to talk to her mother. She wanted Vera. Cait would be on Mike's side no matter what she said. There'd be no unbiased opinions. Coop and Kelly would hand her a soft-furred animal to hold. Papi would listen in silence, then ask her to look into her own heart to make a decision. Right now she needed someone who would have an *opinion*.

She looked around the grounds, saying hello to people and accepting thanks for putting the carnival together. Some said, "See you at the wedding tomorrow." Others mentioned the parade through the center of Mason. "Tomorrow at nine, right?" Mike answered all the questions with a smile.

It was near the cotton candy booth that she saw the two men who had been with Hayes during the archery fiasco. Their shirts weren't as tightly tucked in, and one of them had a smudge on his face, but they stuck out like the oddities they were.

"We met you earlier," one said.

She wanted to get away but she didn't want them telling Hayes she was rude. She nodded.

"We saw you laughing with that guy. He cleaned up but he's the one with the bow, right? The one you beat?" He was smirking.

"Yes."

"So you two made up? You're back together?"

His insinuation was clear. Mike's hands clenched into fists. "He is working for my parents. It's business."

"Sure didn't look like it, from what we saw." They laughed loudly, then had the good sense to hurry away.

Mike stood still for a few minutes, trying to get her anger under control. Jerks! Now they'd run and tell Hayes their interpretation of what they'd seen. Damnation, but where was her mother?

A woman with three kids stopped to ask Mike about the children's pet march tomorrow. It took work for Mike to keep her mind focused enough to answer. Yes, birds are allowed. Yes, parents can help. Snakes only in cages. Yes, Dr. Coop would be there with his bag in case some animal was rabid.

When Mike finally got away, she knew where her mother probably was. The cellar. For the first time, she was glad for the gate Kyle had put in so she didn't have to climb anything. She hurried through, made sure the gate was closed, then ran through the line of trees. As she'd hoped, Vera was sitting at the far edge, under a tree, and reading a book. When she got close, Mike saw it was a history of North Korea. "Planning to go there?"

Vera looked up. "I might. Interested?" She put the book down beside her.

"Maybe. Were you involved in the Falklands War?"

"No. Why?"

"Ask Papi about the little trick he played on me."

"I gave up trying to figure out his mind long ago." She patted her lap.

Gratefully, Mike stretched out on the sweet grass and put her head in her mother's lap.

Vera stroked her daughter's hair. It was so like her own, but tamed by Miguel's sleek black hair. "Has Griff tried to con you into helping him with his bio of me?"

Mike grinned. "I wondered if you knew about that. Will you do it?"

"Miguel says I should. He says the book would actually be about what I've seen and done. It might help if people know what's gone on in the world and the results. You have my permission to tell Griff whatever he wants to know."

"I may not need to. He's already figured out that I went with you and Papi to some less-than-safe places. He knows about Rabaa."

Vera let out her breath at the memory of that horror. "If your father hadn't realized what was about to happen that day... When he saw those bulldozers! And the snipers on the top of the buildings and—"

Mike took her mother's hand. "It's okay. He got us out."

"But so very many didn't survive."

They were quiet for a moment. Then Vera said, "I can tell that something is bothering you. Your dad told me about the archery contest."

"It was all Kyle's fault."

"He's exactly like Robbie. A lovable scamp. But I think your new boyfriend did something Kyle didn't like."

"That's not fair. Hayes never shows his true self to people. He has a guard around himself and only lets in people he truly trusts."

"I've seen women who had to follow behind their husbands apologizing for them. It wears you out, body and mind."

"It's not like that!" Mike said. "I don't have to apologize for Hayes. Most people say he's charming."

"That's good." At Mike's rising temper, Vera changed the subject. "So tell me what you think I should do about this bio. Do I help or not?"

"The problem will be *you*. Griff wants to know about you personally. Not just about some war you covered. He'll want to know what you did in the cellar."

Vera laughed. "We made *you*. Think he wants to hear about that? Your father is a fabulous lover. He—"

"Stop it!"

Vera was smiling. "With your help I could do it. Think you can get along with Griff well enough? Miguel told me you threw lemonade in his face."

"He's okay."

"That's all?"

Mike couldn't help smiling. "We just had some laughs playing the carnival games."

"Games? Forey told me that this morning you did that with your young man. Hayes."

"Yes, he and I went to them, but I didn't play. I didn't want to ruin the day."

"By winning?" Her tone was disapproving.

Mike's face showed her annoyance. "Didn't *you* ever try to impress a man? I'm too much like you. Put me in a contest and I play to win. Cutthroat. I thought it would hurt the romance if I beat Hayes and it *did*. The archery was proof of that."

"What about Griff? Did you hold back for him?"

"Ha! I beat him whenever I could."

"And how did he react?"

"He just laughed." She glared at her mother. "The difference is that I'm not in a romantic relationship with Griffin." She sat up and looked at her watch. "I have to go. I need to find Kelly and see if she needs me."

"You're the one who takes care of us all." Vera frowned. "So much responsibility for one so young. I wish you could have more fun and less drudgery."

Mike stood up. "I do have fun. Lots of it. You'll be at the parade tomorrow?"

"Of course. And you'll be there with your phone and overseeing it all?"

"Yes, I will. Do you need anything? I can get you barbecue or a drink. Pie? Ice cream?"

"Delivered by one of those half-naked firefighters?"

Mike was walking backward. "I'll send Papi with ice cream. Then you two…" She waved her hand at the place where the cellar had been. "I want a little brother. I'll teach him all that I know." She pantomimed using a bow and arrow.

Vera laughed. "Go on with you, but do try to have some fun."

"I'll make it a priority." She threw a kiss to her mother, then ran to the gate.

CHAPTER THIRTY-FOUR

"THERE YOU ARE," KELLY SAID AS SOON as she saw Mike. "The elementary school needs help on their float. I'm up to my neck in wedding stuff. Where's Cait?"

"I have no idea," Mike said. "Where's the float?"

"The old corn depot. The kids are hyped up on sugar. Think you can handle them?"

"Sure. I'll get Griff to help."

Kelly paused. "Is that the guy who had drugs in his backpack?"

"He didn't. It was a misunderstanding. He wants to write a bio of Vera."

Kelly grinned. "Best joke I've heard all day. Do you know where Kyle is?"

"Last I saw him, he was with Griff. They—"

Kelly threw up her hands. "I've got to meet this guy. Go!"

"Yes, ma'am." Mike headed toward the parking lot. When she passed Griff at the firefighters' booth, she said, "Come on. We have a job." He followed her.

They went to her Jeep and got in. As she pulled out, she said, "You aren't bombarding me with questions?"

"I'm willing to follow you wherever you lead. No questions asked. I'll go through snipers and bulldozers. Through—"

Mike groaned. "Vera knows what you want."

"Yeah?" He sounded eager. "What did she say? Did she agree?"

"She—" When Mike's phone buzzed, she took it out of her pocket to look at it, but Griff took it out of her hand.

"No texting while driving. Should I look at it?"

"Sure. It's probably Kelly wanting me to do something."

As Griff looked at her phone, he read in silence. When he spoke, his voice was low. "Hayes says he knows you're worried about what happened, but he promises that everything will be fine. He'll meet you at your house at seven p.m. He says he has something very important to give you." He looked at her. "Sorry. I didn't meant to pry."

Mike didn't want Griff to know her private thoughts. For one thing, she was no longer upset about what had happened. Talking to her parents had given her a different perspective. She'd beat Hayes at archery. That's all. Earlier, she'd felt guilty about that, but now she wasn't feeling bad at all. She thought about Miguel and his talk of patterns and setting a precedent.

"Mind texting him back for me?"

"I wouldn't mind at all," Griff said.

"Tell him I'll meet him at Forey's booth at eight p.m."

"Anything else? Emojis with hearts? Something exploding? I heard the poop emoji is the one most used. Or—"

"Just that. And don't add anything."

As he typed in exactly what she'd told him, he managed to keep his smile under control. He returned her phone. "Back to Vera. What did she say? Anything useful? Like maybe, 'I'd love to help Griff with a bio of me. He can stay in our guest bedroom for as long as it takes.' Something like that?"

Mike pulled into the parking lot, turned off the engine and

opened the door. "Your imagination exceeds your abilities to persuade. Get out. We have work to do."

Grinning, Griff followed her.

An hour later, Mike was exhausted. It had been a very long day. It had been Hayes, then Griff, her father, Griff, Vera, then… Griff.

Kelly had underplayed the chaos at the elementary school float. There were no teachers there, those brilliant people who could calm down a gym full of frantic kids with just their voices. Instead, it was only parents, all of whom had arrived with cupcakes, cake pops and boxes of high-fructose juice.

When Mike saw the chaos of kids screaming and running, some crying at a pitch that could match a tornado siren, she took a step back. Griff pushed her forward. "Don't chicken out now," he said, and they entered.

There were three mothers who had given up. They had flopped down in chairs and were talking with great affection about margaritas. Griff had them put away what was left of the sugary foods, then gave them instructions on which kids to go after. The climbers were top of the list.

He got the kids to run around in a circle, trying to burn off their sugar highs. He sent the crying kids to Mike to distract them with some crafts.

Within twenty minutes, Griff had the place under control.

"Thank you," the mothers were saying. "We didn't know what to do. They—" Griff didn't let them finish. He sent them to Mike to start work on the float.

It was close to finished at 7:45. Most of the kids had been picked up and carried out to cars. They were worn out and mostly asleep.

"You better go," Griff told Mike. They'd hardly spoken

since they got there. Herding young children took precedence over adult talk.

"If you mean go to a hot shower and a bed, I'm ready." When he was quiet, she looked at him, confused.

"Hayes," he said. "The boyfriend, remember? Meet at eight at Forey's, and he has something important to give you."

"Oh!" She had completely forgotten about that.

When she got into her Jeep, what little energy she had left drained from her. First of all, she was filthy. Kisses from kindergartners were lovely except that they left a trail. She had chocolate on both ears, vanilla frosting in her hair and gummy bears stuck to her shirt. She'd never been around Hayes unless she was washed and perfumed. But there was no time to fix herself. Besides, the truth was that she didn't care.

When she got back to the carnival, Hayes was standing twenty feet from Forey's booth and that made her frown. Would it hurt him to buy a slice of pie? For charity?

His clothes were immaculate, not a crease in them. Mike had the wicked idea of hugging him. Maybe the gunk on her would transfer to him. She'd come away freshly clean and Hayes would be…different.

When he saw her, a quick look of shock passed across his face, but he changed it to a smile. "I see you've been working."

"I have. No cleaning Porta Potties yet, but they may be assigned to me next."

He didn't smile at her joke. Instead, he took a step back. "I came to reassure you that everything is okay between us. I know you were worried."

She knew that what he was saying had been true for a while, but it certainly seemed presumptuous. "I've been too busy to worry about anything."

"That's good. But please don't be upset because you kept such a big secret from me."

Mike was genuinely confused. Had he somehow found out about her mom's biological father? That was the only secret she knew.

He seemed to understand her dilemma. "The archery. You didn't tell me about that. You let me go on and on about my small abilities, and there you were, knowing you were Robin Hood."

"Oh," she said. "That. I guess I never thought it was important enough to mention." The spear-throwing incident in elementary school had taught her to not tell people what she could do or where she'd been and what she'd seen.

"But I did think you and I were closer than that." He sounded regretful. "Anyway, I have something to give you." He handed her a little red jewelry box.

Inside was a delicate gold chain with a pretty little heart pendant. He smiled. "It's a preengagement gift."

"I don't know what that means."

"Before…you know, a ring comes this."

Maybe she was too tired to comprehend what he was saying. "Are you talking about an engagement ring and marriage?"

"Well…it's a bit early for that." He was smiling as though he knew that's what she wanted. "This is about exclusivity. That means—"

"I know the word. In this context it seems to mean that I'm not to date anyone else." She glared at him. "I guess your fraternity friends reported on me."

"There was some talk, yes, but I thought of this before I heard anything about what you've been doing." His tone implied that she'd been doing something really bad.

Maybe it was because she was worn out or because she hadn't eaten for hours, but she couldn't take any more. She spoke calmly. "I haven't *done* anything." She handed the box back to him. "Just so you know, there are a *lot* of things I can do better than you."

Turning, she walked away. She feared that at any moment she might cave in and go back to him, but instead her pace increased. The fatigue began to leave her.

When she got to her Jeep she wasn't surprised to see Griff leaning against the driver's door. He held out his hand and she put the keys in it.

"Margaritas?" he asked as he started the engine.

"With nachos."

"And jalapeño poppers."

"Two dozen of them," she said.

"You okay?" he asked.

"I guess." She looked out the side window, then back. "No. I know I'm okay."

"You didn't stay with the boyfriend for long."

"If you expected me to, why were you waiting for me?"

"Hope?" He grinned at her. "So how are things between you two?"

"Great. Fabulous. He's two steps away from a marriage proposal."

At the stoplight, Griff looked at her. "Is that a joke?"

"Not at all. A preengagement necklace leads to a ring, which leads to marriage. I assume. Not sure."

The light changed. "Sounds like he can't make up his mind."

"I think maybe I made him feel that he didn't have to."

"Not sure what that means."

"Me neither." As they pulled into the parking lot of a Mexican restaurant, she asked, "What are you so jittery about? Did something happen?"

They got out of the Jeep. "Remind me not to play poker with you. And yes, something big happened."

"Good or bad?"

"Depends on how you look at it. But we need booze first."

Inside, they were seated in a booth and Griff ordered the margaritas, nachos and poppers. As soon as it arrived, Mike downed half of her drink. "Okay, out with it."

"I've done a horrible thing," he said. "Unforgivable."

"So help me, if you told Kelly that I went to some dangerous places, I'll—"

"I didn't do that. This is much worse. It's about Amazon."

"The river?" She looked at his expression. "Oh. *That* Amazon. Did they mess up your order?"

He looked around as though checking for spies, then spoke loudly. "Amazon never does anything wrong." He lowered his voice. "While you were with the boyfriend, I had a call with my agent. For the last two years, I've been in the running to be the host of a TV travel show. I would explore hidden places, that sort of thing. I was one of the top three contenders. But tonight he told me that Amazon says there are too many travel shows with a single man traipsing through the jungles. They decided they want a Chip and Joanna. I have no idea who they are. Do you?"

"Sure. They're a married couple who remodel and decorate houses."

He looked confused. "What do they have to do with jungles?"

"Nothing so far but give them time. Chip would probably love swinging a machete. I guess this means you won't get the job."

"I, uh…" He took a long drink. "I told my agent about you."

"Me? What do I have to do with this?"

"I said I knew a woman who would be perfect for the show. You're well traveled and the daughter of a veterinarian. He could be on it. Your mother is the great Vera Exton. And your father is a well-known photographer. He could help."

"So both my fathers would be on TV? That would require some explaining." She narrowed her eyes at him. "You and I are *not* a couple. We hardly know each other."

"That was part of my pitch. You and I bicker. We compete. The audience could take sides."

She ate a popper. "It would be sort of a Tarzan *Bachelor* show. Do you give out roses or coral snakes to the winners?"

"You're not taking this seriously. It's a job, not romance. I'm not offering you love and marriage. I'm not even offering sex. Just a *job*. I doubt if there's any female on earth more qualified to do this than you. I bet you aren't even afraid of snakes."

"Of corals, I am. They're deadly."

"See what I mean? You're perfect." He paused. "It would be six months traveling and filming. Then we'd separate. You can come back here and I'll go…wherever. We'd have the other six months to prepare for the next trip. That's when I'll work on the bio of Vera. You and I can correspond while you run the businesses of everybody here in Mason. Not your own, but theirs. Sorry. I didn't mean that to be nasty. But to be fair, people sure do seem to dump a lot onto you."

"Yes, they do." Their nachos arrived.

Griff took some from the platter. "It's the boyfriend, isn't it? You two had a spat and you're using me to get back with him."

"That thought never crossed my mind. Don't forget that this morning I hated you."

He gave a half smile. "So you did."

"Let's talk about something else."

"Okay. Tell me about Vera's cellar."

"No, no." Mike put her hands up. "Leave my parents out of this."

"Then how about I tell you what my plans for my job are? I sent a detailed proposal to my agent."

The rest of the evening they talked of where they'd been and where they'd like to go.

For Mike it was anywhere peaceful. "Running ahead of bulldozers and dodging bullets was a once-in-a-lifetime experience for me. Never again!"

They toasted to that and ordered dessert.

CHAPTER THIRTY-FIVE

GRIFF WOKE EARLY SATURDAY MORNING and he wasn't in a good mood. His trip to Mason had started out so well. He'd received a call from his literary agent saying Vera was in Kansas. He'd jumped in his van and driven straight there, not even bothering to shower or shave.

And that had led to the archery disaster.

After that, he'd found out that Vera would refuse to help him with a bio. People had even laughed at the idea that he thought he'd be able to persuade her to agree. Without her help, if he did manage to write a bio of his grandfather, then segue into Vera's career, it would be one of those "unauthorized" books about a living person. Dismissed by critics, not included in any official histories. Deemed worthless.

His misery had been lightened by getting to know Michaela. To him, it was like meeting the other half of himself. She was someone who'd traveled, seen things, and she knew about journalism. He began to fantasize about working together and not being alone on his trips.

When his LA agent told him what was wanted for the travel show, he knew Mike was the perfect solution.

Griff didn't tell her what he'd said to his agent about her. "You should see her. She's tall and beautiful. She'll look great on a camera."

"Sounds good. So let me talk to her."

"Uh." Griff hesitated.

"She hasn't agreed to this, has she?" He was getting angry. "But you're asking me to present her as half of the deal. If she has a brain, she'll say no to this. Snakes and bugs and no cell service. Of course she'll say no." He took a breath. "I'll tell them you're single and—"

"Give me forty-eight hours to try to talk her into this. I just need to deal with the boyfriend and—"

He exploded. "She's not even your girlfriend? I'm calling this off before I lose all credibility in this business."

"Monday!" Griff shouted.

"Okay. Monday." His agent hung up.

After that call, Griff went to Mike's Jeep and leaned against the door. She'd come back to it eventually unless she spent the night with the boyfriend. *What* did she see in him?

To his disbelief, Mike showed up minutes later and she looked angry. He'd wanted to do a dance of delight.

Instead, he tried to play it cool and let her tell him what was wrong. His hope was that it was over with the boyfriend. But her talk of marriage and rings nearly made him lose his confidence.

He was dying to tell her about the job offer. He had fingers crossed that she'd like the idea and say she very much wanted to take on the project.

But when he told her about it, she gave him some excuse about helping everyone, saying she had to do everything for everybody—just what Kyle had told him. And as far as he could tell, she and the boyfriend were still a go.

His phone dinged with a WhatsApp message. It was used

around the world, and he could keep up with people wherever he was.

It was Miguel. They'd been texting since they met.

Breakfast? the text read. **Unless you want to go to the parade.**

Griff nearly sneered. To see Mike with the boyfriend? Would they be kissing and making up? No, thanks. He texted back. **Great idea. Know where I can buy a suit for the wedding?**

Yes. I'll meet you at First Watch in OP, Miguel wrote.

"And what is OP?" he murmured, but didn't ask. He'd find out from the motel manager. Minutes later, he was dressed and on his way to Overland Park. He had on a plain blue shirt—no more khaki. Too many safari comments.

Miguel was already at a small table when he got there. He looked as glum as Griff felt. He took a seat across from Miguel and placed his order. As soon as the waitress was gone, he said, "Vera went to the parade?"

"I should be so lucky. She's doing something in secret. Probably arranging a job. If she doesn't tell me what it is, that means it's dangerous. 'One last time.' How many times I've heard that! But maybe I should just give up and go with her." He looked at Griff. "I'm sure we'll end up like your grandfather. We'll step on a mine and boom! It'll be all over."

He took a drink of his coffee. "I don't fear dying, but what I hate is missing out on my children. I got to be with Cait until she grew up but I missed a lot about Michaela. She's an adult now and she'll get married and give me grandchildren! Is it too much to want them so much that I'm like a drug addict needing a fix? I want to spend time with Cait and Michaela and some grandbabies. Michaela's children will probably look like Vera and…"

He stopped talking and looked down at his plate. "Sorry

for dumping this on you. You said you need a suit for the wedding."

"Mike turned down my job offer," Griff said softly.

Miguel looked up. "What job?"

Griff told him about the offer in detail, even admitting that he'd volunteered Mike before asking her. "To be fair to myself, I thought she'd love the idea. But she laughed at me. She said all of you will be here and everyone needs her. She said she *can't* leave."

"That's true. Even if Vera and I go away, we'll need her. All our writings and photos are sent to her. She's a whiz with Photoshop and she makes Vera's scribbled notes into comprehensible stories."

Griff sighed. "Mike's problem is that she's too good at everything. Even archery. I hoped that would turn off her arrogant boyfriend, but it didn't. He asked her to marry him."

Miguel showed his surprise. "Are you sure of that?"

"Not exactly, but I know they talked of marriage. Last night she was upset about it, but all I could think about was the job offer. I think she plans to stay here and marry him." Griff leaned forward. "I really don't like him."

"Neither does Forey. She called me last night and said Mike and Brookside Boy had an argument. Something about a piece of jewelry."

"Yeah, an engagement necklace."

"Have I been out of the country so long that that's changed? It's no longer a ring?"

Griff fell back against the seat. "What do I know?"

"I think you should find out," Miguel said. "You can't give up after a single day, can you?"

"But she—" he began, then blinked for a few moments. *Was* there hope? "Where can I buy a suit? What does Mike like?"

"Black, conservative, but with a flashy vest."

"You *want* her to take the job, don't you?"

"My daughter is much more like Vera than she knows. I don't want her to lock herself into a life because other people need her." He paused. "She'd be good at your job and I think she'd come to love it."

"So do I," Griff said.

"Go get your suit and meet her at the wedding." He looked at his watch. "I'm going to the parade." Miguel grinned in a sly way. "Adam Hatten has to ride on a float. He will hate it. I plan to photograph every second of his misery. I'll frame them and hang them above my desk."

Griff laughed. Miguel had told him about their decades-long rivalry. "Ha!" Vera had said. "They're best friends. Always have been."

"I wish you luck in getting great shots."

"And I hope you and my daughter settle your differences."

Griff groaned. "I don't think that's going to happen. She seems to have made up her mind."

"Just don't quit trying."

They left the restaurant, Miguel heading back to Mason and Griff to Oak Park Mall.

CHAPTER THIRTY-SIX

MIKE WAS IN HER BATHROOM GETTING ready for the wedding. She was putting on a smoky eye, the way her friend Laurie had taught her. Her dress, a silvery gray-blue, was hanging on the door.

When she'd bought her gray couch, Forey told her that gray was the color of change. She said, "If you make a gray room, you want to change things in your life." Mike told her that she liked her life just as it was and didn't want any changes. Forey had laughed.

The parade had been exhausting. Mike had had to run everywhere to keep people and machines on track. Thank heaven that her mom had taken care of the Heritage Harvests wagon! Adam and the other past mayors looked great on their float. They'd smiled and waved. The kids were crazy with laughing and yelling. Luckily, there'd been only one breakdown and it was easily fixed.

Miguel didn't show up until the parade had already started, but he had his camera with him.

Good! They'd have pro photos to show.

That Griff wasn't there had annoyed her. She told herself she was being ridiculous and that she'd grown too involved with him in just one day. But still, he could have made an effort.

By eleven, the parade was over and Kelly and her cleanup volunteers took over. Mike went to check on the carnival. It was going well. Kids with painted faces were running around and laughing.

There was no sign of Griff. Now and then, Mike saw Vera and she was always on her phone, which wasn't good. As soon as Mike had a minute, she planned to ask her what she was up to.

At one, Hayes showed up. Behind him were his two buddies. For the first time, Mike's heart didn't escalate at seeing him. In fact, it seemed to slow down. He had on his "serious face." She wondered when she'd started naming his moods.

He ignored the six kids who were surrounding her and asking questions. He talked over the top of them. "I want to apologize."

Mike pulled a pile of tickets out of her pants pocket and gave them to the kids. No skinny jeans for her today! With cheers and squeals, they grabbed the free passes and ran away.

She gave her attention to Hayes.

He continued as though nothing had happened. "I didn't represent myself well. I was so embarrassed at being made to look bad in front of my girlfriend that I couldn't think straight. I'm very sorry." He put his hands on her shoulders. "What if some woman had shown you up in front of me?"

Mike had to admit that she wouldn't like that.

"Can you forgive me? Please?"

Mike wasn't sure what to say. Hardly twenty-four hours ago she'd been hoping this man would propose marriage to her, but now... Now she wasn't sure about anything. "I think..." she began, hoping the words would come to her. "Maybe..."

A few feet away from them, a fight broke out. It was three

kids, about eleven, and they were going at each other. Their punches were awkward, but they were really angry about something.

Hayes took a step back, his upper lip curved into a sneer. "Call Security," he said to the two silent frat boys who were flanking him.

"To put them in jail?" she asked angrily. It was one thing to call Security on an adult, but children? She didn't wait for a reply but hurried to the kids.

Cait and Dr. Coop grabbed two of them, while Mike pulled a girl to her. She could feel the child's heart beating hard.

"How about popcorn, and want to see a really big snake?" Coop asked loudly. "You can watch me feed it mice." The two kids he and Cait were holding nodded. As they left, they gave a threatening look to the girl Mike was clutching.

She crouched down to talk to the girl. "What do you want to do? Go to your mom?" The child's eyes widened as she shook her head no.

"Okay. How about ice cream and you tell me what happened?" The girl nodded.

Minutes later, they were holding huge cones and were sitting near the booth at the far end of the carnival. "It wasn't my fault," the girl said. "I don't like Tommy anymore but Ashlee says I do. But I liked him before she did."

"That sounds complicated," Mike said. "You know what? I think I'm in the same place that you are. And I think maybe I just broke up with my boyfriend. How about you? Ready to give him to Ashlee? Break with him completely?"

With a smile, she said, "Oh, yeah."

They finished their cones and parted ways. When Mike passed Hayes, he started to speak. *More apologies?* she thought. She cut him off. "I think you should go home and stay there."

"But what about the wedding?" he asked.

"I have a date," she said, and kept walking.

That was hours ago and it was just now hitting her that it was all over with Hayes. She was back to being alone. Her dream of being "settled" was gone.

And it was all the fault of Griffin Harding! If he hadn't wanted to show up Hayes in archery, none of this would have happened.

Mike put her hands up on the sink and took some deep breaths. She could almost hear her father say, "Would you rather find out the truth *after* you married him?"

"No," she whispered as she blinked back tears. But whatever the reason for the breakup, it still *hurt!*

CHAPTER THIRTY-SEVEN

BY THE TIME GRIFF GOT TO THE CHURCH, most of the people were seated. It had taken a while to get a suit. Then he'd had to unpack his van to find the vest he'd bought in India. It was emerald green silk with big water lilies embroidered across it. He'd bought it years ago, thinking he'd someday have a place to wear it, but there'd never been one. The vest had been shoved deep into his van, under equipment and work clothes.

When he finally dragged it out, he saw it was a mass of wrinkles. Ironing clothes wasn't something he knew how to do, but the motel owner's wife helped him.

By the time it was all done, he had to rush to the church. Inside, he stopped and stared. It was so covered in flowers he could hardly see the people. There were even flowers hanging from the ceiling.

He saw Mike at the far end of a pew in the front. Griff recognized the extended family.

Adam and Kelly, the parents of the groom, were at the end nearest the aisle. Vera and Miguel were next, then Cait and Dr. Cooper.

For a second, Griff stood back and looked at them. They were like one family but only Vera and Kelly were sisters. What kept them so closely together?

"Bride or groom?" an usher asked.

"What? Oh, groom. I see my place." Griff slipped away to go down the side. He didn't want to be seated in a back pew. He wanted to be right next to Mike.

He sat down between her and the oak side of the bench. Mike hardly glanced at him. "You have to have an invitation."

"Kyle gave me one. Was this seat saved for your boyfriend?"

"He's not coming." She was looking straight ahead.

"Oh. Did he—?"

Mike turned to him in anger. "We broke up. Are you happy now?"

"Was it the archery?" Guilt ran through him.

"That didn't help, but if you must know, he called Security on three eleven-year-olds."

"Oh." Griff worked hard to not let his face show any emotion, but inside he was jumping up and down. Dancing. Arms waving about in happiness. He frowned seriously. "Was it drugs?"

"It was an argument over a *boy*!" Mike looked to the front as Kyle came out and stood quietly waiting for the ceremony to begin.

Griff couldn't stamp his jubilation down. Without a smile, he said, "Did the guards use itty-bitty handcuffs on them?"

Mike turned to him with a face full of fury. "He stuck their wrists together with cotton candy."

Griff let out a snort of laughter so loud that the groom's whole side turned to look at him.

"Sorry," he murmured, but he was having a hard time controlling his laughter. With a huge grin on his face, he looked toward the front. Kyle was looking at him and he gave a subtle thumbs-up to Griff.

At Griff's laugh, Vera took Miguel's hand and squeezed it. "He's good for her," she said quietly. "I think she should take the job."

"I do, too," he said. "But she won't do it."

Vera looked at him, her eyes full of the knowledge of their years together. "Don't let her do what you and I did. We felt we had to give all of ourselves to others. I thought I had to stay where I didn't want to be so I could spend my life with you."

"And I thought I couldn't have both you and Cait."

"We lost so much time."

For a moment, tears were in their eyes. Then the music grew louder and attendants began the march down the aisle. They turned to the front, but they didn't let go of each other, not in time or distance.

After the wedding ceremony, Griff and Mike walked out together. All around them floated the word *beautiful*. The bride, the decorations, the vows read—it was all "beautiful."

They walked to Mike's Jeep. Cars were jammed as people tried to get out of the parking lot. "I guess every girl wants a wedding like that," Griff said as they waited to leave.

"Not me! Too much work, too much money spent."

"Yeah?" His eyebrows were high. "What kind of—?"

She didn't let him finish. "I'd be barefoot and the music would be bells."

"Perfect," Griff said. "Where is the reception? The invite said 'Frog Pond' but I don't know where that is."

"Aunt Kelly's favorite place, but the parking is along the road."

"Maybe we should go so we get a place." He was psychically sending her the word *together*.

Mike still looked less than happy but a tiny sparkle flitted through her eyes. "Leave that monster van of yours here. We'll take my Jeep. I know a back way."

"Of course you do." He was grinning.

Mike edged her vehicle across a muddy field, then between a close-planted forest to stop under some trees. In the distance they could see a huge white tent with beautifully dressed people entering.

"Wow. This is some show," Griff said.

"It's what Kyle and Becks like." She got out of the Jeep. "Oh, hell!"

He went around to see what was wrong. Good ol' Kansas mud. Rich, black soil. "Don't give me any argument."

"What does that mean?" she asked.

He swept her into his arms and started carrying her toward the tent. He expected her to demand that he put her down, but she didn't. It was subtle, but he could feel her relax against him, and his steps slowed. "I'm sorry about your breakup. It must have hurt."

"Yeah," she said. "But I think I had on blinders. Maybe I was impressed that such an elegant man liked *me*. It was flattering."

Griff couldn't control his frown. "Did he earn that place or was it given to him by his daddy?"

She smiled up at him. "Good point. You can put me down now."

Griff gave an exaggerated sigh. "If I must."

Standing, she smiled at him. "Thanks. You've made me feel better."

He put his hand to his heart. "I have now achieved nirvana."

She shook her head. "Come on. Let's go eat."

As she hurried ahead, he followed her. "Let me guess what the menu is. Fried tofu? Cauliflower crust pizza? I know! Sushi."

"You idiot," she said, laughing. Inside the tent, she saw that Griff's place card was next to hers. "How did you manage that?"

"Kyle. We hit it off." He was smiling innocently.

"So what did he do with Hayes?"

Griff looked around the room. There was an empty chair at the table full of children. "Not sure." He was grinning wickedly.

"I'm definitely going to murder Kyle," she murmured as she took a seat.

"Let him have his honeymoon first," Griff said.

They were at the second-most prestigious table. Miguel and Vera, Cait and Coop, Jared and his wife, and the other Hatten son, Sean, and his wife were at the first table.

Mike and Griff were seated with Mason dignitaries—the mayor and his wife, and two prosperous business couples. They'd known each other all their lives.

Griff was a stranger, so they zeroed in on him. As the thick steaks from Hatten cattle were served, they fired questions at him. Who was he? Why was he here? Who were his parents? On and on.

When Griff said his grandfather was Joe Harding, there was a collective sigh of recognition. Vera was the town celebrity. A Pulitzer Prize winner!

"Sorry," Griff said, "but I never met him." Their faces fell. "If it helps, my dad always said I was just like Granddad. Yup. Whenever I did anything Dad had told me not to do, he said I was just like Granddad."

They laughed at that, then increased their questions.

"Granddad got my father a job at Sony right after college, so we ended up living all over the world. Hong Kong, Bangkok, Kyoto, South Africa and—"

"You didn't tell me that," Mike said.

"We haven't exactly had a long heart-to-heart, have we?"

"But you sure know a lot about *me*."

"Didn't know you could shoot an arrow like Katniss Everdeen."

She grimaced. "Really! I'm nothing compared to the men I learned from."

"Bhutan, right?"

"How do you know that but didn't know I can shoot a bow?"

"You—"

One of the men spoke up. "So how long have you two known each other?"

Griff smiled. "About thirty-six hours."

The women were smiling sweetly.

"It's not like that," Mike said. "He works for Vera and Papi. He wants to do a bio on her." Mike said it as though expecting a laugh, but no one did.

Mrs. Anderson looked at Griff. "If Vera can be persuaded, you're the one to do it. You're quite a charming young man."

"Thank you." Griff was smiling.

"He's not as he appears. He's—" Mike broke off at the clinking of glasses. The speeches were about to begin.

While dessert made with Heritage Harvests produce was served, the families of the bride and groom gave toasts and funny little talks about the couple.

There was nothing but triumph about Becks. She'd accomplished a lot. For Kyle, there was a sense of relief.

Griff leaned forward to whisper to Mike. "Sounds like they expected him to marry a convict."

"From his own cell," Mike replied.

With the meal done and the speeches given, the band set up and music began. There was a sweet moment with Becks and her father. He was a handsome man and they looked like something in a Disney movie. A teary Kelly danced with Kyle.

Next came Kyle and Becks. Halfway through, he motioned for everyone to join them. He loved company!

Griff stood up and held out his hand to Mike. "Shall we?"

"Gladly."

Two hours later, they were still dancing. They allowed no cuts, no interruptions. Mike wanted to hear more about Griff's childhood and he wanted to hear more about…well, anything at all about her.

They talked and laughed and danced.

At about nine, they glided past Miguel and Vera. They were seated close together against the tent wall and were in an earnest discussion.

"What do you think they're talking about?" Griff asked.

"She wants to go somewhere and he wants her to stay here. It's the only argument they ever have."

"Who will win?"

"Vera. Papi only puts his foot down when it's absolutely necessary, which means that I'm involved."

"But now that's not true?"

"No. This time Vera will go without him. She'll say it's for 'one last assignment.' I've been hearing that for the last four years."

Thirty minutes later, they came back around, and this time Vera and Miguel had calmed down. They were sitting quietly and holding hands. Her head was on his shoulder.

"They seem to have reached an agreement," Griff said.

"It looks like Papi lost. Hell! That means they're going to leave."

They danced for another twenty minutes. The tent was clearing. Kyle and Becks had left and young parents had taken their overly excited children home to bed. But there were still several couples. Adam and Kelly, and Cait and Coop, were dancing slowly, looking like newlyweds on their honeymoon.

As they passed Vera and Miguel, Griff gave a wave to Miguel, but he didn't respond.

He turned Mike around so he could see Miguel. His eyes were blank. Like something was missing from them.

Griff looked at Vera, her eyes closed as she leaned on her husband's shoulder. Griff knew what was going on. He wrapped his arms around Mike, pinning her arms to her sides.

"Hey!" she protested, and moved to free herself.

He didn't let her break away as he put his lips to her ear. "Please stay calm. Vera just passed."

"Passed? You mean as in...?"

He nodded.

"No!" Mike said, then turned her head.

Papi was holding Vera. She was smiling and she looked like she was sleeping.

Griff still held Mike. "I'm going to help your father get her out of here and you have to stay calm. Your mother wouldn't want the attention turned to her and certainly not have the happiness of everyone thrown away. Okay?"

All Mike could do was nod.

Griff kept his mouth close to her ear. "I want you to go with us and, as Miguel and I help her out, smile as you explain that Vera drank too much. We'll get her to the hospital. They'll—" He was choking on tears.

It was Mike's turn to give comfort. She put her hand on the back of his head and he loosened his grip on her. "We can do this. It's for Vera, for my mother. All right?" She pulled away from him, took his hand and led him to her parents. Mike sat down in the chair on the other side of Vera and held her mother's hand. Griff moved behind them, one hand on Miguel's shoulder, one on Vera's. With a sense of absolute peace, they turned to look at the dancers.

And that's how the photographer took their photo. Mike and Miguel holding Vera's hands, Griff behind them. It looked to be a sweet family photo, with Vera smiling in her sleep, close to the people she loved the most.

"It's time," Griff said. He was trying to be strong but he didn't feel that way.

But when he looked up, they were there. Somehow, they all knew. Adam had sent the remaining guests and the band away; Kelly had already made some calls.

Standing before them were Adam and Kelly, Cait and Coop, and Forey. There were no tears. They would come later.

Adam put his arms around Miguel to help him up. Friends, enemies, adversaries and now united by grief.

The women managed to get Vera out.

Outside the tent was a silent, unlit ambulance, with two men and a woman waiting to take Vera away.

Miguel started to get inside with her, one last trip with his wife, but he halted, then turned to his daughter. His face with its bleak eyes was furious. "You aren't going to sacrifice as your mother and I did. You aren't going to give up your own life because we all need you so much. I want you to go see the things your mother did and write about them. And while you're doing that, I want you to figure out who you are and what you want in life. Do you understand me?"

"Yes, I do," Michaela said.

He looked at Griff. "Take care of her."

"Yes, sir, I will. With all my heart."

Miguel got in the ambulance and the doors shut behind him.

It was the end and it was the beginning.

★ ★ ★ ★ ★

ACKNOWLEDGMENTS

I'D LIKE TO THANK THE MANY PEOPLE who helped me with this book and told me about the glories of Kansas, and there are many.

Hope and Chance Lickteig. Hope drove me around Princeton and Richmond and told me wonderful stories. Murders, haunted houses, things found in the trash. It was incredible! Thank you.

Bud and Shelly Welch of the Welch Brothers Farm. More stories! My favorite. Shelly showed me family photos, and Bud and I had a good talk about growing marijuana.

Marcia Servatius was my go-to when I needed a quick answer about what was in Ottawa in 1972. Her memory was astonishing. Terry and Nancy White helped me with the history of Ottawa in the seventies and nineties. Thank you.

Thanks to Franklin County Historical Society Archives Center for the historical documents and references that were invaluable.

Most of all, I'd like to thank Laurie Tyner. No question was too frivolous, nothing stumped her. She and her wonderful husband took me out to Kansas barbecue, and I agree that it's the best in the world. And thanks to dear Annelise for being the prettiest and smartest baby ever!

Thank you all very much! Your generosity and kindness helped me to write a true account of how great Kansas is. And the Chiefs won! Hooray!